SOMEDAY JENNIFER

SOMEDAY JENNIFER

A Novel

RISTO PAKARINEN

HARPER**AVENUE**

Someday Jennifer
Copyright © 2019 by Risto Pakarinen.
All rights reserved.

Published by Harper Avenue, an imprint of HarperCollins Publishers Ltd

First edition

HarperCollins books may be purchased for educational, business,
or sales promotional use through our Special Markets Department.

HarperCollins Publishers Ltd
Bay Adelaide Centre, East Tower
22 Adelaide Street West, 41st Floor
Toronto, Ontario, M5H 4E3

www.harpercollins.ca

Library and Archives Canada Cataloguing in Publication
information is available upon request.

ISBN 978-1-4434-5385-1

Printed and bound in the United States of America
LSC/H 9 8 7 6 5 4 3 2 1

To Jessica

SOMEDAY JENNIFER

CHAPTER 1

IT'S A HARD LIFE

THE day the Time Machine arrived started innocently enough. One of my clients (okay, my only client) had asked me to come in for a meeting at three. Perfect. I couldn't have picked a better time myself, even if it was a Friday.

See, I was self-employed, which is how we describe people who once had a job but have been downsized or outsourced and are now "personal brands." I was the CEO of Me Inc. I was also its HR department, IT department, accounts department, and office errand boy. The official name of my company was Webscoe, because when I registered it, back when I was in university, anything about the web was "way cool" (as we said in those exciting days). Plus, Webscoe was what Richard Pryor's character called his company in *Superman III*, a very underrated movie.

Being self-employed was great. I could hit Snooze as many times as I wanted (which is why 3 p.m. was the perfect time for a meeting). I could work in sweatpants and a T-shirt (and I did), and I could listen to Total 80s FM as loud as I liked, all day long. I did that too.

To be fair, being your own boss does involve a certain amount of discipline: taxes, sending out an invoice once a month, remembering to make sure there's milk in the fridge, that sort of stuff. Sometimes I missed the old days at the office—the conversations, the jokes, and the long Friday afternoons when somebody would bring in a six-pack and we'd sit at our desks and shoot the breeze and then head to a nearby pub. I did not miss the bitchy politics and lengthy meetings.

My client's text woke up my dozing sense of duty. I rushed to do some honest research for a new app for a bank, but the fancy algorithms knew me better than I did and . . . well, soon I was deep inside the internet rabbit hole, in the world of eighties music videos, Japanese game shows, and movie gifs. At 2:30 p.m., I watched a fifteen-minute video of a teenage boy—judging by the cracks in his pubescent voice—who'd played through *The Hobbit*, a computer game based on the J.R.R. Tolkien novel, and one that I had once mastered.

Then I ran for the bus.

It'd been a couple of years—a decade, even—since I became a freelance contractor for the company that had downsized me. I still loved the freedom, but I also relished returning to the office to chat with colleagues. As I walked in on the day the Time Machine arrived, Dire Straits' "Money for Nothing" was playing in reception. I wondered if it might be a cosmic coincidence (music always seems to stalk me), or if, more likely, my old boss enjoyed forcing his playlist on everyone who entered the office. Either way, I loved the tune, and the happiness the song gave me silenced whatever bit of guilty conscience its title prompted.

The receptionist greeted me with a broad smile. Like the pot plant behind her, she was fresh and new.

"Hi there. Can I help you?"

I gave her my name and told her I had a meeting with the boss. She mustn't have realized who I was, as she gestured to a couch in the corner and suggested I wait for someone to pick me up.

"Thanks, but I know my way," I said, and kept on walking. I spotted some guys standing around the coffee machine, two of the three leaning on the counter with empty cups in their hands.

"Hey, Pete, good to see you." That was Johan—the only one of the three I knew.

"Hi." I reached for a cup from the pile next to the coffee machine. No herbal teas, I noticed.

"Haven't seen you around lately," he said before turning to the other two. "Peter's our internet guru."

The two young men nodded at me. No handshakes.

"I've been busy with that bank project," I said. "How are things?"

"Same old same old. Plugging away. You know. Clients want more for less, the usual. You?"

"The same, I guess. You should know, *you're* my client," I said.

Johan laughed. Then he pointed at my watch.

"Nice watch. What time is it?"

I checked. "About five to . . ."

As I said it, I realized that I'd fallen for his joke for about the thousandth time.

"Are you sure?" he said with a wink, and then went on to explain his hilarious "joke" to his young colleagues. "Peter here wrote one of the first websites in Finland—the web version of the Talking Clock," he said.

The young men stared blankly at him.

"You know, the number you used to call to check the correct time?" Johan went on. These kids probably had no understanding

3

of life before iPhones, whose time display is constantly synched by the cellular network. "You're literally looking at a piece of internet history."

"Umm . . . awesome," one of them said.

"Is it still online?" asked the other.

"Thanks. I'm not sure. I haven't needed to check it for a while . . . ," I said.

We stood there silently, waiting for Johan to get his coffee, and then the two younger men to get theirs. I regretted my decision to pick up a cup. Now I was stuck in this awkward line while they pressed buttons and muttered something in young-people code.

"Hey," said Johan. "I thought I'd see you at Pauli's goodbye party last week."

My first thought was: *Pauli left?*

My second thought was: *Why didn't I get an invite?*

I hope I managed to keep both from showing on my face.

"Ah, I was busy, you know . . . networking event. Being self-employed, it's all go-go-go."

He smiled like he understood, blew on his coffee, and wandered off.

At 3 p.m. exactly I knocked on my client/boss's door.

He waved me in and gestured for me to sit down. He was a big man with a fondness for pastries and a black belt in management-speak. He was also one of a handful who'd been at the company since the days when the office had a dog-walker-in-residence, so we went back a long way. In fact, I had been his "mentor" when he'd first signed on as a fresh-faced intern with a business-school degree. In the years since he had worked his way up, all the way to the top, but in my mind I still called him "kid."

"Listen, thanks for coming down on such short notice. I didn't want to do this on a Friday afternoon. It's such a cliché, right?"

4

He wiped some invisible dirt off his black Stevejobsian shirt and laughed awkwardly.

"Peter, we're going in a different direction," he said.

"We are? Well, that's a smart move. I think I mentioned that we should focus more on mobile apps in my memo the other—"

"Buddy," he said, and sighed. "There's no *I* in *team*. Except for the *I* in our new Indian team. See, we just acquired a digital design agency, so we'll have that expertise in-house. Well, out-of-house. Bangalore, to be exact."

I sat quietly, reality spinning around me.

"We've been trialing them for a couple of months, and the truth of the matter is they're cheaper than you—"

"Oh. We could look at my fees—"

"They're quicker than you—"

"I could devote more time," I said, worried I was sounding desperate, regretting how much of the past ten years I'd spent on Facebook when I'd been invoicing them for my services.

"And there's *sixteen* of them. Peter, I'm afraid we don't need Webscoe's services anymore."

"Oh."

"Look, Peter, I'm sorry. You've been here since the dawn of time, I know. And we both know that since you took your brand external we're under no obligation to offer severance. But as a gesture of goodwill to my old mentor, I thought maybe you could invoice an extra month. Does that sound fair?"

It didn't sound fair. It sounded monstrously, ridiculously, biblically unfair. But I knew that, legally speaking, he was right. They owed me nothing.

"Um. Sure."

"So . . . that's great news, right? Have some 'me time.' Great news for your other clients too. I've always worried that we hog too much of your time. Am I right?"

I swallowed and tried to find my voice. He pursed his lips and then stared at his phone, as if willing it to ring.

"Look, sorry buddy, I have to take this," he said, and turned in his expensive swivel chair so that his back was toward me.

His phone wasn't ringing.

I was seething, but I somehow managed to keep my cool as I got up, leaned against the desk between me and my—now former—client, and said, as evenly as I could, "I remember when you started at this company. You didn't even know what HTML stood for."

He looked up at me, as if surprised to see me there.

"Well," he said. "We learn something new every day, don't we?"

I scrabbled for a witty retort, but he'd already turned away.

I stormed out of his office, out of the building, and kept on walking until I saw the Central Station's clock tower.

I stopped. Closed my eyes. Took a deep breath.

CHAPTER 2

THE ONLY WAY IS UP

FIGHT or flight. Your choice."

In my head I heard the boisterous voice of Seppo Laine, my old science teacher. I remembered him teaching us about the primal instinct that lurks in all of us, that despite millions of years of evolution, thousands of years of society teaching us to be nice, we're still all basically mammals with self-preservation instincts. When faced with a threat, we fight or we flight. Fly, I mean. I ordered another pint, my second, and noticed that I was starting to feel a little tipsy. I hadn't had lunch.

I spent every Friday evening with Sofie, my niece, while my sister, Tina, went to teach her yoga class and her husband, Tim, "worked late." I was supposed to be at Tina's at six, which meant I had a couple of hours to kill after leaving the office. So I'd headed for a new place around the corner—Retrobar, it was called—pulled up a stool, and ordered a beer.

Retrobar was one of those new theme bars that kept popping up downtown. Eighties movie posters, vintage clothes, and album covers hung on the walls. There was a pinball machine in one corner and Pac-Man and Daley Thompson's Decathlon games in another. Screens were everywhere, like in a sports bar, but instead of football and hockey, this placed showed music videos and movies, straight out of my high-school years.

I was the only customer.

The TV above the bar was playing Bruce Springsteen's "Glory Days," with the Boss and Little Steven rocking in a small bar in Anytown, USA; the one next to it featured *Trading Places*. As I watched Eddie Murphy and Dan Aykroyd head to the World Trade Center, intent on payback, I considered the two options Mr. Laine had presented.

Fight: I wrote a long email to my former boss. I told him exactly how I felt about what he was doing to the company I'd once loved, and I told him exactly what I felt about him, making particular reference to his Steve Jobs fanboyism, and that I had proof he'd taken the subway during the Helsinki City Marathon (I didn't, but I had reasonable grounds and wanted to shake him up a little). I reminded him of my mentorship, and then went on to explain all the benefits I'd brought to the company over the years and how I could still be of use to them. I basically begged for my job back. I saved it in my drafts folder.

Flight: Thinking about it, I realized my job situation had become stale; it really was time for me to move on. In many ways, this wasn't so much a sacking as a liberation. I had a good portfolio, a decent set of contacts, and enough savings to tide me over while I recalibrated, defragged, rebooted (or whatever computing analogy best fit) my life. There was no shame in running, I told myself. It wasn't running *away*; it was running *toward* a new adventure.

Yeah, right.

My savings—even with the generous "severance" offer—weren't likely to last the year. My "portfolio," if I could muster the wherewithal to organize one, would be horrendously dated. My "contacts" were probably stored on an old Nokia phone somewhere.

I'd been working at that company in one way or another since its early days—since *my* early days. I knew nothing else; it was the only "real" job I'd ever had. When I'd finished high school, my grades had gotten me into the best university around. When I aced that, I walked straight into the first job I wanted. When they offered to outsource me, it just made my life even more awesome. At the time, I had felt as if the world was constantly falling at my feet. Looking back, it now seems more like I just went with the flow, took the path of least resistance, never challenged, never strived.

"You can't fire me," I said to myself, "BECAUSE I ALREADY QUIT!"

Too late, I realized I'd shouted that out loud. I looked up at the barman, who didn't even flinch. I expect he was used to daytime drinkers.

When I'd first agreed to stay on as a contractor, I'd imagined building my own company into a web juggernaut. I was going to have numerous clients. I was going to be ahead of the software development curve. I was . . . not sure exactly what, but not this. What I hadn't done was formulate a business plan, or reach out to new clients; I hadn't even built my own website, or followed the tech news, or attended conferences. In short, I'd been complacent. When I'd gone freelance, Dad had advised me to put aside 20 percent of my earnings "because you never know when the lean times are coming." Had I done so? No—but I did have a superb sound system in my apartment.

I mulled over the meeting I'd just had. I tried to see it from a bird's-eye perspective, and I didn't like what I saw. There was me, slouching in the chair, shrinking before the kid, stuttering and stunned. "Oh." "Um." "Sure."

I found myself doing my movie voice-over thing: "Sitting at the bar, Peter wonders what the hell he's going to do next . . ."

As CEO of Webscoe, I spent a lot of time by myself. Some things just had to be said out loud, and why say them in a normal voice when you can drop a couple of octaves and add movie-trailer gravitas?

"In a world where corporations are stomping all over people's lives, one man completely fails to stand up to them . . ."

I pulled out my phone and sent a WhatsApp to my old colleague Pauli: *Congrats on the new job! Don't be a stranger. Beers soon, okay?*

Pauli and I had joined the company at about the same time. We'd worked together on what were, at the time, some fairly cutting-edge websites (although they've since been superseded many times over, and probably look like Windows 3.1 to the modern eye). Pauli was the first person I knew to get an iPhone; we'd spent an entire afternoon downloading apps, and then the whole of the next week emailing each other ideas for new apps. Mine were mostly online versions of retro games, live-streaming music concerts, watching videos—good ideas but things for which 2G service providers lacked the bandwidth. His were more to do with utilizing the phone's GPS and interlinking it with goods and service providers. Pauli probably invented Uber ten years before Uber did. Which probably explains the different paths our lives had taken.

I guess you could say I was ahead of my time. I talked about watching videos on my phone, but instead of dreaming up

YouTube, my solution was more of a VHS and DVD second-hand marketplace, just like my "Spotify" was basically a mix-tape song-list generator rather than a subscription-based content-streaming service. I didn't dream big enough.

My phone buzzed a couple of minutes later. *Thanks, man. Not a new job. They offered me a partnership but I decided to start up on my own. So, super-busy but yes let's definitely do beers at some point soon.*

That gave me some hope. If Pauli was starting his own company, maybe he could help me out with some work.

So I replied: *Well if you need any websites built, be sure to get in touch.*

He came back immediately: *Already got that covered, but I'll keep you in mind.*

Of course he already had that covered. He'd set up his own company. I was the competition.

It did sting that I hadn't been invited to his goodbye drinks, but then again, I hadn't been to the office in . . . months? A year? And it wasn't like I was always out on the town, or inviting people to my place. I knew that a busy social life requires effort, that friendship is a two-way street, and in some ways I'd sort of just faded into the background. My school friends had all dispersed, then my university friends, then my work friends. Walking through the office earlier on, I'd barely recognized anyone. I didn't have a girlfriend, or the couple-friends that come with that. I didn't have any hobbies that brought the opportunity for meeting new people, and calling up old buddies to sit in a bar chatting about how much fun life used to be in our teens and twenties had lost its appeal after a couple of decades.

I ordered another beer, telling myself that I needed to stay hydrated because twenty-four degrees Celsius in September was unseasonably warm—damn climate change—and Retrobar had no air conditioning. Even though I wasn't wearing a jacket, I was sweating.

When I got my beer, I tried to engage the barman in conversation.

"Warm, eh?"

He looked worried. "The beer?"

"No," I said with a laugh. "The weather."

He looked relieved and walked away.

I dug my laptop out of my bag, opened a browser tab—next to the Facebook tab I already had open—and typed in *http://192.168.0.1/~peks/time.html*. I pressed Enter and was doubly surprised: one, that I'd remembered the URL correctly, and two, that I was greeted with a grey screen that had big, blue numbers on it: 15:45:03, it said.

That was all. No date, and with the exception of the small envelope icon on the bottom of the page, no graphics.

I laughed out loud, and then flicked over to the Facebook tab and pasted the URL into my status field. I wanted to show everyone that I had made something worthwhile. That I had been cutting-edge, once. I thought of what Johan had said, back at the coffee machine: "You're literally looking at a piece of internet history."

Deflated, I deleted the post. Closed the Facebook tab. I wasn't going to beg for "likes" on a stupid site. Suddenly, the virtual world just didn't seem . . . real enough.

"Hey," I said. The barman looked up, as if to confirm that I was actually talking to him, and not myself. "Have a look at this," I said, as casually as I could.

"Something wrong with the beer?"

"No, no. Nothing like that. I just want to show you something."

The bartender walked over to me. On the screen above him, "Doc" Brown parked his DeLorean in front of a nightclub in the Huey Lewis and the News music video.

"Do you know what this is?" I said, and turned the laptop toward him.

"The time?"

"Precisely." I grinned.

He folded his arms.

"See, this is a bit of a big deal, because this clock, this site, has been running for nearly thirty years. It's probably the first public website in Finland," I went on, when the bartender didn't say anything. "I built it."

"So you're a dotcom billionaire?"

"I just think it's funny that it's still there," I said, a little weakly.

"So you're not a dotcom billionaire?" he said, disappointed, and walked back to polish some more glasses.

"No, but I could have been," I muttered.

I pulled out my phone and sent another WhatsApp message to Pauli: *First round on me. And the last.*

I kept staring at the phone. One grey tick for sent. Two grey ticks for delivered. Two blue ticks for read.

Pauli is online.

Pauli is typing . . .

Pauli is online.

Last seen today at 3:49.

The seconds on the clock on my screen kept ticking away: 34, 35, 36 . . .

I closed the laptop and picked up a copy of yesterday's newspaper that was sitting on the bar. A diplomatic war was raging between Washington and Moscow. "Sabre-rattling," they called it. The stock markets were jittery and people warned of another recession—"boom and bust can not go on," they said (again). Pollution in the seas was reaching what environmentalists were calling "the point of no return." With a horrible sense of foreboding I flipped to the jobs pages. "Tomorrow," I muttered, and skipped over to the comic strips—at least good old Phantom was still out there, saving the world—and then spent a couple of minutes filling in the crossword. I always managed at least a few of the cryptic answers, and then after that had fun trying to fill the other spaces with any words that would fit. There were no empty squares in my crosswords, ever. It's not like anyone comes around to check the answers, is it?

I took another sip of beer and thought about Tina. Surely Tim, her husband and the father of my lovely niece, didn't have to stay late at the office every single Friday? In fact, I had once—well, twice—seen him in the pub a few blocks from their house, having a quiet pint, but I also knew (probably better than anyone) that Tina could be a handful. As far as I was concerned, Tim earned his Timmy-time. And, thinking about it, Tina probably knew that it was a little white lie, but let it slide. Our family's very good at that kind of thing; the old family rug is lumpy and bumpy thanks to the decades of minor disputes that have been swept underneath.

The thought of Tina made me smile. Although she was the only person in the world who could make me so angry I would throw things, she wasn't bad, as sisters went. And it was nice that I got to see her so regularly, even if spending Friday nights with my family did make me a bit of a loser.

Friday night! I looked at my phone again. Somehow Retrobar had sucked nearly two hours of my life from me.

Running out of the door, I texted Tina and told her I was on my way. It was a sunny early-September afternoon, and from the train window, I could see joggers running around the bay, around and around, thinking they were going forward but always ending up back where they started.

All that work—for what?

CHAPTER 3

I STILL HAVEN'T FOUND WHAT I'M LOOKING FOR

TINA opened the door dressed in a Nike T-shirt and tights. She was wearing a Nike baseball cap, with her ponytail sticking out in the back, and pink Nike running shoes.

"Hey," I said, taking it all in, "congratulations on the sponsorship deal!"

She looked at me with a totally blank expression on her face, the way big sisters do to their idiot younger brothers. "Gotta run, my hot yoga class starts in eight minutes. Sofie's in the living room playing, but she's supposed to stop in ten minutes, so please make sure she does. See you in an hour," she said as she grabbed her hoodie.

"Nice shirt, by the way. What's the occasion?" she yelled as she dashed out.

"Oh, just a meeting with a client," I said. The Retrobar booze was wearing off and I was craving another drink. Unfortunately, that was out of the question. While I didn't exactly think Sofie would disapprove, I also didn't want to be slurring my words and going on about ridiculous stuff. In the kitchen I splashed water on my face and made a coffee.

Sofie was a smart kid, and something of a miracle baby. Tina had been in her late thirties when she'd given birth to Sofie, and by that point she must have thought she was never going to be a mother—especially since she'd spent her twenties doing . . . let's just say "enjoying life": backpacking the world, smoking things, going through a long list of boyfriends. But she was a mother now, and a very proud one at that.

"What are you playing?" I asked Sofie as I grabbed the other controller from the floor.

"*Lego Harry Potter*," she said without taking her eyes off the TV.

"Can I be Dumbledore?"

"If you want to . . . but I only have ten more minutes of game time."

"Well . . . maybe we can stretch it a bit," I said with a grin.

"I'm not sure that's such a great idea, Uncle Peter," she said primly. "Kids shouldn't spend too much time in front of screens. It gives us behavioural issues."

She sniggered.

"Hmm. Okay. But if you think about it, if I'm playing too then you're only doing half the playing, so really you should get twenty minutes."

"Uncle Pete," Sofie said, scandalized. "You're sneaky. But I like the way you think."

"So, can I be Dumbledore?"

She raised an eyebrow, shifted along on the sofa.

About half an hour later, as we were doing battle with a large Lego troll, she said, "You haven't asked me how school's going."

"Oh. Sorry. Should I have?"

"Normally it's the first thing you say. 'How's school, Sofie? Learn anything interesting lately?'"

I chuckled. She actually did quite a good impression of me.

"How is school?"

"Boring. Can't we talk about something else?"

"Sure . . ." My mind swam. Perhaps it was the beer fighting with the coffee, but I couldn't focus on anything other than trying to avoid the troll's massive Lego club. Embarrassed, I decided it best to embarrass her. "Got a boyfriend yet?"

"Of course. But I'm not telling you about him, because you'll tell Mom."

I was shocked. "No I won't!"

"You tell Mom everything."

"Not if you don't want me to. Of course I wouldn't." Distracted, Dumbledore took a direct hit and spun into a wall. Sofie giggled.

I loved the sound of her laughter, so I did it again.

She giggled again.

"Anyway, you never tell me about your love life, Uncle Peter, so why should I tell you about mine?"

I tried to distract her by crashing Dumbledore into a wall again. This time, though, she didn't giggle, and with no energy left, Dumbledore lay down and died. Sofie looked away from the screen long enough to raise a cold eyebrow at me.

"That seems like a natural break in play," she said, zapping the TV off.

EVEN since Sofie was little, Tina had made a point of supplementing her education so she could "reach her full potential."

Each morning, Tina would open Wikipedia, click on "random article," and then teach Sofie about the fact that turned up. It was a trick she'd learned from our father, except that he had used random articles in *Reader's Digest*—although sometimes he just read the jokes out loud. Since I'd been forbidden from asking Sofie about school, I asked about the day's Wikipedia lesson instead.

"Oh, it was really interesting. It was about the human brain. Do you know the peak age of human brain processing power?"

"Not sure, because I haven't reached it yet," I said, trying to duck the question. But when she looked at me with her big blue eyes, I had to give it a shot.

"Yeah, no, I don't know. I guess your brain stops growing at the end of your teens? And then maybe you spend a few decades filling it with facts and learning how to use it before you get too old and you start to . . . I don't know. Maybe sixty?" I finally replied.

"Do you want to know the answer?" Tina asked from the kitchen. I hadn't heard her come back in, and was secretly relieved that we'd already switched off the television.

"Sure," I said as Sofie and I mooched toward the kitchen like cats hoping to be fed.

"It's eighteen."

"Long time ago for you then," I said, in an effort to gain the upper hand.

"Not as long as it's been since your last date," Tina shot back.

"Woah, pump the breaks there."

"Sorry, but it's true, isn't it? You haven't had a girlfriend since . . . whatshername? Johanna?"

"I remember Johanna," said Sofie. "She always wore those funny dresses."

"Wow, you *have* got a good memory," said Tina. "You must have only been five or six."

When she put it like that it did seem like it had been quite a while.

"Come on," said Tina, reaching for her laptop. "Let's create a dating profile for you. Let's do it right now."

"What? No." I laughed weakly. "What is it with you guys tonight? Can't a man have a non-existent love life in peace?"

Tina fired up her laptop, slid on her glasses, and looked at me over the top of them in a way that was 100 percent Mom.

Tina and I couldn't have been more different. She was a tall, blonde hippie girl with big brown eyes and the mouth of a sailor. She'd tried to curb her swearing when she became a mother, and then again when Sofie was old enough to repeat words back to her, but it hadn't lasted long. I was a short, quiet, rational, dark-haired, blue-eyed boy. Tina had been the school figure skating star; I was the guy who worked part-time at Video 2000, the local video store. In the Hollywood high-school movie of our teens, she was the nice, kind-of-popular girl, and I was the shy, kind-of-nerdish boy. And when I say "kind-of-nerdish" what I mean is that I was a straight-A student with an encyclopedic knowledge of pop culture who was (as Dad would put it) "a champ at those computer things"; I wasn't the most sporty, or good-looking, or popular, but I had some good friends, and if you wanted your Spectrum computer modified, I was your geek.

"Right," Tina said. "We need to make a list of your best qualities."

"Oh, stop it. I don't believe in internet dating. First, I know how algorithms work. Plus, I'm old-school that way. I'll meet someone if and when it's meant to be—"

"What, working from your living room? Ms. Destiny isn't

going to just ring your doorbell one day. You need to be proactive, Peter."

"Plus, I could never write one of those embarrassing sales pitches anyway—there's nothing special about me."

"I can do it," Tina said, and mimicked typing on her laptop. "A somewhat attractive professional—what are you again, a 'web architect'? . . . I'll drop 'web,' too geeky—architect in his mid-forties seeks a special someone to . . . what is that you like to do?"

"I'm not doing this, Tina."

"He likes to play video games with me," Sofie chirped in. "We nearly got past the troll."

" . . . someone special to adventure through magical lands with. Guaranteed reply to . . . who's your favourite actress?"

"Ally Sheedy. Lea Thompson. Rachel Ward."

Tina stopped her fake typing.

"Wow," she said, and looked at me over her reading glasses again. "Just wow."

"Wow what?"

"Are you living in 1985 or what?"

I felt myself blush.

"What's wrong with 1985?"

She put down the laptop. "Nothing's wrong with 1985. Apart from, you know, the hair. The clothes. The music."

"Hey! Some of the best music—no, *the* best music was made in the 1980s."

"People always say that about the era they grew up in. Look at Dad."

"Pah. What does he know? It was all old crooners and doo-wop. And what do the kids have now?"

"Katy Perry, Taylor Swift, Ed Sheeran," said Sofie, not looking up from her phone.

"I rest my case," I replied, not really familiar with anyone she'd just mentioned.

Tina rolled her eyes.

"Hey, do you remember Seppo Laine?" I asked. "The science teacher?"

"No. I had Hilda something for science. Why?"

"Oh, nothing. Just thought about him earlier." I sighed, sinking back in my chair. "I've been thinking a lot about the past today."

"Why?"

"No reason, just . . . it just seems so long ago."

"That's why it's called the past."

I was trying to open up to her, but she was—either ignorantly or willfully—failing to help.

"I was thinking about some of the choices I've made. Things I could have maybe done better."

"Oh, *tell me* about it. Do you remember that time I wore my bra over my clothes because I wanted to look like Madonna?"

Sofie looked up from her phone.

Tina didn't flinch. "You'd have done the same, darling, only I doubt you could have carried it off."

Sofie went back to scrolling.

"What about movies, then? Surely you agree they were better when we were growing up. They had proper storylines—adventure, romance—not just special effects and mindless action."

"Can you guess who I'm going to say you sound like? I'll give you a clue: it starts with *D* and ends with *ad*."

I groaned. She was right.

Tina got up, put the laptop away, and began to prepare for dinner—which for her meant opening packages. Unlike our mom, Tina wasn't much of a cook. Then again, she was Tina, so her precooked meals were low-carb, low-fat, high-octane. Thinking of Mom's cooking—meatballs and "smashed" potatoes—made my stomach growl.

"But don't you think it would be nice to go back?"

"Back to Kumpunotko? That's a good one."

"Well, why not?"

"Think! Tim and I in Kumpunotko? Next door to Mom and Dad?"

She had a point. Tina and Mom had always had a fairly tempestuous relationship—mostly down to Tina, I seem to remember—and I could hardly picture them settling down as happy neighbours. In fact, they hadn't spent much time together at all in recent years. Of course, Mom loved being a grandmother to little Sofie, but there was a certain frostiness between Mom and Tina. I wondered if there was something under that old family rug that I didn't know about.

"That's not what I meant. I meant, wouldn't it be great to be back there? Life was easier back then, without, you know, social media and the constant over-analysis of things . . . and the idea that North Korea might nuke us all at any moment," I added, slightly more miserably than I'd intended. I could see Tina losing patience with me.

"Listen, Peter. When you have kids, you stop looking back. You look forward to watching them grow."

"But you must be worried, no? I mean, climate change, wars, spies, missile tests. I have to say, I never thought we'd be back to giving people instructions on what to do during a nuclear attack," I said.

"Of course I worry. But"—she tilted her head in Sofie's direction—"the only way is forward. You have to focus on the future."

"But life was so much easier back then," I tried.

She sighed, hands on hips, a gesture as familiar as Mom's raspberry quark pie. "Was it really, though?"

"Yes! Just two TV channels, rock shows on the radio on Thursdays, no internet—the pace was slower."

"Maybe life was easier for you, Peter. You were just a kid. Your job was to sit in your room playing boring video games and developing strange new smells. But don't you think that life for the grown-ups then was just as troubling as it is for you now? Jobs and bills. Taxes and death. It's always been the same."

We stared at each other.

"Things change when you get older. It's called 'growing up.'"

"Oh, please. Who are you to say! You were off chasing gurus in India."

Sofie looked up again, a bemused smile on her face.

"You're so annoying," snapped Tina. "Are you trying to pick a fight? If that's what you want, I'll give you a fight, and don't think I can't take you down anymore!"

I knew she could.

"No. Not really. But I've been thinking about it a lot."

"Fighting me? Think again."

"No, not fighting you. How things used to be."

"Peter, have you been drinking?"

"No, I've been *thinking*."

"You have. I can smell it on you. Don't come around here like this again, please. Drunk and obnoxious."

"I'm not drunk."

"But you are obnoxious."

"Fine, I'm going. Don't bother making dinner for me."

"Fine, go."

"I will."

"Bye."

24

I grabbed my coat.

"Are you not going to say goodbye to your niece?"

It's hard to storm out when you're giving a kiss–cuddle–wave to a twelve-year-old.

I didn't slam the door, but I did glare at Tina on my way out.

When I got to the end of the path, she opened the front door and called after me in a voice loud enough for half of Helsinki to hear. "Do you remember that poster you had on your wall for a few months? Cyndi Lauper, wasn't it? And do you remember why you took it down?" My look didn't shoot daggers; ICBMs tore across the front lawn from my eyes to hers. How did she know about that!? "Yeah, they didn't make posters *tongue-proof* in the 1980s, did they?"

Slam.

My sister Tina. If anyone has ever had the last word against her, I've yet to hear about it.

FRIDAY afternoon had turned into Friday evening. The sun was still out and there was a group of teenagers throwing a Frisbee in the park. I hadn't seen a Frisbee in years.

Just as I turned the corner toward the train station, I bumped into Tim. He was obviously leaving the pub, but we both pretended that he'd been walking home from the station.

"Long day, eh?" I said.

"Yeah, busy keeping. Aren't you dinner staying for?"

Bless Tim. He always tries to speak Finnish, and then always looks relieved when I switch to English.

"Um, no, I have to get home to fix something."

"How are things?"

"Oh, same old same old."

"I hope it's a good same old?"

"Yeah," I said flatly, not wanting to tell him that his wife was the big sister from hell.

In fairness, he probably already knew.

We stood there, silent, for what felt longer than it really was. Then Tim cleared his throat, slapped my back, and said, "Thanks for helping out with Sofie. See ya later."

Although I certainly didn't need them, I grabbed a couple of beers for the train home and jammed in my headphones. I turned on Elvis Costello's *Goodbye Cruel World* and settled back into the eighties. I was done with the day. In fact, I felt done with the whole decade.

CHAPTER 4

DON'T YOU (FORGET ABOUT ME)

W HEN I got home, the Time Machine was waiting for me. I walked (okay, stumbled) through the door and there it was on the mat. An envelope postmarked Kumpunotko with an unfamiliar return address.

Dear Peter,

I do hope that this letter arrives as a complete surprise. That was the purpose of the exercise, do you remember? Let me jog your memory. Kumpunotko High School, English class, January 1986. We were doing an assignment on current affairs, and I thought it would be fun for you all to write to your future selves. As promised, I haven't peeked—I know it's personal. The envelope is still sealed.

As an aside, I've retired now, and it's been a lot of fun going through the class list, remembering all the names and faces. It's also been fun tracking you all down. Some are still living in Kumpunotko. Some, like you, living in Helsinki, were easy enough to find, but some of the class are now in Dubai, Thailand, Scotland, the USA! Many have new names too, and not just the girls.

Anyway, I hope that you enjoy opening your little "Time Machine," and I hope that you are well and enjoying life. I always had high hopes for you, Peter.

Fond regards,

Your teacher, Hanna

I must have stood in my hallway for a full five minutes, frozen in time and space, a streetlight streaming through the kitchen window and casting a long shadow into the living room/office area. All I could do was stare at the letter and marvel at how a few sentences can bring back to life a person you hadn't thought about for decades.

Hanna . . . My first thought was that she must have been pushing eighty! My second was that I was now probably older than she had been when she'd stood at the front of the class and asked us to write the letter.

How did *that* happen?

And the Time Machine . . . ?

I wasn't sure quite how to approach it. I started with the music, turning on Total 80s FM. "Happy Hour" by the Housemartins—a song that never fails to make me smile—blared out of my small, surprisingly powerful speakers. Then I slipped my shoes off, lay down on the couch, and looked at the envelope, addressed to me in my own always-sloppy handwriting. "Personal," Hanna had called it.

Peter Eksell, c/o The Future!

Just the look of the envelope took me back to my high-school days. First of all, it was brown. Nobody used brown envelopes anymore. And nobody licked their envelopes anymore, either, and I could tell the sender had done just that. That was my spit, my three-decades-old spit, holding it shut.

I ripped the envelope open and unfolded the paper.

Dear Me!

It's me here—the 1986 you! Remember me?

Hanna has asked us to write a letter to ourselves in thirty years' time, as part of a book project. She chose H. G Wells's The Sleeper Awakes. In class we've been talking about how events that seem massively important can fade and be forgotten altogether, while one tiny thing can stay with us forever. And how we can't always tell which are going to end up being which. Like, I'm sitting in this classroom now, with certain things on my mind (how cold it is, the dance next month), but by the summer they won't be important any more, and next January I'll have other worries (finals, UGH), and in fifteen years I won't remember what school was really like (as if I could forget!) and in thirty years the things that are currently current in my life will all be history, forgotten. That's the theory anyway. I mean, I can't imagine a day going by without Mikke's stupid grin (he is very funny though). Or how I will make sense of life without talking the day through with Jennifer.

So anyway, I'm supposed to write about a thing that happened that's really important to me, and then see if YOU can remember it. Mine's the hard part—I have to write it down. All you have to do is remember it. Plus, Hanna says you won't be tested on it! (Not by her anyway.)

So here's the important thing that's happened. Three weeks ago, Tina and Mom had a massive argument. Plates smashed, rude words, the works. And Tina stormed out of the house, slammed the front door, and shouted, "THAT'S IT, I'M LEAVING!" Again. I mean, she's probably run away from home more times than I've played The Hobbit on my Spectrum. In fact, one of my/our youngest memories is of the police bringing her back after they found her asleep at the back of the coffee shop next to the Atlas. She'd have been about seven. But I'm getting sidetracked. This time when she ran away, she actually did. Being on a gap year, with nothing holding her back, she walked into Kumpunotko, caught the train to Helsinki, and went to stay with a friend she knew from high school who'd moved there. Normally when she runs away, it takes a few hours or even days for the anger to wear off, and then she and Mom come to some kind of truce, and Dad drives off to get her. Not this time. She'd applied to university and been accepted, and she's got a new job as a waitress in Helsinki until then. And Mom and Dad are both totally fine with that. Dad drove off, but instead of bringing her back, he took a load of her stuff. He said she's got a nice apartment.

I didn't think I'd miss her—she drives me insane, taking my stuff without asking and screaming at me if I so much as look at her room. But it's so quiet in our house now. Like, spooky-quiet, so I won't mind if she comes back to visit from time to time, and I do hope she's okay.

I don't think any of us were ready for the ch-ch-ch-ch-changes. Mom keeps coming into my room to check if I'm okay. And Dad's taken up baking bread. Baking! I just cannot understand how that one thing led to the other, but I suppose a butterfly flaps its wing in Tokyo, and all that . . .

Anyway, Jennifer said she totally understands. She said it's the "small town blues," and that Tina was right to get away before she exploded. I suppose she has a point. She always does. She's smart that way, but I help her out with school stuff, so it all balances out. She says she can't wait to get out either. She says she has no doubt I will. "You're going places, Peter," she said to me the other day.

I mean, of course I'll move to the city and get a job in computing and be the big success everyone says I'm going to be. But I'm happy here in the meantime. I'm in no great hurry. I'll get there.

Anyway, Hanna is handing out the envelopes for us to seal up our Time Machines, so I'd better sign off. Did you remember the World War III that blew the Eksell family apart? The whole thing? Parts of it? Or was Tina's dramatic departure just another forgettable episode? (She would hate that. Personally, I'm guessing she'll be home within a week once she realizes she can't work the washing machine.)

Before I go: How did you do with life? Did you come up with a way-cool game or some totally crazy invention to change the world of computing? Do you have a flying car? A video Walkman? Pizza pills for lunch? Did you get the dream girl? Man, I hope so. Can't wait to find out!

Live long and prosper!

P

I sat there for a while, blinking. I couldn't remember the lesson itself, or the exercise, and even the explosive episode in Eksell family life had mostly faded from my mind. As far as I could remember, Tina did move out around then, but of the departure itself, her storming out . . . nothing. But I did remember one thing from that time very clearly: the way I'd felt about Jennifer Berg.

CHAPTER 5

HOLDING BACK THE YEARS

ONCE, when I still had a job, we had a team-building event where we all had to put cinnamon in our mouths and hold our noses. It was weird, but without the smell I couldn't taste it. I just knew I had something powdery on my tongue. When we were told to let go of our noses, all sensations came rushing in at once.

And that's exactly what happened when all those memories came flooding back. Not just the music and the films—they still featured in my everyday life, nerd that I am—but the cafeteria smells and the little background sounds: Converse squeaking on the basketball court, my locker door rattling, the smell of paint thinner in our art class. I saw faces: Mikke copying my English homework just before class, our math teacher shaking her head at me in disbelief, in a good way, and our gym teacher shaking his head at me in disbelief, in a disappointed way. But what flooded back the most were the feelings.

Academically, there was the pressure of meeting my teachers' expectations. And socially, there were moments when I worried that everyone else had been to some kind of special training day where they'd learned to be cool. I, too, wanted to say funny and clever things to make people like me. To make a certain person like me.

Then came other memories, rolling out in an eighties-TV-show-flashback sort of way—old scenes viewed through a soft lens. Riding my bike to school. A teacher writing on the transparent sheet of an overhead projector. Whispering Battleship coordinates to Mikke in class. Sami getting busted for stashing a copy of *Playboy* inside his geography textbook.

It took no more than a nanosecond ("a one-thousand-millionth of a second," I heard our math teacher's voice say in my head), but suddenly, I was back in school. It was totally amazing—and what struck me most, after just a few moments of reminiscing, was how *rich* my life had been back then.

When we're at school, we take it for granted that, each day, we're part of a close-knit network of friends (well, not all friends, but y'know . . .), and that each classroom is part of a larger system, with thousands of interwoven connections. That life, from 8 a.m. until 4 p.m., is a well-ordered chaos of different subjects: academic, practical, artistic, sporty.

My life had been so colourful, so wonderful, so . . . full! And that Time Machine, which blasted me right back to the eighties, was the most exhilarating thing that had happened to me in, well, longer than I cared to think about.

I read it a second time, pacing around the apartment.

First, I read Hanna's letter again. And then I read mine. Hanna's. Mine. Again and again. That Hanna had written "*I always had high hopes for you, Peter*" put a smile on my face. She was the sweetest person. And then Jennifer saying, "You're going places, Peter." Those sentences were like an elixir—an intravenous shot of espresso, a reboot of all my youthful optimism.

Total 80s FM had switched gears to a more big-hair list with some great guitar songs. And as Bon Jovi's "Livin' on a Prayer" reached its massive guitar riff, I pulled out my air guitar and played a solo that would have made Richie Sambora proud. My fingers were fast, my overbite mean—"Whooooooooah!"—and my head-banging fierce, even if my hair wasn't quite what it had once been. I dropped to my knees and brought the solo to its climax just as Total 80s FM's automated DJ-bot hopped coldly to the next song.

I took a photo of the letter so I could post it on Facebook, which is what you do when interesting things happen, right? But then I read it again and pocketed my phone. As Hanna had said, this was "personal."

I thought about the other thing she'd written, that she'd "always had high hopes" for me.

"Peter always had high hopes for himself too . . . ," I said in my movie-narrator voice, but the words trailed off as I looked around my little world.

My apartment. It was a nice one-bedroom flat in a good suburb of Helsinki, decorated in a minimalist, ascetic style (read as: I can't be bothered with interior design). A big fifty-four-inch TV and my couch took up two-thirds of the living room, the remaining third being my office. I didn't have curtains in the windows but I had a rug on the floor. My CD towers were still on both sides of the TV, even though I no longer owned a stereo. Since buying the small but surprisingly powerful speaker system that streamed any song I wanted from the internet, opening a CD case seemed hopelessly archaic. And let's not even talk about my vinyl.

The kitchen only had space for a table and four chairs, three of which may as well have still been in their flat-pack boxes. The fourth was also practically new, as I usually read my morning paper standing up at the counter by the window, and had my evening meal on the couch, in front of a movie.

I gave my own letter another read, and the line about Dad's bread baking made me chuckle. I'd forgotten all about it, but I bet my parents had neighbours who still remembered the time the fire department came to our house twice in a week.

I read the line about flying cars and crazy inventions and I sighed. And then the line that hit me like a cold slap: "Did you get the girl?" I sat back down and flipped the music off.

Jennifer. Around the time I wrote the letter, the knowledge that I'd see her at school was what got me out of bed in the morning. She made me feel good about, well, most things. She even made me believe that my ramblings about the deeper meanings of Spandau Ballet's lyrics were interesting. "You're going places," she'd said. Of course, my parents and teachers said that too—expected nothing less—but she seemed to really believe that I could do whatever I wanted in life.

I chuckled again and shook my head. The things we say and do when we're young.

"One day, in a small town in Finland . . . ," I started, but nothing followed. My mind was still on Jennifer. Thinking about it now, I realized that there had only been one thing I'd really wanted to do in life, and I *had* really put my mind to it—in fact, I'd thought about it endlessly. I'd wanted to cross the threshold from friendship with Jennifer to something else.

But I'd seen what Tina did to all the guys who pushed too hard, and I didn't want to end up like them. (Some of them, I expect, are still in therapy.) So I hadn't pushed at all. I didn't dare. Besides, I'd always thought it was about destiny.

★ ★ ★

I needed some air. And by "air" I mean "more beer." I left my apartment and headed for the store on the corner.

Sitting outside was a group of hoodie-wearing teenagers—hoods up, of course—passing cans of beer to each other. I'd seen them there before, and I knew one of the kids lived in my building, so I nodded to them and smiled. I may even have winked.

"Hey, old-timer," said one of the kids. "Wanna join us?"

I stopped in my tracks, my heart suddenly thumping. Sitting on a Friday night with a can of beer in my hand, just hanging out, chilling with the boys? I was tempted.

"Isn't it nearly bedtime?" I quipped. "For me, I mean," I added lamely, not wanting them to think I was telling them off.

Silence followed me inside.

Under the glaring neon, in front of the humming fridge, I looked at the rows of cans. A couple more would be enough for me. I could feel the lure of an uncomfortable night's sleep on the couch calling. But then my thoughts returned to the boys outside. What if I *did* roll up with a six-pack, join them on the curb, offer them the wisdom of my forty-six years in exchange for the wisdom of their sixteen? What if I bonded with them? What if we got a bottle or two and all headed back to my place, and they called some more friends over, and we danced into the night to the greatest tunes of the eighties, and the party went down in local legend? What if I did something *spontaneous*?

The door to the store whooshed closed behind me and I walked to the corner, the weight of the extra cans like a trophy in a proud hunter's hands. I just about caught sight of the last of the boys, sloping off around the corner a few blocks away.

"Hey," I said softly. "It's Friday night."

As I walked back home, humming along to John Fogerty's "The Old Man Down the Road," something the kid had said echoed in my mind. He'd called me an "old-timer"! I was *not* an old-timer. I was forty-six, just like Christopher Lloyd had been when they shot *Back to the Future*—probably the best movie ever made.

Granted, he did play "Doc" Brown, the crazy-haired . . . old-timer.

CHAPTER 6

PHOTOGRAPH

B ACK in my apartment, the streetlight was throwing a yellow glow on the Bryan Adams T-shirt I'd bought at my first rock show in Helsinki. I'd framed it and hung it on the wall when I moved in.

Well, the shirt was coming down. It came down from the wall, it came out of the frame, and I slipped into it. I say *slipped*, but perhaps *struggled* would be more to the point. It had obviously shrunk while up in the frame. Oh well. I shoved the letters into my back pocket and headed down to the Garage of Good Intentions, along with my six-pack.

I had been so excited when I moved into my apartment and discovered that not only did it have a parking lot, but I also got my own personal garage. I had so many great plans for that space.

It was at the other end of our white-brick building, which meant I had to walk out and along the full length of the apartments, running the risk of an encounter with Mrs. Hellgren. She was in her eighties, and the unofficial queen of the building (official, if you asked her). She made it her business to know who everybody was, as well as everything they did and everything they didn't do. "I've lived here since the 1960s," she would remind me every time I broke one of her unwritten rules.

I walked next to the wall, where she couldn't see me. I knew she'd probably hear my garage door opening, but by then it would be too late.

I pulled the handle, opened the dark, wood-panelled door about a third of the way, and snuck underneath it like Indiana Jones. I reached back for my imaginary hat and quickly closed the door.

Safe.

In one of Malcolm Gladwell's books, he writes about a study in which strangers got fifteen minutes to examine a person's apartment before they filled out a questionnaire about that person. When they compared the strangers' answers to those provided by the person's close friends, they learned that the strangers were more accurate at predicting the person's emotional stability and their openness to new experiences.

A stranger spending fifteen minutes in my garage would have had his work cut out for him. He would have seen the weights stacked neatly by the bench and deduced that I was a keep-fit kind of guy. He would have seen the electric guitar and the small Marshall amp and concluded that I was perhaps an amateur musician. He wouldn't have known that I'd once binged on the *Rocky* movies and thought I could easily bulk up, or that I'd wasted a few hundred euros on the assumption that I could easily learn how to play like Prince in *Purple Rain*.

And so on.

I cracked a beer.

Over the years, things add up. There were boxes of Webscoe

stationary, and smaller boxes of my Webscoe CEO business cards, all pushed away, out of sight, under a bookshelf in the back.

Not everything in the garage was there to enshrine another failed attempt at self-improvement. The stack of cardboard boxes along the walls was testament to a different kind of laziness; there had been one or two moves when I'd just carted the boxes from one storage place to another without even bothering to open them. I wasn't even completely certain what some of them contained.

That was about to change. In just a few hours, I had lost my only client, had a stupid argument with my sister, and received a strange letter from the past. I was angry and sad. If for some reason I'd tried to explain this all to Tina, she likely would have talked about how the universe would even things out. But I resented the universe. I didn't need the cosmos; I was going to create order in chaos myself.

I was going to clean up the garage.

I lifted the bike up to a hook in the ceiling, put the guitar in its case, and made a slightly neater pyramid of the weights. Pleased with the good start, I picked up one of the dumbbells and did a few curls. I glanced at myself in a dusty mirror on the wall and quickly put the dumbbell back in its place. The Bryan Adams T-shirt wasn't a flattering look.

I swept the area in the middle and moved on toward the back, where the pile of old boxes lived. Moving half a dozen of them revealed a wooden bookshelf, and on it, a black JVC CD/cassette player, which I remembered buying in my late teens for what now seemed an obscene amount. It had a five-band graphic equalizer and Dynamic Bass Boost. I wiped off the dust, plugged it in, and pressed Play on the cassette deck. The guitars on Rainbow's "I Surrender" startled me, and when I took a step back, I tripped on one of the boxes and ended up sitting in it.

When I finally got up, I picked up the plastic case next to the player. I couldn't remember exactly who the intended recipient of this particular mix-tape was, though I did detect a certain theme: "I Surrender," "Move Closer," "Every Breath You Take."

Yes, it was the theme shared with every other mix-tape I or anybody else in the world has ever made—love. And the fact that it was gathering dust in my garage, rather than in a certain someone's tape collection, was a good indicator of my success in that department.

On the same shelf, next to the cassette player, was a pile of my old vinyl records—once my most prized possessions. I didn't have a turntable in the garage, but that didn't stop me spending a while looking at the artwork, the track listings, the sleeve notes. I remember the frustration of the journey home from the record store, finally having the new Queen compilation but not being able to listen to it yet; the tingle of anticipation.

Fifteen minutes later, I cracked another beer and got to the last three boxes. They were among the oldest in the garage; I hadn't seen them in years. Humming along to my excellent mix-tape—"Who Can It Be Now?" by Men at Work—I looked inside the first one. It was full of VHS tapes, some home-recorded, many of them rentals I had "borrowed" from Video 2000.

In the same box, as padding, were three of the promo T-shirts we had to wear at work. They each had a movie slogan in the back. One of them announced that the heat was on, another asked, *Who ya gonna call?* and the third, cleverly, had *wax on* on the front, and *wax off* on the back.

Under all of that was an old Rubik's Cube, and next to it the screwdriver I'd used to take it apart so I could "solve" it. There were some old coins, novelty mugs, video game cassettes, pencils, pens, and a copy of Jules Verne's *Around the World in Eighty Days*, my favourite book growing up.

Seeing all that old stuff took me back to my little room in Kumpunotko, crouched over my Sinclair ZX Spectrum+. It was nothing, ridiculously feeble, an eight-bit computer with forty-eight kilobytes of memory—about enough to hold a low-res thumbnail JPEG—just a keyboard connected to a little TV set on my desk, but it opened the door to a new world.

The world of *The Hobbit*, for example, a game I loved. Just the thought of playing eighties games again made my fingers twitch, literally. I was sure there was a *Donkey Kong* game somewhere in the boxes so I dug deeper, but all I found was more junk: old magazines and comics, and a few newspapers I'd saved for no apparent reason. "Kasparov and Karpov End 11th Game in Draw" read one headline; "Soviet Offers Trade: A-Site Inspection for End to Blasts" proclaimed another; a third announced, "Star Wars 'Ballet' Scheduled."

Whatever was in the third box would have to wait, because when I picked up Verne's book, something flew out. It was a photo I hadn't seen in decades.

There were two people in that photo, a young man and a young woman.

He has his arm around her as they both look straight into the camera with big smiles on their faces. They're in a school gym, but he's wearing a tuxedo with a turquoise cummerbund. On his hands, white gloves. She's wearing an electric-blue Victorian gown. The satin dress has short, puffy sleeves, so she's wearing long gloves, the same colour as her dress. The front of the gloves, and the square collar of the dress, are decorated with black lace. Her dark blonde hair is in an elaborate bun, and to top it off, she's wearing an elegant hat with peacock feathers.

She is absolutely gorgeous. A knockout. A beauty. Stunning.
It was the only photo I had of her, but that didn't matter.
I didn't need photos.
I remembered everything about Jennifer.

CHAPTER 7

WALKING ON SUNSHINE

I'M so happy you're not freaking out about the dance like everybody else," Jennifer said. It was a warm September afternoon, and I was leaning on my bike outside her house, while she sat on the big rock next to her mailbox. Our usual setup.

"Why would I be? It's months away."

"I know, but my parents are already planning for it. Mom's going to take me to Helsinki to see some gowns, and Dad's got a big pile of camcorder brochures on his desk."

"Wow, that is serious."

"Yes," she said gravely. "It is *tradition*. And *tradition* must be *respected*."

"I still don't get how the Viennese waltz is a Finnish tradition," I said glumly.

"Ours is not to question why," she said, doing a passable impression of AJ, the gym teacher whose job it was to teach us the ancient dance routines. "Ours is to follow the steps of our forebears." I had to laugh—whenever AJ said that, Mikke and Sami would growl and do bear impressions behind his back.

"Aren't your parents the same? I thought your mom would love the sense of ceremony."

"Not really. I think Tina made sure they didn't get anywhere near her plans."

"Lucky you. Hey, send her over to deal with my parents."

The thought of Tina reading the riot act to Jennifer's parents made me laugh. Although Jennifer's dad was tricky, known for his temper.

"Didn't your sister wear pants to the dance?" she asked.

"Mm-hmm."

"What a rebel!" said Jennifer with a grin.

"Yeah, but the teachers didn't even bat an eyelash. Nobody minded. She was so angry!"

Jennifer laughed. "I know some of the girls in our year want to wear pants too. So *progressive*. So some of the boys are talking about wearing dresses, just to annoy them. But I think it's cool to dress up once in a while. I just don't think it's worth spending a year panicking about."

"Of course," I agreed.

I mean, of course I agreed. I always agreed with Jennifer. Not out of awe or whatever, but because we were in tune with one another. We thought alike.

"So," she said with a conspiratorial smile. "How's your partner?"

That was *the* big issue, of course. Having learned from past experiences, AJ had come up with a system for keeping the teenagers' courting period as short as possible: he assigned everybody their practice partners at the start of the school year, and if anybody wanted to switch, they needed to let him know on or before December 1 so he could ensure everybody still had a partner. A daylong transfer window, just like in the hockey season, only shorter and more hormonal.

"She's good. She can dance. Yours?"

"He's no Kevin Bacon. Not yet, anyway."

"You can always get another partner. I bet most guys would want to dance with you."

"Most guys?" she repeated, and gave me one of those mischievous smiles I loved and hated to see (mostly loved).

A month later, the leaves on the birches in Jennifer's yard had turned red and yellow, and then fallen off. Jennifer was wearing a white sweater as she sat on the rock; I was leaning on my Crescent's saddle.

"Have you asked anyone to the dance?" she said, apropos of nothing.

The moment I had been waiting for, hoping for, praying for—had it actually arrived?

"Not yet," I said, trembling slightly.

"Well you'd better get a move on, silly, or all the good ones will be taken."

A beat. A surging confidence began to build in me.

All through the autumn, I'd known this moment would come. Each time we'd talked about the dance I'd seen that playfulness in her eyes. And now here she was, practically asking me to ask her.

She sighed and a note of sadness crept into her voice. "Sami asked me," she said. "And I said yes. AJ's already found a new partner for my guy."

"Oh," I said, as brightly as a flickering bulb. "Great!"

Somehow I fought off the urge to run screaming for the hills. "That's great!" I said again.

Jennifer stared off into the distance.

I took that as my cue to leave.

And as I rode away, Bryan Adams's "Jealousy" started to play in my head.

THE day of the dance was February 14, 1986, Valentine's Day, except that the tradition hadn't made its way to Finland yet. English was the last class of our already shortened day, and since Hanna knew our minds were on the dance, she let us go home at noon to prepare.

Jennifer and I walked together to the bus stop.

"Are you all set?" she asked. "I have so much to do! I never thought I'd care this much about the dance. Tell me not to worry. Tell me not to care."

"Don't worry, don't care," I said flatly. She forced a laugh. "Honestly, you don't have to worry about a thing. I've seen you at practice—you're doing great."

I wasn't just trying to make her feel better. I had watched her at our rehearsals, and she was wonderful. Graceful. Beautiful.

"Besides, if anybody is going to rip his pants and fall on his face, it's going to be this guy," I said, and pointed my thumb at myself. "And you," I said, now pointing at her with my index finger, "you'll be perfect—as usual."

"Oh, stop it," she said.

So I didn't say anything.

"No, don't actually stop it, silly," she added with a laugh, looping her arm through mine. "You're the best."

"I suppose it is a little easier for us guys. I'm just going to pick up my tuxedo on my way home," I said. "Then I'll only have about five hours to do my hair, so I'll be cutting it close."

Her giggles made me feel like I was Eddie Murphy, so I walked with a little spring in my step the rest of the way.

Around us, snowflakes were falling slowly. The days were getting longer again, but the winter was still bleak, especially the snowy days. Kumpunotko's downtown was small, only a few blocks wide each way, but everything I needed was right there: the bookstore, the record store, the newsagent's, the video store, and the movie theatres (Kumponotko, despite having only one set of traffic lights, had two movie theatres).

It was weird to see Kumpunotko in the middle of a weekday. I'd only really seen it on the weekends, never when I should have been at school. People were out and about, working, running errands. Mothers with preschoolers filled the pavements; a man was blocking traffic while he unloaded boxes of fish; outside the Atlas, one of the theatres, two workmen were unrolling a red carpet.

I waited at the stop with Jennifer, and when she climbed into the bus and waved goodbye, wiggling her fingers, I held a smile until the bus drove off.

I pulled up my coat collar and headed for the only dry cleaners in town. The owner was a friend of my dad's, and he had a tuxedo for me.

An hour later, I was back home with the tux, getting ready to get ready for the dance. I didn't know what all the fuss was about. All I had to do was shower and get dressed.

Since I had some time to spare, I went to my room to play *The Hobbit*. The game had been Tina's Christmas present to me, but in the month and a half that I'd had it, I'd only solved 25 percent of the adventure. Frustrated at my slow pace, I'd even read the Tolkien book that came with the game, but it hadn't helped much.

I'd just switched to *Hungry Horace*, Spectrum's version of *Pac-Man*, when Mom knocked on my door. She opened it carefully, pushing a pair of sweat pants on the floor out of the way with her foot.

"Did you get the tuxedo? Are you nervous? Would you like a sandwich?"

Mom didn't waste any time.

"Yes, I did. Not too nervous. And it's okay, I'll come down in a second and grab a bowl of cereal or something."

"Cereal," she scoffed. "You need to eat real food. Can I see the tuxedo on you? Come downstairs and I'll make you a sandwich."

She closed the door. I turned off my Spectrum and tore open the plastic bag the tuxedo had come in. I had never worn a tux in my life. I had never even worn a real suit, to be honest. When I saw myself in the bathroom mirror—or, the two-thirds of myself I could see while standing on the toilet—a sense of power and pride filled me.

I looked good.

Mom called me from the kitchen and I walked down like I was Roger Moore in *For Your Eyes Only*.

"Oh my goodness," Mom said as I made my entrance. "You're a regular Philip Marlowe."

"The namesh Bond," I said, politely but firmly bringing her up to date. "Jamesh Bond."

Mom laughed. I liked it. I liked to make Mom laugh.

Then she made me sit down at the table and eat. When Dad saw that I was about to be handling food, he rushed out of the room and returned with a white bedsheet, which he wrapped around me.

"You don't want to go to the dance with sauce on your shirt," he said. "Take it from one who knows."

After I'd eaten, he offered to help with my bow tie. He spun me around because he only knew how to do the tie around his own neck. I had a brief memory of when he used to sit me on his lap to do my shoelaces. He stood behind me and hummed an old-timer song right into my ear. He seemed to be way more excited than I was about the school dance.

After that, I went back upstairs to . . . well, to look at myself in the mirror some more.

"Ah, hello, Mish Moneypenny," I said, throwing my imaginary hat onto an imaginary hat stand. I reached for the imaginary diamond-studded cigarette case in my inside pocket. To my surprise, the pocket wasn't empty. I pulled out something that looked like a postcard.

The card was two-toned blue and white, and featured two logos: the local appliance store's at the top, and JVC's at the bottom. In the middle were the words *Back to the Future*, styled just like the movie poster. I flipped the card over.

To celebrate the exciting new range of JVC products arriving at our shop this spring, we are delighted to invite you to a private sneak preview of the
Hollywood blockbuster
Back to the Future
Friday, February 14, 4 p.m.
Atlas Theatre, Kumpunotko

My mind raced. I knew about *Back to the Future*. Big Hollywood films always took a few months to make it over to Europe, and then a few more months to creep from the cities to our little backwater. Even so, I'd heard whispers that the film existed—excited whispers too. I didn't have a clue what the title meant. How could you go back to the future? Surely you had to go *back* to the past and *forward* to the future?

Minor details.

This was big news!

A sneak preview of a "Hollywood blockbuster" was happening in my little town, on that very day, and I held in my hand an invitation.

If I even for a moment entertained the idea of doing the right thing—which would have been finding the true recipient of the invitation—it flew out the window when I remembered what I'd seen in town earlier and realized I would be walking the red carpet, in a tuxedo, like a Hollywood star.

Slight problem: the sneak preview started at 4 p.m. and our dance began at 6 p.m. I could make it from the Atlas to school in ten minutes—if I ran.

My dance partner was Sara. She was a much better dancer than I was. We didn't talk much during the rehearsals. I was generally too busy counting one-two-three-four, and she was too busy sighing at my incompetence.

She was a petite blonde, one of the smart girls in class. I could have done a lot worse, in terms of potential dance partners, but let me put it this way: I was ready to miss the first dance with Sara for a great movie. Had my dance partner been Jennifer, I might not have taken the chance.

In retrospect, I'm glad I did. In fact, seeing *Back to the Future* that February day in 1986 was so integral to my personal space-time continuum that I can't imagine how my life would have turned out if I hadn't gone.

CHAPTER 8

SWEET DREAMS
(ARE MADE OF THIS)

Q UARTER to four, I was outside the Atlas. Of the two movie theatres in Kumpunotko, it was the smaller. And since people often take bigger for better, the other one had become more popular. I liked the Atlas, though. It was in a beautiful two-storey brownstone on Main Street, sandwiched between the appliance store and a coffee shop. It had opened in the early 1920s as a large-ish bakery before some visionary entrepreneur—or a developer—decided to turn it into a smallish movie theatre.

It also had one of those gorgeous neon signs so that at night, you could see *Atlas* written in red lights above the town.

For reasons I didn't fully understand, the most popular seats in the house were on the balcony, and the front-row balcony tickets always went first. But I thought the best seat was downstairs, right in the middle, in front of the thick pillar that supported the balcony.

The red carpet was there, and outdoor torches were burning, but I didn't see any people outside. Where were the camera-waving press? It finally dawned on me that it was ten below zero, and there wasn't likely to be any Hollywood A-listers at Kumpunotko's second-best cinema.

My dancing shoes were slippery on the snow, so instead of walking like a proper person, I had two options: to shuffle my feet as if cross-country skiing, or to waddle like a penguin. I shuffled to the red carpet. I'd brought proper footwear in my bag, for the run to school, but I didn't want to make my grand red-carpet entrance in big winter boots.

"The fans have been waiting for hours," I said in my movie-narrator voice, "and there he finally is. Peter Eksell, the hottest actor in town, is about to cut the ribbon to the premiere of his latest hit."

I pulled open the massive glass door and walked into the lobby. A few people were milling about. The box office was closed, presumably because no tickets were being sold. On the walls were large posters promoting the other features—*Star Trek III, Rambo II.* The tiny lobby had been turned into a showroom, and I could see the appliance store manager standing behind what looked like a school desk.

A young lady—I imagined her to be the manager's daughter—stepped up and welcomed me to the theatre.

"Thanks, here's my invitation," I said, my voice slightly deeper than usual. I was anxious to get past her, worried that I'd be exposed as an impostor. I didn't even have a backup story to explain my presence. My mind was racing, creating all kinds of scenarios around what might happen next, but they had one theme in common: she was going to laugh and throw me out.

She smiled and barely glanced at the invitation.

"Welcome, step right in! Have a look at the JVC products in the lobby, and try some snacks, sir," she said.

Sir? I thought, but what came out of my mouth was, "Thank you, I will."

And that was it. I was in. I didn't know exactly what I'd done to deserve this stroke of good fortune, but it hardly mattered. I grabbed a brochure and, to avoid suspicion, examined the camcorders and walkmans (lowercase *w* because they weren't real Sony Walkmans) on stands in the lobby. After a minute or so, I couldn't take the suspense anymore. I walked in to the theatre. There were a couple dozen people dotted around, but nobody had yet taken "my" seat, so I darted for it and made myself comfortable.

A few minutes later, the man from the appliance store walked to the front and coughed to get everybody's attention. He gave a short speech, mostly about the resilience and economic benefits of JVC electrical goods. There were a couple of pauses, in which I think he expected people to laugh. He looked nervous.

" . . . And without any further ado, please enjoy the movie. Roll the tape," he said in what I guess he thought was a director's accent, and walked off the stage.

The lights went down, the curtains went up, and the Earth in the Universal logo appeared on the screen. The seat next to me was empty. I stuffed my big yellow down jacket on it and waited for the movie to cast its spell. My only regret was that I hadn't taken some of the candy in the lobby.

Steven Spielberg presents . . .

Definitely a good start. Spielberg was the man behind *Jaws* and *Raiders of the Lost Ark*—both on my Top 10 list, and both of which I had watched on tape while "working" at Video 2000.

A ticking sound. The screen's still black.

A Robert Zemeckis film . . .

The ticking sounds got louder, with more clocks added to the choir. The word *Back* appeared from the right, with *to the Future* underneath it half a second later. I still didn't know what that meant. I briefly wondered if the film was going to be a total load of nonsense, and if I would somehow get in trouble for sneaking out early.

Whatever doubts I may have had were mostly gone by the time the next line appeared on the screen:

Starring Michael J. Fox

I was a huge fan of *Family Ties,* and had once, inspired by his character, worn a knitted tie to school. Once.

By the time Marty got blown away by the gigantic guitar amplifier and raced to school on a skateboard, I was deep inside the movie's world.

I cheered for Doc when he successfully completed his first time travel test. I laughed when Biff got buried under a truckload of manure. I squirmed a little when Lorraine Baines, played by Lea Thompson, looked at Marty *like that*, not realizing she would one day be his mom. I cackled when Marty played "Johnny B. Goode," and my heart melted when he got back to the Lone Pine parking lot and Doc showed him the letter.

An hour and fifty-six minutes later, my life had changed. No longer did I want to be Alex Keaton of *Family Ties*; I wanted to be Marty. I wanted to look like him (and, frankly, I thought I did look a bit like him); I wanted to dress like him; I wanted to be just as quick-witted as him. The fact that I lived in Kumpunotko, which is basically Finnish for "Hill Valley," was surely a sign. Destiny, right?

And then there was the not-so-small matter of Jennifer, Marty McFly's beautiful girlfriend. She's the first thing Marty mentions as a reason to get back to his own time. Doc Brown asks him if she's pretty, and Marty says she's not only beautiful, but she's also crazy about him.

I, too, had a girl friend—not a *girlfriend*, of course—named Jennifer, and I liked her very, very much. And she, too, was beautiful. Was she crazy about me?

Surely.

I took it as another sign.

All I wanted to do was sit there through the final credits and then have the projectionist reload the first reel so I could watch the movie all over again. I wanted to stay in the darkness of the Atlas, with my new friends Marty and Doc, and Lorraine, and Jennifer. I wanted to hear the whirr of the projector and feel the full blast of a movie audio system. I wanted to be taken somewhere else.

Somewhere else! That's exactly where I was supposed to be.

I slipped off my dancing shoes, climbed into my boots, skipped out through the lobby, and started to run, wishing I had a skateboard so I could grab the back of a passing truck and get pulled along the street.

I was so full of energy that I sprinted full out to the first intersection, about eighty metres away. The market square was empty and dark, just like the parking lot of the Two Pines Mall had been in the movie. A car full of guys was driving slowly along Main Street, probably the local Biff and his gang.

I ran a little faster and glanced at the big clock on top of the bank building. It was not a majestic nineteenth-century clock tower like the one in the movie; it was a gigantic twentieth-century digital clock with red numbers. Right then the numbers that were glowing were five and fifty-eight. The dance would begin in two minutes, and I was at least five minutes from the school.

I made a sharp right turn and sprinted as fast as I could until my lungs were burning. I ran by my friend Mikke's house on Maple Street and saw that it was dark. Sometimes, when I walked by their house in the winter, I could see his mom in the kitchen. She was always baking. But Mikke was obviously already at the school. His dad was surely there to take photos, as usual, and his mom was there with a freshly baked apple pie, just in case.

"Great Scott!" I yelled, and pumped the air with my fist.

I could see the school building ahead.

CHAPTER 9

LET'S DANCE

I was a little late, yes. I stuffed my jacket into my locker and ran up to the first-floor ballroom—formerly known as the gym. From elsewhere in the school I could hear the hubbub of voices. It was odd to be in the building outside of normal school hours; it added to the special feeling of it being *our* night. The seniors had left the school to prepare for their final exams, so the place was ours now—hence the traditional dance to celebrate.

Sara was waiting for me on the landing, her arms crossed, tapping her fingers on her arm. She was wearing a long carmine evening gown, but true to her New Wave style and philosophy, she was also wearing fingerless gloves, and chiffon scarves around her wrists.

"Finally!" she said.

"I'm . . . so . . . sorry," I gasped, panting and leaning against my knees. I managed to straighten up, get my breathing back under control. "Care to dance?" I said, and offered her my arm.

I had no clue where that came from. I didn't usually have such confidence with anyone other than Jennifer, and Sara seemed as

58

surprised as I was. She stared at my arm for a few seconds before smiling and locking her arm onto mine.

"Let's dance," she said.

We were the last couple to arrive in the small backstage storage area behind the gym. AJ raised his eyebrows at me, but fortunately, there was no time for questions—right on cue, the prelude for the first music began. AJ huffed, turned around, and started to guide the dancers out into the ballroom to the gentle applause (and camcorder whirrs) of our parents.

Sara and I were at the back of the line, which gave me ample time to observe my schoolmates as, in pairs, they left the dark backstage area and entered the ballroom's bright lights. We didn't have a real band to play the tunes—most of the people in the school band were on the dance floor—so Hanna had been put in charge of the PA system.

It's funny, because for the previous few months, since September, we'd practised for this moment. Every other gym class was devoted to rehearsing the archaic dance steps. The two classes in our year—about sixty teenagers—gathered in the gymnasium and shuffled their feet around the basketball court, their eyes firmly on the ground, counting the beats, trying to stay in line, tripping, guffawing, starting over. And as the weeks had passed, and the partner-exchange transfer window closed, we'd had drummed into us the seriousness of the situation, the importance of getting it right, of not messing up in front of our parents, of not letting down the school and the tradition and the expectations of the generations who'd gone before us. Pressure? Well yes, a bit. But as we lined up to file through that door, I felt nothing but a sense of pride. It was *our* turn. We'd gotten this far. We'd survived.

I watched Jennifer walk in with Sami. Just seeing the back of her head made me smile. Her hair was up in an elaborate bun and she was absolutely drop-dead gorgeous in her long electric-blue Victorian gown and long gloves.

Sara grabbed my hand and pulled me closer to her, and to the door, and we crossed the threshold to the strains of the "Blue Danube Waltz" by Johann Strauss, the younger.

I enjoyed dancing with Sara. And importantly for a klutz like me, she was a good leader. I'm sure that traditionally the males lead the females, but sometimes needs must.

In the middle of one dance, she surprised me. We were formed up in a ring, boys around the outside. The girls would go into the centre of the ring, do a step of their own, and then come back to join us, a move that was repeated four times (or eight, or sixteen—I wasn't sure).

"Hey, give me a high-five," she said as she approached, holding her hand up high.

"A what?"

"A high . . . next round!" she said, twirling away.

I had never seen anyone do a high-five before. I wasn't sure that AJ, who had taught us all the steps, would approve—but admittedly, it was also funny.

A few moves later, she came twirling back toward me, her hand raised again.

"High-five! Raise your hand," she commanded.

I raised my hand, and she slapped it with a big smile on her face.

"Yes! Next time, low-five!"

Her smile caught me off guard. She'd been so serious all through rehearsals, but here she was, grinning, a twinkle in her eye. When she came gliding toward me the next time, I held my hand low and she slapped it, her smile even wider.

As she turned away, she shout-whispered to me, "Next time, both!"

I danced away to do a hand clap with the rest of the boys, and when I returned to meet Sara, I raised my hand to offer a high-five. She slapped it and then held her hand waist high, palm up. When I tried to slap it, she moved it and shouted, "Too slow!"

I realized I was going to miss at the same time I realized I'd swung much too hard. The whole sorry event happened in an instant: my hand sailed past the spot where hers had been, I spun, off-balance, and to the shredding sound of my pants ripping, I ended up in a pile in the middle of the circle of dancers.

I think even AJ laughed.

I got quickly up and caught up with Sara. She apologized profusely, between snickers. The laughter in the gym died down, but I kept my eyes on my shoes for the rest of the dance, my face as red as a fire truck.

WITH the dance behind us and our parents on their way home, we could finally relax. The guys loosened their bow ties, or just took them off, and most of the girls changed into something more twentieth-century—stonewashed jeans and sweaters.

The student council had arranged for us to have the second-floor physics classroom to ourselves, and four desks were pushed together to create a space for a potluck buffet: lots of chips, soda, and popcorn. Someone's mom had insisted on being sensible, and a lone salad sat at the edge, unloved.

Officially, there was no alcohol, but groups of people disappeared at regular intervals and showed up again wearing big grins. Some went to the library to "look for maps"; others spent a lot of time in the bathroom.

My mind was still on another dance: the "Enchantment under the Sea" dance where George McFly kissed Lorraine for the first time—a kiss that changed their lives, their future.

Just then, I felt a hand on my shoulder. I turned around and saw the sweetest blue eyes I knew. Jennifer was wearing blue jeans and a saffron-yellow sweater, with the lace collar of her indigo blouse showing from underneath. She'd let her hair down, literally and figuratively.

"Hello, friend," she said.

"Hello, friend," I replied. "What's up?"

"I know you said that if anybody was going to fall flat on his face, it'd be you, but you didn't have to do it just for me," she said, and smiled.

"Oh, please. You know I'm a man of my word. It was the least I could do."

"What a fun night, right?" she said. "Look at you all handsome in a tuxedo and everything. I was almost jealous of Sara, snapping you up like that."

Almost jealous? Was she for real? Was she teasing me?

I realized that I hadn't seen Sara since the end of the dance; I briefly wondered who she'd snuck off with.

"Ugh, I want to get changed," I said. "Whoever designed the tuxedo obviously never had to sit down."

"What about me?"

"What about you?"

"Was I pretty?"

"Oh," I said. "Of course."

"Ally Sheedy pretty?"

She knew Ms. Sheedy, star of *WarGames* and *The Breakfast Club*, was one of my favourite actresses.

"For sure."

"What more can a girl ask for?" Jennifer said as she took me by my wrist and led me toward the couch in the lobby, where a group of friends, including Mikke and Sami, were sitting and chatting. Mikke and Sami made room for Jennifer on the couch; I found a seat on the windowsill.

Sami was the cool kid, the leader of the pack, the king of school, the Fonz and Sonny Crockett all in one. (Well, in his opinion, at least.) He was tall, dark, handsome. He was also one of few boys with a moustache, even if it was nothing like Magnum's cookie duster.

"What's up, Oddjob?" he said. This was his latest nickname for me, a reference to the pint-sized Bond villain (or the Bond villain's assistant; however you want to see it). Sami called everybody names. He said it was his way of showing affection. I'm not sure AJ would have appreciated being called "Conan the Destroyer" behind his back—but then again, he did take a lot of pride in his physique.

"Hi, Sami," I said, but he wasn't paying any attention to me.

"Having fun, Jenny?" he asked.

I grunted. Of all Sami's nicknames, "Jenny" was my least favourite. Who was he to give her a pet name?

"Of course she's having fun now," Mikke chimed in. "She doesn't have to stand next to you anymore."

"Funny," said Sami flatly. "God, I can't wait to get out of this shitty place in the middle of nowhere."

"It's not even in the middle of nowhere," I said. "It's on the *outskirts* of nowhere."

Everybody chuckled.

"Right on!" said Sami. "Hey, have some of my special apple juice." He sent his flask my way.

I took a sniff. It was sickly sweet, and strong. I tipped it up for a hearty swig but only let a little into my mouth. It burned. I wiped my lips with the back of my hand.

"Attaboy," Sami said. I passed the flask back to him, and he held it up for Jennifer. From her look of disdain I thought she was going to decline, but instead she grabbed it and took a few long glugs. "Steady," said Sami. "Save some for the rest of us!"

A couple of hours into the party, the few that looked old enough to get served at a bar—and the few more that had convincing fake IDs—left the school; some others took advantage of the empty classrooms to get better acquainted.

I was leaning against the door in the physics room, where the buffet tables had been pushed aside to create a dance floor. A lonely DJ was sitting in the corner, surrounded by three crates filled with records. I knew him; he'd graduated from our high school together with Tina two years earlier. Though the music was loud, people were just standing around in clusters, boys on one side and girls on the other. Nobody was dancing to "We Built This City," because, really, how can you?

The DJ spotted me and beckoned me over.

"Hey, you," he said. "Tina's brother. Come here." I went. "Want to do me a gigantic favour and play these two records while I run to the bathroom?" He pointed at two vinyl singles on his side table.

Before I'd even said yes, he was halfway out the door. I took my place behind the record player. He had lined up "YMCA" by the Village People, and Paul Hardcastle's n-n-n-n-"19." I didn't even consider whether the DJ might be offended as I politely slipped the records back into their sleeves and then thumbed through the crates to find some decent floor-fillers.

Twenty seconds later, the snappy synth intro of "Girls Just Want to Have Fun" was echoing off the physics classroom walls, and a "Whoop!" went up from the girls, who stormed the dance floor, their hands in the air. When David Bowie's "Let's Dance" came on, the boys found something they could strut to, and pretty soon the dance floor was full.

I was on my third song—"Relax" by Frankie Goes to Hollywood—when the DJ came back and waved at me to leave the seat. By then, my schoolmates were so excited about my work behind the turntable that they loudly heckled him. Sami put his arm around the guy and walked him toward the door. Just before they walked out, I saw Sami pull his flask from his pocket.

Mikke jumped to the middle of the crowd and threw himself on his back on the floor, like a break dancer, only he needed a couple of other boys to spin him around. He looked like a turtle stranded on his back. Everyone went wild.

Somebody handed me a baseball cap, which I put on backwards. I looked at Jennifer dancing and having fun on the floor—I couldn't really keep my eyes off her—and I realized that I was creating the perfect mix-tape for her, right there and then. There were a couple dozen kids in the crowd, but she was the only one I was playing for.

Next up: "You're the One That I Want" from *Grease*, a good song to dance to, and with the right message. As it kicked off she laughed and winked at me. Was she showing appreciation for the tunes, or that she understood my hidden message? I made a not-so smooth transition to Rainbow's "I Surrender" and let Ritchie Blackmore's guitar (and Joe Lynn Turner's voice) say what I couldn't. She rocked out to that one, hair wild, singing along. Then I took the beat down a notch with Hanoi Rocks's "Don't You Ever Leave Me." Any real DJ could've told you it was way too early for such a smoochy glam-rock ballad, and when our DJ returned to the classroom, he was shaking his head. All that mattered to me was that Jennifer was still on the dance floor, her arms crossed, moving a little like the *Back to the Future* Jennifer had done at Marty McFly's audition.

When I put on Madonna's "Crazy for You" and let the DJ have his seat again, Jennifer was gesturing for me to come to the dance floor, and—possibly fuelled by Sami's special apple juice, possibly by the adrenaline pumping through my veins—I couldn't resist the pull of her curled index finger. Not that I tried.

"Surely I get at least one dance with you tonight," she said.

I swallowed, my mouth dry.

"Of course, and don't call me Sh—"

"Shh. No jokes," Jennifer said, and closed her eyes.

And we danced. We swayed and moved around the classroom floor in small circles, my hands around her waist, her arms around my neck. Before the song was over, Jennifer took me by the hand and walked me out of the classroom.

"You leavin'? We're just getting the party started!" I heard Sami shout to me.

"I'll be right back, Biff . . . um . . . have a great night!"

Jennifer led me to a doorway next to the cafeteria, where nobody could see us. She was a bit tipsy.

"I can't believe we're going to be seniors next year. And then we graduate. Everything's going to change. You'll be just fine though, friend, because you're so smart."

"And you're so . . ." I tried to think of a nice adjective that would describe her. Funny, intelligent, brave . . . I wanted to say she was beautiful, but couldn't.

" . . . much better than you at finishing sentences?"

"Yes, that."

She kept her deep-blue eyes on me for so long that I started to worry I might fall into them.

We heard a honk from outside, and then another.

"I've got to go," she said finally, with something like a shrug. "Can't keep Dad waiting."

I didn't want her to go. Didn't know what to say to make her stay.

"You're something else," she said.

She flicked her hair away from her shoulder, stood on her tip-toes, and gave me a kiss on my left cheek. Then she turned around and, walking backwards, she waved, wiggling her fingers. I waved back and watched her walk out the door. I waited a minute and then left the party as well.

I hummed Madonna's "Crazy For You" all the way to the bus stop, my left cheek burning. I was confused, but also elated and happy.

She'd kissed me.

Jennifer had kissed me.

CHAPTER 10

WHO CAN IT BE NOW?

I stared at the photo in my hand, shaking my head slightly at the memories it had unleashed. Of course I'd instantly recognized those kids, even though I hadn't seen the photo in decades. On closer inspection, its glossy finish showed considerable signs of passing time. It had faded a little, and there were scratches and grease marks on it, but most of them were on the boy's face. Jennifer's smile, eyes, cheekbones, and hair were flawless; she was just as perfect as she had been on the fourteenth of February 1986. Frozen in time.

And the young man in the photo, the one with the moustache? Not me. That was Sami, Jennifer's dance partner that day.

The photographer behind the Agfamatic 3008—the guy pressing the magic red button? *That* was me. Why I'd kept the photo, and not given it to Jennifer, I didn't remember, but I was happy I'd found it.

"Hello, friend," I said to the Jennifer in the photo.

That was our standard greeting. Mikke overheard Jennifer say it once and immediately launched into a long speech about how

I'd "never get anywhere" with her. She'd pegged me as a friend, he said, and that was all I'd ever be.

"Girls can be friends with guys without wanting more," he said, as if he were an expert on the subject or something. "It's weird, but that's how they are. Just remember that once she's told you she wants to be your friend, that's all you'll ever be." He added: "In case you ever thought you'd be more than that."

I stood the photo on the shelf, leaning against the tape player. As the mournful opening piano bars of Lionel Richie's "Hello" crackled through the speakers, a knock sounded on the door. I turned down the volume, and immediately regretted giving the person outside such an obvious confirmation that I was in here.

My only hope was that Mrs. Hellgren was too deaf to notice such things. If there was one person in the world I definitely didn't want to talk to right now, it was her. I held my breath, trying to be as quiet as a mouse at the back of the garage.

Knock, knock. Again.

"Hey, open up," I heard Tina shout.

For a second, I considered staying put, but I knew Tina wouldn't give up. She was going to stand outside the garage banging on the door and yelling until Mrs. Hellgren joined her.

I pulled the handle, and Tina slunk in under the door almost as soon as I could see light.

"Are you all right?" she asked.

"I'm fine. Just doing some cleaning," I said, as matter-of-factly as I could. I walked to the tape player and pretended to be turning the tape over while I knocked down the photo of Jennifer (and Sami).

"I was worried. I called you a dozen times."

"Oh, I must have left my phone upstairs."

"Nice T-shirt."

Tina sat down on a stool. She folded her arms, leaned forward, and looked me straight in the eye.

"I'm sorry about the way we argued," she said. "It was just silly."

"It's okay. It's not exactly the first time."

I rearranged some boxes and, with my hands on my hips, looked around the garage as if deciding what to do next.

"I heard you bumped into Tim," Tina said.

"Yeah, he was coming home from work."

"We both know he's not at the office. It's just that . . . it's hard for him. It's complicated."

"What is? Does he not like me?"

"Actually, he *does* like you, which is what makes it complicated. It's not fun to feel unwanted, and when he sees you and me together, he feels like an outsider, so he'd rather just stay outside."

Tina sighed and got up.

"Anyway, Tim said you seemed a little upset. He thought maybe you needed to talk to somebody. Call it male intuition— it's possible such a thing could exist. What do I know? Anyway, here I am." She took a few steps and picked up an old blue Adidas sports bag with white ends.

"What's in this, I wonder?" She unzipped the bag, pulled out an old grey sweatshirt, and dropped it on the floor.

"Eww."

Apology over, she was back to the old business of antagonizing me. I smiled and passed her a beer.

"It's just old clothes. Probably from when I moved from the university dorm to my first apartment. I moved everything on public transit, so I probably just stuffed some of my clothes in that bag," I said.

"And you haven't opened it since?"

"It's possible," I said, sheepishly.

Tina laughed.

"What else have you got here?" She peeked inside the box where I'd found Jennifer's photo. "Photos!"

There were half a dozen other photos at the bottom of the box. One was from the Bryan Adams concert we'd gone to together; it had been taken from so far back in the stands that it was basically a ball of light in a sea of blackness. The rest painted a picture of a pleasant small-town upbringing. There was the family outside the high school after Tina's graduation; the family outside the same school after my graduation—Dad wearing the same suit and tie; Mikke and I sitting on the floor in my room with album covers all around us, stonewash and big hair; me sitting with my feet on my desk, the Spectrum on my lap, grinning stupidly; Tina and I in front of the Christmas tree, my arm around her neck.

They weren't the exact six photos I would have chosen to represent my life, but they weren't a bad selection.

"How on earth did Dad let us wear those clothes?" Tina said.

"I wonder where that Boomtown Rats album is . . ."

"The school's the same, but look at the cars. They're so boxy!"

"I loved that Spectrum. I loved it."

"See how you have your arm around me, but I don't have mine around you?"

"Mikke's mullet, man . . ."

"I bet he's bald now. All the guys with the best mullets are now bald."

"Look at the posters on my wall: *Ghostbusters, Purple Rain, Back to the Future.*"

"You used to love *Back to the Future.*"

"Best film ever."

71

She was about to say something—presumably to contradict me—but caught herself.

"Hey, remember that time we fought over a poster? On one side, there was Axel Foley from *Beverly Hills Cop*, but on the other side was Kajagoogoo. I totally wanted that," Tina said.

"Yeah. Who got it?"

"Nobody." She dropped the photos back into the box. "The poster ripped."

"You know, I really would love to go back there. I would love to be back in that time."

"I wouldn't, but I think I understand you. I really do."

She walked back to the sports bag and put it on the stool in the middle of the garage.

She pulled the clothes out of the bag, piece by piece, and with each new shirt or pair of pants, she grinned, and she giggled, and then she laughed—until I started to laugh too. And then, between bursts of laughter, Tina whispered, "You know what would make you feel better? A makeover. I know it's nonsense girly therapy, but it really does work. Please?"

I laughed even harder. Tina picked up a green sun visor and put it on, and then, looking through the transparent green plastic, said, "Pleeeeease?"

"Really? Come on! I'm not a doll you can dress up. Not anymore."

"It'll be fun! It'll be like taking a trip back, like you were saying. Come on. Just one outfit?" She held out a bundle of clothes. "For old times' sake?"

"Fine!" I said, in mock annoyance.

I built a dressing screen out of a few boxes and disappeared behind it. Three seconds later, I walked out in my stonewash jeans and *Frankie Says Relax* T-shirt.

"Nailed it!" Tina said, with a surprised chuckle—generously ignoring the fact that I couldn't do up the top buttons on my jeans.

She rummaged through the bag and threw me another pile of clothes.

"Now let's go for something similar but distinct."

I'd told myself I was going to draw the line at one outfit, but when I saw what she'd found I couldn't help myself.

I disappeared behind the boxes and put on a black-and-white three-quarter-sleeve shirt with black sleeves. On the chest, it said *FINISHED the FAB 5K: 1986*.

Tina threw a pair of Nike running shoes over the boxes, narrowly missing my head.

"These too!" she shouted.

When I walked out, Tina gave me an appraising look.

"Perfect. This would be your street-casual look, a.k.a. Alex Keaton casual."

In the time I'd taken to change, she'd prepared the next outfit, and soon I was in blue jeans with a loud Hawaiian shirt and white tennis shoes.

"Not so sure about this one," I said.

"Me neither." Tina laughed. "And you *still* wouldn't be able to grow a Magnum P.I. moustache."

"What's next? Is there a Maverick flight suit in there?"

"Listen, I'm in charge, and don't you fargin' forget it," Tina said. By the tone of her voice and the fake swear words from *Johnny Dangerously*, I could tell she was really getting into it.

"Get back in there," she said, tossing me another outfit. It wasn't quite a flight suit, but the leather bomber jacket and fake Ray-Ban Aviators made me a pretty slick Maverick.

Next up was the Springsteen look: faded blue jeans, bandana, a (tucked-in) plaid shirt with rolled-up sleeves, and boots.

"Hold it! Take the guitar!" Tina said, her phone in hand. "This is too good! Pose like a boss . . . the Boss!"

Click. Click.

"Perfect."

I morphed the Springsteen look—via a trench coat and fingerless gloves—into *Breakfast Club* bad boy John Bender. I punched the air and held the pose, imagining the credits rolling over my liberated, freeze-framed image.

We went on like that for a while, adding *Footloose*—high-waist jeans, tank tops, and T-shirts—and two different *Miami Vice* looks featuring pastel shirts. She held a Clark Griswold–style sweater in front of me.

"Now, tie this around your neck," she said. "Obviously."

I was beginning to worry that she was taking this a little *too* seriously.

She told me to go back behind the boxes one more time and wait. I heard her huffing and puffing, opening boxes and lifting bags while humming the last song on the mix-tape: "Automatic" by the Pointer Sisters. Finally, a pile of clothes sailed over the boxes and landed on top of me.

I sifted through it, pulling out a lavender T-shirt, a white-checkered short-sleeve shirt, high-cut Guess blue jeans, suspenders, Nike sneakers, a Guess two-tone denim jacket, a Casio digital watch, mirrored sunglasses, and a burnt-orange down vest.

There was even a pair of Calvin Klein underpants.

"The Marty McFly," Tina said with a grand finality.

I put it all on, and when I stepped out, Tina shrieked with laughter—not mocking me, but amazed. I caught my reflection in the dusty mirror. The jeans didn't quite do up at the top, and the hair wasn't right, but apart from that it was pretty much spot on.

"Well, that was fun," Tina said eventually. "But I should be getting home. I totally lost track of time."

I laughed, and thanked her for coming.

"I'm so glad to hear you laugh," she said as I changed back into my old (new) clothes. "I told you the makeover would help. Maybe you just needed to have some fun. I mean, I get it. You're probably lonely, and you know, you're at a certain age . . . Don't forget that you can always call me."

"I know."

"Don't do anything silly," she said. "Do I have to worry about you?"

"No, no," I said, swallowing an unexpected lump in my throat. "I'll be fine."

"Anything else I should know about?"

I thought about the letters in my back pocket, but said nothing.

She patted my back and told me to call her anytime I wanted to talk. And that maybe Tim and I wanted to play squash or something.

"We'll see."

"Try not to worry so much," she said.

After Tina left, I cracked another beer, took a sip, and stared at the photo of Jennifer. I folded it in half. A casual, almost accidental fold, so that Sami was now facing the wall. I wagged my finger at her. "You know what? You're something else."

I folded the photo in with the letters and headed back up to my apartment.

CHAPTER 11

ALL NIGHT LONG (ALL NIGHT)

THE hour spent with Tina had put me in a better mood. Yes, she was bossy, and she was definitely a know-it-all, but she did care for me. Also, goofing around with her like that reminded me of some of the fun times we'd had growing up. The fondness threatened to overwhelm me for a moment—or maybe that was just the beer.

I put Hanna's letter—my Time Machine—on my desk, next to a new can of beer, and logged on to Facebook. I got the usual warm tingle when I saw the red notification bell, but rather than instantly clicking it, the first thing I did was unfriend my former boss/client. Which left me with 127 friends, so far, in this lifetime.

The notification, when I did click on it, told me that Tina Eksell-Smythe had tagged me in a photo.

"Wow. What happened here? LOL. #tbt."

She'd made a composite photo that featured me as a seventeen-year-old on the left, and me as "Springsteen," circa forty-five minutes ago, on the right. The teenage me was also wearing faded blue jeans, a (tucked-in) plaid shirt with rolled-up sleeves, and a bandana, but he wasn't holding a guitar. And the man on the right? Well, apart from the mean overbite, he didn't seem to have much in common with the Boss.

I let my cursor hover over the "like" button and selected "haha." A laughing emoji appeared below the photo. To my slight dismay, I noticed that fifteen of Tina's friends had already "liked" the picture.

I scrolled.

One of my Facebook friends, a Canadian wannabe triathlete, was addicted to Facebook tests: "What Cheese Are You Most Like?" "What Tree Represents Your Character?" In the latest one, she'd spent several of her numbered minutes on this Earth getting an algorithm to tell her which of the Seven Dwarfs she would be. She'd gotten "Dopey." She seemed proud of the result, and for good reason. She was kind of dopey.

I quickly flew by a set of baby photos and a link to a blog post by another friend. He'd written about how becoming a vegan had changed his life, which was great for him, but with a zeal that would have made a fundamentalist missionary feel lazy, he seemed determined to convert the whole world to a plant-based diet. I felt a bit sorry for the hopelessness of his cause, so out of pity I gave his post a "like." Then I worried that Facebook's algorithms would start filling my timeline with ads for meat substitutes and thought about "un-liking" it, but then I worried that he might be one of those guys who's set up push notifications, and so gets an alert on his phone every time someone likes something, and then I worried that I might be worrying about stupid things. And then I composed a status update about the pointlessness of worrying about worrying, but then I worried nobody would like it and deleted it. I finished my beer, crushed the can, and sauntered to the fridge for another, vowing to never go on social media again.

I wondered why it is that people—or the people I followed, anyway—tended to only share positive news about themselves, and only link to negative news clips, and articles of doom and gloom.

It had been fun in the beginning, back when I'd first joined Facebook and you could only have statuses like "Peter Eksell is . . . at the office" and "Peter Eksell is . . . not at the office" and "Peter Eksell is . . . smiling at the office," but as the platform had improved and adapted so that more of life could be posted on it, it had turned into a cause of stress and distress—and yet, I couldn't stay away.

I scrolled back up to the Seven Dwarfs test. I got "Bashful."

I quickly got tired of my timeline. I only seemed to see the same dozen people, and they were always doing the same old things, mostly eating fancy dinners and working out, all of which had to be documented in the tiniest detail, from the number of calories burned to the ingredients of their dark-chocolate mousse.

I went back to Tina's photo of me and changed the "haha" to a "wow," which replaced the laughing emoji with one that had a wide-open mouth. I closed the Facebook tab.

My homepage was Google News, and as I cracked the next beer, I scanned the headlines. My mother always said there's nothing in the dark that's not there in the light but, to me, the news always seemed more depressing at night. Violence in the Middle East, a mass shooting in the United States, a tennis player's racist tweet, and a Russian submarine in the English Channel. Same old same old. Russia news somehow always stuck out; living in Finland, the big bear on the other side of the border could not be ignored. Social media had brought that issue a little too close to home again. Literally.

Tina had told me not to worry so much. Easier said than done.

I glanced at the clock in the upper-right hand corner of my laptop, squinting so I could see straight. It was 11:20, the time for great ideas, and I got one. Hanna had mentioned the fun she'd had tracking down my classmates. And here I was, with the internet at my fingertips. The largest accumulation of information ever amassed in human history, and how was I taking advantage of it? I was scrolling through kitten pictures.

I punched "Mikael Lund" into Facebook's search window. None of the photos that popped up with the results looked right, and of those that could have been possibilities, none shared mutual friends with me, which seemed unlikely. Perhaps (just perhaps!) Mikke didn't have a Facebook profile. Some people, I hear, do not.

So I tried Google—and 0.52 seconds later, I had almost 600,000 hits. The first-page results (does anyone ever look at the second page?) included links to several LinkedIn and Facebook profiles. One Mikael Lund seemed to be a professor in Sweden, another a priest in Michigan.

It was impossible to know which one of the thousands was my old high-school buddy, although I had a pretty good idea it wasn't the priest. After all, Mikke had been sent home from school for his "horny Jesus" Halloween outfit. Then again, people change.

I clicked on Images, hoping I'd recognize Mikke if I saw a photo of him. Another half a second later my screen was filled with male faces, mostly white, mostly European, but none that looked like that crazy, big-haired friend of mine.

But then, suddenly, there he was. His big cheeky smile, his face fatter than it had been, and—Tina had nailed it!—his head bald! I clicked on the photo and it took me through to a website, the homepage for a church in Michigan. Well, I never.

I raised my beer and toasted the photo on my screen. The Church of Holy Rock was a denomination I hadn't heard of, but it was obvious that Mikke had done well for himself. According to the site, he was the head priest. Next to his photo was a PayPal button people could use to donate money for the men and women on a mission from God. I never understood why, if God moves in mysterious ways, he didn't move some mysterious money into the church coffers. "But what do I know?" I mumbled.

I spent the next forty-five minutes trying to remember the names of my former Kumpunotko friends and then googling them. Total 80s FM was playing Queen's "Friends Will Be Friends." I was becoming convinced that the station's computer algorithm was stalking me.

My search results were interesting. I had known a couple of goofballs and a girl who was too shy to speak in class, but when I googled them, I found a celebrity chef, a math professor, and a start-up guru.

And yes, they did live in Dubai, Scotland, and Thailand.

"Good for them," I muttered.

It did sting a little that I was sitting in a tiny apartment in Helsinki, barely two hours from Kumpunotko. I gave my head a shake to dislodge the negative thoughts. No, I wasn't an inter-national jetsetter, but I was still relatively successful. Well, I had been. Until that afternoon. And while I wasn't technically unem-ployed, since I had my own company, the fact of the matter was that I didn't have a source of income.

"So they moved? Big deal." More muttering.

Where had the time gone? How had I gone from the per-son Jennifer thought had all the answers, the guy who was going places, to this guy—this guy who couldn't fit into his favourite jeans any more, sitting alone at home on a Friday night drinking beer in his underwear?

A movie tagline of the story of my life would have been something like, "He was here? Who knew?"

It was midnight and I was wound up! I was also nearing the end of my six-pack. There was a bottle in the freezer, vodka that I'd been holding onto for a special occasion, and it was calling my name.

I found a few more old schoolmates on Facebook and scrolled through the updates of their glamorous lives: their summer cottages in Lapland, mansions in Florida; their honour-roll-student children, their flourishing businesses, and oh, all the fancy food they ate.

I clicked back to Mikke's church site but couldn't find a phone number anywhere, so I tried one that was listed in the meta-data on another of the Google results. That Mikael Lund had definitely not gone to Kumpunotko High, and he let me know it. Apparently, he had gone to bed, though. "It's the middle of the night, idiot," he said, and hung up on me.

I flipped back to Facebook and changed the laughing emoji underneath Tina's photo of me to a basic like. Thumbs up, everybody. Ironically. Twenty-seven people had now reacted to the photo, and a few too many of them were crying with laughter.

I slumped on the sofa.

Hours before, the Time Machine had made me euphoric. Life had shown me a glimpse of happiness and then, when I'd bent down to look at it, had given me a kick in the ass. All at once, I was frantic. I didn't know what to do, but I knew I had to do *something*. Something had to change! Tina had said I should be be proactive, and she was right. I could not waste another day/week/

month just going through the motions. Tomorrow was the first day of the rest of my life. My future!

The only problem was that I didn't know what to do. There were so many signs, but I didn't know where they were pointing. Was Hanna's letter—no, *my* letter—important, or just a fun thing? What about the photo of Jennifer? Why had I held on to it for so long? Why had I found it on the same day the letter arrived? Was that a coincidence, or some kind of cosmic message? And what about the clothes? Tina's visit? Her photo? I was confused, and sad, and a little bit lost.

There was nothing else for it.

I poured myself a generous slug of the vodka, pulled my *Back to the Future* trilogy DVD box off the shelf, and inserted the first disc into my DVD player. I turned off Total 80s FM—which, in the style of a good human DJ, had dipped from high-energy disco to smoochy slow dances—and turned up the sound on my surround system. I sat back and watched my favourite movie of all time. My guide to life, if you will.

I know people speak in hyperbole these days, but *Back to the Future* truly did change my life. It made me believe that anything was possible and that nothing was set in stone. That every day, I could change the course of history and create my own future. My grades got better after I saw it, and I grew almost ten centimetres that summer—though that may have been just a coincidence.

And I did believe that anything was possible. I truly did. I just never did anything about it. Because I also believed—as everybody spent my childhood telling me—that I was destined for great things. And if you're destined, it's going to happen anyway, right?

Right?

I knew *Back to the Future* by heart. I could have performed the entire movie by myself, and often did. All by myself. As I did that night, sitting on a worn-down couch in a Marty McFly outfit my sister had put together (minus the restrictive pants, but with the Calvin Klein underwear).

Sure, I was a little heavier than back in the day, and maybe I'd never had a talent for skateboarding or guitar playing. I definitely ate poorly and drank too much. I didn't sleep well or enough, and that showed too. And yet, none of that mattered when I was back in Hill Valley.

I picked up my guitar from the floor and entered Doc's lab. I grabbed a hold of the end of my couch as Marty gave himself a free ride holding onto a pick-up truck. I delivered a poor rendition of Huey Lewis and the News's "Power of Love" at the audition and I kicked dirty laundry off the floor as I walked with Jennifer afterwards, miserable. I sat on the end of my sofa and gazed far into the horizon and slurred, "Someday, Jennifer. Someday."

That's how I acted out the whole movie, with certain modifications made along the way. At Lou's Café, I didn't get a Tab or a Pepsi Free. I had another vodka. As Doc and Marty and Jennifer flew away in the time machine, and the promise of *To be continued* . . . appeared on the screen, I was hunched in the corner of the couch, an empty glass in my hand, staring at the rolling credits.

All I wanted—and surely it was not too much to ask—was a real time machine.

I wanted a Doc, and a DeLorean, so that I could go back in time and get my Jennifer.

So that I could roll up in 1986 Kumpunotko and grab young Peter, in the summer when he finished high school, and give him a good shake. So I could tell him how to get it all right, how to make all the decisions I'd made, but better. So that when I woke up on the sofa tomorrow I wouldn't be this lonely old loser any more. Sunlight would stream through the window, and Jennifer would bring me a coffee and chide me for staying up late watching silly old movies again, and the kids would run in and jump on me, and we'd all laugh and laugh in soft focus about nothing much.

I flipped the TV off, wiped my eyes.

"Why can't you, though?" a voice asked.

It was my voice.

"Because I don't have a Doc Brown, or a time machine," I replied.

"Don't you?"

"No. I need the flux capata . . . flux capacitator . . . flux capacitor. That's how you time travel!"

"But is that the *only* way?"

I opened my mouth to argue with myself, but then I realized that I had a point. Which is why, right there and then, I decided that I *was* going to become a time traveller—however I could, whatever it took.

I just didn't need all the gloom of my 2016 life. Nothing was keeping me here. I was free. I could do whatever I wanted. There was no reason whatsoever that I couldn't go back to a happier time, a time when I'd had friends and love and been a superstar DJ. I picked up a piece of paper and wrote *Memo to self* at the top of the page, surprised at my inability to form the letters properly.

"You're drunk," I told myself. "Drunker than you think. Plus it's late, and dark. Your mind's playing tricks on you."

Silence.

"Shut up," I replied. "This is a great idea."

I poised my pen, ready to write out my plan. I turned my mental amplifier up to full blast, knowing full well that the first power chord was going to blow me away.

I couldn't wait.

CHAPTER 12

ABRACADABRA

WHEN I woke up—or maybe "came to" is a better way to describe what happened the next morning—I could hardly move. The sun was beaming down on my face, which meant that it was already afternoon, and I was still on the sofa. As soon as I moved my eyes, I felt a pain like someone had taken a knife and cut through the middle of my head. Thinking? That made my head hurt even more.

This wasn't a regular hangover; I'd had those before. This one was special.

For a second, I was afraid I was paralyzed, and in my panic I tried to wave my arms. Unfortunately, my gross-motor control hadn't quite woken up yet, so one of my hands hit the floor, hard. I lay there on the couch, cradling my injured appendage, as my blood circulation slowly returned. This allowed me to sit up, and when that didn't kill me I managed to stand up and walk to the bathroom to get something for my headache. Also, I was so hungry my stomach was growling, and I realized that I hadn't eaten a single thing yesterday, but had drunk an awful lot. Deep in the recesses of my still addled brain was a nagging feeling that I'd forgotten something.

I walked back to the living room and looked around. The *Back to the Future* DVD box was on the table, my laptop on the floor next to the table, and my clothes on another chair. Nothing special there. Absently, I turned on the TV and grabbed my laptop. On the screen, a man was gulping down huge bottles of water—at least six litres—and just as he wiped his mouth after the last one, there was a freeze frame, and a slick presenter walked into the picture asking contestants to bet on what would happen next . . . I managed to flick the TV off in time, before my stomach turned itself inside out. I reached for my laptop instead, but closed the lid as soon as I saw the screen.

I had googled Jennifer.

My heart stopped, and then started racing. Then it stopped again. I got up, the laptop hit the floor, the blood rushed to my brain, and I got dizzy. I sat back down on the couch and lay on my back.

I had to think, hard and painful as it was. Obviously, there were one or two (or several) gaps in my memory from last night. I dug my phone out from between the sofa cushions, worried sick that I'd find outgoing calls to numbers I didn't know.

There was one. I had a vague memory: *It's the middle of the night, idiot!*

I swiped left and deleted it immediately. Gone.

Out of sight, out of mind.

The fact was that I hadn't been in touch with Jennifer since high school, so I certainly wouldn't have had the guts to contact her out of the blue last night. Would I?

I didn't know anything about Jennifer's life since 1986. I hadn't tried to track her down in any way, and we weren't even Facebook friends.

Why not?

Well, it was partly to do with the way we'd parted. She'd cut me off, not the other way around.

But why was I so afraid to send her a friend request? What was wrong with me? Was I . . . chicken?

I closed my eyes. Took a deep breath. Ignored the voice.

I told myself, in a loud and clear voice, that it wasn't that I was too *afraid* to find her; I told myself that she'd find me when the time was right.

We'd find each other, if it was meant to be. If she was my destiny.

That had been Jennifer's answer to most things back then. Things that did happen—her getting a summer job at an ice cream stand, for example—were meant to be, while disappointments, such as my being sick and missing a Bond premiere, were brushed away with "It wasn't meant to be." Not then, at least. There would be other opportunities, other chances, she said.

That's how I explained my inaction with Jennifer to myself. If it was going to happen, it would happen—somehow, somewhere, sometime. All I had to do was wait.

I had been waiting a long time.

Behind the Google tab, I found a Facebook page open, displaying search results for "Jennifer Berg." I quickly navigated away from that to neutral territory: my timeline.

As soon as I saw the first posts, I knew it was a mistake.

I closed the tab, closed the laptop, closed my eyes.

I sat there for a while wondering if there was a welcoming room somewhere near me where I could stand up in front of my non-judgmental peers and say, "My name is Peter and I'm a Facebookaholic."

As I struggled to get up from the sofa, something on the table caught my attention. It was Hanna's letter, but it looked a little different from how I remembered it. As I picked it up, I realized that there was writing on the back page too:

Memo to self
Subject: Change your life

Why? Because it's shit.

Drivers
A. I'm not happy. (I'm drunk, but that's not it).
B. Everything is shit, or mostly shit (in survey terms).
C. The world's gone crazy.
D. I'm:
i. 46
ii. single
iii. lonely
iv. stressed
v. drunk

Action plan
A. To go back to when life was awesome.
i. Build time machine
ii.

Ugh. I grunted and gave myself a whack on the side of the head. I just hoped I hadn't posted *that* on Facebook! I picked up the laptop again to check.

I hadn't.

But while I had the computer on my lap, just for kicks I googled "time travel."

Ever since that sneak preview of *Back to the Future*, I'd been fascinated by the concept of time travel. Not enough that I'd undertaken a PhD in quantum physics or anything, but I did understand math and had read any articles I could find about it, over the years.

For instance, I knew that I had gone from being the cool, skateboarding McFly to the crazy-haired Doc Brown, and that real scientists would call that time travelling—because it's "time travel into the future." We are all time travelling, all the time. But that's not what I had in mind. I wanted to go *back* in time.

I got up, flicked on Total 80s FM (a-ha, "Take On Me") and got a big glass of orange juice from the fridge. The hangover was still making me move slowly, but I knew I was onto something. I had been to the well of great ideas, deep in the black hole that contained everything that was and is, and I had returned with some kind of ore that might contain gold. It just needed refining.

Doc had the flux capacitor. In *Terminator*, they had the Time Displacement Equipment, but in both films the technical details of the hardware were fairly thin on the ground. In *Star Trek IV: The Voyage Home*, they did a slingshot run around the sun to get to the speed of light and into a time warp, which is all well and good as long as you have a spaceship.

I found a *Scientific American* article about time travel and got excited when I saw a short item about "existing forms of time travel" because they listed "airline flight" as one of the methods. Could a jet plane travel around the world so fast that it would stop time? That's *almost* how they did it in *Superman*, except that he flew around the Earth, opposite to the way it was turning, so fast and so many times that he forced the entire planet to spin backwards, which somehow resulted in time rewinding like a VHS tape. And I'm just not sure where to start in deconstructing that theory.

Unfortunately, back in reality, I learned that an eight-hour flight would only slow time by ten nanoseconds.

I needed more than that. Besides, I needed to *reverse* time, not just slow it down.

I knew Phileas Fogg had won his bet about travelling around the world because he moved back a day by crossing the international date line. I'd need to cross the date line an awful lot of times. I wondered what would happen if I went to the North Pole and ran around it in circles for a few hours. No, surely someone had thought of that already.

There was the wormhole theory, of course, but that didn't seem feasible, mostly due to financial constraints. And time constraints. Paradoxically, it takes a lot of time to build a time machine, and I didn't have it. Time.

Nor did I have a linear accelerator, a wormhole collection ring, or (again) a spaceship.

Moving on.

With a grunt, I lay back down on the sofa. I read the letter all the way through again, and then spent more time reading the back page, my memo.

I remembered that Bob Gale, the *Back to the Future* screen-writer, had gotten the idea for the story after he found his father's old yearbook in the basement and learned things he hadn't known about him. It made Gale wonder if they would've been friends had they been in high school together.

I wondered if I would have been friends with my dad if I'd gone back in time to Kumpunotko High, circa 1955. I don't know; my dad's a bit of a strange one. I then wondered if I would have liked me—or if 1986 me would have liked this lonely old lump of present-day me.

And that's when it hit me.

"And that's when it hit him," I said in my voice-over voice.

I got up. I didn't need a flux capacitor or a wormhole. I sat down. I didn't need money, or a spaceship. All I needed was determination. I got up again. I had the answer; it had been there all along. It was so obvious! As Doc Brown said, "If you put your mind to it, you can accomplish anything."

"Anything!" I shouted, my fist raised.

CHAPTER 13

SMOOTH OPERATOR

I pressed Play on my boom box and the speakers crackled to life. There was a minor audio cough, where the maker of the mixtape had pressed Record, and I tingled with anticipation, waiting to see what the first track would be.

Before the first note was even fully formed, a massive grin had spread across my face.

"Kids in America."

The rapid, urgent synth beat was strong, and I nodded my head to the pulsating, swirling sounds of metropolitan life. I met Kim on the first line and sang along, word-perfect, until the drums kicked in, and then I clapped and danced around the room like a maniac through to the first chorus. Prince met my eye from the *Purple Rain* poster, sitting astride his purple motorbike with a look of steely approval. I grabbed my mirrored shades from the lamp on my desk, tied my bandana around my head, and hopped over a pile of *Mad* magazines as I rocked over to the mirror.

From over on the *Ghostbusters* poster, Venkman grinned indulgently.

My Casio calculator watch told me it was 10:02, and that the date was September 5, 1986. I checked on my ZX Spectrum+ but *The Hobbit* was still loading. Above the TV set was a picture of Axel Foley in *Beverly Hills Cop*, giving me a cheesy grin and the hand signal for a-okay, and a postcard in which three monkeys played poker (I'd wanted a poster with the tennis player scratching her bum, but Mom's frown had ruled that out).

I picked up my Polaroid camera, pointed it at myself, and gave the widest smile yet.

I was here, in good old 1986; if ever there was a moment for a celebratory selfie, this was it.

Click. Click. Nothing. The film must have run out. I checked, but the dial indicated that there were three exposures left. Maybe the battery had died? I popped the hatch open and found that the batteries hadn't just died—they'd leaked and encrusted the terminals with battery acid, which had long since dried.

My Spectrum announced that it had finished loading, and I sat down to continue my progress through the eight-bit rendering of Tolkien's Middle Earth.

Five minutes later, there was a knock at the door.

"Come in!" I said, not even turning around.

"Hi, Peter. I thought you might be hungry so I made a little something downstairs."

It was Mom.

"Oh, thanks," I said, my eyes still on the TV.

"Do you have to play that game all the time?"

I didn't say anything. She opened the door carefully, pushing a pair of sweat pants on the floor out of the way. She demonstratively picked up a few *Mad* magazines from the floor, put them in a neat pile on my desk, and sat down on my bed.

"Is everything all right, Peter?"

"Sure, Mom, everything's great."

"Can you stop playing the game for a second, please, and look at me?"

"I can't. There's no pause, Mom."

"I'll wait."

I could tell by the tone of her voice that she was getting angry, so I switched off the Spectrum and the TV—there was no point saving it; the save process took longer than the turn I'd just had, and I hadn't made any progress anyway.

"Peter," Mom said. That sounded ominous.

"Mom," I said, trying to keep things light.

"What's going on?"

"Nothing's going on! I'm just hanging out in my room, reading magazines, and playing video games. Awesome."

"I know, and your father and I really like having you here. But . . . it's just a little surprising. Have you lost your job? Are you in trouble? Do you need money?"

I'd known this little chat was going to come along, eventually. They'd been surprised when I showed up at their door, but we'd all pretended that my visit was nothing special. Mom had gestured me in and then extended her hand to shake mine. We weren't a family of huggers. "A firm handshake will get you far in this world," my father used to say, and as I walked in, they both stood in the hallway, looking slightly surprised but also as if they'd been waiting there for me since I'd left home: Mom, a mix of Judi Dench (of *A Fine Romance* era) and Betty White (of *The Golden Girls* era), fussing about and helping me with my duffel bag, and Dad standing with his hands behind his back, nodding and looking like Steve Martin in *Father of the Bride*, his handshake at the ready.

I didn't know what to tell them. I *did* know that I couldn't just come out and tell them straight that I was a time traveller, trying to give myself a second chance.

"Everything's good, Mom. Just taking some time . . . off. I'll be here for a while, if that's okay with you and Dad."

"Of course. Let us know if you need help. You know we don't have a lot of money but if it's money you need . . ."

"Mom, I'll be fine."

I used the future tense to cover my behind. I hated lying to my mother, but when I put it like that, I could still look her in the eye—which she always made me do if she suspected I was lying to her.

"Fine. Anyway, come eat . . ."

She got up and walked to the door. Right then, the upstairs phone rang.

"I'll take it here!" Mom shouted to Dad downstairs.

"Okay!" Dad yelled back.

"Hello?" she said, and then, "Oh, hello." A flat response, as if some bureaucrat had rung to arrange a drain inspection.

Then: "Nice of you to call."

Then: "Uh-huh, since Sunday."

Then: "No, I don't know. He won't talk to us."

Then: "Anyway, how's Sofie?"

So it was clearly Tina on the phone. And I was clearly right about there being some unspoken frostiness between them.

"Yes, he's right here, hold on. Give Sofie a big hug from Granny!"

Mom walked into my room with the receiver in her hand. The cord was stretched a little but not even close to the max; we had swapped the manufacturer's cord for a ridiculously long one so Tina could have some privacy in her room during her marathon calls.

Mom handed me the receiver and left my room, closing the door as far as the cord would allow.

"Yes, this is Peter," I said, as if I had no idea who was on the other end.

"Peter, what the hell?"

Tina was raging mad.

"What?"

"I've been worried sick! I've called you a thousand times but your phone's off. I've emailed you. I would have sent you a Facebook message, but you seem to have deleted your account. I even went by your house and that creepy old lady told me you'd packed up and left."

"Why did you call here then?"

"Oh, believe you me, this was my last resort. But they *are* our parents and if you *had* gone missing—since you *have* gone missing—I thought they needed to know."

"I'm sorry," I said sheepishly, but then composed myself. "I'm sorry, I don't know what this Facebook thing is that you're talking about."

"What? What is up with you?"

I sighed. Tina wasn't going to let this go until she had got an answer. Usually, she wanted an answer that she could be happy with, but I was afraid that just wasn't in the cards this time. Even so, she deserved an explanation.

"Tina, you know what's up. I told you I wasn't happy when I was," I said quietly, in case Mom was snooping in the hall.

"You weren't happy *when* you were? Can you start making sense, please?"

"It does make sense. I was sick of *when* I was, of modern life, of the mess I'd made of everything. So here I am now, back in good old 1986. And thanks for the makeover; the outfits are working nicely so far."

"Wait . . . what!? You told me that life was simpler back in the eighties. We had a makeover. You didn't say you were going to *give up on life and disappear*!"

"I haven't disappeared. I've travelled through time."

"*What?* How does that even work?"

"Well, it's already going fairly well, thanks for asking. Not using my phone was the hardest thing. It's fascinating, the reflex to 'post' everything and then see how many people 'like' it. Bizarre. I still reach for the phone whenever I see something interesting, but now, if I feel like checking Facebook, I do ten push-ups. My arms are a little sore."

Silence at the other end.

"Anyway, I left my phone in my garage in Helsinki, along with my futuristic car. I don't watch the news, I'm off social media, I play my old games, and I read old papers at the library—that's how it works," I went on.

"Basically, you're just going to live in the past? Please," Tina said.

"Hey, the Amish do it! And they're happy."

"*That's* your argument for this? Are you crazy?" she yelled.

"Actually, you know, I don't think I am? For the first time in a long time, I have absolute clarity, and I know exactly what I'm doing."

"I've heard of mid-life crises before but this one . . . man, this takes the cake! Why didn't you just buy a motorcycle like everyone else?"

I didn't say anything.

"You come home, right now!"

"Tina, Tina," I said, as calmly as I could. "You don't seem to understand."

As I walked out of my room and back to the phone's cradle, the long cord slithering snake-like behind me, I inhaled and gathered all the mental strength I could, because I was about to do something I had never done in my life.

"Tina, I am home," I said, and hung up.

I skipped down the fifteen stairs between our bedrooms and the living room. Mom was waiting for me in the kitchen with some cheese-and-cucumber sandwiches on a ceramic plate. She offered me some coffee as well, but when I said I didn't drink coffee, she gave me milk instead.

"What did Tina want?" Mom asked.

"Oh, nothing special. She just wanted to chat."

"She didn't say anything about their coming here, did she?"

"It's been a while since they were here," Dad said from his chair in front of the TV.

Mom began to wipe the kitchen counter with a quiet ferocity.

"No, she didn't mention that. Mostly she was interested in my plans."

I saw Mom and Dad exchange a look. They were thinking the same thing. I tried to distract them.

"So, anyway, great sandwiches, Mom."

Nobody said anything. I could hear our kitchen clock ticking, and I followed the second hand as it travelled its way around the clock's black face.

"What *are* your plans?" Dad asked eventually.

I was getting frustrated with the questions. I had only been there for two days.

"Not you too. First Mom, then Tina, now you. Plans, plans, plans! I don't have a master plan. Maybe you all do, but I don't. Things will work out the way they're meant to work out. If you want me to leave, just say so."

"It's not that, Peter, not at all . . . ," said Mom.

I heard Dad chime in: "We're just worried about—"

I didn't hear the end of the sentence because I stormed out, flinging the door open with such force that it shook in its frame.

Parents.

I needed some space.

CHAPTER 14

MY HOMETOWN

I walked out of the house without looking back, and ran to our storage room on the far side of the communal parking lot. I battled all the way to the back and picked up my dusty skateboard. I remember the day Dad brought it home—he had a friend who'd bought a shipment of this newest craze, and I'd been delirious with excitement. Within five minutes I'd fractured my wrist and had never ridden the stupid thing again. I chucked it to the side and pulled out my golden Crescent racing bike with the zebra-patterned drop handlebar.

I really wanted a large triple-shot, no-foam latte, but since those weren't available in the 1980s I went for something else to get my blood pumping: my wheels.

It had been a few years since I'd ridden any bike, let alone this one, so it took me a little while to notice that the ride was bumpier than it ought to have been. After a hundred metres or so, I understood that something was wrong, and when I dismounted, I saw that both tires were flat.

Instead of turning back home and risking running into Mom

or Dad, I kept on walking to the nearest gas station, where I examined the Crescent a little more closely.

I had made the zebra stripes on the handlebars by myself, by rolling white tape over the original black leather grip. The bottle holder I'd screwed on was also still there, but the bottle was gone. On the mudguard at the back was a faded sticker in the shape of the famous London Underground sign, with *Mind the Gap* on it, that I'd bought on a trip to London.

A baby-blue lock was hanging underneath the seat.

Once I had filled the tires with air, I turned up the collar on my denim jacket, turned my baseball hat backwards, clipped the JVC walkman (lowercase *w*) on to the back of the waistline of my jeans, and then carefully placed the headphones over my ears. Without even looking, my finger found Play.

With the tires now rolling smoothly, I found riding the bike was as easy as . . . riding a bike. I could've done it with my eyes closed (but didn't). I did do it without hands, though, as soon as I got to the main bike lane. I put my hands in my jacket pockets and let Queen's "I Want to Break Free" and the late-summer breeze on my face carry me away. I looked at the blue sky above me and smiled, thinking how nice it was that there was no climate change, just a hole in the ozone layer, but that we'd fix that by starting to use roll-on deodorant.

There were no terrorists—except airplane hijackers, and the IRA, and a little bit of Middle East trouble—but those things were far away. They never came to us, and especially not to Kumpunotko.

I switched up a gear. I didn't have a plan but I trusted my bike, which felt almost like an extension of myself, to make the decisions for me.

Kumpunotko was only a small town/large village (take your pick), but even so there were several routes between our house and the market square. The straightest was along the bike lane. It was pretty—lined with birches almost the whole way—and at the halfway point there was a kiosk where I could stop and get a soda.

Then there was the other route. The one my bike had chosen.

On this route, there was no bike lane, only a dirt road, so it took almost twice as long to get to the town square. I'd discovered it during our first year of high school, when Mikke had told me there was a barbershop along the way—the cheapest in town. That sounded good to me, as I was hoping to pocket some of the money Mom had given me for the haircut and put it toward something I needed much more: Phil Collins's new solo album, *No Jacket Required*. The one with "Sussudio," whatever that meant.

I rode along the little track through the forest and marvelled at how everything had completely not changed. I remembered just about every bump, root, and pothole.

After the track through the forest comes the dirt road, and I clearly remembered riding along it that first time, keeping an eye out for a barbershop. I'd seen nothing of the sort, just lots of nice, big houses. The neighbourhood was a little closer to town than ours, and therefore a little bit nicer. We had low, terraced houses, like ours, and apartment buildings; this neighbourhood had only decent-sized single-family homes with porches and verandas and two-car garages.

On that particular day, I was riding past a nice grey house, not too big and not too small, with similar houses in different colours on both sides of it, when I saw Jennifer, sitting on the porch and reading a book. We didn't really know each other so well back then—we'd been in school together but had never really spoken—but I was so surprised to see her that I jammed on my brakes, stopping with a squeal.

She looked up.

"Hi," I said.

"Hi," she said back, expectantly, waiting for me to announce why I was there.

"You live here?" I asked.

"No, I just like to sit on random porches, reading my book."

I couldn't think of a clever reply.

"So, who's the biker?" I nodded toward a yellow Honda Monkey moped that was leaning against their garage.

"That's my brother's."

"I didn't know you had a brother."

"Maybe there's a lot of things you don't know about me," she said. That's when I saw that smile for the first time.

"I'm looking for a barbershop," I said lamely.

She looked around her, puzzled.

"Not one here the last time I checked. Although if you trust me to have a go with the kitchen scissors and the hairspray, I could try for that Flock of Seagulls look?"

"Ha. I'll pass, thanks!"

She pouted, wounded.

"Mikke told me there's a barbershop along this way."

"Keep going that way." She waved vaguely. "Right into town."

"Thanks," I said. I didn't want the conversation to end there. "What are you reading?"

She held it up for me to see and rolled her eyes. *To Kill a Mockingbird*. "Frankly, I might just save myself some time and watch the movie."

"That's exactly what I said! But my dad made me read the book. He kept asking me questions about things that happened to make sure I wasn't cheating."

"So you've read it?"

"Finished it last week."

"No way!"

"Way!"

"And what do *you* think Atticus represents within the context of Maycomb's community?"

I laughed. "I don't know. I'm doing the other question, about how Jem and Scout change over the course of the novel."

"Oh, you're no use," she said dismissively, and then laughed.

I thought about it, the novel's powerful ending still fresh in my mind. "I think he represents the voice of reason, though, doesn't he? He represents logic, while everyone else in the town represents emotion. He thinks things through, while they all act on impulse. He doesn't allow prejudice to . . . um . . . prejudice his decisions."

"My God, that's brilliant, Peter! Can I steal that?"

"Actually, I think that's much better than what I'd been planning to write, about Jem and Scout growing up being like the civil rights movement growing . . . or something."

"Well, it's too late now. That's my essay, and if you write the same thing I'll just tell Hanna you copied me." Her eyes sparkled, and I chuckled along.

I could have stayed and chatted all day. I would have loved to have just parked the bike, and she could have shifted over, making space for me on the porch seat, and we'd have shot the breeze all afternoon—but I knew not to outstay my welcome.

I glanced casually at my calculator watch.

"I'd better be going. This hair won't cut itself, you know."

"Are you really going to get a haircut?" she asked. "I think it looks great the way it is."

I turned my eyes to my bike and pulled the brakes a couple of times, as if to test them. They made a squeaky sound.

"Anyway, I'm so glad you came by," she said quickly. "I was

just sitting here wondering how the heck I was going to make sense of this, and you come by with your clever ideas. It's like it was meant to be. Like destiny or something."

I grinned. "Pleased to be of service."

I got on my bike and rode for a bit before turning back for one last glance. I saw her wave goodbye, wiggling her fingers. I rode on, and eventually took a left turn toward the record store, my mullet flowing in the wind.

I didn't have a mullet now. Not yet, anyway.

I stopped outside Jennifer's house to turn the tape over in my walkman, but I took my time about it. The house was just as I remembered it, except that there was no Jennifer on the porch, or in the window, or sitting in the backyard swing, or even in the awesome old orange Saab 96 that was parked outside the garage.

I reattached the walkman to my jeans and got back on the saddle.

Eight minutes and two songs later, I was riding through downtown Kumpunotko for the first time since my arrival.

There was the old wooden building with the bookstore and the realtor, and after that the bank's cream-white stone facade, then the dry cleaners, and the general merchandise shop that did an odd sideline in curiosities like old coins, cannon balls, and military clothing.

On the other side of the street was the men's clothing store, the barber shop, the small record store, and the comic book store. There were other stores and shops too; I'd never been to them, but it was good to see that they were still there.

After that, just next to the only traffic light in town, was the bus terminal, and then the main square.

I left my bike leaning against a no-parking sign and walked around for a while. It was a warm day, so I took off my denim jacket and let my T-shirt remind people to *Choose Life*. Around my head, I wore a black-and-white checkered scarf, like tennis ace Pat Cash, the coolest cat I knew. My fake Ray-Ban Wayfarers—like the ones the Blues Brothers wore—were the icing on the cake.

I bought an ice cream and sat on a bench. A man walking by nodded and said hello. I wondered if I knew him, but I didn't think so. A couple of minutes later a young woman, leading a toddler, gave me a smile and said good morning. At first I thought my excellent eighties clothes were attracting people to me, but then I remembered: in small towns, people say hello to each other.

The Kumpunotko market square, the town's epicentre, was the site of a real market, with fishmongers and people selling berries and potatoes and such, and that hadn't changed at all. The introduction of plastic shelters in the previous century may well have been the only significant change since the last ice age. In the middle of all the red and orange market tents was a red, round, giant umbrella that I recognized.

I only saw the umbrella, but I knew full well that under it would be an old man, sitting on a bar stool, selling lottery tickets. Next to him would be a car, a beige Lada, once popular in the Soviet Union and Finland. It wasn't a great car but it was better than nothing. Even though I loved my Crescent, I had bought my share of lottery tickets trying to win that thing. And each time I didn't, the old man told me it just wasn't meant to be.

The car was different today, a grey Škoda, but it was still the same guy.

I reached for my phone, planning to snap a photo and send it to Tina. But the square thing in my back pocket wasn't a phone:

it was my backup tape. I gave my head a shake, as if to physically reset my brain.

"Hi, kid, you feeling lucky today?" the man said in a loud, hoarse voice, shaking a red plastic basket filled with lottery tickets.

"Sure, why not?" I handed him a coin and chose a ticket.

"Maybe a car, or maybe a stereo . . . a camera would be great," I muttered as I rolled open the ticket.

"Thank you for your support," I read out loud to the man.

"It wasn't meant to be," he said.

"Maybe tomorrow," I said with a laugh, and continued my walk.

On my way back to the bike, I made a stop at the Atlas.

I pulled at the door but it didn't open. No real surprise there: Who went to the movies in the middle of the day? I pressed my nose against the glass door, trying to see inside.

There was something off about the scene. Everything was tinged with grime. As I squinted into the darkness, trying to achieve focus, I realized it was the window; it looked as if it hadn't been cleaned in years. I wiped my nose with my jacket and leaned in again.

Even through the layers of dirt, I recognized the old lobby. The box office was in its place, but behind the concession stand, the candy was gone from the shelves. Outside, the poster frames outside were empty, and somebody had taped a sign on one of them, advertising a church's flea market. The Atlas seemed to have closed down—and some time ago, by the looks of it.

I walked backwards onto the street to get a better look at the building. The sign was still there, though it looked beaten up, especially in the daylight.

A car honked at me and I jumped back to the sidewalk, too shocked to even wave my fist at the driver.

The image of the ghost theatre bothered me. Instead of getting my bike, I walked to the coffee shop next door. It was in one of the oldest buildings in town, and I had once seen Jennifer and her mom there as they'd sat by the window in the fancier part of the shop, upstairs, drinking hot chocolate.

Before the young lady behind the counter had time to ask for my order, I blurted out, "Hey, what's up with the old movie theatre?"

"Which one?"

"Um, the one next door?"

"I don't know. It's been empty for a while . . . I think. How can I help you?"

"I'm not sure . . . Do you know why it's empty?"

"I mean, can I take your order, please?"

"Oh," I said. "A hot chocolate, please."

I took my drink and walked up to the second floor. I glanced around but didn't see Jennifer anywhere. That was fine. I had stuff to think about.

Something about the Atlas being closed down had shaken me to the core.

CHAPTER 15

START ME UP

I got my bike and rode it all around Kumpunotko. It only took about twenty-five minutes, and as I rode back past Jennifer's house, I found I was calm again. The house looked just as quiet as it had on my way in to town. No lights were on, and I didn't see anybody moving inside, but I didn't let that disappoint me. Somewhere deep inside, I had the sense that something important—something that could help me to take hold of my life and turn it around—was beginning to form, like an itchy little seedling.

I couldn't quite grasp it, or formulate it, but it felt important. I was on the verge of having . . . a . . . mission, and that gave me such energy that I pedalled like an Olympian all the way home.

Dad was still sitting in front of the TV, news blaring. I turned away so I wouldn't see the doom or the gloom of current affairs. Mom was sitting in the kitchen working on a crossword. We didn't talk about my leaving the way I had left; we just all shifted slightly to allow for the new lump under the old family rug.

I knew what Dad would have said, had we talked about it. He

would've quoted a song, probably the Beatles, and reminded me of what had happened with the upstairs bathroom.

It was the smaller of the two in the house, just a sink and a toilet, and the door bore the signs of an encounter with Hurricane Tina. Once, when I had been in there for way too long (in her opinion), she almost punched her fist through the door. Dad made her fix it, but all she did was put some tape on it. He let it stay that way as a reminder to us all (not because he was too lazy to fix it properly himself).

"Let it be . . . a lesson to you now. Every time you come in here you'll see the door, and you'll think of two things. You'll think about managing your temper, and you'll think how important it is to put in a real effort to make things better after you've misbehaved," Dad told us.

I couldn't take my mind off the Atlas, and I knew Dad would know what was going on with it. He probably knew the previous owner, or the manager, or the guy who cleaned out the popcorn machines. He'd know somebody. Dad knew everybody in Kumpunotko.

He was watching the news. I asked if I could talk to him, and he asked if it could wait. Happy to leave the room, I chatted with Mom for a couple of minutes, and then bounded up the stairs.

I loaded up the first Spectrum game I had ever played, *Thro' the Wall*. I always found that while one part of my brain was focused on moving the paddle and breaking the colourful brick wall, another part was puzzling through something completely different. It had worked for me in school—thinking up the solutions to math problems as I tapped away at the keyboard.

At least, that had been my excuse for spending all that time in front of the screen.

"Yeah, right," Tina had said.

"As long as he keeps his grades up," Mom had replied, choosing to think the best of her son.

So many ideas were percolating in my brain that I lost track of time and stayed upstairs until dinner. I also got the new high score, beating every single score I'd achieved in my teens. So much for Tina's Wikipedia theory about peak brain power!

Mom had made my favourite food, meatballs and mashed potatoes—smashed potatoes, as Dad called it—and I knew that was her way of sweeping things under the rug. In return, I ate three platefuls.

Between the first and second, I got to the point.

"Dad, I have a question," I started, "and I don't know anyone else who might have the answer."

"Oh, interesting," he said.

"You know the old movie theatre in town? The Atlas?"

"Yeees," he said, stretching the *e* to indicate that I should go on.

"Did you know it's closed?"

"Yes."

He didn't elaborate, so I pressed on.

"Do you know who owns it?"

"The theatre? Yes."

"I knew it! Who?"

He gave me a puzzled look.

"It's the ... or at least it used to be the guy whose brother had the video store you used to work at, I forget the name."

"Video 2000," I said.

"I meant the brothers' names. Their sister was actually at university with me. But they closed it down. The movie theatre, not the university."

"Exactly. I know that. Do you know who owns it now?"

"I think a developer bought it recently."

My hand went to my back pocket, but all I found was the receipt from the coffee shop. No mobile phone, no googling to find out if what my father said was true.

I slammed the table with my hand.

"Not good?" Mom asked. She offered me some more food.

"They're probably going to tear it down, right? That's what developers do; they won't want to run a movie theatre."

"Probably. It's a good spot for an apartment building, right downtown. The town council approved the sale not so long ago," Dad said. "Yes, I remember now. I read about it in the paper."

I felt all the blood drain from my face. I leaned on the kitchen table and tried to get some air into my lungs.

Damn. Of course. Stupid me. I was such an idiot, thinking I could just waltz into town and do whatever I wanted.

"But a friend of mine told me they won't be able to tear it down until they get the council's approval. He works at the town hall. He said that some people will surely file complaints." Dad balanced the last morsels of food on his fork. "You know, some people don't like change. Always trying to slow down progress."

"Are you feeling all right?" Mom asked me.

"I think I am," I said, when Dad's last words had finally registered.

"That's so you, Peter. Only an architect would pay attention to a rundown movie theatre," Mom said.

"I'm a *web* architect, Mom. Not exactly the same thing."

"Sounds the same. I just meant that you've always had the eye for that sort of thing. And you have always enjoyed the cinema. More food?"

Dad excused himself. He sat down in his TV chair again and started to flip through the channels. Mom cleared the table and loaded the dishwasher.

"What would you say if I told you that I'd like to reopen the Atlas?"

I don't know which one of us was most surprised to hear those words come out of my mouth. I certainly hadn't been aware of thinking about it until I heard myself say it. Mom looked at me and smiled. Dad said nothing.

"Did you hear that?" Mom asked Dad, louder.

"What?"

"Peter wants to reopen the cinema."

Dad looked at me from the chair.

"I think it's a fine idea," he said. "You've always liked the movies, haven't you?"

"And your father and I love having you at home," Mom said.

Again, it felt like my brain was cooking; I had such a flurry of ideas, and yet nothing I could really pin down. Reopening the Atlas was a great idea, and Mom and Dad were right about my love of the movies. I had always wanted to if not *own* a movie theatre than at least work at one.

I ran upstairs to my bedroom, not even looking at the Spectrum on my way to the desk. I grabbed a pen and started to fill the pages of my old spiral-bound math notebook with thoughts and drawings.

My brain *was* cooking.

By the time the shadow of the pine trees hit the wall of our house and Mom came knocking to tell me she had made tea, the entire floor was covered with pages full of numbers, arrows, short sentences, bullet points, circles, squares, my signatures, and pictures of Smurfs (the only thing I could draw).

Mom and I had tea in the kitchen while Dad watched TV in the living room. Afterwards, I brushed my teeth, dropped my toothbrush in the yellow plastic mug with my name on it, and retired to my room.

I decided that writing to Tina would help me formulate my thoughts. In one of my desk drawers, I found a postcard with a picture of Snoopy sitting on the roof of his doghouse, typing *It was a dark and stormy night.*

> *Have arrived safe and sound. Did notice one major disturbance in the time-space continuum and will have to take care of it. You'll thank me later when I save the world. (Seriously, all is well. Trust me.) P.*

Tomorrow I would mail it to Tina.

I pulled the cords from the Spectrum and reconnected the TV to the VHS.

I chose a tape at random and started an episode of *Hill Street Blues*, but I couldn't focus on the story and had to rewind the tape several times. I was too distracted. Something out there was calling for me.

The sun had set, but I had to get out of the house.

I needed a bike ride.

CHAPTER 16

(I'VE HAD) THE TIME OF MY LIFE

WITH the dance firmly in the rear-view mirror, we were all expected to immediately get back to our studies, ignoring our newfound sense of maturity and importance. One day we're in tuxedos and ball gowns, the next it's "Sit down, children! Stop fidgeting."

The arrival of spring didn't help.

There seemed to be a new energy in the air. We were the top dogs now, and some of the teachers seemed a little less able to handle us. Especially teachers in subjects that didn't require the same kind of discipline as, say, math. Seppo Laine, our science teacher, didn't let up; he made sure we were preparing for the finals. But others, like our art teacher, just didn't command similar respect. Her name was Siri, and she was, in a word, "bird-like" (yes, I know that's two words). She was small, and frail, and she resembled a crow every time she lost and looked around for her keys—which happened every day. The fact that she was always dressed in black didn't help. Nor that when she got annoyed with us, she would squawk.

She didn't have the stamina or the willpower to fight Sami's arguments, so she often sent us out into the world to do art projects. That day, the task was simple.

"Go out and document Kumpunotko's history," she told the class.

"How?" yelled Sami.

"Any way you want to. Paint, draw, make a collage of picked-up litter."

"But . . ."

"Just get out there and have fun," she said, and added under her breath, "Just get out."

Mikke and I walked to the park across the street from the school. There was a soccer field, and a wading pool that smaller kids used in the summer—although there wasn't any water in it yet. There were also half a dozen swings and some other playground equipment. Mikke and I sat on the swings and talked about movies. He had just seen *The Karate Kid*, so he walked around with a scarf around his head, striking dramatic karate poses and squaring up to imaginary adversaries with an intense warrior look on his face—all while trying to sound profound.

"It's all in here," he said, and pointed to his temples. "All your potential is here. And all the obstacles too. All in your head."

Then he jumped up in an attempt to do a helicopter kick and fell down in the sandbox. I was laughing so hard I nearly fell off the swing.

"Hey guys, what's so funny?" said a voice from behind us.

Jennifer. She was in a blue-and-white striped sweater, blue jeans, and high-top sneakers. No makeup. She didn't need it.

"Hi," we said in unison.

"We're just goofing around," Mikke went on. "That was a move from *The Karate Kid*."

"Yeah, I've seen it. It was okay. The movie, I mean. Your technique, less so."

Mikke rolled his eyes and sat on a swing to my right. Jennifer sat down on the one to my left.

"What are you doing for art class?" she asked me in a way that made me think I was the only person in the world.

"Nothing," said Mikke. He scooped a handful of sand from the ground. "I'll glue this on a piece of paper."

"Very mature," said Jennifer.

"It's art."

"If you say so," she said, and turned to face me. "What are you going to do?"

"Not sure yet. Maybe take photos."

"Great idea."

"Would be even better if I had my camera with me."

"So you're not going to do anything?"

She had me there, but I didn't want to disappoint her like Mikke obviously had, so I told her I was going to write a poem about the playground in the spring.

"I'll call it 'Boys of Summer,'" I said. "What's your plan? Draw something, obviously." I nodded at the big sketchpad under her arm.

"That's right. Hey, can I draw you?"

"Are you kidding me?"

"No! The light's perfect. I like the shadows," she said.

Mikke got up and put his hands in the kangaroo pocket of his hoodie.

"Well, that's my cue," he said. "See you later, Pete."

As soon as he got behind Jennifer, he turned around and winked at me. I blushed and hoped that Jennifer wouldn't notice. Mikke then started licking his lips, blowing me kisses, trying to look like Madonna. I looked away, off into the distance, trying to be the perfect model. Jennifer didn't seem to notice Mikke; she just took my hand and moved it slightly higher on the swing's rope, making me sit just right.

She sat down on a bench in front of the swings and started to sketch. I just sat there on the swing, frozen in place, staring off into the distance while sneakily looking at the way she moved her pencil, with another pencil held sideways in her mouth.

"You can schpeak," she said.

"I don't know what to say."

"Anything. You work at the video store. What's the best thing you've seen lately?"

"*Beverly Hills Cop.*"

"And the worst?"

"I've seen so many bad movies since I started working at Video 2000, but let me think . . . It would have to be this B movie I saw a few weeks back. I still don't know whether it was supposed to be taken seriously."

"Hand up, please," she said, as I'd let it slip. She smiled. "Tell me about it. Let me be the judge."

I told her what I recalled of the plot, which was fairly negligible; all I really remembered was that at the end of the movie a severed head flies through the air and lands in the hands of a mob boss who looks down at the head, surprised.

"Eww," she said.

"And then the head says, 'Sorry, boss.'"

Jennifer started to laugh, and the pencil in her mouth dropped out. I broke my pose so I could pick it up for her, and was just carefully rearranging myself on the swing when the air-raid alarm went off.

I hopped off the swing, swore, took Jennifer's hand, and

started to run. I saw that her sketchpad had fallen to the ground. I didn't want to stop—"Nothing's worth getting evaporated for," they always said—but it was Jennifer's, so I ran back and grabbed it. We sprinted through the soccer field and across the schoolyard, straight to the back door and down the stairs to the basement. The door to the shelter was closed, and nobody else was clamouring to get in. I was so tired from running that I just leaned against the wall and then slid down to the floor. Jennifer looked at me and did the same.

"What was that all about?" she asked me.

"The air-raid siren?"

"But it's the last Friday of the month! It's just a test."

My face turned red again, and she patted me on the shoulder.

"It's okay to be afraid," she said. "Nobody wants to get nuked."

"I know. Sorry. I just panicked. It's so annoying, this constant *will we get vaporized on the way to school* thing," I said.

"I don't know if this is something I should even say, but I don't mind the Cold War—as long as it stays cold. If it gets hot, that's when we'll all be in trouble."

I managed a laugh. "I know. But, you know, my sister's figure skating team had some visitors from the Soviet Union last Christmas, and I felt bad for them. They had nothing—no money, no decent clothes; they knew Wham! but they didn't have the tapes. One of them brought over a full set of crystal glasses! They'd had them in the family for years. And she traded them for a pair of Tina's jeans. Mom was so angry! She told Tina she was taking advantage of the girl. But it was what she wanted. Their lives are so different from ours. But they're still just people like us, you know?"

We were silent for a while.

"You always have your heart in the right place, Peter, and you're not afraid to show it. I like that."

Jennifer finished her drawing there in the basement, from memory, and when the school bell rang, we handed it in as a joint project. Then we got our stuff from our lockers and walked toward the bus terminal together.

"Sorry, boss," she said suddenly, in her best mob voice.

I chuckled.

"I'm curious now. I want to see the movie," she said.

"Come to Video 2000 and I'll loan it to you. For free."

"Can you do that?"

"Sure."

"You're there on the weekends, right?"

"Every Saturday, and sometimes, like today, on Friday afternoons."

"Are you going there now?"

"Yeah. I start at four, work until ten."

Again I hesitated, but this time Jennifer didn't bail me out.

"Do you want to come and get it now?"

"Sure, I don't have anything else to do."

I wasn't sure if that was such a big compliment, but I let it pass. I had mustered up the courage to ask her to Video 2000, and she had said yes. It only took us fifteen minutes to walk to the store, and we stayed side by side, not touching, not even brushing shoulders, just talking the whole time.

We walked past the record store and talked about music. We walked past Burgerland and talked about food. We walked past the bookstore and talked about our favourite books.

And when we got to Atlas, we stopped and looked at the posters outside. *Supergirl* was opening that day.

"*Supergirl!*" Jennifer exclaimed.

"Do you like Supergirl?" I asked her, surprised.

"I don't know anything about her!" She laughed.

"She's Superman's cousin. And Clark Kent's, of course. I don't know Helen Slater, but Mia Farrow, Faye Dunaway, and Peter O'Toole are amazing, so the cast is great."

"You know a lot about movies, don't you?"

"I love movies."

"Must be a dream to work at a video store then."

"Yeah, but nothing beats the cinema. You have to see films in a real theatre and experience them with all of your senses. It's not just about seeing the moving pictures—you have to see them larger than life. The sound isn't like your TV at home; the explosions shake your body. It's like you can smell the gunpowder."

She giggled, and I wondered if I'd gotten carried away.

"Still, a cinema's where magic happens. It really is. Don't you think? A group of strangers getting together in a dark room, ready to be transported to another world where everything is possible."

"Where even women can be superheroes," Jennifer said.

We kept on walking.

"It's not always strangers," she said. "I usually go with a friend or two. Nobody goes by themselves, do they?"

"I do. I go to movies by myself."

"Really? Why?"

"I just told you. I want to get transported to another world. I'm not there to talk, or chat with friends. I want to enjoy the film."

"But don't you like to have someone to talk about it with afterwards?"

"Of course," I said, thinking how nice that would be.

We arrived at Video 2000. I opened the door, like a proper gentleman, and saw Matti, the manager, sitting behind the counter, watching a Chevy Chase movie—I couldn't tell which one.

"Hi, Matti," I yelled out, in a more casual way than usual.

"In a minute," he replied, waving vaguely.

I made my way to the action section and gestured for Jennifer to follow me. I walked along the shelf with my head tilted, trying to find the movie I was looking for. When I found it, I pulled it out and handed it to Jennifer.

"Here."

"Hey, this isn't a B movie."

"I know, that one's rubbish. I wouldn't want to inflict it on you. Try this. It's *WarGames*. Have you seen it?"

She shook her head.

"It's great. You'll like it, for sure."

I walked behind the counter and opened the huge drawer where we kept the movies, found the VHS tape with the corresponding number, opened the plastic case, and put the tape inside. Then I slid it across the counter to Jennifer.

"You'll like it. Yes, it's about nuclear war, but the hero is a girl called Jennifer."

She grinned. "Thanks, Peter."

Jennifer left and I went to the back room to get changed. I was putting on my black T-shirt with *The Heat Is On* on it when I heard Matti shout from the other side of the curtain.

"I hope she's worth it," he said. "It's on your tab."

JENNIFER returned *WarGames* on Monday, two days late, and I was afraid Matti was going to take the late fee from my salary. I decided that I could live with it if he did.

"I'm not surprised you're scared of Armageddon if you watch movies like this," Jennifer said as she handed the tape to me during recess.

"But it's good, right?"

"It is. And you were right about Jennifer being the hero."

"I hope I didn't spoil the surprise."

"Mom and Dad liked it too."

"Oh." I was speechless. I hadn't imagined that Jennifer would go home with the tape, gather her family around the TV, and watch it with her parents. What had she told them about it? About where she had gotten the tape, and why?

"But my brother thought it was goofy. Unrealistic, he called it. A kid playing tic-tac-toe against a supercomputer."

And her brother too!

"Yeah, well. You can tell him it's actually totally plausible. I mean, I have a modem and a computer in my room and I can dial up any computer in the world."

"Is there anything you can't do?"

I blushed, and Jennifer did too—presumably because she thought she'd embarrassed me. She quickly changed the subject.

"Anyway, I was wondering if you'd want to see *Supergirl* with me," she said, and then opened the door to an honourable retreat: "You don't have to if you think it's silly, but I remember you saying you'd want to see it."

"I would! I would. Like to. See it," I stammered. "With you."

"Excellent. Tonight?"

We walked to the bus together and agreed to meet at the Atlas fifteen minutes before showtime.

I showered and played Spectrum until it was time to go, and then got on my Crescent and rode to town in record time.

So that's how I ended up sitting in a dark room with a group of strangers, eating candy and quietly cheering Supergirl on with the hottest girl in the school sitting next to me.

We got seats under the balcony, and for the entire duration of the film, I kept my hands on my lap and stared straight ahead.

Jennifer did the same. Together, we followed Supergirl into a new and exciting world.

"DON'T you think it was strange that her hair color changed when she wasn't in her Supergirl costume?" Jennifer asked me afterwards as we sat in the coffee shop next to the Atlas drinking hot chocolates with extra whipped cream.

"She's Supergirl, nothing's impossible. Maybe she just removed her wig at lightning speed?"

Jennifer laughed. I took a straw and blew bubbles into my hot chocolate.

"Well, I had fun. Did you?" she asked me.

"Are you kidding me? So much fun."

"I think it's time to go home, though."

I glanced at my watch. It was eight thirty.

"Yeah. You're right. I'll walk you to the bus."

Jennifer patted my hand. "My hero."

We strolled through Kumpunotko toward the main bus stop next to the square, reliving the various good and bad bits of the movie. She was right; it was great to have someone to talk about it with afterwards, just as it was great to have someone to laugh with in the darkness, and reassuring to sense her tensing in anticipation at the scary parts. Also, who knew we could split a bag of licorice allsorts so perfectly: she loved the aniseed jellies (which I hated) and hated the mint licorice (which I loved). I waited until the bus arrived, leaning on my bike, chatting about this and that.

"There it is," she said as the diesel engine growled around the corner.

Hot coals glowed in my stomach as I remembered that kiss

at the dance. It had been a few weeks and nothing. Not even a mention.

I wasn't sure what to say; I didn't know if this was a date, so didn't know if I should be asking her out again.

The bus pulled up, and with a loud hiss the doors opened.

Jennifer gave a little shrug. "Well, bye then."

Battling my cowardice and summoning every atom of courage, I leaned forward to reciprocate that kiss on the cheek from February, but she'd already turned to climb aboard.

"Bye," I whispered.

As she got on the bus, she turned around and wiggled her fingers. "See you later, friend."

"See you later," I said, adding "friend" just as the door closed.

CHAPTER 17

AGAINST ALL ODDS
(TAKE A LOOK AT ME NOW)

I could have dropped Tina's postcard into any of the three yellow mailboxes between our house and the market square, but I didn't, and fifteen minutes later, I was back on the dirt road I knew so well. In the dark, when colours turned to grey, all of the houses looked the same, but I knew exactly which one was Jennifer's.

I rode past, giving the surroundings a cursory look. I didn't see anybody in the yard, or even on the road. The house looked quiet except for a light in the downstairs window. I circled around to do a second pass, and when I was about a hundred metres from the house, that light went out. Moments later, another one was turned on upstairs.

"He didn't know what he was doing, and he didn't know why he was doing it. He just knew . . . he had to do it." My voice-over voice had dropped to a whisper, a sign that I was nervous.

I stood in the same spot I'd stood in so many times before,

never crossing the line between the road and Jennifer's yard. The road belonged to everyone; their yard belonged to them.

This time, I wasn't going to wait for an invitation.

I had waited long enough. It was time.

I tiptoed to the front door to get a better look at the sign on it. It said *Welcome*.

I had expected to see a family name, something personal. Something that would at least give me confirmation, one way or the other, as to whether or not Jennifer still lived there.

What was I doing? I was a grown man, snooping around like a lovesick teenager.

Frustrated, I turned around and walked back toward the road as quietly as I could, cutting across the lawn to the spot where I'd left my bike.

"He crept with the stealth of a highly trained ninja."

A few steps from the street, I stepped into a hole. My ankle buckled, and to keep my balance, I had to leap sideways. I landed on something hard and spiky, but before I could tell what it was, something hard and solid shot up and cracked against the side of my face, filling my head with white-hot sparks of pain.

A rake. Someone had left a rake on the lawn.

I may have screamed a little as I collapsed, clutching my face, my ankle, my dignity.

Who am I kidding? I know I screamed, and not just a little bit, either. The reason I know this is because a moment later I heard a front door opening behind me and someone shouting.

"Hey, what's going on? Why are you screaming on my lawn?"

"I think I stepped on something," I whimpered.

"What are you doing here anyway?" said the voice, big and male and now right behind me.

I looked up and saw a man, a big man, standing above me.

He made no effort to help me up from my knees, not that I could blame him. I wouldn't have rushed to help a suspicious man sneaking around my house in the dark either.

"I'm sorry, I'm sorry—I'm lost. I was looking for a place to get my hair cut. I used to live around here, and now I'm back, and I remember there's this place on the way into town—and it's obviously not this place, this is a house, but I was trying to see what door number it was so I could see if I was going the right way."

"Isn't it a little late to be getting a haircut?"

"Yes, of course, but you never know, small-business owners work weird hours. I also like to get a haircut late in the day because you get the most value for money that way. If you cut it in the morning you pay full price but then it'll grow back all day and ..."

"Can you get up on your own?" His voice was gentler now.

I added another item to Mr. Laine's list of primal instincts: fight or flight or roll around on the floor babbling nonsense in the hope that your attacker takes pity on you.

"Probably not, but I'll try," I said, and that's when the man stepped forward. I could see his face better, and he could see mine.

"Don't I know you?" he said.

"Don't I know *you*?"

"Are you ... ," he tried, prompting me to say my name.

"And you must be ... ," I shot back.

He said nothing. Folded him arms. I interpreted it as my turn to speak.

"You're Jennifer's brother!"

"What? I guess, yes, I have been known as my sister's brother. And you are ...?"

"Oh, I'm Peter, I'm Jennifer's classmate."

"You are?"

"Yes, we sit together in English class. I *thought* this house looked familiar! Yes, of course, the barber is that way . . ."

"How hard did you hit your head?"

He extended his hand and helped me up, which is when I found out I had sprained my ankle really good. I couldn't put any weight on my right foot, and I winced in pain the moment I tried.

"All right. I don't see any blood, or bones sticking out through your skin, so you'll probably be fine," said Jennifer's brother, whose name still escaped me.

I was racking my brain to remember it. I must have known it.

I wasn't ready to go yet. Jennifer's brother was here, so maybe Jennifer was inside the house too, right that second. Maybe she lived here and had sent her brother out to scare away a weird man. Or maybe they were both visiting their parents, for one day only, and she wouldn't be back in town for another year or two?

I found myself straightening my spine and putting on a winning smile.

"Thanks, I'm fine now. Um, sorry to bother you. I'll let you get back to your family get-together."

"What family get-together?" he asked. "Are you sure you don't have a concussion or something?"

"Oh, I just assumed that you were visiting your parents here, and maybe . . ."

"Listen, I'm going to bed now. In my bed, in my house, which is this one right here. Which is my home."

"Oh, so you live here now? I'm sorry."

"For what? That I live here? Oh, man . . . I think we're done here."

"No, no, sorry for bothering you, sorry for the misunderstanding."

"That's fine. Goodnight."

"So, wait, does Jennifer live here too?"

He stopped, turned back to me.

"Yeah, sure. I have a really cozy relationship with my sister."

"What?"

"No. She lives across town. She moved back to Kumpunotko when she got a job at the hospital. Anyway, if we're done here?"

"Jan!"

He stopped again. "Yes?"

"I just remembered your name. Jan. Janne and Jennifer. Simple!"

"Yes, it made labelling our school clothes a lot easier. Anyway, goodnight."

I watched Jan close the door and the lights downstairs flick off. I saw his figure at the upstairs window. He put his hands on his hips and stared down at me. I gave him a friendly wave. His wave back was more of a gentle go-away, which reminded me that I probably should.

I hobbled over and picked up the bike.

Getting onto the bike, I felt something in my pocket and remembered the postcard I had meant to send to Tina. My ankle was hurting really badly now, and I had to pedal using just my left foot, but I still took a short detour to post the card.

Sitting on my bike, leaning against the yellow mailbox, I reread the card before dropping it in. The closure of the Atlas now seemed irrelevant; I'd just made a much more significant discovery. Jennifer was in Kumpunotko! And Kumpunotko was where the Atlas was. Where I was. Opening the Atlas was meant to be! It had to be. It was the portal through which Jennifer would appear, my *Field of Dreams*. If I renovated it, she would come.

I didn't need to stalk her online or look her up in the phone book; this, surely, was destiny.

A half hour later the Crescent was leaning against the wall outside our front door and I had pulled myself upstairs, like a movie villain who refuses to die.

I was man with a plan now, and the plan, which I wrote down on a piece of paper as soon as I got to my room, looked like this:

1. *Get Atlas.*
2. *Fix Atlas.*
3. *Open with a sneak preview of* Back to the Future.
4. *Invite Jennifer.*

I stuffed the paper in the pocket of my jeans so that I'd always have it with me. Then I took a painkiller, curled up under my *Ghostbusters* covers, and pressed Play on the VCR again.

I fell asleep to *Hill Street Blues*.

The last thing I remembered hearing was "Let's be careful out there."

CHAPTER 18

LIVE TO TELL

I'VE never looked forward to getting to the hospital as much as I did that morning. My ankle had swollen to the size of a grapefruit, I needed to have somebody take a look at it.

Even more than that, though, I wanted to find Jennifer.

I found it odd that she was working at the hospital. Growing up, she'd wanted to be an artist. Also, she hated the sight of blood. But then, working at the hospital didn't mean she was a doctor or a nurse; she could be a receptionist, a porter, an ambulance driver. Maybe she was a hospital clown?

I should have asked Jan.

I cringed, recalling the way I'd babbled, squirming there at his feet. I must have looked like a deranged stalker. *I* knew that wasn't what I was, but it must have looked a little like it to him. I told myself that I'd meet him again in time, and we'd look back on the whole episode and laugh.

Although my ankle felt a little better as I sat down at the kitchen table, it was obvious I wouldn't be riding my bike to the hospital. I'd have to ask Dad if I could borrow his precious VW

Beetle. He'd had the car for as long as I could remember, and both Tina and I had been allowed to drive it once we got our licences because Dad didn't want us driving his Volvo.

Once you hold on to something long enough, it becomes cool again, and that's exactly what had happened with Dad's Beetle. He never even considered selling it, despite several offers. He only drove it a few times each year, on perfect summer days, and he liked to tinker with it, keeping the engine in good order and the body rust-free.

Dad had already eaten breakfast when I came down, and he was sitting in his TV chair, watching reruns of *Candid Camera* with a stony, impassive face. For some reason, that really made me chuckle.

"Mom already left," said Dad when he realized I was there, "but she left you some breakfast in the fridge."

"Where's she gone?"

"She went to . . . oh, I forget."

Mom had stopped working two years earlier. Some people slow down when they retire; I was worried that this was happening to Dad. Other people do the exact opposite, and when they're no longer obliged to sit at a desk eight hours a day, they fill their lives with fun and variety. That was Mom. There wasn't a club or an event in Kumpunotko in which she wasn't somehow involved.

While I ate the porridge she'd left me, I carefully brought up the topic of the car with Dad. I didn't want a ride to the hospital any more than I would have wanted to be dropped outside school by a parent, and I especially didn't want a ride in a 2014 Volvo V70, for the very obvious reason that in 1986 they hadn't been invented yet.

"What do you have planned for today?" I said, casually.

"Nothing. I'll pick up your mother at some point."

"How do you know where to pick her up if you don't know where she is?"

"She'll call."

"Could I borrow the Beetle?"

So much for careful.

"Sure."

"Are you sure?" It seemed too easy. When I was a teenager, he would inspect the car every time I returned it, like a beady-eyed car-rental clerk.

"Of course. The keys are in the cupboard by the phone. Hope it starts," he said, and turned up the volume.

The maroon car was in its usual place, under the shelter of a carport to the side of the parking lot; this was supposed to protect it from the elements, but a family of birds was nesting in the beams and had given the car a fair splattering—particularly the windshield. I didn't have the energy to hobble back for a bucket of soapy water, so I decided to try to find a car wash in Kumpunotko. I slid into the old Bug, which smelled of dust and oil and old leather, and gripped the steering wheel, smiling. I tried to remember the very first time I'd sat there, but couldn't. As a child, I'd slide over to the driver's side when Dad went into the shops, turning the wheel and wiggling the gear stick, driving off on epic adventures—I particularly liked jumping the Beetle over the dunes of the Sahara—until he returned.

The driver's seat had a sixties-style rug as a cover, and the steering wheel had a fluffy purple protector, making it look like something out of *The Muppet Show*. I turned the key and pumped my fist when the engine started on the first try.

I had taped my right ankle so tightly with electrical tape that I couldn't move it at all, which was fine for walking but made using the gas pedal impossible. And since balancing the clutch is really a two-footed job, I was going to have to improvise. After a quick glance around I found an umbrella on the back seat, and that did the job perfectly. With my left foot operating the clutch and my umbrella operating the gas and the brake, I was motoring!

Fortunately, Kumpunotko is a one-traffic-light town, and as the main "rush hour" had passed already, traffic was fairly light. It felt great to be back in the old Bug, trundling along the familiar streets, each umbrella-push of the gas pedal creating a metallic roar that had birds wheeling from the trees.

The Beetle had some trouble climbing the road toward the hospital—a great white building on top of the highest hill in town. I was almost all the way up, ready to make a right-hand turn into the parking lot, when I saw a car coming out. I stepped on the clutch and the Beetle slowed, but as I jabbed at the brake pedal with the umbrella, the handle came off in my hand and the umbrella fell down into the footwell. As I began to roll backwards, I managed to yank the car out of gear and shift my left foot over to stamp on the brake pedal, only to find I'd already stopped.

I looked back to see a large silver Saab, far closer than it might normally have been.

My first thought: *Dad's gonna kill me!*

In my panic, I thrust the car into first gear and stepped on the gas pedal with my bad foot. Pain shot through me and the car stalled. In the rear-view mirror, I saw a hand come out of the driver's window of the Saab, waving at me to turn into the parking lot.

"Defying the monstrous pain that shook his body, he somehow kept going," I narrated.

The Saab followed parked in the spot right next to me.

Fight or flight?

Neither.

Out of the corner of my eye, I saw a figure get out of the Saab. I stayed put, frantically trying to kick the incriminating umbrella under the seat with my left foot. The figure walked around to inspect the front of the Saab. As the figure moved closer to my window, I pretended to be searching for something in my glove compartment. When I looked up, I saw a woman's stern face on the other side of the glass. She stood with her arms folded across her chest.

Fight or flight? I smiled and waved.

In puzzlement, she tilted her head. She was a sporty-looking woman in her forties, I guessed. I reminded myself that, despite my best efforts, that made her about my age. Grown-ups: I always forget I'm one of them now.

She had blonde hair that hung to her shoulders, and laughter wrinkles around her eyes— or maybe "anger wrinkles"? I couldn't tell. She was about my height, maybe a little shorter. She had blue eyes, and she was wearing a denim jacket, blue jeans, and green Converse sneakers. And she was chewing gum. She looked like Olivia Newton-John in the last scene of *Grease*.

I sighed and got out of the car.

"What just happened there?" she asked, sounding like an annoyed teacher, like Tina asking Sofie why there's popcorn all over the sofa.

Fight or flight?

To be honest, I was bored of finding a third option, because it invariably meant humiliating myself. So I decided—for once—to stick up for myself.

"Oh, hey, it's the lady who rear-ended me. Do you know how brakes work?" I said.

"Well, excuuuse me. As a matter of fact, I do," she said, and paused for effect. "In fact, it looked to me like you were rolling backwards. So perhaps you're the one who doesn't know how brakes work?"

Should have chosen flight. While I tried to come up with a respectable way out of the situation, she pressed on.

"Are you suggesting that it's my fault you can't stop your vehicle rolling backwards down a hill?" She looked around. "There are a few people around. I wonder if anyone would act as my witness."

"No, hey, come on," I said, my hands up, gaze down, palms to her, in my best impression of Columbo. "No need to get the cops involved here, right? I mean, I bet your Saab didn't even get a scratch."

She chuckled. "Actually, yeah, not a scratch. I'm only teasing. Sorry, I didn't mean to sound aggressive. It's just that I think my arm may be broken, so I'm in quite a lot of pain."

I gave her what I thought was a piercing look. "How do you change gears with a broken arm?"

She laughed nervously. "Well, I doubt it's *actually* broken. Just sprained. And what's wrong with you? You look like you're hobbling?"

"Yeah, twisted my ankle." I realized too late that she'd tricked me. "But I was doing fine with driving until the handle came off the umbrella . . ."

She laughed, and then mock-whispered, "We probably shouldn't be driving at all?"

Eager to smooth things over, I one-upped her: "We're idiots!"

Her smile dissolved, and an eyebrow crept upwards. Deciding to quit while I was behind, I said, "Anyway, no harm done, eh?" and started to limp toward the entrance. Just as I walked through the sliding doors, she speed-walked through in front of me with a chuckle.

I may have been hurt but I still had the eye of the tiger. I took longer strides and, defying the pain, started to walk faster toward the registration. Just a few steps later, she was ahead of me again. She turned around and blocked my way.

"You don't remember me, do you?" she said.

Everything went still.

Jennifer? My eyes were as big as plates and I had chills going down my spine.

Jennifer!? I was squinting to see better. The chills were multiplying.

I stroked my chin. A thousand thoughts went through my head. I was so elated and so disappointed with myself. Here was Jennifer, and not only had I crashed into her car, I'd also spoken to her for at least two whole minutes without recognizing her.

Frantically, I tried to reconcile the spritely teen face with this stern middle-aged woman. Both blonde-ish. Both had . . . eyes . . . noses . . . ? It was hopeless. I was hopeless.

"Jennifer?"

She frowned.

"No, Sara. Remember? We went to high school together."

Oh god. Of course. Sara the New Wave girl. My wrong dance partner.

"Um, you're Sara? Of course, I *am* an idiot. You've hardly changed," I lied, transparently. "Good to see you!"

"You too. Wow, what a surprise. I didn't know you were in Kumpunotko."

"Yeah, I just got here."

"Are you back for good? Where have you been? What do you do? Sorry, too many questions!"

I laughed. "Let me just register first, and then I'll tell you everything."

"Way ahead of you." She turned around and walked briskly to the registration window.

As we waited for our names to be called, we gave each other the short version of our life stories, the public version—the one we give to distant relatives or old friends from school.

In my case, it went from high school to university to a successful career in IT to being an entrepreneur and an adventurer.

Her story began with being an au pair in Sweden, then studying music, and after that I tuned out a little bit, wondering if Jennifer was somewhere close. Not the receptionist, she was too young . . .

" . . . so now I'm a policewoman here."

I was back in the conversation.

"Wait, what? I crashed into a cop's car?"

"Yes, sir, you did."

"Oops. Am I in trouble?" I asked with a laugh.

She didn't laugh back; instead, she took out her pocket notepad.

"Do you really have to report it?" I asked.

She shrugged her shoulders, as if there was nothing else she could do.

"Oh, come on! There was no damage!"

"No," she said, and laughed. "I just wanted to see you dance a little."

"Dance! With this ankle?"

She looked at me slyly. "Well, I'd high-five you if my arm wasn't hurting so bad."

So she remembered the dance, remembered my split tuxedo pants, the gymnasium echoing with laughter. Fine. That gave me an opening, which I jumped into casually.

"Who else do you see from the old days? You know Mikke's a priest now, in America somewhere."

"I didn't know that."

"I heard Jennifer's still in town—do you remember Jennifer? I bumped into her brother yesterday. He told me."

Sara got up from the wooden bench to throw her chewing gum in the trash can a few steps away.

"Yeah, I've seen her," she said when she sat back down. "It's not like we're friends or anything, but I've bumped into her around town."

"Oh well, I guess I'll bump into her eventually then. Not that it matters. You know. Whenever. Or never," I said.

I was very casual on the outside, but inside, the voice-over man was in high gear: "Firmly settled back in Kumpunotko, our hero knew he had every chance of bumping into her . . ."

Just then, the doctor called Sara in.

"Good luck," I said.

"Thanks," she replied, and disappeared into the doctor's room. I'd hardly had enough time to pick up a magazine when Sara walked back out and toward me.

"Listen, if you want to go grab some pizza or something, just text me, okay? Here's my number." She handed me a page torn from her pocket notebook.

"Will do. Thanks," I said. "My number's in the phone book. Well, it's under my father's name," I added, but she'd already closed the door again.

I lingered outside the doctor's office for a while longer, but I didn't see Sara again. The doctor who called me in was too short and too old to be Jennifer. She shook my hand in a way my dad would have loved and asked me to sit on the bed. She looked at my ankle and told me that nothing seemed to be broken, so she just taped it properly—with medical tape, not the electrical kind I'd used.

"Take it easy now. Just give it some time," she told me.

"Thanks." She seemed nice, like someone I could talk to. "Hey, Doc. You don't happen to know Jennifer Berg, do you?"

She looked puzzled. "Is she a patient? Because obviously I can't talk about . . ."

"No, she works here. At the hospital. I thought you might know her."

"Sorry," she said with a smile. "Lots of people work here."

Her smile remained. I left.

CHAPTER 19

SMALL TOWN

SARA'S Saab was still parked outside the hospital when I limped out with a prescription for painkillers. It was almost four in the afternoon, and Kumpunotko was at its best. The view from the hospital was beautiful, the houses and the town's buildings laid out below, little people in little cars trundling here and there along little roads.

I stood by the low stone wall at the edge of the parking lot and looked at the hills around the valley, the sunlight bathing the fields in green and casting long shadows from the patches of woodland. With some trouble, I climbed up on the wall to get an even better view.

"It's not bad, you know." The voice came from behind me, startling me so that I almost fell down.

Sara.

"It looks pretty nice from here," I said.

"Should you really be standing on that ankle? Sit down instead." She climbed onto the wall too, and then sat down on it. "It's small, I think, but it's mine."

I realized she was referring to Kumpunotko, and nodded. "We were in such a hurry to get out of here. I used to think that living in the city would make my life exciting, that I'd make it big and be happy, but all it did was make me realize how many more strangers there were."

"True."

"And sometimes it's nice to be in a place like this," I said, nodding down toward the town.

"Where everybody knows your name?"

"Yeah. Who said that?" I asked, wondering if she knew.

"I think it's from an old TV show."

We sat in silence for a while.

"Don't you think the clock tower looks so much bigger from up here?" I said.

"Funny how it makes a bigger impression from afar."

I wasn't sure what she meant by that.

"What's your favourite place here?" she asked. "I love the market square. It's so full of life and colour."

"And that guy is *still* there, selling lottery tickets."

"I don't think anyone's ever won."

"Somebody must have. The car's changed."

"Oh no, that got stolen. Pretty much the crime of the century around here."

I laughed. "Mine's the movie theatre. The Atlas."

"Why?"

"Don't you just love the magic of the movies?"

"Sometimes. It's so expensive though, when you can just watch it at home a year later. You used to work at that video store, didn't you?"

"Video 2000. Yeah. You know they're planning to knock it down? The Atlas."

"I heard a rumour."

"I don't think it's just a rumour."

"Oh, that's a shame. Still, there's always the other one."

"I loved the bookstore too," I said, suddenly keen to change the subject but not wanting the conversation to end. "I like the way I can trace my life through the different departments. The kids books are in the back, with the little chairs and sofas."

She laughed. "I used to always make my mom read *Goodnight Moon*. Even though we had it at home. God, I loved that book."

"And then you move to the front of the store, the teen fiction. Then, when you grow up, you move up into proper fiction—action and thrillers."

"I never went there," Sara said.

"I guess you get enough of that at work."

"No. I've just never liked thrillers. I don't find them particularly realistic. And I don't like the idea that something awful has to happen in order for it to be entertaining."

We sat in silence for another while. Not exactly awkward, not exactly comfortable.

"Anyway, as exciting as this is . . ." She grinned and swung her legs around, climbing back over into the parking lot. "See you around, Peter."

I waved and watched her walk back to her Saab. She had another look at the front bumper, then waved her fist at me, then grimaced in pain. I laughed and waved again.

I sat there for a little while longer and then limped back to the car. Just before I hopped in I cast a look back over the little town of Kumpunotko. I gave the movie theatre a small wave. I couldn't see it, but I knew exactly where it was.

"It will be mine," I said in my narrator voice. "Oh yes, it will be mine."

★ ★ ★

I drove out of the parking lot, then shifted into neutral and just cruised down the hill, the car speeding faster and faster, past the burger joint, the train station, the bank, the pizza place, and then slowing down until it stopped right in front of the record store. I took it as a sign from the universe and steered the car to the side of the street, into an empty parking spot.

A small bell jingled as I walked in. A big man behind the counter looked up from a newspaper but didn't turn down the music—Simply Red's "Holding Back the Years."

"Good tune," I said, raising my eyebrows and nodding up toward the ceiling, where the speakers were.

"Yeah," said the man. The name of the store was Kim's Basement, and while I assumed he was Kim, the store wasn't in a basement, so I couldn't be sure.

He sold only second-hand records, with CDs on one side of the store and vinyl on the other. I moved to the vinyl side and started to go through the crates. My muscle memory was still there, and my fingers flipped from one cover to another in fractions of a second, bypassing records I had no interest in as they were either rubbish or, having been released after the mid-1980s, didn't technically exist to me.

Every once in a while I stopped and let out a surprised gasp when I found a record I had coveted during my high-school years but hadn't had enough money to buy. They were all marked at just a few euros—yes, I know euros didn't exist in the mid-1980s, but come on—and pretty soon I had a decent-sized stack of LPs set aside.

When I finally approached Kim at the cash register, I had thirteen records in my hands, all of them great eighties classics.

"Great store," I said.

"Mm-hmm."

He flipped through my selection and stopped at Dire Straits' *Brothers in Arms*.

"Not their best," he said.

"No?"

"No."

There was a slightly awkward silence.

"Can I still buy it?"

"Up to you."

"Would you?"

"I guess," he said. Without another word, he lifted the counter-top and walked past me, heading to the records. He pulled one directly out of the crate and handed it to me on his way back.

"But that's the one you really need," he said. "Where it all began."

It was called *Dire Straits*. I did that thing where you look at an album sleeve and nod, as if you're appreciating the music therein. I turned it over and read the track listing.

"Sultans of Swing" caught my eye.

"Okay," I said. "I'll take that one too."

He bopped his head to the beat—he'd put on some Ultravox—as he punched the keys on his old cash register, and then pointed at the total.

"Cash only."

"Suits me!"

I rummaged in my pockets for some money. Found a note and some coins, but realized I was a few euro short.

"Um," I said, unsure what to do. "I'm a little short."

"Yes, but size isn't everything."

I grinned.

I had a quick flick through the pile, deciding what to put back.

"You could always open an account," he suggested.

"Really?"

"Really."

"Could be dangerous. I mean, there's a lot of good records in here."

He grinned. "I know. All you need to do is register on our very high-tech database." He reached under the counter, took out a leather book, opened it up, and slid it over to me, along with a ballpoint pen. There were columns for name, address, amount owed, and signature. "Got any ID on you?"

I showed him my driver's licence. He took a quick photo of it with his phone and passed it back. In the book, next to where I'd inscribed my details, he wrote *15 euro*. "Just settle up at the end of the month, yeah?"

As I scribbled my initials in the final column, I realized I could finally buy all the albums I had ever wanted, without batting an eyelid.

I was rich!

WHEN I got home, Dad was still in front of the TV; Mom wasn't home yet. I shouted "Hello!" and went straight upstairs, eager to listen to my new albums, and to take it easy and play a computer game. After all, that was what the doctor had ordered.

As side A of Sade's *Diamond Life* ended, I was still trapped in the Elvenking's wine cellar, inside an empty barrel, hiding from the pale bulbous eyes that were after me. Just as I was about to move, a vicious warg hit a well-placed blow and cleaved my skull in two. *Progress: 12.5%*

The house was eerily quiet. I could hear the ticking of the kitchen clock all the way from my room.

When I got downstairs, Dad was asleep in his chair, the remote in his hand. An enthusiastic salesman was pitching car wax on the shopping channel, but the TV was on mute. I took the remote and switched off the television.

That woke him up.

"Oh, hi, you're home. How's the foot?" he said, too cheerily.

"It'll be fine. What have you been up to?"

"Nothing much, nothing much."

"Have you just been sitting here the whole day?"

"I got the mail."

"From the doormat? It's a beautiful day! Maybe you should get outside a little?"

"I will, when I go pick up Mom."

"By the way, here are the car keys," I said. As I pulled them out of my pocket, a piece of paper flew out and landed on the floor. It was my to-do list.

I picked it up quickly so that Dad wouldn't see it. He saw the note fall but didn't seem overly interested.

"Keep the keys, maybe you'll need the car later today or tomorrow. I have the Volvo," he said.

"Okay. When are you going to pick up Mom?"

"She'll be late today."

"Maybe we can surprise her and make dinner? Wouldn't that be fun?"

"Hmm. I don't think she'd like that. Sit down, the news will be on in ten minutes."

So I sat down. I told Dad about bumping into Sara, and, being very brave and grown up, I told him there was a little dent in the chrome of the Beetle's bumper. I apologized. He waved it away, said he knew someone who could take a look. Then I told him about the doctor, but as soon as I began he unmuted the TV at the start of the news jingle, so I got up and said I had things to do in my room.

I did have things to do. And so far I had done none of them.

1. *Get Atlas.*
2. *Fix Atlas.*
3. *Open with a sneak preview of* Back to the Future.
4. *Invite Jennifer.*

Kim Wilde was singing in the background, but I couldn't focus on music.

All I could think was "Get Atlas! Get Atlas! Get Atlas!" It was going around and around my head like an enthusiastic crowd chanting at a hockey game.

"Hey, Dad! Daa-aad!"

No reply.

My ankle was hurting again, and I wanted to avoid walking as much as possible, but when Dad didn't answer my fourth shout, I had no choice but to grit my teeth and get downstairs. I had a genius idea: I held on to the handrails on both sides and slid down. This worked brilliantly—and looked great—but halfway down I realized my mistake as my hands began to get friction burns, and then—even worse—the impact of landing in the hallway at speed hurt my ankle far more than fifteen smaller bumps would have done. Sometimes I worry about myself.

"Hey, Dad," I said. Not only was I limping, I was also waving my hands to cool them off.

"Hey, Peter," said a voice from the kitchen.

Dad was sitting at the kitchen table in the gloomy darkness.

I turned the lights on.

"Didn't you hear me yell?"

"Oh, sorry. I was just deep in thought, I suppose. What was it?"

"Are you okay? Has something happened?"

"No, no, just waiting for your mother to call. What did you want?"

"Just checking if you know who the developer is, the one that bought the movie theatre?"

"Oh. I think it was the friend of the brother of a girl who went to university with me. That was before your mother's time, of course. She was pretty. I don't think your mother liked her, though."

"But I thought you said her brother had sold the movie theatre. I want to know who owns it now."

"As I said, the *friend* of the brother of the girl. Yes. BBB."

"What?"

"That's the name of the company—BBB. That's what it says on the sign on the roof, I think. You'd have to check. I'm sure it'll be on the internet somewhere."

"Thanks," I said, feeling like I knew less than I had two minutes before. "Would you like me to pick up Mom? Maybe you're tired."

"No, no, I always pick her up."

I found the phone book in its usual place in a cupboard under the downstairs phone. I carefully turned the pages so I wouldn't tear the very thin paper, and when I got to *B*, I ran my finger down the column as quickly as possible to find the correct number. I dialled it right away, hoping there would still be someone there.

After four rings, a cheerful voice answered.

"Hello, BBB?"

"Hello, BBB, I'm interested in the movie theatre."

"Um. How can I direct your call?"

"I'm interested in the movie theatre. In Kumpunotko."

"Ah. Okay. Hold a moment, please."

After a few minutes of listening to a looped instrumental version of Limahl's "Neverending Story," the music stopped and a man spoke.

"Hello, this is Tomi Taimi. I understand you're asking about the movie theatre. Would you like to buy an apartment?"

"No, sir. I'd be interested in running a movie theatre in it."

"Hmm. There must be some misunderstanding. We're about to demolish the building."

"Yes, I heard that. But you can't. How would I show movies there if you'd bulldozed it?"

"Excuse me?"

I realized that—as seemed to be happening quite a lot lately—I was failing to make myself clear. I took a breath and recalibrated.

"Okay, listen. The movie theatre is very important to me, and I'd like to have the chance to save it from demolition."

"But we've been given permission to acquire the land, so we've acquired it."

"Perhaps I could acquire it from you?"

"Perhaps. Do you have six hundred thousand euro? That's what we paid."

I suddenly felt very small, and very helpless, and very silly.

"Listen, the building currently stands on land that belongs to BBB," Taimi continued. "All we need is final planning consent. I think there's an objection of some sort, but that's with the lawyers at the moment. I don't imagine it will be too long before we've overcome that . . . hurdle. And anyway, Kumpunotko has another movie theatre. Why don't you use that one?"

"It has to be the Atlas. I have a plan!"

"What kind of plan?" asked the man, the patience in his voice dwindling. "A business plan?"

"Exactly!" I semi-lied. "A business plan. I've come up with a *great* business plan. It's a win-win situation. You win, I win, the town wins."

The line was silent. I heard Tomi Taimi cough.

"Listen, at the moment, while things are up in the air, we are still technically open to suggestions. We have plans for apartments, but nothing's set in stone just yet. If you have a better suggestion, we would be willing to listen. Would you like to come down and present a feasible plan to me in person?"

"Tomorrow?"

"Tomorrow."

"Ten?"

"Ten."

"Great. See you then."

I wiped the sweat off the receiver before I put it back in the cradle. I jumped for joy, and kicked my leg up like David Lee Roth would have done on stage at the start of "Jump." Well, in my head it was a DLR-worthy kick. In reality, I barely got my foot above my waist, and I landed on the sprained ankle, like Daniel LaRusso when he tries the crane kick in *The Karate Kid*. I howled with pain, and hobbled upstairs to try to think up a business plan.

CHAPTER 20

(JUST LIKE) STARTING OVER

E VERY project starts with a blank piece of paper, so I got one of those from my desk, along with a pen. In large letters, I wrote:

The Altas Movie House: Regeneration Project

Underneath that I wrote my name: *Peter Eksell, CEO, Webscoe*.

I drew a square on the page, and then added some circles of different sizes here and there. I coloured some of them black; others got horizontal, vertical, and diagonal lines.

Mike + the Mechanics' "All I Need Is a Miracle" was quietly playing in my ears, my walkman once again being in complete sync with the universe.

The sun had faded and the sky was fully dark, so I drew my curtains. I looked at my alarm clock. It was 10 p.m. I'd been working on my business plan for three hours and all I had was a bit of nicely shaded geometry. I'd also managed to spell *Atlas* wrong.

I rummaged in my desk drawer for a fresh sheet of paper, and in doing so found my old modem under a pile of ancient cords, hairbrushes, toy cars and sweatbands.

"Hello, old friend!"

I blew the dust off it. This little box of delights—barely bigger than a standard VHS player—had been my first passport to digital connectivity. All you had to do was wait until your big sister was off the phone and then plug it in, dial up, and join the Micronet, where thousands of other young gaming enthusiasts would post messages, and share jokes and cheats for games. Many of my friends from school had computers too—and we all knew who had what; I was in the Spectrum camp, Mikke with Commodore—and we would often meet up and chat on BBS forums about computer games, films, music, and, well, computer games.

I plugged the modem into the phone extension, and then into the Spectrum. I made a wish.

At first, nothing happened. Then there was a beep. A scratchy warble. And then, as if it had been there just yesterday, the BBS welcome screen began to load up on my TV. It was like in *Star Wars* when, despite being unused for decades, Luke's lightsaber immediately spits out a perfect line of blue light.

Crackling with glee, my fingers began to run over the keyboard.

First stop, as always, "Dragon's Lair."

While the modem beeped away, doing its elaborate digital handshake with the host, I picked up a baseball hat from the drawer, flipped it on backwards, and did a little chair dance. I loved the nighttime, when everybody else was asleep. Everything moved slower, everything was calm, and as long as I stayed in my own world—hopefully in "Dragon's Lair"—everything was all right.

But "Dragon's Lair" was closed. I tried "Shack Attack"—out of business. "MAD world"—gone.

After ten handshakes and ten digital "too slows," I was ready to give up, but then one more BBS caught my eye: "I Wanna Rock!"

While the computer did its thing, I rummaged through my box of cassettes and found the perfect one, covered with devil horns and anarchy symbols. I slotted it into my walkman and pressed Play. Big mistake. I'd forgotten to turn the volume down, and almost blasted myself across the room, clutching at my ears like George McFly when Marty dresses up as a spaceman and blasts him with mean Van Halen guitar licks.

My ears ringing, I turned it down a little, then snarled my teeth and banged my head along to Mötley Crüe's "Shout at the Devil."

Several lines of text appeared on the main page, and I saw the system operator's message, dated just six weeks prior. The sysop was called Twisted Sister. Obviously. In her message, Twisted Sister said she'd been hosting the BBS for ages, but there was no traffic anymore. She said she'd pull the plug on the board by the end of September if there wasn't any pick-up.

There were only four items on the menu: (1) private chat, (2) file download, (3) a public board, and (4) jokes.

Calling myself Pinhead, after Marty McFly's high-school band, I chose the public board and typed my reply, in English, just like the original messages: *Hi, Twisted Sister. I Wanna Rock too! Please keep this humming.*

There weren't any interesting messages on the public board so I read a couple of the jokes, but was interrupted by sounds from the hallway. Dad was heading to bed. Quite late. Must have fallen asleep in front of the TV. Even with my headphones on, I could hear him cough and sigh and then slowly click the bedroom door closed.

I was exhausted, and I still didn't have a business plan. I trusted myself to think it over as I dozed in bed, and then wake up early and write it all down ahead of my meeting with BBB.

I was walking toward the market square, feeling very pleased with myself. I hadn't expected the meeting with BBB to go quite so well, but there I was, holding the deeds to the Atlas in one hand, the keys in the other. I had on my high-cut Guess blue jeans, a lavender T-shirt with a white-checkered short-sleeve shirt over the top, and my hair (getting slightly long at the back now) was combed back in a smart wave.

As I rounded the corner on to the market square I must have been daydreaming, because I walked straight into a woman heading the other way. I knocked her purse out of her hand, spilling its contents all over the sidewalk.

"Oh God, I'm so sorry, I'm such a klutz," she said as we both bent down to retrieve her stuff. And as we did so, of course our heads banged together.

"Oh God, *I'm* so sorry!" I offered. We both laughed and clutched our foreheads. Only when she gingerly took her hands away from her face did I realize who it was.

"Peter?"

"Jennifer?"

My heart started thumping.

She had barely changed at all. Same simple smile, blonde hair, button nose. If anything, age had been generous, and she was even more beautiful now.

"Peter," she gasped excitedly. "Is it really you? What are you doing in Kumpunotko? I thought you were off in the big city, running some kind of web company?"

"Ah, well. I was missing home, so I came back."

"Wow! It's so great to see you. You haven't changed at all."

"That's what I was just thinking about you. If anything, you're even more beautiful."

She looked bashful. "Me? You're just saying that."

"No, really. Listen—there's something I have to tell you. About when we were kids." Her head tipped slightly, a keen, inquisitive look on her face. "You see, I didn't have the guts to admit it back then, but—"

"Peter."

"Yes?"

"Peter!" Her voice had changed, dipping down a little. "Peter, wake up," said Dad. "Your alarm's been going off for an hour."

Cursing my cruel imagination, I bounced out of bed—howling in pain at my sore ankle—and saw that I had barely half an hour to get up, get dressed, and get to the BBB office to present my plan. I hit Play on the stereo, but "I Just Called to Say I Love You" wasn't quite right. I flicked through my tapes, found the right one, put it in, pressed Play, rewound it a bit, pressed Play again. I let the Pointer Sisters' "Neutron Dance" blare as I scrambled to get myself ready.

I pulled on a Hawaiian shirt and climbed into my white linen suit, rolling up the sleeves. I checked myself in the mirror—I definitely needed a haircut, but I didn't have time for that. I grabbed my business plan, hoping BBB wouldn't notice the minor spelling mistake, and padded it with a sheaf of blank paper; I shoved the whole thing into a folder. I grabbed the breakfast Mom had left for me in the fridge and hobbled outside, hoping the Beetle would once again start on the first try.

CHAPTER 21

PLEASE, PLEASE, PLEASE, LET ME GET WHAT I WANT

T HE BBB office was in the old bank building, so it was easy
to find. Tomi Taimi was waiting for me in reception when
I walked in. He was tall and gaunt, with a widow's peak and fra-
meless glasses. His handshake was too strong, like he was trying
to prove something. He guided me to a small conference room
where another man was waiting. I was already sweating from the
anxiety of the rush, and hoped none of it was showing through
my linen suit.

The other man had tufty white hair and a heavy white beard.
He wore thick glasses and a rich-blue shirt that had two top buttons open, revealing a chunky gold necklace and more chest hair
than I wanted to see. I thought he looked like Santa Claus on a
day off.

"Peter, this is Kari, our managing director."

We shook hands and sat down. He gave me a patient smile.

"So, I understand you have a proposal," said Kari, and gestured toward the coffee pot. Tomi Taimi took the hint and slid the tray toward himself.

I cleared my throat.

"Yes. As I explained to Tomi over the phone, I would like to rent the movie theatre in town," I said. I wanted to keep things vague while I could.

"Hmm. Why?"

"To show movies! Why else?"

"Why else indeed. The trouble is, that theatre hadn't been profitable in years. I think the old owners only kept it going as a passion project. But when you run out of money, passion isn't going to pay the bills. That's why it closed. And given that it's right in town, it's a waste of good land for it to be sitting there gathering dust. So, the council gave us permission to acquire it."

Tomi Taimi—BBB's deputy director, according to the business card he'd handed me I the lobby—waited for his boss to finish before asking if I wanted coffee.

"No, thanks. Look, I understand all that. And I was thinking about it. And it's like you say—a passion project."

Kari tilted his head, suggesting I should elaborate.

I decided to lay my cards on the table. Kari was clearly a decent man, and the fact that he looked like Santa Claus had already put me in an enormously trusting frame of mind.

"Okay. I grew up in this town. When I was a boy, I worked at the Video 2000 store. Remember that place?"

Kari stared blankly at me , but Tomi Taimi nodded. "I used to rent Sega games there."

"But it was always my dream to run the Atlas." This was an exaggeration, but I seemed to be on the right track, so I pressed on. "I understand that you guys have to knock it down, because you want to build apartments there or whatever. Who am I to stand in the way of progress?"

Kari gave an acquiescent nod. "So, what is your business plan?"

I opened the folder and tipped it upside down. Blank sheets spilled across the table.

"Look, I'm not a business man. I just want a chance to fulfil my dream before it's too late. I understand you're a few months away from sending in the bulldozers. Let me have that few months. I just want to run it as a movie theatre, please."

Kari smiled kindly. "But it's in a fairly bad state of repair. You'd have to fix it up before you could charge people to go in there."

"Then I won't charge people!" I blurted, knowing I was getting closer and closer to convincing Kari. "I just want to create something really special. I don't care if I have to fix it up: I'll fix it up. I have savings. And I don't care if you're going to knock it down later. I just need this now."

I realized I was begging.

Tomi Taimi passed a coffee to Kari, who stirred it gently, looking at me over his thick glasses.

"The trouble is," said Tomi, "it would involve an awful lot of paperwork, organizing the permits and so forth."

"I'd do all that. Promise."

Kari stopped stirring and put down his spoon. He sipped at the coffee, put the cup back down.

"Okay. How about this. We provide you with a short-term rental agreement. *Short*-term," he said, and raised his index finger. "I'll have our lawyers email you something this afternoon. It would have to include certain caveats, particularly that you would be bound to vacate at very short notice, regardless of how many tickets you'd sold or whatever."

"Of course!"

"Remember, this is *our* business. I understand your passion, but we have shareholders, and we also have several people keen to invest in apartments, so we can't have you barricading yourself in there, okay?"

"Of course not! I totally understand."

"Good. Tomi, would you ask Petra to find a suitable short-term tenancy form? We'll make it out until the end of the year. Perhaps longer, if things don't go our way."

Tomi nodded. "Of course, you understand you will be liable for business rates and utility bills."

"Of course," I said, nodding like a wagtail.

Kari finished his coffee and stood up. "Great. And I suppose, given that the building was just gathering dust anyway, we should make the rent nominal. One euro a week, shall we say?"

I was gripping the table so hard I almost snapped a chunk off.

I tried to stay cool and business-like, but instead I jumped up and, barely remembering to hobble, ran around the table to give Kari a great big hug. He intercepted me with a hand, allowing me to shake, and I pumped his arm so vigorously that his glasses began to wobble down his nose.

"Yes, yes, very good. Now, most importantly: What film are you going to open with?"

"*Back to the Future.*"

"Aah, good choice. The whole trilogy?"

"No, just the original."

"Excellent. I always found part two a little too dark. Who needs that?" he said, and nodded to me and Tomi. We nodded back.

"Would there be a red carpet? I don't think there's ever been a red carpet in Kumpunotko!"

Of course, I knew otherwise, but this was not the time for nitpicking.

"There *will* be a red carpet," I said, changing the verb.

"Maybe people can dress up?"

"Maybe? I expect them to! It's going to be a gala opening."

"And maybe they can recite lines from the movie during the performance, like in those sing-along musicals," added Tomi, who seemed to have picked up on his boss's excitement.

Kari and I looked at each other.

"And ruin the movie?" we said in unison.

Tomi Taimi blushed, and Kari smiled and clapped him on the back.

"Come on, let's leave Peter to his plans." He reached into his pocket and took something out, placing it down on the table. He slid it toward me. A set of keys! "I figured I might as well bring them. Just give your email address to the receptionist on the way out and we'll take care of the paperwork."

I froze. "Ah."

Chapter 22

RUN TO YOU

I ran as fast as I could—well, it was more like speed-hobbling—all the way to Atlas. That's the good thing about living in a small town: it only took about forty-five seconds. I sat on the curb across the street, admiring the theatre while catching my breath. I remembered it that February night so many years ago: snow falling, torches blazing, red carpet awaiting. Then I crossed the street and walked around to the side door, the one the crowds of moviegoers would walk through after the film, chatting excitedly, analyzing the plot, talking about the best bits or what they thought should have been done differently. The keys on the ring—dozens of them—were helpfully labelled, and though I could have gone in through the big glass entrance door, I decided to save that for a special occasion.

My hands shaking, I had some trouble getting the key into the lock, but nailed it on my third try. I pulled the door open, noted the sign on the inside that said *Exit: Push*, and boldly stepped into the darkness. The door swung closed behind me, rendering everything pitch black. I stood there in silence for a moment. The sound insulation meant that silence really was silence. All I could hear was my breath and the slight parting of my lips as a huge smile spread across my face.

The Atlas.

Mine.

I allowed myself only a few moments of glory. There was work to be done.

I pushed the door back open and wedged it in place with a garbage bin until I could find a light switch. Thankfully, the power was still connected, and I flicked every switch on the large bank, the building humming to life around me as power surged to the various strips and bulbs throughout the place.

I was in a little corridor that connected the lobby, the auditorium, and the balcony. Right in front of me were the stairs up to the balcony, and a little to their right, the door to the main lobby, through which excited moviegoers would come, clutching their tickets and candy, taking off their coats, perhaps holding hands. I turned left and walked down the sloping corridor that ran the entire length of the theatre until I came to another door, to my right.

Behind that door was a sight that made me gasp for air. A single tear ran down my cheek, and it wasn't an allergic reaction to mould.

The sea of red velvet seats in front of me was the most beautiful thing I had ever seen, even with a hideous painting of a dragon on the back wall.

I walked all the way up the aisle, turned around, and took in the view. On the way down, I tripped on loose carpet and almost fell. I sat down on a seat in the first row, stretched my legs, and shouted "Great Scott!" at the top of my lungs.

I dug my action plan out of my pocket, and with a pencil

I'd taken from BBB, when I blushingly wrote down my postal address, I crossed out item number one.

1. ~~Get Atlas.~~
2. *Fix Atlas.*
3. *Open with a sneak preview of* Back to the Future.
4. *Invite Jennifer.*

"You have cleared 25 percent of the adventure," I said, substituting my usual narrator with a computer-like voice.

I knew there was still a lot to do—a hell of a lot—but the first and most important thing was already clear in my mind. There was a special someone I wanted to invite to opening night. I walked to the Atlas's lobby, laid my business folder on the counter, withdrew a single sheet of paper, and, in my smartest (though admittedly probably not that smart) handwriting, wrote a letter.

Dear Mr. Lloyd,

Thirty years ago, you changed my life with your fantastic performance as "Doc" Brown in Back to the Future. Today, I've made it my mission to turn back the wheels of time and bring movie magic back to my hometown by screening Back to the Future in the same theatre where I once saw it. (Except, now I'm the manager.)

It would be a great honour for me, for the town of Kumpunotko, and for the entire country of Finland, if you would make an appearance at the opening of my movie theatre, the Atlas, on December 1.

Looking forward to meeting you.

Your humble fan,
Peter Eksell
Manager, Atlas Theatre

Marty needed his Doc.

IF ever there had been a piece of news worthy of sharing on social media, surely this was it. I was half-tempted to write a letter to each of my 127 Facebook friends, but that would have been weird (and time-consuming). But I was desperate to tell someone, and having walked around downtown Kumpunotko for fifteen minutes without finding a phone booth so I could call Tina—where had all the phone booths gone!?—I decided to send her a postcard instead.

The Kumpunotko main post office—there were two—was in a big old stone building that oozed importance, which made me feel like a man on a mission as I ran up the steps.

First I selected an envelope, and wrote in large letters across the front:

Christopher Lloyd
c/o Universal Pictures
Hollywood, California
USA

Then I went straight to the postcard racks and picked up a touristy Kumpunotko card with a photo of the town hall, the square, the high school, and naked people in a sauna. I stood up and scribbled a note to Tina—*Per my previous card, I now have the keys to the Atlas. Plan well and truly underway. More news soon. Love to Sofie and Tim*—the chain that held the pen to the desk rattling and swishing as I wrote.

I put the pen down, and as I turned around to take my place in the line, I bumped into something and heard a woman's short scream.

"What the hell are you doing?!" she yelled. The contents of her purse were on the floor and she was scrabbling around to catch rolling coins. My dream from last night came back to me.

"God, I'm so sorry. Let me help." I got on my knees on the floor.

"Please don't," she said, and when she was finished with her purse and saw my face, she added, "Oh, it's you."

It was Sara. She was wearing a white summer dress with a purple flower pattern, and a raspberry beret on her head. Her cheeks were rosy, as if she'd just been outside for hours. Her eyes had that same sparkling and suspicious look as the last time, making me think she was teasing me and accusing me at the same time.

"I'm so *so* sorry. I just didn't see you there. So clumsy of me. Idiot, idiot!" I said, and slapped my forehead a couple of times.

"That's right. Let me help," Sara said, and started slapping my forehead too.

"Thanks. Nice hat," I said.

"Dude, nice suit," she countered.

"Why, thank you."

"What's the occasion?"

"Oh, you know, big important meeting in town."

"Oh yeah, what about?"

It didn't feel right, telling a stranger my exciting plan before I'd at least told Mom and Dad that it was *actually going to happen*, so I just smiled ambiguously and tapped the side of my nose. "That's for me to know and you to find out."

She laughed. "Well, whatever it is, you seem in a much better mood."

"I suppose I am."

"Well good! Then you won't mind me going ahead of you. It's just that I'm in a bit of a hurry."

"Be my guest," I said, beaming.

We switched places in the line. While we waited, Sara told me a story, in hushed tones, about how one of the "elder gentlemen" of the town had just been busted for running an illegal still.

"Very naughty."

"Exactly. I don't think anyone *really* minds, if it's just for your own consumption. I mean, if you want to go blind and mad that's your business. But sticking labels on it and trying to sell it from under the counter—that's just dangerous."

I shook my head sagely. "I must have been viewing Kumpunotko through rose-tinted glasses all these years. Turns out it's a hotbed of crime. Illegal distilleries, car thefts."

"*A* car theft."

"Well. It's practically a crime wave. I'm surprised you even get a day off."

"How do you know I'm not working?" She lowered her voice. "I could be in plain clothes, undercover."

"Are you?"

She gave me a beguiling smile and tapped the side of her nose just as a counter came free. She sauntered up to talk to the lady.

We both finished up at the same time, and walked out together. I held the door open and she skipped through.

"Well, have a nice afternoon," she said.

"And you. Hey, by the way, have you seen Jennifer Berg?"

"What? No, why?"

"Oh, no reason. I just remembered your talking about her."

"Really?" Sara said.

"Didn't you?" I asked weakly.

"Nope. As I said, I've seen her around a few times, you know, in the decades since we left high school."

"Ah. Right."

"Anyway," she said, "nice seeing you. You've got my number. Text me if you want to get a cup of coffee, maybe."

"I'd like that. Maybe I'll call you."

"Take care," said Sara, and then she walked down the stairs and away across the market square.

I took my to-do list out of my pocket again.

Item number one was done, and item number two would probably be reasonably easy. Item three couldn't be too difficult, surely. That just left item four: invite Jennifer.

CHAPTER 23

WAKE ME UP BEFORE YOU GO-GO

SPRING blossomed into summer. A magical time. The snow was a distant memory and the sun was already high in the sky when you awoke, and stayed up there long after bedtime.

I was looking forward to the holidays. The final year of high school was going to be hard work, so it would be nice to spend some quality time mooching around Kumpunotko: riding my bike, completing *The Hobbit*, edging ever closer to building up the courage to finally make the big step—from leaning on my bike on the pavement to sitting *with* Jennifer on the rock by the mailbox. It's important to have ambitions.

There were, however, a couple of flies in the ointment.

The first came in the form of Dad.

"My buddy who runs the warehouse is looking for casual workers over the summer."

"Oh. Did you suggest putting an ad in the paper?"

"No. I thought you might be interested."

"Not really. I have other plans. But thanks."

He frowned.

"It wasn't a question, Peter. Tina had summer jobs every year through high school."

"But I've got a job at Video 2000!"

"A couple of evenings a week? Come on. You need to fill your time doing something useful."

I was about to point out how useful running a video store was when the phone rang.

"Peter!" yelled Mom. "Jennifer!"

And that was the second fly. I was just about to launch into a story about what a bummer it was that Dad was expecting me to get up in the mornings when she told me to come over and say goodbye: "We're going on a road trip. No idea when we'll be back, since Dad's driving. We could end up anywhere. I totally don't want to go, but what else am I going to do—kick my heels in Smallville all summer, waiting for nothing to happen?"

While I appreciated the *Superman* reference, her revelation knocked me sideways. My whole summer, ruined in the space of five minutes.

Still, I managed to survive as best I could.

I spent a lot time playing Spectrum and riding my bike. Jennifer sent me a postcard from Liège in Belgium telling me that she was looking forward to getting to Paris, that it was going to take a day longer because her dad had taken a wrong turn at Antwerp ("we're not happy campers"), that the many bicyclists on the roads reminded her of me, and that she had a present for me.

Of course, I couldn't reply, and I didn't know exactly when they were going to come home, but I kept riding my bike past their house on my way to work, thinking of her. Working at the warehouse was more fun than I had thought it would be, but also harder. The days were long, and I always volunteered to work overtime because I discovered that the longer I worked the more money I got and the more albums I could buy. When I finally got home at night, I barely had enough energy to play computer games.

It wasn't until August that I had my first off day and could, albeit briefly, resume my plan of being a careless drifter in Kumpunotko, just enjoying the summer. I rode my bike around town, but no matter where you started, in Kumpunotko you always ended up at the market square. In the summer, the square was buzzing with action. There were twice the number of stands and tents, compared to winter, and the place was always jolly with the music of a few local buskers, taking turns in one corner of the square. In the other corner, diagonally across the square, was an ice cream stand.

As I got closer to the stand I thought I recognized the person behind the iceboxes. It was Jennifer. I got off my bike and walked it the last few metres.

"Jennifer! What are you doing here?"

"Serving ice cream. The girl who worked here got chilblains and they needed someone. Dad knows the owner. What would you like?"

She gestured toward the dozen boxes of ice cream under the glass.

"Oh. A strawberry and cherry."

Jennifer started to scoop up ice cream. She had a Tricolour wristband around her right wrist.

"When did you get back? How was your trip?"

"Last week."

"Last week? Oh."

"It was amazing," she said with a smile. "Paris is so magical; it's about as far from this place as you can think of. People there are so . . . different. They're thoughtful and yet emotional. And they *talk* about their emotions."

I wasn't quite sure how I felt about that.

"Europe—the *real* Europe—is so vibrant. There's so much *energy*," she went on, and handed me my ice cream.

"I take it you didn't get lost again, then?"

She looked at me blankly.

"On the postcard you said you got lost in Antwerp."

She laughed. "Dad's a terrible driver," she said quietly. "Refuses to let anyone navigate. Just looks at the map in the morning and assumes he'll remember the way. We got lost in Sweden, Denmark, Germany, the Netherlands . . . we even got lost on the way to Helsinki, and he drives that way most weeks."

"Excuse me," said a voice behind me. "This is all very interesting, but can I possibly get an ice cream?"

We both realized there were several people waiting.

"Sorry, you have to work. I'll see you later," I said, and pulled out a wrinkled bill from my pocket. She put it in her cashbox and, as she gave me the change, she smiled at the person behind me.

"Next, please."

Later that day, after more kilometres on the bike than I'd planned, I happened to roll past Jennifer's house. It was the fifth time I'd "happened" along that way in as many hours. Finally I saw her. She was wearing cut-off jeans and a black T-shirt with *Voyage Voyage* written on the front, and a lot of eye makeup.

I stopped, of course. She smiled, and wiggled her fingers, and walked to the rock next to their mailbox.

"Hello, friend," she said.

"Hello, friend."

She gave me the proper beat-by-beat story of their road trip. The sights she had seen, the food she had eaten, the books she had read on their way from Kumpunotko to Barcelona and back. Summer evenings in Finland are endless, and it felt like I could just sit there with her forever.

Every once in a while she paused to ask me if I had been to whatever place she was describing, but when the answer was Copenhagen: no; Amsterdam: no; Brussels: no, she stopped asking.

"Kumpunotko must seem awfully small to you now," I said.

"The whole world is out there, Peter. Listen, this guy I met in Paris, Jacques, he told me you have to follow your dreams. He was from a small town in France, I forget the name, and now he's selling his own paintings by the Seine."

"Was that his dream?"

"He knew what he wanted, and he went after it. I think he's right. You should follow your dream. What's your dream?"

"I . . ."

"Well, we all know you're going to be a big shot in computers, but isn't there something a little more . . . interesting?"

"I don't know . . ."

"You must know! Maybe a movie director? Movies are your passion, aren't they?"

"I can't do that. I wouldn't know where to start, making a film."

"You'd need a script. Maybe be a screenwriter?"

"Maybe."

"Or something different. A set designer? Building all the spaceships. That'd be far out," she said, a faraway look in her eyes.

"Maybe. But . . . computing? I've written some really good code this summer. I got a new computer. It's got MS-DOS, a floppy drive, and so much more RAM than my Speccy."

"I want to be an artist," she said, apparently not even registering what I'd said.

"And you will be. You're so talented; I know, I've seen it."

She sighed, and played with her hair.

"I want to move to Paris. You know they have the École des

Beaux-Arts? So many of the greats studied there. What do we have? Kumpunotko High? I was thinking of transferring there for my senior year. Jacques said I should apply. Do you think I should?"

I didn't tell her what I thought she should do. Instead, I told her what I thought she wanted to hear.

"I think you should follow your dream, Jennifer."

"But it's crazy, isn't it? Am I crazy?"

"I'd do it if I were you."

She gave me a hug.

"I can always count on you, Peter," she murmured into my ear, before turning and skipping up the stairs onto her porch. "See you around," she said.

"See you, friend," I replied.

I knew she was going to do it. Go off and seek her fortune, follow her dream.

I'd have given anything to follow it with her, but I knew that wasn't how it worked. She may have been part of my dream, but I clearly wasn't part of hers. I wasn't a (presumably handsome) French painter called Jacques who (presumably) drank treacly coffee and spoke philosophically while smoking and gazing wistfully into the distance. Besides, I had responsibilities; I had to complete high school, and then do my compulsory national service in some remote province of Finland, if I were to have any hope of going to university.

I watched her go into her house.

A week or so later, at exactly 6:15 p.m.—fifteen minutes after my work lugging boxes at the warehouse had ended—I parked my bike against our house and Dad told me there was a message on the machine for me. I knew what it was before I even pressed the little silver button.

"Hey, Peter, guess what?! The school in France rang—they had a cancellation! It's totally short notice; I'm literally shoving clothes in a bag as I speak. Listen, I wanted to come and see you to say goodbye, but then I realized I don't even know where you live! And I guess you're out anyway. But look, if you get this message before—I don't know, four o'clock?—then come and see me. Would be great to say goodbye—"

I clicked the red button to delete.

That was the last time I heard from Jennifer.

I had gotten into this adventure because I'd received a letter—my Time Machine—from my old teacher, and it had reminded me of Jennifer. I had jumped in with both feet, without thinking, without a plan.

Back then, she was my best friend. After the dance, over those few months, we were as close to being a couple as you can be without actually being one.

She knew that the empty seat next to me on the bus was always reserved for her, and I knew the seat next to hers was mine. She knew that if she needed to talk to me after lunch break, she would find me in the corner of the school library, and that we'd talk about, well, everything . . . except the one thing I was never brave enough to mention.

I knew that if I rode my bike past her house an hour after school, she'd be sitting outside waiting for me, and I knew the red light blinking on my answering machine before a big test was always her.

We were there for each other—like David and Jennifer from *WarGames*: classmates and best friends against the world.

Until we weren't.

176

There was no fight, no argument. I don't think I ever did anything to upset her. Our friendship didn't end; we just went in different directions. She went to Paris; I stayed in Kumpunotko. I graduated. I did my military service. I moved out of Kumpunotko to go to university. She never even sent a postcard.

I didn't know anything about her life after high school.

Not once had I tried to track her down (except on that drunken, best-forgotten evening).

I wondered again why that was.

Was I chicken?

Basically, yes. But there was more to it than that. Something romantic; a silly notion holding me back.

It had to do with . . . destiny.

If Jennifer was destined to be mine, then cyberstalking her was *not* the way things were supposed to be. Cupid never fired a bow down a fibre-optic cable.

If Jennifer and I were supposed to meet, we were supposed to *meet*.

Of course I was also scared that a) she had a husband she was madly in love with, b) she would greet me with the words "Hello, friend," or c) there would simply be no spark.

This terrified me the most. I knew we had only ever been "friends," but I also knew, looking back, that there was more to it than that, under the surface. I knew, from having read articles and websites and novels, from having seen probably more rom-coms than a straight single man ought to watch, that it was just slightly possible that she might have been nervous, that she might have been tongue-tied—that the booze she drank at the dance might have lowered her inhibitions so that she was able to do what she secretly wanted to do—kiss me—and that when she didn't kiss me after *Supergirl* maybe it was because she was scared of rejection. Or, even worse: when *I* didn't kiss *her* after *Supergirl*, she was disappointed and rejected and cried all the way home.

I mean, unlikely. But not impossible.

After all: "Look at you all handsome in a tuxedo and everything. I was almost jealous of Sara, snapping you up like that."

Maybe we'd never had a candlelit dinner, but we'd had something better. We'd had a connection. And as far as I know, it was never officially disconnected.

CHAPTER 24

LET'S GO CRAZY

I was surprised to see Dad's TV chair empty when I got home. I heard the sound of somebody flushing the toilet. Sure enough, Dad walked out of the bathroom—TV remote in hand—said "hi," and walked straight into his precious chair.

"Hey, Dad."

"I didn't hear you get in. Sit down, *Murder, She Wrote* is about to start."

I liked all detective shows, and I liked Angela Lansbury, so I sat down in the other chair—Mom's—facing the TV.

"So, Dad, what have you been up to today?"

"Oh, the usual."

We were silent.

"Wanna hear a joke?"

"Always."

I told him one I had read on the BBS.

"Why did the Swede throw his clock out the window?"

The joke had originally been about a "boy," but I knew jokes on the Swedes were Dad's favourites.

"Heh, why did the Swede . . . ," he said, tapping the arm of the chair. "No, tell me."

"He wanted to see time fly."

"Good one," Dad said, without laughing. "Classic *Reader's Digest*."

"Hey, why don't you just tape the show on the VCR and watch it later? I want to show you something."

"VCR? We haven't used that for years. I just press a button now, store about a thousand hours of TV on the hard drive."

I sighed.

"But I want to watch this now," he said with the air of a man used to getting his own way. "Watch with me."

Right then, Jessica Fletcher started to type and Dad raised the volume. I sat next to him for the entire show, but my mind was elsewhere.

Since being home I had only seen Dad get excited about something once, and that was when he witnessed Tottenham— his favourite team—lose a match. The rest of the time he sat in his chair, watching TV. Frankly, it made me angry. And concerned.

He didn't have signs of Alzheimer's or anything like that, but this was not the Dad I knew. That man was always on the move, always with a plan, pulling strings to make things happen. He knew everybody, and not just in Kumpunotko; his web of connections spread around other parts of Finland, even in Helsinki.

"I bet the wife did it," Dad said. "Her alibi's very weak."

I didn't know what he was talking about because my mind had been wandering, but I didn't want to leave him hanging.

"That's what they'd like you to believe," I said, and wagged my finger.

"I know," Dad said.

A half hour later, as a frozen image of Jessica Fletcher laughing with the sheriff filled the screen, I got up and slapped Dad on the back. "Well, you were right, of course! Anyway, let's go. I want to show you something. Put your shoes on."

He grunted as he got up and walked to the hall. I wiggled the Volkswagen keys in front of him and told him I was driving.

"That way it'll be a surprise to you."

"Can't wait," Dad said. "You seem excited."

There was no traffic, so what would have been a ten-minute drive during the morning "rush hour" now took seven. We sat silently in the car for a bit as Dad checked out his old ride. He picked at a bit of the roof lining that was beginning to fray. Then he leaned back and put his hands behind his head.

"Autumn's coming," he said.

"Coming? Dad, it's September already."

"That's what I said."

I turned on the stereo. The tape was in the middle of Survivor's "Eye of the Tiger." To my surprise, Dad turned up the volume and pumped his fist.

"Wow, I didn't know you liked this," I said.

"It's not Sinatra," he said with a big grin, "but this one's pretty good."

He rolled down his window and stuck his elbow out just as we pulled in to the Atlas parking lot, next to the black side door.

"This is it," I said as we both got out.

"Great spot! I've never thought of parking here."

"No, no, this is *it*. This is want I wanted to show you. The cinema."

"What are you talking about? I've seen it before."

"But do you know who you're looking at now?"

Dad shook his head, a puzzled look on his face.

"The new manager!" I threw my hands in the air. "Ta-dah!"

I walked to the side door, turned the key in the lock, and opened the door. I flicked on the lights and gestured for Dad to come in.

"What's this? You're the manager? What's going on?"

"I'll tell you later. Come and look at this beauty," I said and walked to the main theatre.

Dad was just a step behind me, and I could hear him muttering something to himself.

I did jazz hands again when we got to the main hall and I turned the house lights up.

"This is where the magic happens," I said.

"And . . . you . . . and this? Is that why you were asking about the developers?"

"Yeah! I spoke with them and made a deal. I get to run the place until it's time to tear it down. They reckon around Christmas or so."

"And you're going to do what?"

"Well, obviously I'm going to show films. Lots of films. But first I'm going to have a big gala event, a grand opening. I'm going to give Kumpunotko the kind of event it's never seen before."

He nodded patiently, looking around.

"But, do you know how to do it?"

"How hard can it be?"

Dad sat down on one of the seats in the first row and extended his feet all the way out. He looked around the theatre, humming a Beatles song, nodding, and wrinkling his nose.

"Well, you have your work cut out for you," he said with a chuckle. "How big is it?"

"Ten by ten, downstairs. And the balcony's got thirty seats, so one-thirty in total."

Dad got out of his chair and walked up the aisle in the middle.

He kicked the carpet that I had duct-taped down. I joined him on row six, walked to the middle, and sat down. Dad sat in the seat next to me.

"The cushions are soft, but there are no cup holders. There's enough legroom for you, Pete—you're not that tall—but look at my knees," he said, and pulled his knees almost to his chin.

"Maybe we could put the rows farther apart? We'd have to lose a row, but . . ."

"Nah. Nobody really minds. You know what's always bothered me, though? That I have to keep my jacket on my lap at the movies, or shove it on the dirty floor. Why can't there be a small hook for it? Right . . . here." He pressed his index finger in the middle of the seat in front of him.

"You got it. We'll have that. I'm the boss. Want to see the rest of it?" I got up, squeezed myself past Dad, and led him into the lobby.

"The lobby needs a new coat of paint, I think," I said.

"And some lamps."

"Sure."

"And a red carpet."

"Obviously."

"Do you think all of this can be done by one man?"

"Well, there's the thing . . ."

I let that hang in the air.

He opened and closed the service hatch, which creaked. Ran his finger through the dust on the counter. Blew it away.

"Perhaps you could find someone to help you out?"

"That's what I was hoping."

He put his hands on his hips and looked at me.

"You do realize I've become quite attached to my TV schedule."

I grinned. "That's what the VCR's for, right?"

Dad got on his knees and started to scratch the floor with a key. Then he walked around the lobby, behind the counter, and into the office. He came back out holding a large yellow plush toy in a boiler suit and safety googles, its mouth splayed in a ridiculous grin. "What's this?"

I knew, but didn't want to admit that, so I just pointed to one of the film posters on display—*Despicable Me*—which must have been one of the last movies shown before the place closed down.

He walked to the entrance of the auditorium and yelled "Day-O!" so that it echoed through the dimly lit cinema.

"We can work it out," Dad said. He winked.

"How quickly do you think we can fix it up?"

"Hard to say. I don't know much about running a movie theatre, either. To get the theatre in presentable shape will take weeks. We need to see what has to be done, then get all the material, then do the work. Not to mention all the paperwork."

"The developers mentioned that. I have no idea what they're talking about."

"I assume you'll need all kinds of permits if you want to have a hundred people in here."

I only wanted to have one person in there, but I didn't say that to Dad.

"I don't think it's the government's business to tell me what I can or can't do . . ."

Dad looked at me askance. "This from the man who worries when there's only three months left to file his tax return? You have changed lately, Peter."

I looked down, embarrassed. He continued: "I must say, I admire your libertarian stance, but I think you need to at least file something with the police. And the fire department. They'll

184

probably do an inspection. I know a guy who used to do those. I can ask him."

"That'd be great. By the way, maybe we shouldn't tell Mom about this . . . yet."

He cast me a glance. "Why?"

"I don't know. It doesn't quite seem real yet, and I don't want everyone to get their expectations up."

He frowned, but didn't say anything more.

Five minutes later, I locked the door and we picked Mom up from the library. She had been reading books with little children, one of her many projects.

"What have you been up to today?"

"Nothing much," I said.

"Peter's bought the movie theatre," Dad blurted out.

"What?" I said, angry at Dad.

"What?" Mom said, confused.

"What?" Dad said, puzzled, looking at me.

"It's a project I have. Could be fun," I said. "And I haven't bought it. They're letting me run it until they're ready to pull it down."

"Projects are good for you," said Mom. "Tell me more when we get home."

"Hey, I just had a crazy idea," I said. "How about we get dinner at Burgerland? Like old times."

I looked into the rear-view mirror and saw Mom's smiling eyes look back at me. She nodded toward Dad.

"What do you say, Dad?"

"You're on."

Five minutes later, at Burgerland, Dad held the door open for Mom and me, and told us we could have whatever we wanted. In the old days, when money was tighter, that had been a real statement of generosity, a genuine treat. These days, it was a nice bit of nostalgia, like buying all the records I wanted. I ordered two cheeseburgers and a milkshake, which made Mom shake her head.

"Always the same. And now Dad's going to make you eat another two, I'm sure," she said, and added with mock worry: "No eating contests today, please."

The place looked exactly the same as it had always looked: half a dozen small square tables, ketchup and mustard bottles and a napkin holder in the middle of each one. We sat at a table by the window, because that's what Dad always wanted. He claimed he liked to watch the world go by, but we all knew he was keeping an eye on his car: he would sit up and stiffen whenever anyone parked too close.

After four cheeseburgers and two milkshakes, I slumped in my chair, unable to move.

"Well, isn't this nice," said Mom. "Just like old times. Dad always egged you and Tina on. She had to beat you, even if by just two fries."

"I know! She counted the fries too."

"One time she almost fainted, remember? You had your friend with you, the big boy, and Tina challenged him as well. I don't think she'd anticipated quite how much he could put away. They both threw up afterwards!"

"Mikke had to throw his jeans in the garbage. He sat in the trunk of our station wagon in his underwear," I said, and we all laughed.

"Whatever happened to him?"

"Not sure, we lost touch." I didn't want to mention what I'd discovered, but only because I didn't want to mention how.

"That's a shame," Mom said. "You can never have too many friends. But you were always a loner."

Ouch.

"I mean, Tina always had friends over, but you . . . you've always been very comfortable by yourself, sitting upstairs with your computer, taking sandwiches into your room."

"I had friends."

"Oh, I'm not saying you didn't. Just that you were also happy playing with your computers, content to be alone . . ."

I suppose she had a point, but sometimes moms—or my mom at least—had a way of cutting right to the bone.

"And," she carried on, "you got to make your hobby into your job. Not many people get to do that, do they? And now look at you, following your dream . . ."

Again, she had a point, and I couldn't help but smile.

"Can we go home now?" said Dad. "I don't want to miss the evening news."

We somehow wedged ourselves back into the Beetle and chatted all the way home.

CHAPTER 25

HELLO

THE phone was ringing as we walked up to the front door. Mom rushed in and grabbed it—but not in time. She hardly had time to put the receiver back in the cradle when it rang again. That told me who was calling and, had I had any doubts, Mom's first words, and the way she said them, were a dead giveaway.

"Oh, hello," she said, somehow managing the fine art of a completely polite surface with an undercurrent of disappointment. The buoyant mood of the evening ebbed away.

"Fine. Everything's good. No, no, we just got in. We were at Burgerland." Pause. "Yes, he's here. Give our love to Sofie." She held out the receiver.

"I'll take it upstairs instead," I yelled, hopping upstairs the best I could. My ankle was a lot better, but it still hurt when going up or down stairs. When I picked up the phone and crashed onto my bed, I shouted to Mom that she should hang up.

"I hate calling you on this landline. I'm sure Mom's listening to our conversation downstairs," Tina said.

"No, she's not. I heard her hang up."

"Hope so. Anyway, Burgerland?" Tina said. "And it's not even a Sunday."

"It was a spur of the moment thing."

"Well . . . ?"

"Well what?"

"How did you do?"

"With what?"

"Oh, come on! Just tell me."

I laughed. Tina was such an easy target for teasing.

"Fine. Four cheeseburgers and two milkshakes."

"AND STILL THE CHAMPION!" Tina yelled into the phone.

"Yeah, yeah, yeah. You're still the champ."

"How's life in Kumpunotko? Has our brave time traveller made contact with locals?" she said, her voice dripping with sarcasm.

"It's awesome. You should try it."

"Like I would ever want to live there again. When are you coming back?"

I played with the phone cable, twisting it around my finger, and cleared my throat.

"Not yet," I said after a pause.

"Okay, you need time. I get it. I get it. How's living at home?"

"It's fine. It's quiet here, so I mostly play games on my computer when I'm home. And I read. I found my comics!"

"Well, I'm sure they're about as exciting as they were first time around. And what do you do when you're not at home?"

"I have my bike. And a project."

"What's that?"

"I told you! Didn't you get my postcards? You should have gotten one of them by now."

"Postcards?" She sighed. "No. I didn't get your postcards. Tell me."

"I'm taking over the Atlas. It's closed down, so I'm opening it back up. I'm going to open with a bang, a big gala event."

"Wow, when?"

"Early December, I think. We just need to restore the place first!"

There was a pause, and when she spoke next she sounded down. "So you're staying there for a while?"

"For now, yeah. I think the movie event is going to be great. I'm really looking forward to it."

"What do you know about putting together a gala event? What do you know about running a movie theatre?"

"Nothing, yet. But how hard can it be? It'll be amazing. *Back to the Future*, the way it's supposed be seen. And everybody will be there . . . I hope. You guys'll come, right?"

"Sure," she said quietly.

There was something up. Something I wasn't quite brave enough to confront her about. There was definitely tension between Tina and Mom . . . but it was their tension, not mine.

"Hey, can we set up a time for a call? I'll call you on Sunday, say?" Tina asked.

"Sure. I have no plans. But I'll write it down in my calendar. What time?"

"Um, five?"

I scribbled *Tina call* in a tiny calendar I'd bought at the bookstore. It was the first appointment I added to it. Well, second, because I had written in the meeting at BBB—but after the fact.

"Anyway, I just wanted to check that you're okay. I worry about you, brother," she said.

"Don't. I haven't felt this good in years."

"I'm glad. Listen, I have to run. Sofie needs me. Take care and don't break the time-space continuum," she said.

I could hear her laughing when she hung up.

I stared at the piece of paper with my plan on it, and suddenly realized I'd gotten it the wrong way round. I crossed out the numbers three and four, and switched them around.

1. ~~Get Atlas.~~
2. *Fix Atlas.*
3. ~~3.~~ *Open with a sneak preview of* Back to the Future.
4. ~~4.~~ *Invite Jennifer.*

No point having the gala opening and *then* inviting the star guest.

I needed to do some serious thinking, so I pulled my Spectrum closer and played for a while, but I couldn't concentrate on *Thro' the Wall*, let alone *The Hobbit*.

Something was wrong. Something Tina had said had sowed a troubling seed within me. Not the thing with Mom; I wasn't going to touch that.

What do you know about running a movie theatre?

What did I know? Well, I had seen an episode of *Columbo* in which the murderer makes a mistake with the changing of film reels, which gives the detective the clue he needs. In the episode, Columbo learned to change the reels and flick the switches and turn the knobs just right. So my total knowledge of running a cinema boiled down to watching a fictional detective do a stylized version of one aspect of the whole shebang.

I did have a lot to learn.

I read my plan again. It was too crude. It wasn't even a plan. I felt stress creep up on me. Just like when I'd read Hanna's letter, and gotten all jumpy and couldn't sit still. I got up and paced around my four-pace room clockwise. Then I turned and paced it two laps counter-clockwise. Had I been a smoker, I would have lit one up.

Instead, I did some push-ups. Before the third one, I glanced under my bed and saw the box of comics I'd told Tina about. I pulled it out and picked up the magazine on the top. It was the *Phantom*—the Ghost Who Walks—my favourite superhero. Not even Superman was as cool.

I flipped through the comic but stopped at the letters pages, where they ran jokes and pen pal ads, my favourite. I loved reading them, in part because it was fun to imagine finding my perfect match and in part because they were always so full of hope, but so wrapped up in acting cool. They were all the same, though: a lonely teenager looking for a friend who he knew to be out there somewhere. If only the right person happened to read the comic and see their ad.

The letters made me think of Mom, and how she'd called me a loner. And that made me think of Tina, who had always been the precise opposite of a loner—whatever the word for that is.

Something about our phone conversation had made me sad. I wanted to explain to Tina what I was after, without spelling it out. I wanted her to understand me, to get me.

It was too late to call her back, so I wrote another postcard instead.

Hi Sis,

Kumpunotko's not that bad, you know. Lots of familiar faces made me feel right at home right away. The other day, I bumped into Jan, a classmate of yours. His sister (Jennifer) was in my

class. Sprained my ankle. Long story, but nothing to worry about.
I'm already better.

    You should come and visit.

XO,
    P

I put the postcard in my pocket and went for a bike ride to town. I was in an odd mood, slightly dislocated, and I wondered if it was because of the conversation with Tina or the half-kilogram of meat I'd eaten earlier.

I stood outside The Atlas and admired the building. The sign wasn't in as great a shape as I'd thought, but I couldn't wait to see the massive glass doors after a good scrub. I tore down the flea market signs that had been taped there, crumpled them into a ball and threw the ball in a perfect three-pointer into a nearby trash can.

"And the crowds go wiiiiiiild!" said my sports-commentator voice.

WHEN I got back home, the house was dark. I carefully placed my Crescent against the wall under the kitchen window and tip-toed to my room. I closed the door so that the lights wouldn't wake up Mom and Dad.

I dialled up to "I Wanna Rock!" and saw that the sysop had replied to my reply.

Okay, I'll keep it live for a bit.

I was disappointed that there wasn't more, but right then, a chat window opened. As far as I knew, only one person could do that—the sysop herself.

I figured this was a faster way to chat, she wrote.

Definitely, I wrote back. *Thanks for having this BBS. Good to be back.*

I hit Enter and waited.

It took a long time for me to get a reply. A minute later, text lines started to scroll on the screen, a letter at a time, and a line at a time, as if each pixel had to wait for the previous one to arrive before it started the epic journey down the telephone wire.

I remember I used to thrill at the technology.

Good to be back? So you know how this works. Excellent. You'll find the games under "files," and I'm afraid the jokes are fairly dated. But there's no traffic, so you'll always get through. Tell me what you're looking for here.

I thought about it.

Nothing special. Just wanted to do exactly this. Meet like minds, you know?

Again, I had to wait for the reply.

I see. I agree—the nighttime is the time for some electronic communication. What's happening in your neck of the woods?

Just listening to some music.

What?

Spandau Ballet's "True."

I was worried that Twisted Sister might laugh at me for listening to something that soft, but when her reply came back it made me smile.

Great tune. Weird lyrics, though.

It's about how hard it is to tell someone you love them.

It is?

I think so. Though you're right; it is hard to tell.

It took us forty-five minutes to have that exchange, with the dial-up modem and the computing power of the Spectrum, plus my having to translate everything into English before I typed it in, so we called it a night.

Good to talk. See you around, Twisted Sister wrote.

I logged off and pumped my fist. I had a new friend.

CHAPTER 26

LOVIN' EVERY MINUTE OF IT

THE next morning, I awoke with a clear head. Whatever blues I'd felt had disappeared. In fact, I felt a small inkling of optimism. The only way forward was through, as they say. If I ever wanted to get to item three on my list, I had to get through item two.

Dad was waiting for me in the kitchen. He had a big mug of coffee in front of him, and he was writing something on a piece of paper. For the first time in ages, the television was off.

"I thought we'd go to the hardware store today," he said. "A friend of mine owns it, so we can probably get a deal."

I was still in my pyjamas.

"Come on," he said, throwing me a slightly disapproving look. "This cinema isn't going to fix itself, you know."

He was right. I'd been back in Kumpunotko for ten days now. Though getting the keys had been, thinking about it, a breeze, I hadn't really done anything since, except for inviting Christopher Lloyd to the opening night. I looked at the calendar and did a quick calculation. I had half of September, all of October and November—ten or eleven weeks—to get the old Atlas back on her feet. It was time to roll up my sleeves.

"But we don't know what we need."

"We'll need everything, I reckon. Put your work clothes on. Oh, eat breakfast first. Mom left you something in the fridge. By the way, I had a look at the bumper; it's not too bad. There's this guy I know, he's got a garage, so I called him. He said he'd hammer it out in fifteen minutes and it'll be as good as new. Whenever you have time," he added.

"Wow, you've been busy."

Dad smiled. He tapped his pen on the piece of paper. "Look here."

He had drawn three columns, dividing our work into three categories: 1) Construction; 2) Paperwork; 3) Movie. Then he had written items under each heading: things I had to take care of, I guessed.

"Construction is going to be the easy part, I figure. There's not going to be anything too heavy-duty, so most of it I can do myself. The paperwork? Well, I think I can help there; I know how to grease the wheels in this town. But the last thing—the actual film and running the cinema—is something I can't help you with."

It would have taken me another week to get myself that organized. I wanted to hug him. So I slapped him on the shoulder, which is about as close as our family gets to such things.

AT the Atlas, we walked the same route as on our first visit. This time, though, Dad walked ahead of me pointing at things, and I walked a step behind him with a clipboard, taking notes. He did things I hadn't even thought of, like checking which windows opened, flushing each toilet, and trying each tap. It felt weird going into the ladies', but he just strolled in without a care. I was half-expecting a flustered grandma to hit him around the head with her handbag.

He'd brought various tools with him, and for a while he stood by the fuse box, scratching his head. He had a little machine that he touched against bits of the building's wiring. Sometimes it gave a *beeeeeep*. Sometimes it gave a *bi-bi-bi-bi-bip*. Sometimes it made no sound at all.

"Hmm."

An hour later, we sat on the stage in front of the curtain, our feet dangling in the air, and summed up our inspection. We agreed that most of the work would be fixing up, and when Dad said, "There's nothing structural needs doing," I nodded, as if that's what I'd been about to say.

"Paint the walls. Clean the carpet, at least. Wiring and fuses. Light bulbs. Plumbing." Dad listed things out, tapping his fingers one at a time.

"Plumbing?"

"One of the toilets is backing up. God knows what's been down there solidifying for the last however many years. People will need to use the toilet, with all those big sodas."

He switched hands.

"Tickets. Cash registers."

"I'll do cash only."

"You can't do cash only. People will expect to be able to pay by card. I reckon you'll lose fifty percent of your customers if you insist on cash only."

I remembered Kim's Basement. "The record store does cash only."

"And he probably turns over twenty euro a day. You want a hundred and thirty people in here, ten euro each. You're going to need a card machine."

I said nothing.

"Which will have to be linked to a bank account, which means you'll have to register a company name with the bank, which means you're going to need a company name. Don't worry, I expect you can apply for all that stuff online."

I swallowed the nasty taste building in my throat.

"I already have a company name."

"Well, that's one less thing to worry about. Where was I? That's right, the projection room needs to be checked. At least the projector's still there; you got lucky. God knows if it works, though, so you're going to have to get a film and test it. Do you know how to work a projector?"

"I've seen . . . something on TV."

"Great! You know what? I'm starting to get a good feeling about this."

It was nice to see him motivated, to see him doing something other than working on the butt-print he'd put in that TV chair.

"So, what do you figure . . . how long?"

"A couple of months, give or take."

"Give or take what?"

"If you plan to open it by December 1, you should be fine. That'll give you . . . lots of time."

I flipped the pages on my small diary. My earlier calculation was spot on.

"Eleven weeks."

He nodded. "That seems reasonable."

I grinned. Eleven weeks was surely enough time for destiny to work its magic.

JUST as we were wrapping things up in the auditorium an hour later, I heard a voice from the side door.

"Hello, anybody here?"

"Yes, here, who is it?" I yelled back

I walked briskly toward the side door but had only gotten halfway there when I saw the face that went with the voice.

Sara. Only this time she wasn't wearing a beret, and there was no purse on her shoulder. She was wearing an all-blue uniform, and her shoulder-length blonde hair was pulled back in a pony-tail. There was a pistol on her hip. She looked serious.

This was a Sara I'd never seen. Work Sara.

"What's going on here?" she asked, no glimmer of mischief in her eyes.

"Um, Sara . . . ? What are you doing here? What's going on?"

"I'm a police officer. I saw an open door at what I thought was a deserted building, and thought I should investigate. You'd be surprised what we find in places like this."

I held my hands up.

"Okay, officer. You've caught us red-handed, planning how to restore this place."

Looking puzzled, Sara followed me down toward the front of the auditorium.

"Watch your step there. The carpet's a trip hazard. Sara, this is Dad. Dad, Sara. We're renting this place, fixing it up."

Sara laughed. "Well, now I've seen everything."

"Have you ever seen a movie from the Atlas balcony? It's where the cool kids sit."

"Funnily enough, I have. I did grow up here, you know." She let her gaze wander around the theatre, its seats, the curtain. "You've certainly got your work cut out," she said.

"We know. Come on, Dad. We should be getting to the hard-ware store."

"Right you are."

We began walking back toward the lobby.

"Ask her about the licence," Dad whispered. "She's a cop, she'll know."

But I didn't want to bother her with that while she was working. Her job was busting bad guys, not stamping forms.

When we got to the side door, she smiled and asked me when we were planning to open.

"Not sure yet. We're thinking early December. As soon as we get everything fixed here and I have some movies to show.

I wanted to keep it vague. I had been burned in the past when I told people too early about great projects that had ended up failing . . . and this one definitely had several sensitive parts to it.

"Do you even know anything about how to run a movie theatre?"

I rolled my eyes and gave the standard response. "How hard can it be? Just turn out the lights and press Play, right?"

She chuckled.

"What are you going to open with? Is there a big blockbuster coming up that you've got your eye on? I know you've always loved movies."

"*Back to the Future*," I said. "I'll open with *Back to the Future*."

"Good call," she said. "An oldie. I like that one."

"Would you like to come?" asked Dad. "We could give you a couple of tickets. Like to look after our boys and girls in blue," he added with a theatrical wink.

I blushed and stepped in front of him.

"Nice to see you again, Mr. Eksell," she said patiently.

"And you, Officer."

I was just about to tell Sara she didn't have to call me Mr. Eksell—as a joke, obviously—but she was gone.

When we heard the side door close, Dad shook his head at me.

"You should have asked her about the licence."

"There's time."

WHEN we walked into the hardware store, I asked Dad to be vague about the Atlas project, as I didn't want anyone making a fuss. But Dad was a straight shooter.

"Hey, how you doing?"

"Great! My son's taken over the Atlas." Dad slapped me on the back. "We're restoring it, and then there's gonna be a big gala opening. You should come!"

"That's great, man," said the guy behind the counter. "You know how to run a movie theatre?"

Every single person, the first thing they asked was whether I knew how to run a movie theatre. Except for Sara. It had been her second question.

WE picked up paint, brushes, and masking tape, plus a bunch of electrical stuff, and then we swung by home to collect dust sheets and overalls from the store room. I stood back while Dad rummaged through boxes and crates. At one point he pulled out a camping stove. He popped out the cartridge, gave it a shake, and seemed to be pleased with what he heard. He passed it to me to stick in the car.

"Why do we need a camping stove?"

"In case we need to cook our lunch," he said, as if I were the simplest pupil in the class.

As we were heading back to the Atlas, I brought up my uncertainty with Dad.

"I know you keep telling people that I'm going to open up the movie theatre, but do you really think I can do it? I mean, if I'm honest, I don't know anything about it, and even now, I realize there are so many things I just hadn't even thought that I'd have to think about."

"Peter, you've always been great at whatever you've tried to do. Computers and . . . uh, computer things. If opening the Atlas is what you want to do, of course you can do it," he said. "Besides, word's out now. So you're going to *have* to do it."

I bit my lip.

Dad was humming Sinatra's "You Make Me Feel So Young," but apart from that the journey passed in silence.

"Listen," he said eventually, "a buddy of mine used to run the Atlas. I'll call him when we get home. He'll know what you have to do."

"Wow, Dad. Thanks. Why didn't you say?"

"I did. You know, the brother of the girl I was at university with used to run Video 2000, and the other brother ran the Atlas. I told you. Keep up, Peter."

I laughed, and tried to shake off the doubts. Things were good. If nothing else, I'd gotten Dad out of his TV chair.

"Dad," I said, once we were back home.

"Mhm?" He was rummaging in the fridge for a beer.

"Want to play some chess?"

"Only if I get to be Garry Kasparov," he said with a smile.

"Fine. I'll be Anatoly Karpov," I said, and ran upstairs to get my chessboard.

When I got back downstairs, Dad was sitting by the kitchen table, waiting for me. We set up the board and the pieces. Dad was white, so he got to open the game, and he took his time choosing his move.

"There," he said, at least a minute later. "Kasparov has made his first move."

"Oh, the Arabian opening," I said, as if I knew something about chess. "But you know Karpov's the true champ, right?" I added, and moved a pawn.

The game was cagey at first, neither of us wanting to commit.

He brought both knights out, and I opened up to let out a bishop and a castle. We traded a few mid-range blows, but then, about twenty minutes later, after he'd come back from getting another beer, he needlessly moved his queen's pawn forward, leaving her open to attack from my bishop. I feared a trick. I feared a trap. He poured beer into his glass, allowing a good head to form.

"Sorry, do you want one?"

"Nah."

"I don't want to offer every time I get one. Help yourself, yeah?"

"Of course," I mumbled, staring at the board, wondering what he was up to.

He set down his glass on a coaster, looked back at the board, saw me reach for my bishop.

"Oh," he said. "Oh shit."

The trouble with beating your dad at chess is that no matter how old you are, you never know if he's losing just to make you feel better. Still, he seemed genuinely annoyed, so it did feel good.

CHAPTER 27

HOUSE OF FUN

THE next morning, work began.

"You start with the painting. I'll get on with the electrical stuff. Put masking tape around the edges; we don't want paint on the carpets."

I picked a wall, the one in the corridor between the foyer and the auditorium. It was quite big, but even so I figured it couldn't take *that* long.

Three days later, I finished the corridor and moved into the auditorium. I looked at the size of the room with renewed awe. By a quick calculation, if I kept going at the same rate, I'd finish around February. It wasn't the painting that took so long; it was crawling around with masking tape, trying to get the edges straight. Tomorrow, I thought, as I soaked in the bath that night, I would have to take a ladder. And a bigger roller. And some cod liver oil, to deal with the aches in my joints.

As I was combing my hair, the phone rang. I ran to answer. It was Tina, a whole day ahead of schedule.

"Listen, Mr. Time Traveller. I need a huge favour. Tim's on a business trip and I've accidentally booked a full class of yoga beginners for Sunday. Can I send Sofie to spend some time with her uncle?"

It sounded like a question, but it wasn't, so I gave Tina the answer she was after.

"Of course."

"Great. You can pick her up at the train station tomorrow. She'll be on the 11:07."

I rode my bike to Atlas, and then took the ten-minute walk to the train station. Kumpunotko wasn't the final stop, and I hoped Sofie hadn't fallen asleep or gotten so into a game that she'd miss the stop. That had happened to me a few times in my first year of college, when I still regularly made the two-hour trek from Helsinki.

I looked at the half dozen people standing outside, waiting for their friends and family, everybody with their eyes glued to a small gadget in their hand. One man put it away, looked at me, nodded, and then, thirty seconds later, was back to staring at the phone.

And then there was Sofie, in light-blue jeans that she (or Tina) had rolled up, a *Ghostbusters* T-shirt I'd bought her, sneakers, and a backpack that seemed to be bigger than she was and that bounced from side to side as she ran toward me, her frizzy hair glowing in the sun like a halo.

She gave me a hug. She was nothing like the rest of my family.

We walked back, talking about her trip and how we'd get strawberries from the market—and I couldn't help noticing that she checked in on Facebook as we stopped to wait to cross the street.

"Can I tag you?" she asked me.

I pretended I didn't understand what she meant; I tapped her on the shoulder and yelled, "Not if I tag you first! You're it!" I ran backwards across the street, shooting at her with my fingers.

She sprinted after me, her backpack once again bouncing from side to side behind her.

As we turned the corner toward Atlas, she asked, "And why do you live here now?"

"I wanted to make a change. I was a bit tired of my life. So I'm going to open a movie theatre here. This one, right here. Do you know how movie theatres work?"

"No. Do you?"

"Sure!" I said. "Of course!"

She raised an eyebrow and gave me a look so piercing she may actually have been channelling my big sister. Obviously, I'd been the subject of several conversations at home.

Dad was busy at work when we got back, and after a quick hello and a hug—even Dad hugged Sofie—he got back to it, and I felt that I had to do the same. Sofie sat on the stage in front of the big screen, her legs hanging over the edge. She held her phone in her outstretched arm and smiled for a selfie. Click. Then she turned around so that Dad and I were in the background.

"Smile!" she told us. Dad obliged. I may have been frowning but, as she couldn't tag me, I would never find out.

"Hey, Sofie, I've got a great new game. All the cool kids are playing it. It's called, 'painting a wall.'"

I handed her a brush and took her to the front of the stage. Then I got on my knees—she did the same—and we started to paint the wood panelling, a task that suited both our abilities.

I wanted to stay close to Dad and keep an eye on him. I was afraid he'd set the bar too high and that instead of giving the Atlas a simple polish, we'd find ourselves standing in the middle of a pile of rubble, like the couple in *The Money Pit*.

"Hey, Pete," yelled Dad, after about half an hour.

I put down my brush and stood up, my knees creaking, back aching.

I walked over to where he was, on his hands and knees, tracing electrical lines running behind the wallpaper. A bead of sweat was running down the side of his head.

"What's up?"

"I forgot, I've got news for you," he said.

"Bad news or good news?"

"That guy I know—the movie man—he'll be here today. I bumped into him and asked if he'd be able to have a look at the projection room."

"Okay, and who was he again?"

"He used to be the manager."

"Of what?"

Dad spread his arms wide, a gesture that encompassed the entire theatre. "So he might know a thing or two. His name's Rexi. We made their ads for the paper, and I helped him out a couple of times so he owes me a favour. Or two."

"When is he coming?"

"Sometime today. Listen, do you think Sofie would like to go home? Mom can look after her?"

"Are you kidding me? She loves to hang out with her Uncle Pete, right?"

Sofie nodded, her thumbs tapping the gadget in her hand.

"Except, we have one rule here," I went on.

"What's that?"

I grabbed the phone from her hand and put it in an empty bucket next to me.

"That."

"Awwww."

"You can play with this instead," I said, and took my yo-yo dog for a walk.

"What is that?"

"This? Only the coolest toy ever. It's so cool that just one 'yo' wouldn't do it justice," I said. She stared at me like I was talking gibberish. "It's a yo-yo. That's what it's called."

"What does it do?"

"Nothing. It's what *you* do with it. Put your finger like this," I said, and pointed at her with my index finger. Then I hung the yo-yo off her small finger and gave her instructions. The yo-yo fell down the string, and stayed down.

"You just have to practise," I said.

Dad moved over to the other wall where he continued his little project with the electrical cable and the machine that went *beeeeeeep*.

It was so silent in the theatre that I could hear Dad humming the Monkees' "I'm a Believer" in the corner, which meant only one thing: it was time to turn the tape.

Dad had brought his old transistor radio to the theatre on the first few days so he could get his news fix. Originally, I just took a break every hour on the hour and got myself a cup of coffee from the gas station, but with the summer days turning into early fall, I'd gotten tired of going outside to wait for the news to end. Also, seven cups of coffee a day made me jumpy.

We agreed on a compromise. I brought in my old ghetto blaster and we took turns choosing tapes. It meant that every even-numbered hour, the Atlas echoed with the voices of the Beatles, the Stones, the Who, Sinatra, Paul Anka, and Dad, and every odd-numbered hour, the stage was set for Bryan Adams, Bruce Springsteen, Madonna, Wham!, the Police, Cindy Lauper, Hanoi Rocks, and all the other eighties greats.

Unlike Dad, who could have had a karaoke sing-off with the best of them, I had trouble carrying a tune, so I just worked and listened. Especially with other people around—the friends of Dad's who kept turning up out of nowhere to return favours granted in the dim and distant past.

There was an admirable pile of tapes standing next to the boom box, and I let my index finger slide down the plastic cases, stopping at a couple that had nice mix-tape names: "Ride On," "Daley Thompson's Decadence," or "Black Magic."

"What are those?" Sofie asked, as if she were the time traveller, not me.

"These, my dear, are tapes."

She looked at me blankly.

"They're like playlists," said Dad, helpfully, "but in physical form."

"Wow," breathed Sofie, picking up a cassette case and giving it a little rattle before peering in through the clear plastic. "It's like a cave painting, but in music form."

"And on them," I continued, "I have stored some of the best music ever made."

Dad coughed from the corner, demonstratively. I laughed.

I pressed Eject, returned Dad's Elvis tape to its case, and slid my "Beat Box" mix into the player.

I'd been listening to my old tapes so much since I'd been back that I knew them all by heart. I knew what the opening song was going to be from the first scratchy sound of the needle hitting the vinyl: Eurythmics' "Would I Lie to You?"

Sofie laughed at that, I think, or maybe it was my dancing, but she joined me and we danced up and down the aisle until the song faded away.

We had a fun day, although I felt bad depriving her of her social umbilical cord and then ignoring her in favour of the decorating work. But she was happy to join in and, I have to admit, far better at straight edges than me. She even came up with a clever technique, which involved painting carefully around the edges of an area first, with the brush, which meant when we were filling in the main area with the roller we could do it a lot more quickly.

Mom came out in the afternoon and brought us some home-made pancakes, which we ate sitting in the front row.

"Did my mom ever come here?" Sofie asked me.

"Sure. But she always sat in the balcony. With the cool kids."

"She was cool?"

"She's still kind of cool, don't you think?"

Sofie groaned.

"Someday, you'll be just as cool," I teased.

"Mom says that people who talk about doing stuff 'someday' never do it."

I laughed. "She's got a point. That's why we're doing this today!"

At half past five, I gave Sofie her phone back. She slipped it straight into her pocket, without checking for notifications. I walked her to the station. As the train pulled in, she reached into her pocket and pulled out my yo-yo. She tried to pass it back to me, but I shook my head.

"Keep practising. You never know when it might come in handy."

She rolled her eyes, gave me a hug, and climbed aboard the train.

WHEN I returned to the Atlas, it was my turn to rock the ghetto blaster, and barely had Duran Duran's "Hungry Like the Wolf" gotten to its chorus when it was interrupted by a "Yoo-hoooooo!" from the door.

Dad's old friend arrived. He was wearing camouflage cargo pants and an olive-green army jacket over a grey sweater. His head was utterly hairless, and white spots shone across his scalp as he walked toward me, like the reflections of streetlights on a car windshield.

He waved to Dad, who waved back and yelled, "That's my kid, Pete, the one I told you about!"

I stood up and creaked, and reached over to silence the Durans.

Rexi extended his hand, and as we connected in a firm handshake, he said, "So, you're thinking of being in the movie business."

"Well, yes. Not just thinking anymore, as you can see," I said.

"Your father said you wanted to speak with someone who knew how to run a movie theatre," he said, dismissing my comment.

"People keep telling me I don't know anything about running a cinema. But how hard can it be, right?"

Rexi squinted—not just his eyes, actually, but his whole face—and looked me dead in the eye. I expected him to call me a punk, but it was my lucky day. Instead, he just growled and stepped closer. He wasn't much taller than me (most people are), but he was compact, stocky. He spoke quietly.

"You ever had to aqua-vac eight hundred square metres of carpet in one night? You ever changed the lettering on a billboard, ten metres up, in a force-six gale? You ever spliced together a broken reel while three hundred people downstairs munch popcorn, without even missing a beat? No? I thought not."

He turned and began walking away.

I wasn't quite sure what had just happened.

I realized I was still holding my paintbrush. I put it back down. "Um. Mr. . . . Rexi?"

"What are you just standing there for?" he snapped, without looking back. "Let's have a look at the booth."

As he walked away, I noticed he let his hand trail down and brush against the red velvet of the seat.

UPSTAIRS, Rexi walked into the projection room and switched the light on. I stood behind him, unsure of what, if anything, to say.

The room was about as wide as the theatre, but only about two metres from front to back. In the middle of it, in front of the hole in the wall, stood the projector—a beige box on legs that looked like a seventies' idea of a domestic robot. Behind it stood a huge round table.

He took a deep breath and closed his eyes.

"Oh, how I've missed you," he whispered.

He flicked the light back off and barged past me.

BACK downstairs he made himself comfortable in one of the front-row seats, his legs splayed more widely than seemed feasible. I wasn't entirely sure where to look.

"You wouldn't have lasted a day up there. Not a day," he said, and gestured up to one of the windows in the back of the auditorium. "Up there, there was no room for error. You had to be quick, fast, effective, never miss a beat. It got up to forty degrees in there, and you weren't even allowed to *sweat*."

"I see," I said sheepishly. I didn't want to upset Dad's slightly odd friend.

"Do you think you've got what it takes to run a cinema?"

He wanted me to admit defeat.

"Yes, sir, I do," I said, "but I'm going to need help." I decided on a direct approach. Flatter his ego. "I'm going to need *your* help. Nobody knows this place like you do."

"Now you're talking." He stood back up and swaggered over to me. "Here's my advice, so listen carefully."

I looked at him and nodded, dumbfounded by the whole affair.

"Let me whisper it to you."

I turned my right ear toward him, waiting for the cinema guru to give forth his wisdom.

"DON'T DO IT!" he shouted into my ear.

With my heart in my throat, I jumped and bolted toward the door, tripped and stumbled over the ghetto blaster, and landed in a heap. When I realized what had happened, I looked back at Rexi, who was sitting back in the front-row seat, smirking.

"Ready for more advice, kid?"

I struggled to get to my feet.

"Not sure. Can you tell it to me from over there?"

He pushed down the seat next to him and patted it. "Come on," he said, smiling in a way that suggested he'd had his fun with me and was now ready to help. "Tell Rexi what you want to know."

I pulled out the list Dad had made and went over the items with Rexi. And once he'd stopped being a maniac, he actually became quite helpful. He told me Dad was right about all the licences, and the movie permits, and the marketing plans, and he gave me some ideas for how to go about it all.

"Where are you getting the reels from?"

I shrugged.

He gave me a telephone number and a contact name at a media distributor in Helsinki.

"And you know what type of reel? Changeover or platter?"

"No idea."

"You're crazy," he said, "but I like it. I like it!" He clapped his hands and shouted to Dad that he should have told him I was crazy, and they both laughed.

"It's platter. That's what the big table was. I once had to reassemble a whole movie. The crowds were coming." His eyes took on a faraway look, like a veteran recounting a war story. "They told me they were going to cancel the show. They told me it was impossible." His gaze snapped up to meet mine. "I fixed it. You want to know how long?" I didn't dare to hazard a guess. I was going to say less than sixty seconds, but was worried he might actually hurt me if it was wrong. "An hour and a half," he said coolly. "I dunno, but they told me it's the world record."

"Wow," I croaked.

"Listen, kid, running a movie theatre is hopeless. Your dad told me you love movies and that you used to work at Video 2000. I get that. I love movies. My brother owned Video 2000; I remember you."

He paused and ran his fingers over his scalp. He sighed.

"The thing is, Pete, cinema is dead. People don't want that anymore. They want to sit at home and eat sludge off a tray while they stream movies on a fifty-inch flat-screen or whatever. Fifty watts of stereo sound is good enough for them. They don't care! They fast-forward over opening credits, the barbarians. And don't even get me started on people who watch movies on their iPads . . . goddammit."

As he was speaking, he'd been running his fingers over the red velvet of the chair. Absently he lifted his hand, held two fingers under his nose, and sniffed.

He sighed again.

"In other words, I wasn't kidding when I gave you that piece of advice. Forget about it. Save your money. This is a waste of your time. It's a tough business, and working that machine"—he pointed to the little window—"is art."

I nodded.

"I know. I remember an episode of *Columbo* where he operates a projector, so I think I've got a pretty good idea how it works . . ."

Rexi didn't say a word, but then again, no words could have communicated what his eyes were telling me.

I closed my mouth.

Rexi looked away.

"You have no idea," he grunted. "It'll never work."

"Thanks for your time," I said, swallowing the lump in my throat. "I need to get back to work. I can't let Dad do it all."

We walked to the lobby in silence. Rexi shouted his goodbyes to Dad, who was still working on the wiring somewhere behind the scenes.

"Thanks, Rexi! I'll get you that thing later this week," Dad yelled after him.

I noticed that Dad had switched the tape again. The song that was playing was the Platters' "Great Pretender."

CHAPTER 28

TRUE COLORS

Now that my ankle was feeling better, I decided to start each morning with a good bike ride to get my blood pumping and limbs limbered up ahead of a day of crouching and stretching and repetitive brushstrokes.

I'd ride along the bike path into town, the music in my walkman pushing me on. At the market square I'd go full throttle, and then engage low gear for the uphill climb. It was a couple of kilometres, I think—my Crescent didn't have an odometer, and bike computers hadn't been invented yet—and the first few days it was a killer, and I would arrive at the hospital parking lot hacking and screeching and wobbling, desperate to get air into my lungs and expel it as soon as possible. I'd sit on the wall and catch my breath while looking out over the hills around the valley, casting occasional glances at the main entrance, at the staff getting out of their cars to begin their days . . .

Over time the ride became easier, so I would try it in a slightly stiffer gear, and as my legs grew stronger I found I didn't need the easy gears at all. I noticed one evening that my Bryan Adams

T-shirt, which had previously clung to my belly, was now tight around my pecs.

I learned the route by heart, memorizing the location of each bump and pothole. And I tried altering my start time by ten minutes here and there so I would get to the hospital at different times, but I didn't once see *her*.

They say it only takes a week for smokers to lose the chemical craving for nicotine, but the psychological craving can last for years—a lifetime.

What was I doing?

I'd travelled back in time to the 1980s because I wanted to rake over the coals of a romance that hadn't even been a romance in the first place. But I didn't want to rake over those coals myself; I wanted a spark to smoulder unbidden and bring the fire to life. I desperately wanted it to . . . just . . . happen. I'd come back to Kumpunotko because I believed that Jennifer was my destiny. And, while I didn't exactly *believe* in fate or God or karma or the cosmic forces controlling the universe, neither did I want to tempt fate, to ruin my chances somehow manipulating destiny.

I wished there was somebody I could talk to about it.

I didn't have a best friend any more. And Tina? Well . . . Tina would just laugh. I considered telling Twisted Sister, but having that kind of conversation on a dial-up modem would have taken months. Dad would have plucked some Beatles lyric from his head. And Mom . . . let's not even go there.

So I rode my bike. And, of course, riding a bike up the biggest hill in town was good exercise. It wasn't *my* fault that Jennifer worked in the building at the top of the hill, was it?

Rolling down the hill was my reward for the hard work, and a nice consolation each day when the main prize didn't materialize.

I would roll all the way down without pedalling, and on the days when I managed to roll as far as Kim's Basement, I took that as a sign that I should treat myself.

Kim was my polar opposite. He was a big man, in every sense of the word. He was tall, and I'm guessing he liked his food. Had he given me a bear hug, I would've disappeared completely inside the embrace. I'd let my hair grow; he had a crew cut. He had "ink," as he put it, whereas I was scared of needles. But we both loved our music. And on that point we mostly sort of agreed. Our musical tastes were, it has to be said, both pretty awesome.

Kim liked making lists. I discovered this one morning when I walked in and he pretty much shouted at me: "What's the best song for driving on the freeway?"

"'Road to Nowhere,'" I said, reflexively. Because it is.

"Damn!" he said, scribbling it down. "Why didn't I think of that? What else?"

"'Drive,' by the Cars?"

"Got that. Obviously."

"Um . . . 'St. Elmo's Fire'?" I blushed. What did he expect, putting me on the spot like that?

"Hmm." He looked at me curiously. "'St. Elmo's Fire,' in brackets 'Man in Motion.' Yes. I never would have said that. But I like your thinking."

His other lists have included "Top 10 Songs to Play Air Guitar To," "Top 10 Songs to Cook To," and "Top 10 Songs That Have to Do with the Law (But That Are Not By the Police)."

One morning as I was coasting down the hill from the hospital, I came up with an idea for a list myself: "Top 10 Songs to Look for Your Dream Girl To."

"What kind of a list is that?" Kim asked me. "Sounds a bit niche. Something on your mind, man?"

"You know, what would be the song you'd like to hear in the background when you serendipitously meet your dream girl?"

"Hmm. If it's only one song, why a Top 10?"

"It's more about the time just before you meet her, see. When you can sort of feel it in the air . . ."

"'In the Air Tonight,' for example?"

"Exactly. It has to be on the list. Maybe not number one, but how could you not include it?"

"Not too obvious?"

"Maybe a little . . . but like I said, it's a Top 10 list."

Kim lifted the countertop; he rubbed his chin as he walked around his store. He was mumbling something I couldn't hear.

"'Every Breath You Take?'"

"Isn't that a stalker song? This isn't about obsession," I said, perhaps a little sharply. "It's about, you know, destiny. The guy doesn't even know the girl is there, and then the universe aligns and . . . say . . . 'Abracadabra' or 'Missing You.'"

More chin rubbing. More pacing. More mumbling.

"Does he know her, though? This hypothetical gentleman."

"Maybe. Yes. A long time ago."

"I get it. Here's a good one. 'I Want to Know What Love Is.'"

"Yes. That goes on the list." I pulled out my diary and wrote down the names of the songs we'd already mentioned (except the stalker song).

"You're old-school," Kim said. "I like it."

Forty-five minutes later, we had a list of ten songs, and another hour of heated debate later, we had put them in order.

1. "You're the Inspiration"
2. "Waiting for a Girl Like You"
3. "Saving All My Love for You"

4. "Suddenly"
5. "Dead Ringer for Love"
6. "I Want to Know What Love Is"
7. "If I Was"
8. "Since You've Been Gone"
9. "For Your Eyes Only"
10. "Woman"

We were both very pleased with the list, and Kim told me he had all the songs in stock and that I should swing by on my way home. That evening I did so and was delighted when he passed me a BASF D60 Chrome tape. "No charge, man," he said with a grin. When I got home, I noticed that he'd added Survivor's "The Search Is Over" as the last song on Side B.

In my mind, I thanked him for his encouragement.

As the days ticked by, we moved from September to October, edging ever closer to December. Painting the walls had been the least of our problems, and something we should have left until the end. Dad's creative solutions to some of the electrical issues had been ingenious, but also illegal, as his electrician buddy told him after the fact. And though we poured bleach and drain cleaner and even acid down the blocked toilet, nothing worked, so we had to call on another friend of Dad's to have a look at it.

Dad's plan covered everything from polishing the front doors to buying new garbage cans, cleaning the curtain and carpets, building a new counter, cleaning the seats, and reupholstering half a dozen of the most sat-upon ones.

My biggest decision—and expense—was getting a new sign. The T in the old one was broken; it looked like somebody may have thrown a stone through it. I didn't want people to see *ALAS* glowing in the night, so I decided to order a new one. I found a company in the phone book, rang them up, and explained what I needed.

"Sure, we can quote on that. Can you send through a design? CAD file or high-res PDF."

"Um, sorry, I . . . I'm not a designer. I just want it like the one that's there, only not broken."

"Sure. We can try to copy what you have. Can you email us a picture?"

I had an idea. "Maybe someone could come out and have a look? Maybe the old one's fixable."

"To Kumpunotko? Um, have you tried just replacing the bulbs?"

I reminded her that one of the letters was actually broken. She sighed and said someone would be with me by Wednesday.

Dad fixed the minor issues with the plumbing, replaced broken tiles, cleaned and polished the projectors, and mopped the floors, all the while humming his songs. I generally tidied up after him, passed him things, made tea. One day I was taking a stack of boxes out to the dumpster and spotted something strange.

"Dad, someone's been using our dumpster."

"Hmm?" he said through a mouthful of screws.

"Must have been a local restaurant, only there's a bunch of potato sacks. Unless you're planning on selling chips?"

He laughed and carried on his wiring.

DAD had a new game. Every time it was my turn to play music, he'd come back with examples of 1960s music that had inspired the songs I'd grown up with.

Spandau Ballet: "Nothing without Marvin Gaye."

Kim Wilde: "Nancy Sinatra did it much better."

Bruce Springsteen: "Well . . . isn't that the Animals all over again?"

"It just goes to show that all the best music was made in the 1960s," he concluded.

When he said that, with his arm around my shoulder, I noticed that his posture had gotten better. He was, once again, taller than me.

Mom often came to see us, and she always had sandwiches with her. One day she also brought the mail—a postcard from Tina.

Pete,
Happy to hear you're feeling better. I'm curious about everything.
Please send photos.
T.

"I'm happy too," Mom said as she handed it to me.

There were other issues with the theatre. I had been back to the town hall twice to get my event permit. My application was missing some documentation, and I got into an argument with a young man at the fire and rescue department.

"I don't make the rules, it's the law. It's the Assembly Act," he said, enunciating "act" carefully.

Finding the movie distributor had been much easier, and they were more than happy to help me find the reels to *Back to the Future*, as soon as I sent them the technical specifications of the projector that was going to be used. The film would be sent to me by courier once the invoice had been paid. Oh, and they would take 50 percent of the proceeds.

"Wouldn't have it any other way," I replied, stuffing my fist into my mouth.

THAT evening I called Tina. I couldn't send her photos—I'd taken a full roll, but I wasn't sure there was anyplace to get 35mm film developed in Kumpunotko—but I still wanted to give her an update.

"You'll have to come and see it for yourself."

"Is everything on schedule? Will you be able to open the theatre again?" she asked me.

"Of course! We're almost there. Well, there's still a lot of painting, cleaning, boring admin stuff. But we have about eight weeks now, so plenty of time."

"Is that all you do there? It must be so boring, especially now that summer's over. I bet the streets are empty by six."

"It's not too bad, actually. I've been busy," I said.

"Dancing to Duran Duran? Making mix-tapes? I hear Union Jack tank tops are all the rage there. Yo-yo-yo!"

Tina was snickering. Sofie had been debriefed, I noted. I countered by lifting a corner of the family rug.

"So, have you spoken to Mom?" I asked.

"The usual. She asks after Sofie, passes the phone to you . . ."

"I don't think she's happy."

"Then maybe she should think about things. Maybe she shouldn't freeze people out."

"What?"

"Nothing."

The line was silent.

"Take care, Peter. Thanks for the postcards."

Tina hung up.

I stared at the receiver for a second before putting it back in its cradle.

I logged onto the BBS and chatted with Twisted Sister for a while, comparing notes about the best (and worst) of the early MTV big-hair rock videos. We managed to establish that she preferred those with a narrative, whereas I was more into the live concert footage, before I began to doze off.

CHAPTER 29

SLEDGEHAMMER

Y ou need a haircut, young man," said Mom. It was true: I'd been putting it off for ages.

So the next morning, rather than riding to the hospital, I took my bike past Jennifer's old house and into town via the off-centre route. I parked outside Salon Salon, the cheapest barber in town. The bell above the door dinged as I walked in.

Everything was just the way I remembered it. The same faded black-and-white photos offering the latest (circa 1978) trends. The same creaking pneumatic chairs. And, most importantly, the same slightly hunchbacked barber himself, Stefan.

He barely looked up.

"Hey, Peter, take a seat. With you in a minute."

He was just about finished with an elderly gent who only had hair in a couple of tufts around the ears, so I didn't figure it would take long. I sat on the old hard wooden bench.

For the first time in ages, in anticipation of a moment of waiting, my hand crept toward my phone pocket. I chastised myself for the lapse, and instead reached for a copy of *Sports Car* magazine, but it was from 1998, so I put it back.

Instead, I went through a mental checklist of the things I had to complete before I could finally cross item number two off my master plan. Which then got me thinking about my Time Machine, and how far I'd journeyed, through time and space, since its arrival. Funny how little pieces of paper can be so important to our lives.

Finally, after cropping the wads of hair sprouting from the old man's nostrils, Stefan dusted down the seat and waved me over. I sat down in the comfortable old leather.

"The usual?" he asked, reaching for a thick pair of scissors and a comb. "Short at the top and the sides, long at the back?"

I spluttered. "How the heck d'you remember that?"

He shrugged. "Always remember a customer. Anyway, you been away or something? Not seen you in a while."

Half an hour later, I walked out of the barbershop onto a sunny autumnal Kumpunotko street, my mullet waving in the breeze, feeling like a million dollars. I unlocked my bike from the No Parking sign and was just turning it around to head toward the Atlas when the back wheel banged against something. Or someone, to be more specific.

"Hey, watch it!" he shouted.

I turned to look, and there was a guy with thick, dark hair.

"My trousers, man," he said, rubbing the material vigorously.

"Sorry." I said it more to placate him than anything. There was no dirt on his trousers.

He finally looked up at me, picking up his brief case and straightening to his full, rather large height. It was the moustache I recognized first.

"Sami?"

"Yeah, I'm Sami. And this is an expensive suit."

"Well, maybe you should be more careful where you walk."

His eyes flared. "You swung your bike around without looking, like you own the sidewalk."

"Yes, but you clearly saw me. Anyway, no harm done. How are you?"

"What? I'm fine. Who are you? Do you know me?"

For a moment I was tempted to just walk off, leaving him mystified.

"It's Peter, man. From school?"

He looked puzzled.

"Peter Eksell?" I said. "Look, never mind. You're obviously in a big rush, so I'll just get out of your way."

"Eksell? Yeah. That's right. You're Peter Eksell! What the hell are you doing here? I haven't seen you since . . ."

"Since high school. Well, I was in Helsinki for a few years, running my big IT consultancy, but then I decided—"

"Yeah, anyway, I am in a rush. Great to catch up. Listen," he said, already walking away, "let's go for a beer some time, okay . . . ?"

"Great."

I watched him walk away in his shiny business suit, with his shiny briefcase and his thick, shiny hair. He probably could have grown a proper mullet in a week.

"Hang on. Wait a minute," he said, charging back toward me. "I *heard* about this. You're the guy who's trying to restore the cinema."

I grinned. "That's me."

"You're the guy who's trying to stop the apartments!"

"Well, not exactly."

"Hey, listen. I'm on the council, and we've worked damn hard trying to get that waste of space taken down. It's an eyesore, having a building falling apart like that right in the middle of town. You know, young people can barely afford to get on the property ladder, but there's prime real estate sitting there empty, slap-bang in the middle of town."

I hadn't thought about it like that.

"We don't need another movie theatre," he said, right in my personal space, towering over me. "We need affordable homes. We need investment opportunities. We need development. Progress!"

"Well," I said, as diplomatically as I could, "perhaps if you speak to Kari at BBB you'll understand the situation a bit better. I'm not delaying anything. Anyway, lovely to catch up, Sami. Hope to see you in another thirty years or so . . ."

I climbed onto my Crescent, dinged the bell, and rode past him down the street.

Sometimes I wonder why I'm not in touch with my old friends any more.

Sometimes I realize why.

IT was another tough day at the Atlas, sanding the handles on the glass doors, and part of me was wondering what I'd gotten myself into, and if it was really worth it. In a year's time, all of this would be bulldozed, crushed to rubble, carted off to wherever rubble goes, to presumably be sorted and sifted and turned into new building materials. In six months, this lovely Art Deco door handle could be shredded, pulped, reconstituted as MDF, flat-packed and sitting in a big blue-and-yellow warehouse waiting to be someone's bedside table.

I was tired. Being a movie theatre entrepreneur was a lot of work, but I couldn't let go of the goal. I couldn't let doubt fill me and ruin it. I had a little over seven weeks to go, and I was on track. I couldn't *wait* for the day when I'd be able to roll out the red carpet and welcome the good people of Kumpunotko to the new, improved Atlas.

I bumped into Sara at a hockey game

"The one time I go to a hockey game," I told her, "and who do I see?"

"Meee!" Sara said with glee.

"I didn't know you were a hockey fan."

"Got to support the team, man."

"Of course. Go KP!"

"I never used to come to hockey games, you know. Back then."

"Me neither."

"But it really makes me feel like I belong here, that I'm part of the community. And people can see I'm not just a mean old cop."

I grinned. "I doubt anyone thinks you're mean."

She snarled at me.

"Where are you sitting? I'm on the corner, over there. Plenty of space, if you want to join me?"

"Ah, sorry. We've got front-row seats. My buddy knows the coach, so . . . ," I said, just as Kim returned from the concession stand with grilled sausages and two cups of coffee.

"It's fine. I'll see you around. Go KP!" Sara said, and pumped her fist.

I didn't necessarily like painting the walls, but even I could see that I was getting better at it. And it did give me an opportunity to really think. Every stroke of the brush, every sweep of the roller took me deeper into my consciousness. I wasn't a religious or even a spiritual person——I never did yoga and I didn't believe in meditation——but when I was painting over the dragon at the Atlas, I was at peace.

Until the music stopped.

Dad went on humming for a few bars, but I turned around and saw Tomi Taimi standing in front of the curtain.

"I guess you didn't hear me come in," he said. He walked toward me with his hands crossed, twiddling his thumbs nervously.

"You boys have done wonders here. It's hard to believe this is the same place it was when I checked it out in September," he said, wringing his hands.

"Thanks. It hasn't been straightforward, but we're happy with the way things are going," I said. "Coffee?" I nodded at a Thermos next to the radio.

"No. No, thanks." He cleared his throat. "I'm afraid I have some bad news. We just heard back from the town hall. The council have apparently been working hard behind the scenes, and we won our case against the last complaint. Therefore . . ." He looked really uncomfortable, like he was trying not to cry. I almost felt sorry for him. Almost. "Sorry, guys. The bulldozers will be here in about three weeks. November 1, to be exact."

I dropped my roller on the ground. I glanced at my left wrist, but I wasn't wearing my calculator watch. It didn't matter. When I heard "three weeks" my heart skipped a beat.

"I think I have to sit down," I said, and did so, on the carpet. All I could do was stare ahead.

Tomi Taimi sighed.

"I'm sorry. I thought you'd like to know in person, rather than in writing."

"We appreciate that," said Dad, emerging from the shadows. He got down on his haunches and put a hand on my shoulder. "Maybe there's still time to do one show?" he said softly.

"Maybe . . ."

THAT evening, I paced around my room and the house like I lion in a cage. I'd start to do something, drop it, and start something else. Rinse and repeat.

I'd lost a month. Maybe even more than that. Worse, the little notion I'd always carried—that somehow the demolition would be stopped and the cinema saved forever—faded to black, crushed by a big yellow bulldozer. Now everything would have to be ready by the end of October.

October 26! The date hit me like a bolt of lightning. Of course! I would move my gala opening to October 26. It was the perfect date—the same day that Marty McFly travelled back in time, met young "Doc," and—

The lightning hit a second time. I had told "Doc" that I'd like to see him in Kumpunotko on December 1.

In a frenzy, I took the first piece of paper I saw on my desk and, as carefully as I could in that state of mind, wrote a second letter to Christopher Lloyd. It was shorter than the first one.

Dear Mr. Lloyd,

Please accept my apologies, but there has been a change of plans. I would appreciate it if you could be in Kumpunotko on October 26, a date I am sure you know well.

I apologize if this means you have to change your flight booking. I'd be more than happy to cover the cost of doing so.

Very much looking forward to meeting you.

Humbly yours,
Peter Eksell
Atlas

I put the letter in an envelope, sealed it, and went downstairs for dinner.

CHAPTER 30

HERE I GO AGAIN

MAYBE you won't have the theatre for long, but I'm sure it will still be an unforgettable night," Mom said.

"Yeah," added Dad gruffly.

"Dad and I will help you the best we can, of course."

"Yeah," said Dad.

"Don't give up."

" . . .Yeah."

They reminded me of an elderly Finnish version of the two jailbird thugs in *Trading Places*. Which made me Billy Ray Valentine. But I wasn't feeling very lucky that evening.

I mumbled some sort of a reply, but my mind was elsewhere. It was everywhere. I sat down to play a game, and to think, but my hands were twitching. I logged onto the BBS to see if Twisted Sister was there.

While the Spectrum loaded the software, and the modem hooked up onto the BBS, I berated myself for being so stupid. My inner narrator was mad; he was mad as hell.

"He thought he'd found the perfect way to go back in time,

and to get his girl. What he forgot was that he was a *slacker!*"

My breathing got heavier and heavier.

The "I Wanna Rock!" logo appeared on my screen, followed by the menu choices. Before I'd had time to check for new messages on the board, Twisted Sister began a chat.

Good evening. How are things with you today?

Hi, I typed back.

I needed air. I inhaled as much as I could but nothing was enough. The walls started to close in. I heard another chat message rattling onto the screen.

That was short. Are you okay?

I sat down to write.

Had some devastating news today. Trying to digest everything.

A minute later, a reply:

I see. Remember that at a time of stress, you have two choices: fight or flight. Just remember that it's a choice. Your call.

What the hell? Was Twisted Sister actually Seppo Laine? I tried to picture the old man hunched over a keyboard, sporting a massive perm and shock-rock makeup, but my brain couldn't take it any more. *I* couldn't take it anymore. I needed air and I needed space. I ran downstairs and was headed toward the front door when something stopped me in my tracks. Dad's computer screen was shining in the dark study, and I stopped at the threshold for a second, staring at the machine humming softly on the table.

Dad had been looking at Tina's photos of Sofie on Facebook. She was cute, and Dad's computer was gorgeous. It was a laptop, no bigger than my Spectrum, but so much faster and more powerful. It had better graphics, better software, and . . . a fast internet connection. If I just borrowed it for a few minutes I could go online and fill in all the forms I needed to finalize my permits; I could do all the other admin that was clogging up my time—I could do days' worth of work in minutes. I could type "Jennifer Berg" into a search engine and see what came out . . .

I grabbed the Beetle keys from the hall table and ran.

I drove first toward town, and when I came to the intersection that would have taken me to Jennifer's road, I pressed the gas pedal to the floor and continued straight ahead.

I sped past the Atlas and the record store and the market square, and, ten minutes later, I sped past the City Limits sign. My heart was racing, and my poor brain couldn't keep up. To make sense of things, I decided to sing.

I reached for a new tape in the glove compartment, but my hand hit something else. Paper. The Time Machine. "The fargin' Time Machine," said Tina's voice in my head. The stupid piece of paper that had gotten me into this stupid mess in the first place. I pushed it back in and, instead, pressed a tape into the Blaupunkt stereo that Dad was so proud of.

I hit Play and a powerful guitar chord struck out, but then crunched slightly and warbled, and—"Noooooo!" The machine was eating my favourite tape. I clicked Eject and the stereo spat out the cassette, the magnetic tape still tangled in its guts.

I didn't need music; I could sing.

But nothing came to me.

There was no song for this moment.

I couldn't think of a thing.

My brain was like a jukebox with a stuck mechanism.

I let out a long, deep scream as the Beetle roared along the highway toward Helsinki.

I pressed that gas pedal with everything I had, as if pushing it harder would somehow make the car go faster. Dots of rain began to fall and were picked out by the Beetle's headlights, whizzing past me like stars at warp speed.

"Come on, move!"

The speedometer's needle was creeping upwards, past fifty, climbing toward sixty. At seventy, the steering wheel started to shake. I shook it some more, leaned as hard as I could on the gas, jumped up and down on the seat, trying to make the car go faster. I wanted warp speed. I wanted light speed. No—I wanted something better than that.

"Give me eighty-eeeeight!" I screamed.

The lights of a gas station blurred by. A truck going the other way barely registered. The car was shaking, rattling, and rolling as the needle edged past eighty, eighty-five, creeping up . . . toward . . . ninety . . .

And then all around me were blue and red and white flashing lights, and I thought for a moment the car had done it—ripped a hole in the space-time continuum—until I heard the siren.

I finally lifted my foot—it felt dead, like lead—and the car slowed down. I steered to the side and stopped. I closed my eyes and shook my head in disbelief. It wasn't the middle of the night, but it was late and the road was empty. Didn't the police have anything better to do? I opened the glove compartment, chucked the Time Machine aside, and found my registration. When I sat back up, I saw the police officer standing next to my car, giving me the "roll down your window" gesture.

I rolled down the window.

"Good evening, sir," said the officer. "Would you mind stepping out of the car? You may have noticed that you were speeding."

"Sara?" I said, astonished.

"Hello, Peter. Step out of the car, please."

"This is weird."

"Just get out of your car and into ours."

I did as she asked. I couldn't really see what the problem was.

The road was deserted, but her partner was glaring at me like I'd driven at ninety through a school zone.

I looked back up the road. In the distance, by the village we'd just passed through, I saw the unmistakable yellow glint of a school zone sign.

Ah.

Sara escorted me to the police car. She opened the back door and I hopped in. She then sat down in the passenger's seat while her colleague punched some numbers on a big computer console in the front.

I thought it looked a bit like the set-up in the car in *Knight Rider*, but kept that to myself.

"Didn't you see the school zone signs?" Sara's partner asked.

"I'm sorry, Officer. I didn't."

I wanted to point out that it was 11 p.m, but I didn't think that would help my case.

"And I bet you didn't think you could drive so fast in one of those old Beetles, did you?" He glanced at me in the rear-view mirror.

"I wasn't thinking. Period." I bit my lower lip. I wanted to say as little as possible.

"I mean, fast enough to lose your driver's licence," he added gravely.

"Lose my licence?" I whimpered.

"Two months maybe," he said. "Profession?"

"Right now, unemployed," I said, partly because I was feeling sorry for myself and partly because with no income I would get a smaller fine.

Sara turned around and looked at me; she grimaced.

"It's true, isn't it? I don't have a job."

"Do you know each other?" asked the other policeman.

"We went to high school together," I said.

"Oh."

I slouched back, not paying attention to what the policeman was saying as he droned on; something about no street lighting and elks going through windscreens and blah. Sara didn't say anything either, and after they had checked my details on the computer, I was given permission to leave.

Sara escorted me back to my car. She seemed to be appraising me. I wasn't much to look at. I had paint stains on my hands and my face, and I was wearing faux Adidas sweat pants—two stripes only—a dirty T-shirt, an orange hoodie, and a denim jacket. And deck shoes.

"Are you okay, Peter?"

"I'm fine."

"You don't look fine."

"Thanks."

"Let me know if you want to have that cup of coffee sometime. Maybe you need to talk to somebody? "

She handed me the ticket.

"You know I saved your butt here, right? My partner wanted to drop the hammer on you. It's not every day we have car chases here," she added, and waved my driver's licence in front of my face.

"Thanks. It was stupid of me."

"Very. Drive safe now."

I promised her I'd do that, and when I saw her get back inside the police Volvo, I looked at the ticket. The fine was 250 euros.

The limit had been fifty kilometres an hour. My speed? Eighty-eight.

CHAPTER 31

DON'T TALK TO STRANGERS

T HE next morning, I woke up to a knock on my bedroom
door. It was Dad.

"Hello, sleepyhead, time to get to the Atlas!"

"Really?"

"Of course! You heard Taimi. We're in a bit of a hurry now.
Better get a move on! I'm heading out now, so I'll see you there.
Mom left your breakfast in the fridge."

Then he was gone.

When I walked into the Atlas fifteen minutes later, Dad was
already busy at work, unclogging the toilet. Again. "Can you see
if you can find me a coat hanger? Must be one somewhere . . ."

I walked to the office and looked around. I'd given it a good
tidy up, throwing away all the promotional material for nineties
films that didn't exist yet, and I didn't remember seeing a coat
hanger. Then I remembered the storage room, accessed through
a little door under the stairs up to the balcony. When I got there,
though, a shiny brass padlock prevented me from checking it out.
I didn't remember that being there before, and none of the keys

on my key ring seemed to fit it. I was just heading back to ask Dad about it when I head a toilet flush.

"Eureka!" he yelled, and then came out to find me, holding a plunger aloft.

"Dad, why's that door padlocked?"

"What door? Oh. I was going to ask you, have you spoken with the film distributors? When are the reels coming? What about tickets? Do you have tickets?"

"Yes, they'll be here shortly, they said. The bookstore sells generic numbered tickets we can use, I think."

Dad continued his rapid-fire interrogation.

"How are you going to let people know about the event? What about the lobby—are you going to get to work on the walls today? And who's going to take care of ticket sales? What about candy? Will there be candy?"

I shook my head. "I don't know, Dad. I don't know."

He put his arm around me and pulled me closer.

"Hey, Pete. I get it. But today's a new day. And don't worry: we can work it out. Oh, and I'll let you choose the music all day," Dad said.

"Deal," I said, and got changed into my overalls.

By noon, Dad had moved to the balcony to bolt the chairs into place.

"I don't know what people have been doing up there, but some of those chairs are really loose!"

I was at the far end of the hall, under the balcony, operating a carpet-cleaning machine. It was a rental from a friend of Dad's.

"That looks like fun," someone shouted over the noise of the ten-amp electric motor, startling me. "And it's probably safer than trying to break the land-speed record in a Beetle."

It was Sara. She was back in her civilian clothes—jeans and a leather jacket.

"Let's not talk about it," I said, aware of my dad working above our heads.

"Understood. Listen, would you like to grab a pizza with me?"

"What, now?"

"How about in an hour? Or do you have other plans?"

"Well, Dad and I always . . . ," I began to say, but was interrupted by a hoarse man's voice yelling something from the balcony.

"I forgot my lunchbox at home. I'm going to drive home and eat there," Dad said.

Sara looked up and waved.

"La Favorita it is then," she said. "See you there at one."

La Favorita, run by a Greek guy, was Kumpunotko's first pizza place. It was also the best.

The walk from the Atlas to the corner of Main and Market only took five minutes, but I left early to make sure I wouldn't be late. I checked the big digital clock on top of the bank building on my way there: 12:50 p.m.

I waited for Sara outside, like a true gentleman. After what I estimated to have been ten minutes, I started to look around to see if I could spot her. After another ten minutes, I took a peek inside the restaurant, but no Sara there, either. I walked back toward the square to check the time. It was now 1:11 p.m.

I couldn't understand why Sara would have stood me up. But I'd waited too long to just leave, so I walked back to the restaurant. When I got there, Sara was standing outside, tapping her watch.

"It's polite to text if you're going to be late," she said, and before I could protest, she added with a smile, " . . . but I don't have your number."

As soon as we sat down, Sara cut the small talk.

"How are you doing? Are you okay? How's the project going?" she asked. "When will you open? I want to come to the premiere. There'll be a red carpet, right?"

"October 26," I said, as casually as I could.

"That soon? Great!"

"It's the date when Marty McFly goes back in time," I said.

"Nice touch. You must be almost finished then."

"Almost, but even in the worst-case scenario, we should be ready in a week or two. I hope," I said, and felt cold sweat running down my temples.

We sat there silently for a while. Sara fidgeted with her left ear; I looked around the restaurant. The walls were covered with photos of local celebrities smiling with the owner, and newspaper clippings from Kumpunotko's two papers, with reviews and stories profiling the owner on his fiftieth and sixtieth birthdays.

"I haven't been here for a while, but this is the first place I ever saw somebody roll up an entire pizza and eat it like that," I said. "Actually, the only place," I added.

"Who eats a pizza like that?"

"Mikke," I said.

Sara couldn't help but laugh. Mikke had been such a joker. I felt a tinge of sadness that he'd moved to another continent. Why couldn't he have been here instead of Sami?

"Do you remember when he went to school dressed as Horny Jesus?"

"Ha! Do I ever. And do you remember—maybe you weren't there—when he sat in chemistry with a garbage bag over his head? He pinched it tight under his nose so he could breathe in through his mouth and inflate it through his nose. It swelled up like he had a massive head, and he'd even drawn a smiley face on it. Even Seppo Laine was cracking up, though of course he was trying to tell him about the dangers of suffocation . . ."

The waiter came and took our orders, and we both knew ours without looking at the menu.

"Hey, I had this great idea back in high school and I think it'd still work. Want to hear it?" I asked.

"Of course."

"What if there was a phone number you could call to get an answer to any question? Like, anything. 'What's the capital of Jordan? I'll hold . . . oh, it's Amman? Thank you.'"

Sara looked at me, her mouth open.

"And if they can't give you the answer immediately, they'll call you back," I said.

She closed her mouth but said nothing.

"Good idea, right?" I said.

"Well, hasn't it sort of been done?"

I wasn't aware that any such phone service existed.

Sara slid her phone out, pressed a button, and then spoke. "Siri, what's the capital city of Jordan?" She stared at me while the phone bleeped, thought for a second, and then gave the reply in a cool, digitally helpful voice.

I pasted a polite smile on my face, like a reformed alcoholic might do when his companion orders a triple vodka.

"Peter, why did you move back to Kumpunotko? Are you sick? Is your mom sick?"

"Why did you?" I shot back.

"I asked you first."

"I have a project here."

"But you didn't have the project until you got here, right?"

244

"Okay. I needed a change."

"You call moving back to your old hometown 'change'? Living with your parents? To be honest, you don't seem to have changed that much at all, and frankly, that's a little scary."

"What do you mean?"

"Well, let's begin with your clothes. I swear you wore that same sweater in one of our high-school class photos. And last night—"

"No, no, not 'last night'—"

"Yes, Peter, last night you looked like something straight out of, I don't know, a bad eighties music video. Seriously, what's going on? For God's sake, Peter, look at you! You have a mullet!"

I flipped my hair with my hand and smiled.

"I just wanted to get back to my roots, find the person I used to be and the people I used to be with. Why do you care so much about why I'm here?"

"Maybe I'm just curious," she said.

"Are you?"

"Hell, yeah. You have to admit it's strange behaviour."

I laughed. "Okay, but I don't know what else to tell you."

She shook her head, looked away; she may have even cursed.

"It's just that," Sara began, "you seem to be moving backwards, and it's not natural. You're supposed to go through life *forwards*. Nature wants you to evolve."

She cleared her throat. She seemed to be about to say something, but I didn't hear it.

Because someone had just come in and sat down at a table across the restaurant.

It was Jennifer.

I don't know how many hours I spent watching the back of that head in high school. I watched her move it side to side as she listened to the teacher, and I watched her fix her hair when she got bored in class. She had the best posture of anyone I'd ever met; I always thought I could pick her out of a lineup just by her posture.

I mumbled a quick excuse and stood up. I took a couple of quick steps toward the woman's table, with both my arms extended in a surprised greeting. When I got there, the woman looked up from her newspaper and—

It wasn't Jennifer.

I muttered an apology and thanked the heavens that the bathroom was in the same direction. I kept going, stumbling through the door, until I found a cold tiled wall against which to rest my head.

Funny how you can go from pure bliss to bewilderment to panic to shame in five short seconds. I washed my hands and my face with cold water to calm myself down before walking out, trying to act natural.

"Are you okay?" Sara asked.

"I'm fine," I said as breezily as I could. "Why do you keep asking?"

She looked over her shoulder at the lone diner and then shrugged.

"You look like you've seen a ghost."

"No, no. Just went to the bathroom. You were saying?"

"Hmm. I think I was saying that I'm not sure why you're putting so much time and effort—and however much money—into a project that's basically doomed. But I hope you're getting out of it . . . whatever it is you're hoping to get out of it."

I picked up the salt shaker and gave it my full focus. I twisted and turned it in my hand, afraid to look at Sara. I really, really didn't want to think to deeply about what she'd just said. I had no idea how much of my savings were left, as I had no real way to check.

Thankfully, she diverted my attention.

"Can you at least tell me what the deal is with you and Jennifer?"

I dropped the salt shaker, spilling salt all over the table. I brushed it off with my arm.

"There's no deal . . . How could there be a deal between me and somebody I haven't seen in thirty years?"

"Stop it. I may not be that smart, but I'm not that stupid either. You've brought her up almost every time we've met." She stopped herself—but I saw it—from glancing at the lone diner again. "She does look a bit like her."

I shrugged, as if I'd barely noticed.

"Okay, look," I said. "Jennifer and I were pretty good friends back then, you know that, and . . . I simply lost track of her after she moved to Paris. We were friends. That's all."

"Paris? Yeah, right," Sara muttered, and went on in a louder voice: "Have you googled her? Facebooked her?"

"It's not that important."

Sara laughed, but not in her usual charming way. "If it's not that important, why have you asked me about her, twice? I don't know her; we're not friends. In fact, we've never been friends."

I didn't know what to say, so I said nothing.

"I can probably find her for you," Sara said after a short pause. "Even if she's not on Facebook, I can just look her up at work. I'm not supposed to do it, because every single search I do on the database is logged, but I can have a look. If you want me to," she added.

"Oh, no, no, no, no. No. I'm sure I'll bump into her, you know, when the time is right," I said.

"Okay. Whatever. Up to you. Your call."

We got our pizzas. Sara rolled hers up and stuffed it in her mouth, and then laughed so hard she almost choked. We paid and walked back toward the Atlas.

"Want to watch a movie tonight? My place?" I asked Sara outside the theatre.

"Which one?"

"How about *Trading Places*?"

Sara laughed so hard she had to wipe the tears off her cheeks. I wasn't quite sure what was so funny.

"A classic eighties flick. Of course. Listen, Peter, I would love to, but I can't tonight. Tomorrow?"

"Tomorrow it is."

I pulled out my calendar and wrote in *Sara*, trying not to see the big red circle around October 26 a few pages later.

Sara shook her head as she watched me jot down the diary entry. Then she gave me a hug and walked away.

CHAPTER 32

CARELESS WHISPER

Even though we parted as friends, Sara's words had put a dent in my self-confidence. I told Dad I wasn't feeling well and rode home.

All I wanted to do was curl up in my bed and watch TV all day. I didn't need other people, and I especially didn't need doubters. Sara had to have known that I was feeling down and that all I wanted was some sympathy. Instead, she'd grilled me like a cop in a cheap novel.

Some sympathy. Was that too much to ask?

I threw off my blanket, got up, dialled Tina's number, and walked back to bed. I put my pillow behind my back and sat against the wall.

"Hi, Tina."

"Hi, Peter, how's it going?"

"Could be better. Got a speeding ticket last night."

"That's a bummer."

"Yeah."

I didn't know what to say so I said nothing. I could hear Tina whisper something to another person.

"Hey, Peter, if you wanted to talk you'd better talk. I'm in the middle of something here," she said. She covered the mouthpiece again, and I heard something about Wikipedia.

"It's just that . . . a friend of mine pretty much called me an idiot today."

"Poor baby, are your being bullied in Kumpunotko?"

"Please. I'm serious."

Again, I heard her speak to someone, and again, it had to do with Wikipedia.

"I'm sorry. Okay, I think Sofie can work on her own for a minute. Tell me everything."

"Well, there's been a bit of a disaster thanks to an idiot at the council—who was an idiot at school too, now that I think about it—who's taken a dislike to me, and so the developers now have full planning permission and I only have two weeks to get the Atlas ready, and as things are now, I have a senior citizen working on the theatre's plumbing on his own, I don't have a film to show yet, and I haven't even started with the advertising or anything like that."

"I see."

"And I had pizza with an old high-school friend today, and she told me that—"

"She? Who is she?"

"No, nothing like that, she's just an old schoolmate. She was actually the cop who gave me the ticket, and I guess she felt bad about it."

"Do I know her?"

"I'm sure you do; you knew everybody. It's Sara—the girl I went to the school dance with."

"Small? Punk rocker, I think?"

"New Wave, actually."

"Same, same."

"Actually, it's not the same thing. Punk was far more—"

"What did she say?"

"What?"

"What did she say that got you so upset?"

"Well, basically she says I'm regressing, that my ideas are stupid. And she made fun of my clothes and my hair."

"Really? That sounds horrible!"

"I know!"

"Maybe she was trying to 'neg' you; you know, make you more interested by pretending she's not? Maybe she's playing hard to get. Girls can be horrible and manipulative creatures sometimes, trust me."

"She said my mullet was idiotic."

"Wait, what? You have a mullet?"

"Not a good one, unfortunately. She said I wasn't evolving. Like I was a case of arrested development or something."

Tina didn't say anything. I heard her inhale and sigh. She was clicking her tongue in an effort to find the right words.

"Well, you aren't evolving, are you? Isn't that what this whole thing is about? Going back in time and all that? Isn't that, by definition, going backwards. Regressing?"

"No!" I shouted. "Time travellers don't just regress; they do things that change the future! Marty McFly's life got better. He became cool and his parents started to play tennis!"

"Take it easy, Peter, I'm on your side."

"Sure you are."

"Do what you have to do," Tina said. "Finish what you started."

"Don't worry," I pouted, "I fully intend to. Anyway, the grand premiere is in two weeks. October 26. I hope you guys can make it here."

"We'll see. It's not that easy if you don't feel welcome, but I'll try . . ."

I heard the front door open and some noises from the downstairs hallway. It was Mom, coming back from the church flea market.

"Hello!" she shouted.

Now it was my turn to put my hand over the receiver.

"I'm on the phone, I'll be down in a sec!" I yelled at the top of my lungs.

"Listen, Tina, I have to go, I'll talk to you later," I said, and hung up.

Mom was in the kitchen when I got downstairs. She'd put two tote bags on the kitchen table and was unpacking groceries from them.

"Who was that?"

"Tina."

"What did she want? Did she call because she knew I wasn't at home?"

"Actually, Mom, I called her, and not because you weren't at home. I wanted to talk to her because I wanted to get her advice on something, and to see if they might want to come for a visit."

Mom said nothing, but closed a cupboard door slightly harder than necessary.

"I don't know what your problem is, Mom, and neither does Tina! She's doing her best."

When she was almost done putting vegetables into the fridge, she spoke to me from behind the refrigerator door.

"Maybe Tina understands you and supports you, but she

doesn't seem to have a lot of sympathy or empathy for the rest of the family," she said.

"What do you mean? She's always put the family first."

"Her family. But maybe not *this* family."

"You've lost me, Mom. I don't know what you're talking about."

"You know, Peter, I may be provincial and a bit old-fashioned, but I pride myself on certain things, and my cooking is one of those things." As if to demonstrate this, she brought out a home-made pie from the fridge and set it on the table. She turned and got down a couple of matching plates, and spoons, and a knife. Without asking, she began to serve.

"I'm not following," I said to break the silence.

"It's just because my father liked my cooking, and my little sisters did too, when I had to take over when your Mummi, God rest her soul, passed away. And your father has never turned away anything I've put on a plate in front of him. And you and Tina, growing up, always licked the plate clean. But . . . ," Mom said.

"But? Mom, what are we talking about?"

"Tim, of course. He puts on a good show, but I know," Mom said, and tapped her temple with her finger.

"Look, Mom . . . Tim's English. They eat boiled vegetables and kidney pies and ginger ale. He wouldn't know a good blueberry pie if you slapped him around the face with one."

"I've a good mind to," she said. I was shocked.

"Mom?"

She got up and turned away, apparently unable to look at the pie on her plate. Instinctively, she grabbed a dishcloth and began wiping away non-existent dirt.

"It's not about that. He told Tina . . ." She composed herself, took a deep breath. "He said to Tina, and I heard . . . he said I cooked like an old hag." She began to wipe the kitchen counter with such ferocity that I half-expected the cloth to catch fire.

I think I saw her wipe a tear from the corner of her eye, and that made me sad. And angry. I needed to take it out on something, and sandpapering and painting a wall seemed like just the thing to do. After giving her shoulder a comforting squeeze, I hopped on my Crescent and pedalled hard to the Atlas.

CHAPTER 33

WHEN THE GOING GETS TOUGH, THE TOUGH GET GOING

I walked in through the side door—I still wanted to save main entry for special occasions—and immediately, a smell hit me. Underneath the pervasive stink of the paint, something else. Not mould. Not sweat. Somewhere between mould and sweat. I made a mental note to talk to Dad about the toilets again. Or maybe the cleaning agent in the carpet machine had accidentally reawakened the long-forgotten stenches of days gone by. The guy in the shop had said it would be best to air the place out. I wedged the side door open with a garbage can.

Looking around, I realized for the first time that Dad and I had really made progress. The carpet-cleaning machine had done wonders. The seats were bolted down again and in straight lines. The walls that I'd painted looked smart and new. Dad had even re-panelled the ticket office booth, and fitted a new counter.

The film reels were supposed to arrive at any moment. I looked around the theatre, and where before I had seen only problems and obstacles, now I saw challenges, things I could deal with. In my estimation, we had more than a fighting chance of getting everything ready by October 26.

I didn't have a choice. I had ten days, and I had to make the best of those ten days.

Renovating the place with Dad had been a lot of fun. It had definitely been good for Dad to have a project, and I think it had been great for us to work on it together (although I was, basically, his lackey). I probably hadn't had a decent conversation with Dad since I'd left home. I thought again about Bob Gale, the writer of *Back to the Future*, and wondered if he would have gotten along with his teenaged father. And while Dad and I were both long past our youths, we did find a lot of common ground, shared jokes, had fun—even if he did have terrible, old-fashioned taste in music. I also hadn't realized exactly how vast his Kumpunotko network was. He really did know everybody, and somehow had pull everywhere, even at the town hall. Having moved to the Big City, I'd often thought of his life as small. I couldn't have been more wrong.

I hadn't ever spoken to Sara about the public-event permit, but that was fine because the police chief's son turned out to have been an intern at the ad agency where Dad had worked.

"People will do anything if you're nice to their children," he told me when he handed me the envelope that held the permit with the correct stamps and seals.

Dad had always been something of a renaissance man, having first dropped out of high school—or been kicked out; the story changed—and then gotten his diploma at night school after he met Mom. He then went on to get a college degree, all the while having different kinds of jobs. He had been a construction worker, a chef, a substitute math teacher, a football team mascot, a car salesman, a classified ad salesman at the local newspaper, and, finally, an account manager at an ad agency, where he stayed for the rest of his career.

In the last few weeks he had been all that again (except for the football mascot, though he'd certainly been cheering me on in other ways). Dad must have cashed in a lifetime of favours. Every day somebody new showed up at the theatre with something.

There was Antti, the giant from the lumberyard who delivered new things almost daily, and Marko, a small and smelly man who cleared all the drains in Kumpunotko—and the toilets at the Atlas. We had Anna from the dry cleaners (the daughter of the man who'd lent me the tuxedo that fateful night), who helped us clean the curtain, and Jenni, who did the fire and safety inspection the same day Dad called her, rather than after the four-to-six-week wait she'd quoted me.

With the exception of Anna, they all were closer to Dad's age than mine. And with the exception of Anna, who silently went about her work, they all stayed for a while, chatting with Dad and me, having a poke around.

In fact, Marko took to hanging around the theatre even after he'd cleaned the pipes, and once you got used to the smell that lingered around him, he was great company. He was, surprisingly, also a big Frankie Goes to Hollywood fan, and had even seen them live in Brighton once.

"I've never seen anyone as charismatic as Holly Johnson. He had the audience right there from beginning to end," he said, gesturing to the palm of his hand.

"George Michael?" I'd said.

"Not even close. Maybe Princess Diana. Maybe."

"She wasn't a singer."

"No," he'd said. "But she had character."

I finished my inspection, and as I made my way back toward the lobby, I heard Dad chatting with someone. Assuming the smell I'd noticed might have something to do with Marko, I popped in to say hello.

But it wasn't Marko. Dad and his buddy Erik were sitting on small stools in the lobby, just outside the bathrooms, chatting. Erik had come in to fix the mechanism behind the massive red curtain. Both sides now moved at the same speed and met in the middle, which meant I wouldn't have to have somebody crank it open at the start of the film. The glide of the curtains; it's just not something you think about, but it really is part of the magic.

"You've got to get your masking right too," he'd told us, pointing to the bits of curtain at the sides and the top and bottom of the screen. "It's a nightmare. That stuff slips off all the time, and then your picture looks off-centre. And nobody wants to watch a wonky film. Makes you feel seasick."

He greeted me with a wave.

"All done, boss! Functioning like clockwork!"

"Thank you so much for your help, Erik," I said.

"You're welcome. When your dad called me, I told him I'd do it right away."

I tapped my fingers against each other, nervous about taking the next step. But it had to be done.

"Thanks again. Um, how much do I owe you?"

I had asked Dad at one point how much his wheeling and dealing was going to cost me. I'd been prepared to clean the carpets by hand myself, but he had insisted on renting the machine. I'd imagined we were going to build a few new benches, but he had ordered a whole new suite of furniture for the lobby. When

I asked him, he just grinned and started singing an old crooner about money burning a hole in his pocket.

"Don't worry about it," said Erik. "It was my pleasure. Your dad and I will figure things out somehow." He winked at Dad.

Dad just grinned back.

"Maybe you can give Erik a couple of tickets to the show?" he said.

That was another thing: he promised tickets to all his friends and acquaintances who had helped us, which was fine, but it reminded me that I didn't yet have physical tickets to sell. Nor had I even begun to advertise.

Whenever I thought I could see light at the end of the tunnel, it just turned out to be the headlight of an oncoming express train.

"ANYBODY here?" I heard somebody yell at the door, but I didn't do anything because I expected Dad would go out to meet yet another one of his friends.

I went on with my painting until eventually Dad called for me.

"Hey, Peter. You have to sign for something here," he shouted.

I knew perfectly well that he could have signed for it, so I went out to see what the fuss was about. A courier driver was waiting for me. After I'd signed his papers, he asked me where I wanted the delivery to be dropped off.

"We deliver to the doorstep," he added helpfully. "Not inside."

Apparently, his helpfulness had its limits.

"What is it?" I asked.

He gestured with his thumb over his shoulder to where a wooden crate the size of a small refrigerator was standing up on a trolley.

I asked him to walk around the corner so that we could take the crate in through the main lobby doors. When Dad and I opened the doors, he arrived pushing the trolley with one hand and holding the crate in place with the other.

"This good?" he said, and without waiting for my reply, he tilted the crate a little, pulled his trolley from underneath it, folded it up, and walked back to his van.

"What's inside?" asked Dad.

"It looks like the crate in *Raiders of the Lost Ark*. The one that holds the Ark of the Covenant," I said.

"Let's open it up then."

Dad set to work with a screwdriver and a hammer. Inside the crate were six smaller containers, and inside each one of those was a film reel. We were going Back to the Future!

We carried them, one by one, upstairs to the projection booth and stacked them in two piles on the round table inside.

"Don't you want to try it?" Dad asked me.

I thought of Rexi, and how complicated he'd made it all sound.

"No."

"What's the matter? You chicken?"

I scowled at him. Then I thought of Rexi again, and how arrogant he'd been. We'd managed so much, Dad and I—and really, how hard could it possibly be?

I picked up one of the reels, walked closer to the projector, and had a look.

I flicked a switch.

Nothing happened.

I pressed a button.

Nothing happened.

A third, a fourth, a fifth switch all gave the same result.

Nothing.

"Is it plugged in?" asked Dad.

I started to laugh. I staggered over to the table and placed the film reel back into the container, and then continued to howl, leaning on my knees.

"That's . . . just . . . fantastic . . . ," I said between bursts of hysterical laughter. "I have a movie theatre . . . I just don't know how to show movies."

Dad chuckled a little. When I'd stopped laughing and wiped the tears off my face, he addressed me in his concerned-but-helpful voice.

"I know he's a bit of a character, but I think you're really going to need to call Rexi."

"He made it pretty clear what he thinks about all this. I'm not going cap-in-hand to that maniac."

Dad sighed.

"You know, the manager at the electronics store is a friend of mine. He showed me one of those digital projectors once. Just plug in your laptop, stick in a DVD. I'm sure he'd let you use one . . . if you gave him some tickets, maybe."

I glared at him.

"Maybe just as a backup? I'm sure Hugo would be happy to help . . ."

"No way, we're going to do it right—or not at all!"

He glowered back at me.

"Then I guess there's only one thing we can do."

Arms folded, we just scowled at each other for a while.

Finally, I threw my arms up. "Fine!"

★ ★ ★

Rexi lived in an apartment around the back of the record store. I'd tried ringing him on the number Dad gave me but had no luck. Instead, I tracked down his address and rang the doorbell.

Eventually, a skinny woman answered.

"He's at the pub," she said, without even asking who I was or what I wanted. She was kind enough, though, to tell me which pub.

I found him, both elbows on the bar, tracing lines through the rings of beer from the bottom of his bottle.

"Hey," he said. "It's Atlas Boy."

"Hey," I replied as cheerfully as I could. "It's Atlas Man."

"Pssht. No such thing any more. Beer?"

"Thanks, but I'm driving."

"Two beers, Olli."

I pulled up the bar stool next to his.

"So," I began.

"So let me guess. The reels arrived and you don't know which end goes in the damn machine."

I laughed, trying to keep it light. He seemed like a human minefield.

"I don't even know how to switch it on."

"Ha!"

Our beers arrived.

"Will you show me, please? I need to know how to work it. I wouldn't expect you to do it on the night, but if you could at least just show me how the machine works, I'd be really grateful."

He growled.

"Have you lost your *Columbo* tape?"

Damn. He hadn't forgotten.

"Listen, I'm sorry. Obviously, I know nothing about being a projectionist. But I do know that . . . Dad would be grateful too. He thinks a lot of you."

"Your dad," he said, spinning his empty beer bottle. "Your dad."

I wasn't sure what to make of that.

"So . . ."

"When do you open?"

"October 26. Next week. It would be great if you could come by before then, though. I mean, we don't even know *if* it works . . ."

"Oh, it works," he said. "The building, yeah, I may have let that slide a little toward the end. But that machine's as good as the day it arrived. Better, even."

"Great. Do you think you could—"

"Did I tell you about the time we had a hundred school kids coming to watch *Home Alone 2,* and the goddamned sound system packed it in? I had an hour to rewire eighteen speakers and get the surround realigned. What do you think I did, Atlas Boy . . . ?"

I reached for my beer—my first since 2016. I had a feeling I'd be walking home.

CHAPTER 34

YOU SPIN ME ROUND
(LIKE A RECORD)

ALTHOUGH there was still plenty to do as the twenty-sixth drew closer, I left the Atlas early the next day so that I'd have time to shower, rewind *Trading Places*, and do everything else I had to do to get ready for my movie night with Sara.

My first stop was Kim's record store. He was sitting on his bar stool behind the counter, as usual. Normally I waited for other customers to leave so I could sit and hang out with my new friend, but I didn't have time for that, so I got straight to the point, ignoring the man who was going through the old Dylans.

"I'm having a friend over tonight, and I'd like to play something that will set the tone just right. Warm but not sexy," I said.

"Interesting, interesting," he said, and rubbed his chin. "Dance?"

"No. Nothing too slow, but no dance beats either."

"Lyrics? Rule the world, or peace on earth?"

"Peace on earth."

"Album or single?"

"An album with a lead single."

Kim smiled and wagged his finger. He lifted the countertop and walked straight to a crate by the door. His fingers carefully but quickly flipped through the albums until he found what he was looking for.

"Not sure what you have in mind, but according to the parameters you just gave me, this is the perfect album for you," he said, and handed me a brown album cover.

It was the *We Are the World* charity album.

"The best artists in the world," Kim said. "Springsteen, Jackson, Dylan . . ."

"Dylan?" said the man from the other side of the store.

"Not for you," said Kim, and turned back to me. "And," he went on, "on the other side, you have Gordon Lightfoot, Neil Young, and Anne Murray!"

"Kim, you're a genius," I said, and we high-fived.

The thought of Sara interrogating me again made me nervous, so I tried to eliminate all the things that had annoyed her. I wore an ordinary pair of jeans and a plain black T-shirt, with no movie taglines or eighties-band logos.

The mullet stayed.

I was also determined to keep the discussion on the movie and away from Jennifer.

An hour before I expected Sara to show up, the phone rang. I tossed my Spectrum on the bed and bolted to the hallway, but when I answered the phone, I heard Mom's voice.

"Oh, hi, Mom," Tina said.

"Hello, Tina," she said. "How are you? How's Sofie?"

"Hi, Tina!" I said. "Mom, you can hang up."

"Sofie's great. Her science project came first today. She's so clever," I heard Tina say.

"Mom, you can hang up," I repeated.

"Okay, okay, hanging up now," she said. I stayed silent until I heard the click on the line and her steps downstairs.

"Okay, here I am, how are you?" I said.

"Great. Good. Pretty good."

I could tell by her voice and the descending value of her well-being that something was up.

"Are you all right?"

"It's just that . . . you know, we may not be able to come to your screening—"

"What? Why?"

"Because it's a Wednesday and it's a long drive and Tim will have work the next day—they have a big staff meeting and Thursdays are a bitch for him . . . you know."

"Actually, I don't know. I get that it's a Wednesday and that it's difficult, but it really would mean a lot to me to have you guys here."

"It's just, you know—"

"Again, I don't know."

"It's not fair if one of us doesn't feel welcome. Then it makes me jumpy and edgy, and you know how I get when I get edgy. The gloves are off."

"Yes, I know that," I said, suddenly feeling very defensive on Mom's behalf. "But perhaps it's not about you. Perhaps you shouldn't always jump down people's throats when you don't know who's done what to upset whom!"

"What? Who *has* done what to upset whom? As far as I know, Mom's been on Timmy's case for a while now. I don't know—do you think she's racist or something?"

266

"No, I don't think she's racist! I think you need to talk to your husband about how he talks about his mother-in-law."

"What? Peter, can you stop being so damn cryptic, please? I know in our family we're incapable of speaking directly about anything, but can you please just say what you mean!? Argh!"

I held my breath, my ear ringing. It wasn't unusual for Tina to yell down the phone at me. But for me to detect a quiver in her voice, the suggestion that she was holding back tears . . . That was unheard of.

"Look, Tim said something snide about Mom's cooking, and she heard him. Something about her cooking like an old hag. You know how she takes pride in that sort of stuff."

"What? Tim would never say that! He loves her cooking. He thought all we Finns ate was rotting herring and salty licorice; he was amazed by her cooking."

"So why say that then?"

"I don't know! I don't know what you're talking about. Besides, it's not like I haven't had to endure years of little put-downs about him, little remarks."

"No. But I bet I know which came first."

"Oh God," she said softly. "This has been stewing for too long. I have to talk to Tim about this."

"Probably a good idea."

"And look, we'll try our best to come. Maybe Tim can drive back late and we'll get the train or something. We'll try."

"Thanks, sis."

"I've gotta go," Tina said, and hung up.

I tiptoed to the hall to put the phone back, and heard Mom's quiet humming from the kitchen.

I still had some time to kill so I dialled up on the BBS to see if Twisted Sister was around. Just seconds after the "I Wanna Rock!"

logo had scrolled up on my TV screen, a chat window popped up. I wondered if Twisted Sister ever left her house.

Hello! What's new? I read the words out loud as they appeared.

Just bought "We Are the World." Your take?

The answer came while I straightened the rug on the floor and opened the narrow ventilation window to let in some fresh air.

Great single, strong album. Lots of top artists. Springsteen and Perry crush it.

I've got someone coming over tonight. Thought it would make a good soundtrack.

Before I hit Enter, I added: *It's not a date.*

Sounds like it. ;o)

I chuckled.

Thanks, Twisted Sister, gotta run.

I had just pressed Enter when I got a new idea and started to type again.

A crazy idea: Would you want to come to my cinema opening in Kumpunotko, Finland, on October 26? This is an official invitation. Would be fun to see you here.

I waited for the reply to come back. Had I overstepped? Was I officially asking Twisted Sister on a date?

Kumpunotko? Finland? Ha ha. Are you kidding me?

I wasn't sure what to make of that. That old uncertainty surfaced; the words in an online chat lacked nuance, and offence could be read into the harmless. Was she mocking my town's name? Admittedly it did sound funny in English, but you try saying "Chicago" in Finnish without it sounding like "Sicker-cow."

All true. It's a little town in Finland. I've renovated the old movie theatre here and will have a grand opening on October 26. Just thought, if you're not doing anything else that day . . .

I waited to be laughed at, to lose one of the only new friends I'd made since this whole adventure began.

Which movie?

"Back to the Future." *Doc Brown is coming too . . . I hope.*

This is too much. Doc Brown in Kumpunotko, Finland? That alone sounds worth the airfare.

I didn't know what to say to that, so I signed off and disconnected the modem from the wall.

CHAPTER 35

TALK TO ME

MID-OCTOBER. The leaves on the trees behind our house had mostly fallen, and through my window I could see that the wind had swept them into a pile underneath the Beetle, which sat patiently in its carport, that sad and put-upon look in its eyes. I saw Sara make her way up the small walkway between the houses. She was looking at each door, searching for ours.

I went downstairs to open the door for her and decided to remind Mom and Dad of my plans. Dad asked me if we needed the big TV, and when I told him we'd watch the movie upstairs in my room, he gave me the thumbs-up from his chair.

"Do you know if she's allergic to anything?" Mom asked.

"I don't, sorry."

"What's her favourite food?"

"I'm not sure."

"Not sure? What kind of a boyfriend are you? Do you know anything about her?"

"Oh, she's not my girlfriend . . . but she likes pizza," I said sheepishly.

"I hope she's not a vegetarian!" Mom said, and disappeared into the kitchen.

A second later she was back, clutching an egg whisk. The doorbell rang.

"That must be her!" she shouted, and clapped her hands, disappearing back into the kitchen.

I opened the door and ushered Sara in. She was wearing a nice Norwegian wool sweater and, if I wasn't mistaken, a little bit of makeup.

"I took the bus; I had a glass of wine earlier. Anyway, here's a little something. I was taught that you should never arrive empty-handed."

She handed me a bag of chips.

"And listen, I'm sorry about giving you the third degree before. I was out of line."

"Don't worry about it. This way, please," I said, but before I had the chance to show her the way upstairs, Mom walked back out of the kitchen, wiping her hands on her apron, her eyes on Sara.

"Peter, aren't you going to introduce us to your friend?" she said.

"Sure, where are my manners?" I said. "Sara, this is my mother. Mom, this is Sara."

"Pleased to meet you," they said in unison, and then Mom added, "I made some warm sandwiches, they're ready."

I couldn't say no to my mother, and Sara obviously didn't want to either, so the four of us sat down and ate the sandwiches.

"How lovely that you two are partners again," said Mom.

Sara and I shared a look. *Partners?*

"You did look wonderful when you danced together," Mom said. "And I do like that you're back in Kumpunotko. It's good for young people to remember where they come from. Your mother must be thrilled too."

"She is. Although she likes to remind me of all the times I vowed to leave town and never come back."

I figured it was time to make our escape, and I tried to signal that to Sara by rolling my eyes, tapping the table, and even making strange head gestures, but she went on chatting with Mom and Dad. Mostly Mom. When Dad had finished his sandwiches, he excused himself and left. A few minutes later, I showed Sara my upstairs room.

She stopped at the threshold.

"This is like stepping inside a time machine," she said. "Everything's so . . . eighties."

"Thanks," I said.

"Maybe you shouldn't take it as a compliment."

Sara walked around my tiny room as if she were making an inspection. She laughed at the *Ghostbusters* and *Purple Rain* posters on the walls, ran her finger over the picture of Axel Foley and marvelled at my ZX Spectrum. Then she noticed the VCR on my desk, next to the fourteen-inch TV screen.

"VHS?" She shook her head. "I hope that's a colour TV at least."

"It sure is," I said.

"This is . . . something else, truly," she said, and sat down on my bed.

I shifted the TV closer to the edge of the desk and turned it so she could see it better. Then I pulled out a cardboard box with all my VHS tapes from under my bed.

"Wait, what? There's more?" Sara said. She was giggling.

She hopped off the bed and got on her stomach on the floor. She reached under my bed and pulled out another cardboard box, the one that was filled with comics. "Hey, I'm not going to find anything naughty in here, am I?"

I feigned outrage—and then wondered if *not* having anything naughty in there made me a little boring. Next she pulled out a box full of junk: newspapers, some tapes I had, and an old electronic typewriter.

"Does that tunnel go all the way to 1979?" Sara asked me.

"Oh, it's just some old stuff. Mom and Dad don't like to throw anything away. Let's roll the tape now, okay?" I sat on the bed with my back against the wall and set the bag of chips Sara had brought between us.

I had seen *Trading Places* a dozen times and thought it was funny every time, but Sara's laughter made it even funnier.

As each of my favourite jokes approached, I watched her out of the corner of my eye to see if she'd find it funny too. I don't know why I felt the need for her affirmation. I mean, *Trading Places* is funny. Fact.

And then my favourite bit came along—Dan Aykroyd as Santa, drunk on the bus, trying to eat a stolen side of salmon through his false beard. Sara was howling with laughter, squirming at the awfulness of it, slapping her thighs and wiping away tears.

It was such a happy vision that I couldn't take my eyes off her, even though I was supposed to be watching Dan Aykroyd.

After the movie was over, I rewound the tape, pressed Eject, and slipped the movie back into its cover. Sara pulled up her feet and crossed them in front of her. She looked me in the eye and sighed, like a parent who doesn't know what to say to her child.

"Listen, Peter, obviously you don't want to talk about what's going on, but you should know that when things bother me, I want to get to the bottom of them. I guess that's part of the training, or maybe why I chose to be a cop. So, please explain." Once again, she gestured around the room.

My silence pushed her on.

"Do you think you might be having some kind of breakdown? Is that why you're in Kumpunotko? And if you are, that's fine, I'm not judging. I want to help you. Really. I'm on your side," she said.

I wanted to choose my words carefully, but I didn't know whether to just tell her everything or try to change the subject. The look on her face made my decision easier: she was not going to let me change the subject.

"Have you ever felt stuck?" I said. "In your life, I mean."

"Maybe."

"Have you ever looked back at the good old days and wondered what might have been?"

"Of course."

"And have you ever just looked at the world and thought that everything's going to hell, that there's trouble everywhere, that . . ."

I stopped and took a deep breath. I smiled.

"See, this is what I'm talking about. I'm getting agitated just speaking about it. Anyway, I always thought things would get better and that there would be progress and then, suddenly, Russia annexes Crimea!"

"Go on," Sara said gently.

"You think humanity's making progress, and then it all slides away. It just got to be too much. Also, you're a policewoman; your work has a purpose. Mine didn't. Nothing I did mattered and nothing was going right."

I paused.

"And what does that have to do with you living with your parents with a picture of Axel Foley on your wall?"

"I don't know. I guess I just thought . . . I was explaining it to Tina—my sister?"

"Yes, I remember Tina."

"I was saying, wouldn't it be great to be able to go back? To be living thirty years ago, but safe in the knowledge that—"

She gasped and put her hand on her mouth, then pointed at me with her other hand.

I nodded.

"Yeah," I said. "That's right. I'm a time traveller."

She began shifting backwards on my bed.

"Listen, listen, I'm not crazy. I know time travel may not be possible. I did a lot of research into building a time machine and I know you probably need a wormhole—which I don't have."

Sara was leaning against the wall now.

"So, basically, you move back in with your parents, into your old room, play with your old computer—"

"Yes, yes, I know all that. But I promise you, I'm not crazy."

"—and you think that by watching old movies and listening to a bit of New Wave you'll actually be back in the eighties? Don't you see the obvious flaw?" Sara said, the softness gone from her voice.

I put my head in my hands. "I'm not crazy, okay?"

"I may not be a doctor, Peter, but I think you are nuts; and that's the technical term for your condition," Sara said. "Nuts."

"I'm just getting away from the problems that torment me. Who doesn't do that?"

"Kind of like an ostrich sticking its head in the sand."

"That's a myth. Ostriches don't do that."

"Let me rephrase it then. You have stuck your head where the sun don't shine."

"Maybe," I said. "Maybe I am nuts, but I'm also happier. I'm ignorant. I haven't got a clue what's going on in the world, and I'm happy. All I have to worry about is getting the Atlas fixed up," I said.

Sara said nothing for a moment.

"And what about Jennifer?"

I cleared my throat.

"What about her? She was an important person in my life back in the eighties, and it's only natural that I'd like to have her in my life."

"But you haven't met her?"

"That is correct."

"And you haven't bothered to even try to find her?"

"That is also correct."

"What's with the movie theatre then? As far as I can remember you didn't own a movie theatre in high school."

"I still don't. I rent it. But yes, I improvised that part."

"And that doesn't mess with the . . . what's it called . . . time-space continuation thing?"

I said nothing. I took my head out of my hands and looked at her.

"Sorry," she said. "It's just that . . . this is the weirdest thing I've ever heard and, somehow, I feel sorry for you."

"You don't need to."

She got up and put on the Norwegian sweater she had taken off when the movie started.

"I have to go home now. Thanks for the movie. It was very funny."

"Hey, let me at least drive you. I'm not sure if the buses will still be running."

"Thank you. That's sweet."

While I was putting on my shoes by the door, Sara said something about having forgotten her purse in my room. She ran up the stairs and came back a moment later.

"Oh, please thank your mother for the sandwiches," Sara said.

"You're very welcome, my dear," Mom shouted from the kitchen.

The evenings had gotten colder, and the Beetle's windshield was foggy. I wiped the fog off with my hand, enough for me to see through my side of the windshield. Sara had her arms wrapped around herself, as if she was cold, or needed comfort.

I turned the key. The car coughed but wouldn't catch. I pumped the gas pedal and turned the key again. Nothing.

"Oops," I said, and tried again.

"Don't flood it, easy on the gas there," Sara said.

"I know, I know."

I tried again, but the Beetle wouldn't start. Then Sara wanted to give it a shot. We switched places, but no matter how forcefully she turned the key, the car showed no signs of life.

"Is there another car you can take?" Sara asked me as we got out of the Beetle.

I stole a glance at Dad's Volvo at the far end of the parking lot. Being from 2014, it didn't exist yet.

"I'm sorry," I said to Sara.

She looked at the shiny Volvo, looked at me, and sighed.

"It's fine," she said, tapping at her phone. "The buses are still running. I'll walk to the bus stop."

We just stood there for a while, looking at each other. Sara shook her head and smiled a little.

"I had fun," I said. "Will I see you again?"

"Oh, you'll see me," Sara said. Then she put her hands in her jacket pockets and headed over to the main road. I watched her disappear behind the neighbour's house, waiting to see if she'd turn around to see if I was there.

She didn't.

When I got back inside, Mom was up, watching TV.

"She seemed very nice," she said. "She reminds me of someone."

"Yeah, Mom, she is really nice. Demi Moore, maybe? But blonde," I replied.

"I was thinking of Doris Day."

I said good night and walked upstairs. I threw the empty bag of chips in the garbage, pulled out my box of comic books from underneath the bed again, and put on the Police's *Synchronicity*. That's when I noticed a small piece of paper on my pillow.

Peter, I don't understand your time travelling, but I do wish you happiness and hope that you get what you want. Here's Jennifer's address. Sara.

CHAPTER 36

WORDS

I grabbed the note, got up, and left my room.

My heart was racing.

I had Jennifer's address.

I hadn't even looked for it, but there it was, in my hand. It was like it was meant to be . . .

When I saw that Mom had turned off the lights downstairs, I took the first stairs three in one and then slid on the handrail the rest of the way, put on the shoes that were fastest to get into—my flip-flops—and snuck out. I got on my Crescent and pedalled toward town.

A few minutes later, there it was, right in front of me. Jennifer's building was on the same street as the high school, only farther away from the square, and closer to the sports centre.

I parked my bike against the wall.

Her building was one of a few high-rises in Kumpunotko, and the only one with an elevator. I knew because I had delivered advertising flyers one summer. I tried to open the front door but it was locked. I pressed my face against the glass door and held my hands close to my eyes to cut the reflections. The hallway was dark, and I couldn't even see the resident directory.

I walked backwards to the other side of the street, my eye on the few apartments where the lights were still on.

"He had almost given up hope, but he knew deep down that one day, destiny would answer . . ."

I saw the curtains move at one of the windows and my pulse quickened. An angry-looking man stared down at me. I froze, thinking that if I didn't move he might not see me. But when I looked up he was still there. He pointed two fingers at his own eyes, and then turned those same fingers and pointed at me.

I ran to my bike and rode away.

BACK home, I got to work on the invitation. I could have rung the doorbell, but that seemed like cheating. And hanging around outside hoping to just "bump into her" seemed more than a bit like stalking, and I didn't want to send that signal.

What I wanted to send was a beautifully crafted invitation that would convey my feelings in a precise manner, that would surprise her and make her curious. I started in longhand, and it took me half an hour just to get a few lines of text on paper. I couldn't get it right. Part of me still wanted the opening night to be a big reveal, in which Jennifer would realize that I was her destiny. So I wanted to be, at best, vague about the sender.

My first draft was a letter informing Jennifer that she had won two tickets to the show in a random draw, but everybody knows that unsolicited prizes are generally not to be trusted, so I trashed that. In draft two, she had won the tickets as a bonus from a book club (that didn't exist), but that was even more dubious. Draft number three was an anonymous letter from a "secret admirer," but that one flew into the garbage can straight away. I pushed the pen and paper away and pulled the Spectrum closer.

It looked at my alarm clock. It was 2 a.m. I heard Dad's snoring from the other bedroom. I should have been sleeping too, but there was too much nervous energy bubbling inside me, so I played a few games of *Thro' the Wall*, then solved another 5 percent of *The Hobbit*.

I quit the game and started to type something—anything—in an effort to see if I was more creative at a keyboard than with a pen and paper. Before I knew it, though, I had dialled up to "I Wanna Rock!"

Twisted Sister had posted something on the message board.

Out of action for a bit. Please keep it clean here.

I slammed my desk, which made the Spectrum jump; as it landed, the BBS program crashed, and I could see just red, blue, and green pixels on the screen. Worried that I had broken my computer—my precious computer!—I frantically turned it off and on again, and when I saw the familiar grey screen with the 1982 copyright notification, I dialled up the BBS so I could reply to Twisted Sister's message.

Just then, a chat popped up on the screen.

Hello, I just posted something on the public board but nice to see you here.

Are you okay? I replied. Generally speaking, I was the one on the receiving end of that question, so it felt nice to deflect the concern elsewhere.

Yes, just going on a trip, ha ha. How are things?

I'm trying to write something but can't get it right.

Write what? A letter? An essay?

A letter.

While I waited for Twisted Sister's replies, I jotted some notes down, but nothing made sense. I wanted it to be short but not too short, witty but also warm, and mysterious but still crystal clear.

Love letter to a ladybug or a cover letter to a job application?

Neither, I typed reflexively, . . . *but maybe closer to a love letter to a ladybug, as you put it.*

The next reply took a long time to hit my screen, so I guessed that either Twisted Sister was thinking, and thinking hard, or it was going to be a long message. Or both.

Pinhead, just write down what's in your heart. Whatever you want to say is in your heart. Just let your fingers dance on that keyboard and let them lead the way. If you really like the ladybug, you have to tell her that. Otherwise, you'll never get anywhere.

I read the message several times; it took so long that Twisted Sister got tired of waiting for my reply.

Pinhead. I have to go. Good luck.

I looked at the different drafts scattered around my desk. I closed the BBS software and stared at the grey screen. And I did what Twisted Sister had said: I let my fingers dance on the keyboard.

Jennifer,

This is Peter, your friend from high school. I'm back in Kumpunotko and heard that you are too. On October 26, at 9 p.m., I'm reopening the Atlas movie theatre.

I have reserved two seats for you for our special screening of Back to the Future, *and I would love to see you there.*

It's been too long since we last spoke.

I first signed it *Love, Peter* but changed my mind, deleted *love*, and wrote *Yours, Peter* instead.

Then I copied the text onto a blank sheet of paper, by hand, folded it carefully, and put it inside a stamped envelope. Jennifer would get it just in time for the premiere.

Perfect.

CHAPTER 37

THE FINAL COUNTDOWN

TOWARD the end of *Back to the Future*, there's a scene in which Marty McFly almost fades from existence because things he's done in 1955 directly impact the events that would have led to his very existence. But when his (future) parents kiss on the dance floor at the "Enchantment Under the Sea" dance, he comes back to life, with a vengeance.

I was that guy.

Just days earlier I had been ready to throw in the towel, but now I was full of energy, taking care of all the things I should have taken care of days and weeks earlier.

With the letter to Jennifer safely in the inside pocket of my jacket, I rode my Crescent around town. First stop was the post office. The letter was too important to be dropped in a roadside mailbox. I wanted to take it as far into the postal system as possible, preferably handing it to the actual mailman.

I was behind a few people in the line. That didn't stress me out at all. I was calm. I even whistled a few bars of Europe's "The Final Countdown," although I had to stop when the man in front of me turned. The frown on his face turned into a smile when he saw that the person whistling into his ear was me.

"Hey, kid, how's the movie business?" he asked, and slapped me on the shoulder.

It was Erik the Electrician, and I felt really pleased to see him. Like he wasn't just Dad's friend, he was my friend too.

"When's the big day?" he asked.

"Wednesday," I said, a grin on my face.

"Can't wait. Your dad promised me a few tickets, you know."

"Oh. Of course, absolutely," I said, nodding.

"I'm sure you're in a hurry. You can go before me," he said, and gestured me forward.

From the post office, I rode straight to the local paper, Kumpunotko's *Sun*. It wasn't a seven-day newspaper, but its Sunday issue was delivered to practically every household in town, and there was no better way to spread the news about the Atlas.

I locked my bike to a No Parking sign and walked into the office. It was in the same building as La Favorita, in a small second-floor office with only two windows, both of which faced the backyard. There was no reception, and no receptionist, but I had barely gotten through the door when a middle-aged lady, about to scurry past me, saw me and stopped in mid-stride.

"Yes?" she said, and smiled.

"I'd like to place an ad in the paper, in Sunday's issue."

"This Sunday?"

I nodded.

"Too late, I'm afraid."

"Too late?"

"Too late. We've already sent most of the pages to the printers. Unless you have a print-ready PDF, with crop-marks and bleed," she said.

"Hmm. And there's no way to get something in the paper? No way?" I said.

She shook her head, sadly.

Right then, a man walked into the room. When he saw me, he, too, stopped.

"Peter?"

He was shorter and fatter, and his hair was in a strange pony-tail, but it was definitely him.

"Matti?"

"Hey, how are you doing?" said my old boss, coming over to grab me in an enthusiastic hug. "I heard you were back in town. How's the Atlas going? And how's your old man? You take it easy on him, will ya? Oh, and if Rexi starts to boss you around, just tell him you know his big brother."

"If I see him I will. He's supposed to be coming to show me how to work the projector."

"Rexi—a law unto himself." He turned to the lady. "This guy's going to reopen the old movie theatre," he said.

"Interesting," said the lady. She turned to me. "Why haven't we written about you? My name is Minna. Can I interview you now?"

"I guess."

"That way you'll get your story in Sunday's paper too. Matti, we can just bump the story about the hockey-playing dogs, right?"

"Sure."

"Great. Let's go to the conference room. It's a little quieter there."

"I'll see you later," said Matti. "Rexi said you'd get us tickets."

AN hour later, having told most of my story to Minna (leaving out the stuff about my miserable life in Helsinki, being a time traveller, hoping to bump into Jennifer, et cetera), I pedalled as hard as I could to get to the Atlas on time to meet the guys who were delivering my new sign. As it turned out, the *T* had been damaged beyond repair, and it was so old-fashioned that it would have been more expensive to attempt to replace it with something similar than it was to just buy a whole new sign. Even so, it was more expensive than I'd expected. I'd finally braced myself and called the bank to check my balance. It wasn't looking good, though I wasn't quite in the red yet. And so I'd allowed myself one little (big) luxury and splashed out on a new sign. I knew Dad was going to be at the theatre, but seeing the sign go up was a moment I didn't want to miss.

When I closed my eyes and dreamed about the Atlas, seeing the red neon sign glow in the dark was the second thing that came to mind.

Dad and I stood outside, Mom's sandwiches in our hands, and admired the new neon sign, with its cursive *Atlas*, going up on top of the canopy.

"Almost there, Peter," Dad said.

"Almost. Have you talked to Rexi?"

"Haven't heard from him since the other day."

"There's going to be a story in the paper on Sunday," I told him.

"Excellent. Rexi's brother runs the paper now."

"I know. I just saw him. He also told me you had promised Rexi some tickets. And Erik."

"I did, I did. You don't mind, do you?"

"No, I don't mind. I don't even know how people can book tickets. Except by talking to you, I guess," I said, and laughed. "I do have the tickets, though. And I'll buy candy and soda next week."

"Are you nervous?"

"About the opening? A little bit," I said, refining Dad's question so I could tell him the truth. The screening made me a little nervous; thinking about Jennifer showing up plunged me into a pool of anxiety.

"Good. Nerves will make sure you pay attention. Come on, I want to show you something."

I followed him as he made his way inside, walked up to the cassette player, turned the volume button all the way up, and pressed Play. The theatre echoed with a familiar bass line, shortly followed by a delightful tambourine that opened the door to the singer.

Dad clapped his hands and did some slow upper-body dance moves, his eyes closed as he swayed to the sounds of "You Can't Hurry Love." I was astonished to hear he had chosen the Phil Collins cover from the eighties, not the Supremes' original.

"I like this version," Dad said.

I laughed. "Is that what you wanted to show me? That you've developed better taste in music?"

"Ha! No—this."

He pulled the hammer from his utility belt and then drew a few nails from his breast pocket. He got down on his knees and hammered a row of nails across the seam of the carpet, to stop it from bunching at the bottom of the slope, as it had been doing since we first arrived at the Atlas. He then stood up, gave a little wiggle to check it was holding firm, and put the hammer back into his utility belt. I watched all this with quiet intrigue.

"GREAT SCOTT!" Dad shouted. "We're done!"

There he was, a crazy-haired man in white overalls, doing a little dance and pumping his fists in the air.

"What's that, Dad?"

"That's it. That was the last thing. That bit of carpet—it's been annoying me since we got here. I mean, maybe you need to stock the fridge or something, but as far as I'm concerned, we're done," he said.

"But, what about 'Great Scott'?"

"What? Who?"

"You just yelled 'Great Scott!'"

"I did no such thing," Dad said with a laugh. "I don't think I said anything."

It occurred to me that maybe I had been exposed to paint fumes too often over the last few weeks. But I knew what I had seen. I had seen Doc Brown.

I had seen Doc Brown! I didn't need Christopher Lloyd; I had my very own Doc.

"Anyway, I'm proud of you, you know." He put his arm around my shoulder. "I've always said, if you put your mind to it, you can accomplish anything."

I said nothing.

I was speechless.

I knew that putting up the sign was like turning on the Bat-Signal. It would tell the whole town that the Atlas was back, and because I wanted to savour the moment, I decided to wait until Monday—a couple of days before the screening—before I let it shine. I closed the side door, and Dad and I drove home.

In the darkness of the car, with Sade playing in the background, Dad and I chatted about the little things we still had to do.

"Rexi is important, because without a film, there's nothing," I said.

"Right, but he'll be there."

"Are you sure? He seems a bit unreliable."

"Rexi is a lot of things, but I wouldn't call him unreliable."

Dad must have phoned ahead and told Mom the news, because

when we got home she had a surprise waiting. My favourite food for dinner—meatballs with smashed potatoes. And once I'd eaten that, Dad got up from the table and walked off into the study. He came back with something behind his back.

"You can tell me if you don't like it."

"He'll love it, dear, of course he will."

"Nonsense. Peter, this is your project, and I for one know how important these things are. Perhaps the most important thing of all, because if nobody comes there's no point even having the reels and the seats and the candy."

"Just show him!"

"Yeah, Dad, just show me."

"Okay."

He pulled from behind his back an A3 sketchpad. He set it in front of me and opened it up.

There, in faint pencil sketch, with sharp ink lines over top, was a rendering of Marty McFly, looking at his watch and holding open the gull-wing door of the DeLorean DMC-12. The picture was drawn in Dad's own style, and looked like something from a DC Comics graphic novel. Emblazoned across the top, in lettering true to the original film poster, was *He's BACK!* Under the image, in smaller font, Dad had neatly written out the date and time of the showing. *At the Atlas Movie House*, it said along the bottom. *For a limited time only.*

I wasn't sure what to say.

I didn't know how to . . .

Dad had . . .

"I copied the poster, you know, from the internet."

"Do you like it?" asked Mom, but I couldn't reply because I couldn't speak.

"Hey," she said. "Be careful you don't drip tears on it!"

She gripped my shoulder tightly, her other hand on Dad's. By our family's standards, it was pretty much a group hug.

WHEN I'd brushed my teeth, I went back downstairs. Dad was sitting in his TV chair but the set was quiet; he was reading a sci-fi novel. Mom was in her chair, working on a crossword puzzle. Dean Martin or Bing Crosby or someone (I found it hard to tell them apart) was crooning softly in the background.

"Dad?"

"Mm?"

"Can I ask you one more favour?"

"Wow, you don't ask for much, do you?"

"Will you be my Doc Brown? I invited him—the actor—but I don't think he's going to make it."

"Is he the hero?"

"Yes, very much so. Without him, there's nothing."

"Then yes, I will."

"Fantastic. And I was thinking, maybe Tim could be Biff."

Mom looked up sharply. "Are they coming?"

It wasn't anxiety in her voice. It was hope.

"I hope so, Mom. I think so. Maybe."

"And who can I be?" she asked.

"Actually, I was hoping you'd run front-of-house. Selling tickets, you know? Only Dad's given most of them away to his friends, so I'm not sure there'll be much for you to do. But you can definitely dress up. You and Tina."

"That would be nice," she said.

★ ★ ★

BACK in my room, I took out my plan. I grabbed my BBB pencil.

1. Get Atlas.
2. Fix Atlas.
3. ~~3.~~ *Open with a sneak preview of* Back to the Future.
4. ~~4. Invite Jennifer~~

"You have cleared 75 percent of the adventure," I said in my computer voice. So why did it feel like I still had so much to do?

CHAPTER 38

MANIC MONDAY

O N Monday morning, I got in the Beetle and drove to the library. Mom had phoned ahead and spoken to her former colleague, who smiled secretively and pointed me toward the photocopier. It was a huge white behemoth, with in-trays and out-trays and all the latest scanners and features.

"I'm sorry, I don't know how . . ."

She sighed and left her little book trolley parked at the end of a row, and then came over to help. She was a tall lady in her fifties, I guess. She wore lots of natural fibres and smelled nicely of mint. I stood back and twiddled my thumbs.

"So, movie posters, right? How many?"

"Is twenty okay?"

"Are you sure?" she said severely.

"Ten?"

"Don't be ridiculous. How are you going to tell the whole town? I'll do you fifty. But don't tell anyone. Our budgets are being slashed left, right, and centre, and they make us use these cards so they can track who uses the machines the most. Who knew Big Brother cared about copier budgets?"

She slid three different cards from her pocket and chose which one to use. "I think the town planning department can pay for these," she added with a smirk.

Ten minutes later she shoved the pile of posters into my arms and shooed me away, heading nonchalantly back to her book redistribution task.

"Oh, Peter," she called as I neared the exit. I turned. "Your mother said something about putting me down for a couple of tickets."

I grinned and left, stopping only to stick up my first poster on the library notice board. As I did so I noticed that Dad had added a little something over the weekend. In the top corner, set in a bold star, were the words: *Meet the superstar: DOC BROWN.*

I sighed. I couldn't have that on the poster. What if people turned out to see him? What if they got angry that the Hollywood star wasn't there?

I thought of heading back into the library and telling the nice lady I'd dropped all my posters in a puddle, and could I have some more please. And then colouring in the star so it just looked blank on the next batch of copies. But that was all a bit far-fetched. Besides, it wasn't even raining.

Surely nobody would notice.

Next stop, the supermarket. I stocked up on juice, water, and soda. We didn't have a soda machine, so we'd have to sell it out of bottles, by the cupful. I bought the biggest cups they had. We also didn't have a booze licence, so I rolled the trolley past the beer section without a second glance. I figured if people wanted to bring booze, they would just sneak it in like people have always done in cinemas. I threw in candies of all shapes and sizes, filling the trolley with stuff. I knew I was being reckless with money, but I was so close to my goal that none of that mattered any more. Besides, cinemas tend to charge about quadruple what shops charge for candy, so as long as people showed up, surely I would make my money back.

I put a couple of posters up around the parking lot at the supermarket and then, with the Beetle fully loaded, I headed back to the Atlas to unload.

On my way there, I stopped at Kim's to leave a poster for him to put in his window.

"Can't I have two? One for the window, one for my memorabilia collection? This is history in the making, dude."

The market square was half deserted. Some of the vendors had already left, and the ones still there had started to pack up their tents and caravans. On the same side where the taxi drivers wait was a big notice board, and I taped up two posters there.

I was on my knees with a roll of tape in my mouth, about to stick another poster on an electric utility box, when I felt somebody tap my shoulder. I struggled to get up, but before I could see the person behind me, I recognized her voice.

"Drop everything! You're in violation of the town code, paragraph forty-one, subsection twelve."

It was Sara, in her police uniform again. I took the poster down with the hand that was behind my back, away from her.

"How are you?" I asked.

"Not many days left now. I saw the story in the paper. No mention of you being a time traveller, though."

"No," I said. I didn't want to elaborate.

"Let me see the poster," she said, and grabbed the one in my hand. I didn't struggle, given that she was a cop.

"This is awesome. Did you draw this?"

"Dad did."

"But you never told me Doc Brown is going to be here. That's huge! It's probably the biggest thing that's ever happened to Kumpunotko," she said. "A real Hollywood star—are you kidding me? You might even get the network channels here!"

I swallowed. Sara noticed.

"What's wrong?"

I sighed and shook my head.

"Doc Brown is Dad."

"What?"

"The Doc Brown that's going to be at the premiere is my father. Not Christopher Lloyd, the award-winning actor. I wrote to him, but he never responded. It's Dad. My dad," I said, with enough panic in my voice for Sara to pick up on. "Let's hope the networks *won't* be here."

"I'd kind of like to see that: your father giving interviews, signing things, waving to crowds, kissing babies."

Sara paused.

"Look, the poster doesn't say that the actor, what's his name—"

"Christopher Lloyd."

"—Christopher Lloyd is going to be there, just that Doc Brown will be. And he will!"

"But if the networks come . . ."

"So what?"

"Then when he's not here they'll go away again."

"So? You're not doing this for the fame, are you? It's not even about the money, as far as I can tell, is it?" Sara looked me straight in the eye.

I cleared my throat and started to fiddle with my backpack, hoping for a change of subject. Sara gave me one.

"Listen," she said. "I just came from the Atlas because I was looking for you. I wanted to give you this, as a good luck charm—or something."

She handed a small red box to me. It had a golden ribbon around it. I opened it quickly.

"I wasn't sure if you already had it but . . ."

"I don't! I actually never owned this," I replied and took the *Back to the Future* soundtrack cassette from the box.

"Something for you to listen to on your headphones while you ride . . . although as a police officer I should warn you that riding on the road without due care and attention—"

"I love it! It's perfect, thank you."

"So . . . friends?"

"Of course," I said, stunned by her question.

"I know I said some harsh things over at your place, and that was probably stupid. Sorry, but it's part of the training; I don't really do small talk, and tend to just get to the point. So I'm sorry for calling you crazy," Sara said. "Even if you clearly are," she added with a grin.

"No harm done. I know you mean well. And I probably do need to be told. I appreciate it, I really do."

"Good luck with the show. Truly. I hope you get whatever it is you want. And, well, I've enjoyed bumping into you around town . . ."

"We can still . . . ," I started. "Wait, you're not coming?"

"I'm not sure if that's a great idea."

"You *have* to be there. I'll give you two tickets, on me. Please come?"

She smiled.

"Well, if you insist . . ."

"I do."

"Great! See you there."

I waited until Sara's cruiser had disappeared around the corner before I taped the poster on the box. I was lightning quick with them, taping one on La Favorita's door, two outside the bookstore, several on the various bus stops around the town centre, and a few on the posts holding up traffic signs. The man at the appliance store wasn't interested, he told me, in promoting other interests, but the lady at the coffee shop was happy to put one up, as long as I bought a hot chocolate. I put two up in the movie poster frames outside the Atlas, on either side of the door. I unloaded the drinks and candies into the foyer, and spent a while writing up a price list on a large sheet of paper.

No Rexi.

I drove around Kumpunotko, stopping here and there and wandering around neighbourhoods, putting posters up on community notice boards and bus stops. I went and knocked on Rexi's door. No answer. I went around the pubs of Kumpunotko, and though the staff were all happy to put up my posters, none of them had seen Rexi.

As it got dark, and I ran out of posters, I headed home.

I lay in bed that night, pondering the imponderable: if Rexi didn't show up to teach me how to work the projector, would I compromise everything and use a digital projector, laptop, DVD?

It was an agonizing decision, but I knew the answer.

The screening must go ahead.

THE next morning I woke up early, too early, and felt like I hadn't slept. I tried to get back to sleep, chasing the slumber deep under the pillows, but I couldn't find it.

I showered and dressed and left the house quietly, Dad's snores punctuated by the tick of the kitchen clock.

There was barely anyone about as I rode along the cycle path, through the town, and up the hill to the hospital. I barely had to change down a gear now, and I made it to the hospital parking lot with my heart thumping but not trying to explode out of my chest. I stood on the wall and looked down at my sleepy little town, delivery vans chugging about, the earliest commuters heading out of town for jobs elsewhere.

I got back on my bike and rolled down the hill.

First job: investigate digital projectors.

I walked my bike around the corner to the Atlas's side door. A man was standing there, leaning against a car, his hands in his pockets, bald head shining in the sun.

"Okay, kid, let's do it."

"Let's," was all I could say. I opened the door and followed Rexi up to the projection booth.

CHAPTER 39

EVERYBODY WANTS TO RULE THE WORLD

REXI walked in with an air of authority, as if he owned the place. He took off his coat and hung it on a chair, and then rolled up his sleeves. He closed his eyes, spread his arms, and took a deep breath.

"Can you feel it in the air?" he asked me, his eyes still shut.

"What's that . . . sir?"

"Movie magic," he said, and exhaled. "Movie magic."

Rexi opened his eyes and clapped his hands. "Okay, enough of that clap-trap! Let's get to work."

He looked at the film reels on the round table and then walked around the projector, flicking switches and opening compartments I hadn't noticed and then slamming them shut. He made "do-bi-do" sounds, and snapped his fingers, and then, with a sniffle, turned to talk to me.

"I love this machine," he said, and slapped the projector. "I don't care what anyone says about the printing press, the telephone, the modem; this machine changed the world."

I tried to look suitably impressed.

"Anyway, I have good news and bad news," Rexi said. "Which one do you want to hear first?"

"The . . . the bad news," I stuttered.

"Okay. The bad news is that you'll never be able to put these reels together."

I sighed and buried my face in my hands.

"And the good news?" Rexi said quietly. "The good news is that you've come to the right guy. Well, that and the fact that some *genius* decided to invest in a platter system, even though this wasn't a multiplex." The volume of his voice went up with every word toward the end of the sentence.

"Would that genius have been you?"

He waved away my praise.

"And what exactly is a platter?"

"That large pizza plate over there," he said, and gestured loosely toward what I'd thought was a large table.

"See, back in the old days, I had to be here in the projection booth and make the reel and projector changes, and there was no margin for error. If I missed a change, the audience would have been left gawping at a white screen."

This was what happened in the episode of *Columbo*, but I thought it best not to mention that.

"Of course, I never made a mistake. I could have made a projector change in my sleep, my eyes closed, one hand tied behind my back."

I nodded politely. I wasn't following Rexi's train of thought, but the last thing I wanted to do was say something he'd interpret as an insult, causing him to storm out and leave me in the booth. I was, however, starting to wonder if he'd ever get around to showing me which was the Play button.

"But then came these platters—those things, the non-rewind

systems," he said, and again nodded toward the large table. "That way, the projectionist could put the movie together in advance. Then you only needed to do it once. You just splice the reels together and play it, and since the film runs all the way around, there's no rewinding, no changing of reels."

"Oh. That sounds easy enough."

Rexi looked at me. He looked tired and his face was lined, but there was a fiery intensity burning in the centre of his pupils. He smiled a crooked smile, shrugged his shoulders, and took a step toward the door.

"I guess you won't be needing me then," he said.

"No!" I shouted. "I mean, please don't go. I didn't mean it that way, just that it must have been easy for somebody like yourself." I pulled out my little diary and a pen. "I don't expect I'll remember it all. I mean, how could I? Don't worry, I'll take notes."

He pursed his lips, and when he thought I'd squirmed sufficiently he nodded and resumed his lecture.

"Well, kid, even with the spliced reels there's still a craft to it, still no margin for error. It's not just about the assemblage. You do all that in advance. But you've got focus, aperture, light levels. And God forbid you ever dropped one of those things," he said, pointing to the reels. "I know other theatres had two men do the assembling, but I always did it by myself," he said.

"Why two men?"

"Because they weigh so much," Rexi said coolly.

He looked at his wrist as if to check the time, but he wasn't wearing a watch.

"You know what time is?" he asked. "It's time to get to work." He grabbed one of the film reel canisters and read the title of the movie that was written on it. "*Back to the Future*? Good choice."

"Hey, Mr. Rexi, sir, what can I do?"

302

"You can get me a cup of coffee. Large. Black."

Then he opened the first canister and got to work. I put my diary back in my pocket and scurried away.

ONE cup of coffee wasn't quite enough for Rexi who, three times, sent me out for more. When I wasn't on a coffee run, I sat next to Rexi in the projection booth, listening to his war stories, careful not to touch anything, move anything, or do anything unless specifically told to do it.

When he took off his olive-green army jacket, I could see large sweat stains under the arms of his brown-khaki T-shirt.

"Are you sure there isn't anything I can do?" I asked him.

"I've got this," he said, like a bomb disposal expert hovering over the task at hand, eyes fixed, hands steady. "It's just that each one of these reels has to be spliced and transferred on to the plat-ter, so it takes some time," he added, and bobbed his head toward the pile of film canisters. "I could do it quicker, but I want to do it right."

"What if the film breaks?" I asked him.

Rexi laughed. "It won't. I've tried to break it by pulling it apart as hard as I can; even I couldn't do it." I got the feeling I could trust him on that one. "And then, once I've done this, you're set. I'll add the auditorium light cues as well," he went on.

"Okay, great. Thanks," I said, writing *light cues* down in my notes. "Is there anything you'd like me to do?"

"Why don't you get me a cup of coffee?"

I put on my jacket, again, and walked to the gas station, again. Downtown Kumpunotko had gotten quieter with each of my coffee runs, and now the streets were completely deserted, not a person in sight. The sun had set a couple of hours earlier, and

303

when I looked at the clock on top of the bank building, its big red digital numbers shone in the darkness: 6:05.

I walked back with a large paper mug in my hand. When I got within a couple of blocks of the Atlas, I stopped to admire it from afar. The streetlights shed some light on the façade, and the light from the lobby came beaming out through the glass door, creating dramatic shadows. The cinema was alive again; it was the place to be, where people could come to forget their worries, escape from reality, go on an adventure with their friends and dream themselves away with a loved one. It was a bittersweet feeling, knowing that all of this was only temporary.

I looked at the big clock again, and that's when it struck me.

It was 6:11, but that wasn't it. It was the way the clock glowed over the market square that stirred something inside my brain.

It was time. It was time to tell the good people of Kumpunotko that the Atlas was back. I ran in through the side door, straight through the little corridor, and into the lobby, where I found the switch for the neon sign.

It was only a little switch, an old-fashioned turn-switch, but somehow it felt like it represented the culmination of everything I'd set out to do—well, not *everything*, obviously, but since I'd first looked through the grime-streaked lobby windows and seen my old movie theatre in a state of ruin, it had all been building toward this. I'd set out to accomplish something, and it had worked.

I turned it on.

Nothing.

But that's because I was inside the building.

I jogged back through the theatre, out the side door, along the alley, and onto the street.

And there it was, glowing bright across the town.

Atlas.

"He was back," I narrated. I ran a few steps back and forth and even let out a scream, like Doc Brown after he's sent Marty back to the future, and in the process, spilled Rexi's coffee on my hand. I hurried back to give it to him before it got cold.

He was still hunched over the side table, assembling the movie. I put the cup down on the table in front of him.

"Thanks," he said without lifting his eyes from the film.

He spent another few minutes focusing on a very precise piece of celluloid.

"Hey, listen, there's somebody here to see you. Got in just after you left. Downstairs," he said.

"Oh, okay. That's weird," I said, and left the booth. Partly weird that someone—probably Sara—was back to see me. Partly weird that Rexi had let me stand there for five minutes before he told me.

I walked back downstairs and checked the lobby—still empty—then headed for the auditorium. I couldn't see anyone, at first.

"Hello?"

"Hello, friend," said a voice in the dark.

My heart skipped a beat and then went into overdrive. My legs were like cooked spaghetti, my mouth was dry, and all I could hear was a whooshing sound in my ears as all the blood in my body went rushing through my head in every direction at once.

"I'm sorry. I mean, it's me, Jennifer," she said, clearing her throat. "From high school?"

She was leaning against the column, her hands behind her back, her long overcoat open. Her hair was shoulder-length, and it cast a shadow on her face. "Jennifer?" I managed a whisper. I stood in one place, my arms by side, not moving, a silly grin on my face. "Jennifer *Berg*?"

She smiled and stepped into the half-light.

"I got this invitation in the mail," she began. "I just wanted to stop by to make sure it was really you. Peter *Eksell.*"

She held her arms out, and I stepped forward into them. She pulled me into a polite hug. She smelled of a soft perfume; I couldn't quite place it. As if speaking would have destroyed the magic, I just nodded, vigorously, and then out came a whisper, "Yep. It's me."

She let go of me and stepped back.

"How was Paris?" I blurted, and she burst out laughing.

Her skin looked smooth, her hair cut to create a dark frame around her beautiful face. Around her neck, under a silk scarf, was a simple golden chain. She was wearing black dress pants, in a very Diane Keaton kind of way, and like the true lady I knew her to be, a pair of black leather gloves.

"It was very sweet of you to think of me. Thank you," she went on. Her voice was deeper now. It still had the same sweetness, but underlined with maturity. There was a huskiness to it, like peppered honey. "I hope it's okay that I came by; I know the invitation said Wednesday. I'll come, of course. It was just such a surprise!"

"You look . . . fantabulous." I finally managed to get some words out of my mouth.

Jennifer blushed and looked at her feet.

"Thank you. You look good too, Peter. It's been a while."

"Thirty years," I said, almost in my movie-trailer voice.

"And now you run the movie theatre. That's great. You always did love movies. It's like it was meant to be."

"*Supergirl,*" I said, and then chided myself. Why was I only capable of grunting single words? In the old days, Jennifer was the only one who'd made me feel at ease, the only girl in school I could speak to without mumbling. I cleared my throat. "Remember when we came here and watched *Supergirl*?"

"That's right! We sat over there," Jennifer said, and pointed at the row behind her. She let out a nervous giggle and played with her hair. The giggle made me relax. It was the same old infectious Jennifer giggle that had always made me laugh.

"And you wondered why her hair changed colour whenever she put on her superhero suit."

"Oh yes! Isn't it funny the things we remember."

"I can't believe you're standing there. Jennifer Berg! I mean, I hoped you could come to the premiere, but . . . I think I'm in a state of shock."

She giggled again. "Anyway, I just wanted to stop by and thank you for the invitation," she said, and pressed her hands against her chest, one on top of the other. "I won't keep you longer, I'm sure you have a lot of work to do."

"Oh, it's fine."

"I should be going, though." She buttoned her overcoat and picked up her purse from the floor.

"Of course," I said. "Thanks for coming. I'll walk you out. You've been here before, I know, but still."

"Ever the gentleman," she said with a grin.

We walked up the corridor, Jennifer in front, me two steps behind. She pushed the door open and the cool autumn air blew her hair onto her face.

She brushed it aside and turned around.

"I'll see you tomorrow then. Good luck, Peter."

I stood by the door and watched her as she walked to the sidewalk and turned back to look at me. Then she waved, wiggling her fingers, and disappeared around the corner.

I stood at the door for a long time, hoping that the cool air would clear my head and settle my heartbeat.

It didn't.

I walked back inside and stopped at the exact spot where Jennifer had stood, replaying my painstakingly embarrassing lines in my head over and over again.

"They say no battle plan survives contact with the enemy," I narrated. "His plan didn't even survive contact with a friend."

I climbed the stairs to the projection booth to see how Rexi was getting on with his assembly of the reels.

"That went well," he said, "I guess."

"Yeah?"

"Yeah. I think she likes you. Anyway, I'm done. Do me a favour. Go sit downstairs in the centre seat."

I didn't need to be asked twice.

I skipped down the stairs two at a time, ignoring that annoying sweaty smell that still lingered in the little corridor, and pushed through into the auditorium.

As I sat down in the best seat in the house, the curtains began to glide open.

The screen, usually a dull grey, jumped to life: first a luminous silver-white, then a rich, deep black.

There was a crackling *woof* from all around as the speakers hummed into action.

A scratchy scribble of letters appeared on the screen, totally out of focus, and I think I heard Rexi swearing. Then the letters came into focus.

Universal Pictures, Inc.
Universal Pictures, Europe, GmbH.
Universal European Distribution, SARL.

Next, a large diamond shape appeared with a square inside it, and a circle inside that. The circle was like a sniper's scope, with alignment lines top to bottom and side to side. And inside that circle was a number 5, which became a 4, then a 3, 2—

Then it all cut, and the curtains began to close.

I heard Rexi shuffling around upstairs.

"We're good, kid. She's loaded and ready to go. Time for a beer."

I locked up and rode home, my head spinning and my heart beating faster than ever before. Just before I got to our street, I took a sharp right toward the football pitch. I threw my bike onto the ground and started to run toward the stands, and then up into them, hopping from one row to the next. Once I got to the top, I ran on the spot for a few steps, and then—in a glorious *Rocky* moment—raised my arms toward the sky.

CHAPTER 40

UNDER PRESSURE

W HEN I woke up on the day of the big event, my mind was at ease. I was so calm that it scared me; it occurred to me that I might be in a coma. I lingered in bed for a while, trying to come up with the thing I had forgotten to take care of, but I couldn't think of anything.

I played back my meeting with Jennifer. While I'd basically wanted the ground to open up and swallow me, I thought that my general muteness had at least prevented me from saying anything I might regret.

I could hear noises from downstairs, the sound of people talking, but the voices didn't sound like Mom and Dad's. The sun was shining into my room, casting a long shadow of the TV onto the poster in which the monkeys were playing poker with big grins on their faces.

I looked at my clock radio. It was 11:02 a.m. I had slept for more than twelve hours, probably for the first time since my teens. I dragged myself out of bed, picked up my jeans from the floor, and climbed into them. I felt a familiar lump in one of the pockets.

Since being pulled over by the cops, I had carried the Time Machine with me. I knew it by heart by now, and I reread it again, muttering the words, almost as if it were holy scripture. Then I folded both letters and put them back in my pocket.

I considered loading up *The Hobbit*. I'd gotten to 82.5 percent of the adventure before I'd passed out last night. It would have been nice to get it all done today, would have felt significant somehow, but I decided not to. Today there were more important things than computer games.

When I walked downstairs to get some breakfast, Mom was at the kitchen table working on a newspaper crossword puzzle. Dad was sitting in his TV chair, watching a movie. A musical refrain caught my attention, and I whipped my head around to see Marty driving the DeLorean to the start line Doc had painted across the street.

"Are you watching *Back to the Future*?" I asked. "Spoiling it for tonight!"

"I wanted to see who the Doc person was," Dad replied. "I don't think I've ever seen this movie."

"Well, what do you think?"

"It's fantastic so far—don't tell me how it ends," he said, and raised the volume. I glanced at the TV and saw Doc hanging from the clock tower.

"Won't say a word. What do you think of Doc?"

"He's the best. I'm just not sure about that Biff character."

"Biff!" I said, and slapped myself on the forehead.

I ran upstairs, dialled a number, and, like Michael Jackson on a dance floor, spun into my room to talk to Tina. I had told her about my idea that Tim could dress up as Biff, and she'd said she would discuss is with him, but she hadn't got back to me. She also still hadn't told me for sure if they were even coming. I knew she wouldn't want to let me down; I also knew she and Mom were still trying to out-stubborn one another. I realized that in my rush to paint walls and get forms stamped, I'd left it too late to fix my own family before the big night.

Why hadn't that been on my list? Jennifer—yes; Atlas—yes; mother and sister can barely talk to one another—deal with it later.

The phone rang eleven, twelve times. No answer. I waited another ten seconds, and then hung up and dialled the same number again, standing next to the phone. Still no answer.

I put the phone down and shouted down the stairs.

"Mooooom! Have you talked to Tina lately?"

"No!" she shouted back.

"We're just going out," called Dad. "Do you need anything?"

"No thanks," I shouted back down.

I went back into my room. Suddenly, I had a splitting head-ache and felt slightly sick to my stomach. In the bathroom I ran my wrists under the tap and did some deep breathing. That seemed to calm me down.

It was just nerves, surely. Last-minute nerves. Tina was sure to come . . . right?

I decided to distract myself with some final admin work.

On my desk was the set of mustard-yellow perforated tickets I had bought at the bookstore. Next to it was Dad's list of people he'd promised tickets to. I sat down to finally count them.

There were forty-two names on the list. I had seen about a dozen of them at the Atlas, doing different things, delivering machines or other things, talking to Dad outside the storage room. With two tickets each, and five to Rexi, that was eighty-nine.

Then there was Mom and Dad, Sara plus one, Kim plus one, and of course the owner of La Favorita, to whom I'd promised a couple of tickets when he'd let me put up the poster. Plus the library lady's two. And Tina and Sofie. And Tim. And Jennifer's two. And me.

There weren't going to be many left to sell to the good folks of Kumpunotko.

I dialled Tina's number again. Still no answer.

I resumed my counting. Eighty-nine plus . . . I tapped each name on my own list with a pencil and counted them one by one, ninety, ninety-one, . . . ninety-three, . . . one-oh-four.

I didn't have a ticket sales problem because I basically didn't have any seats left.

My headache was getting worse. I could hardly move, but I had to try Tina's number again. I let it ring until the line was disconnected. They didn't even have an answering machine—were they living in the past or something?

A little voice in my head: "Why don't you just call her cellphone?"

I shook my head. Not her cellphone, that was impossible.

"Oh, *come on*. Surely this is more important."

I shook my head again.

Even if I'd wanted to, I couldn't call the cellphone. I remembered the number of Tina's landline because I'd dialled it so often. I had no idea what her cell number was. I'd never physically dialled it; it was stored on my own cellphone, which was locked in my garage in Helsinki.

I walked slowly into the bathroom and took a painkiller. When I got back to my room I put on my headphones and lay on the bed. When I woke up two hours later, the house was still empty and the sun was about to disappear behind the horizon.

I took a quick shower and then got into my premiere costume.

I had given my clothes a lot of thought. I'd tried my best to look the part since being back in the eighties, and I didn't think I was a particularly vain person, but nobody puts on a gala screening at the reopening of the town's second-biggest cinema without at least wanting to look smart. A part of me wanted to go with a tuxedo to complete the circle. After all, that's what I'd worn on the red carpet when I first saw *Back to the Future* at the sneak preview.

But I was meant to be Marty. The guy I'd spent a good portion of the eighties (and, let's be honest, my whole life) wanting to be.

I took out my Guess jeans. The ones I'd tried on back in the garage when Tina had given me her makeover. The ones I'd actually worn, back in school. The ones I hadn't fit into since college.

I sat on the bed and gave them a shake. Put my left leg in, and then my right leg. Stood, up, pulled them up, and fastened the button fly.

The pants sat loosely around my waist. Almost too loosely. My morning rides on the Crescent had done wonders, even with all of Mom's cooking. I was back.

I didn't want to be seen with my pants around my ankles, but thankfully the costume included suspenders, so I slung those over my shoulders and clipped them in place to hold the trousers up. I completed the outfit with a lavender T-shirt, a white-checkered short-sleeve shirt, and white Nike sneakers.

After another failed attempt to get in touch with Tina, I headed out to the Atlas. Just as I got on my Crescent, I met Dad walking from the parking lot back to the house. He was grinning.

"Hey, Dad, one thing, just so you know. Remember how you wrote 'Doc Brown' on the poster? People may get upset when they realize it's you and not Christopher Lloyd. The actor, I mean," I warned him.

"If it's Doc they want, they won't be upset," he said. He spread his arms wide and yelled, "GREAT SCOTT!"

I laughed. Ah well. What was the worst that could happen? Pretty much everybody in the audience was a friend of his.

"I have to get going," I said, "but one more thing. I've tried to get in touch with Tina, but she isn't answering."

He shrugged. "She's probably driving. Hey, she is coming, isn't she?"

"I think so," I said, and got on my bike. "I'll try her again later," I yelled as I rode away.

THE premiere was set for 9 p.m. Mom and Dad said they'd come at around eight to help with the last-minute preparations. Rexi also said he'd come in "early," but hadn't specified a time. I had no reason to doubt him because it had been the same with the film reels; he'd shown up when he said he would.

With so much time to spare, I took the longer route to town, but rode quickly past Jennifer's brother's house, giving the yard only a quick glance, happy to see nobody on the porch, nobody on the swings, nobody on the rock by the mailbox.

The first thing I did when I got to the theatre was turn on the sign. Then I locked up the side door again and walked to Kim's to give him a ticket.

Of course, Kim didn't need a ticket—nobody was going to need a ticket—but I wanted to give him something.

He was playing Huey Lewis and the News when I walked in.

"Trying to get into the mood," he said. "Can't wait, man. Did you know that 'Power of Love,' the song in the movie, wasn't on the version of *Fore!* that was released in the US?"

"Actually, I did."

"It's crazy. This is awesome."

"It's like 'Crazy for You,'" I said. "Great single, but not on any of Madonna's studio albums."

"Same story with 'Boys Don't Cry' and 'Love Will Tear Us Apart.'"

He grabbed a pen and paper and we made a quick list: Top 10 Stand-Alone Singles. Before we knew it, it was 6 p.m., and Kim said he had to go home to get changed.

I walked back to the Atlas, following the beacon of the red neon sign glowing above the town.

I had done everything I could. All that was left was to wait for the clock to strike nine. I wanted to get into a time machine, but this time I wanted to drive into the future! Two hours, so that I could get to the big event. Or maybe even four hours, so it would all be over.

CHAPTER 41

IS THERE SOMETHING
I SHOULD KNOW?

Rexi was the first to show up. I was surprised to find him in the projection room on one of my rounds of the theatre. I didn't ask how he'd gotten in. I didn't want to know. An even bigger surprise was that he wasn't wearing army fatigues but black dress pants, a dark brown jacket, a white shirt, and a grey-and-black checked bow tie. I didn't have the guts to ask him about it, so I was relieved when he volunteered the information in his own inimitable way.

He stepped out from behind the projector and loomed toward me, his shiny bald head centimetres from my face. "Hey, what do you think of my outfit, *slacker*?"

I couldn't help but laugh. He was Principal Strickland.

"You laughing at me, slacker? Get it? Slacker?" Rexi looked at me, nodding, and with a smile on his face. "I'm Strickland."

"Of course. Perfect. Thank you."

He looked very pleased with himself.

"So, will you show me your secret tricks?"

Rexi looked at me, the smile gone from his face. He squinted his blue eyes, and if I wasn't mistaken, I heard a low growling.

"Basically, this goes against everything I believe in, and if you were somebody else's kid, I'd tell you to go to hell," he said, "but . . . you're not."

"All I need to know is how to start the movie," I said. "How to press Play. Nothing more."

"See, that's the problem. I've put the reel on the projector, but how does the focus get set? How does the aperture get set? Who switches on the audio? Who dims the lights?"

I held up my diary. "Tell me what to do. I'll take notes."

He held a finger up and tapped at the side of his head.

"You think you can fit everything that's in here onto that pad?"

"Well, no. But just give me the basics."

He turned his back on me and started turning dials on the machine.

"Get outta here, kid. This one's on me. You go and have fun. I'll run the reel."

"Seriously?"

"Get out," he snapped. "Before I change my mind."

I slowly retreated from the room. As I closed the door, I'm sure I heard him whisper, "I missed you, baby."

MOM and Dad showed up at around 7:45 p.m., Dad in his Doc Brown overalls and boots, his white hair tousled up, and Mom in a fifties dress with a blue scarf around her neck.

"I'm Old Lady Number Two," she said before I even had a chance to ask.

Dad and I rolled out the red carpet and lit the outside torches, and just as we got back inside, in came Tina, Tim, and Sofie. Tim was dressed in a grey jacket, black shirt, and silver tie. He'd had his hair cut short and, with the help of about a tonne of grease, was a pretty convincing Biff Tannen. Tina was dressed up in a white blouse and eighties high-waist jeans. Sofie was wearing a ball gown and a tiara, and her hair had been curled. And while many twelve-year-olds might rather have died than be seen out in such an outfit, she went with it, grinned, and looked amazing.

"This place is *sick*," she said. "And that means good," she added, giving me a massive hug.

"I've been trying to call you all day," I said to Tina.

"We were on the road. Why didn't you call my cell?"

"I couldn't remember the number," I said, lamely. She rolled her eyes. I didn't push it.

There were greetings all round. Mom gave Tina a short hug, while Dad shook Tim's hand and punched him on the arm. Then they swapped, and Dad gave his little girl a bear hug while Tim moved in to peck Mom on both cheeks.

There was no sign of Mom's usual brittleness.

I pulled Tina aside into the auditorium.

"What's going on?" I hissed. "Why didn't you call me? Why are you all here?"

"You invited us," she said simply, touching the side of her massive hair, releasing a waft of hairspray.

"Yes, but what's Tim doing?"

"He's being Biff. Like you asked, remember? Because he's a very nice man and wanted to help his family."

"Yes, I know, I just didn't know that you'd—anyway, why is Mom being *nice* to you?"

"Oh, that?" She threw her arms up. "Peter, you're such a drama queen! I spoke to Tim and it was all just a misunderstanding. He said to me, in English, 'Your mom's a witch in the kitchen'— apparently, it's something his grandpa used to say. It means she's a demon cook. But Mom heard and Google-translated it, except 'witch' turned into 'old crone' or something. Basically, she was a little too smart for her own good. Anyway, we spoke the other day and straightened it all out. Come on, Peter, keep up." She sniffed the air. "What *is* that smell?"

She walked along the corridor, and under the stairs up to the balcony she found the storage cupboard. The padlock was off and the door hung open. We peered inside. The camping stove and several large pots were sitting against one wall. There were pipes and wooden spoons and airlocks and bottles of sterilization fluid arranged on shelves. Tina stepped into the space and picked up a potato masher. I stepped past her and picked up a bottle of clear liquid. I popped the top and took a sniff. It had no scent. Water? I took a sip and my mouth exploded—and I sprayed Dad's illicit potato vodka all over the place.

"Um, you might want to take it easy with that stuff," said Dad from the doorway. "I'm not sure quite what proof it is, but you may not be able to drive for a few days."

I didn't know what to say. I almost lost my temper, shouted at him. He could have got us into so much trouble—an illegal still, on *my* business premises? But then I thought of all the work he'd done, of how he'd gotten himself out of his rut and helped me bring my dream to reality, and I couldn't be angry. Besides, I saw the cheeky smirk he was trying to hide and couldn't help but laugh.

"You lock that door," I told him. "We don't want the council inspector seeing that if they decide to pay a surprise visit."

"Right you are, boss."

We headed back to the lobby, where Mom was showing Sofie some ballroom dancing moves, and Tim was tucking into Mom's bilberry pie. Dad, looking a bit sheepish, disappeared behind the counter to do some last-minute pretending-to-be-busy. Tina and I stood off to the side.

"So, when do I get to meet your mystery woman?"

"Soon, I hope. She was here yesterday, and she said she'd be here tonight."

"And you already went out for pizza with her? Sounds serious."

"No, no, that's someone else."

She raised an eyebrow. "My little brother, the ladies' man."

I couldn't be bothered to argue.

"And you're still a time traveller, I suppose, since you couldn't call my cell?"

I shrugged. "I love it back here."

"You look good. You've lost some weight. I can barely look you in the eye though because of that ridiculous mullet," Tina said. "But I'm happy that you're happy."

"Really?" I said.

"Really," Tina said. "I hope this doesn't mess up your time-space continuum."

And we hugged.

"Hey," we both snapped at the same time, "watch the hair!"

Our hug was brief, but it was cut even shorter by Mom's shriek from the other side of the lobby.

"Peter, I think you should see this," she yelled.

I left Tina standing there and in two long leaps, jumped toward Mom.

"What's wrong? What's happened? What's wrong?"

Mom was standing at the door, her head tilted to her right, her nose against the glass.

"Look." She took a step back and pressed her index finger where her nose had just been. "They're here."

"They are here," I said.

"Who's here?" Dad asked.

"Everybody," Mom said.

Outside, on the red carpet and beyond, was a line of dozens of people, many of them dressed up as *Back to the Future* characters, others in their best eighties outfits, and others yet in fifties clothes. Kumpunotko had never seen such a concentration of hair and makeup. A sense of panic began to creep in.

"How am I going to know who's who, and who's got a ticket?" I screamed.

"Just let everybody in," Dad said. "What does it matter? They're all from Kumpunotko. We know most of them."

"I guess, but how do we know how many there are?"

"Why don't you stand here, welcome each one to your theatre, and give them a firm handshake," Dad suggested. "And Tina, you stand with him and keep a count. Remember, there are one hundred and thirty seats. What did the fire inspector say about people standing at the back?"

"That it wasn't allowed."

"Fine. Stop at one-fifty."

Dad guided me to the right spot and opened the door.

"Welcome!" he shouted.

It took me thirty-five minutes to greet everybody.

Kim came with his partner.

"Top ten movie songs?" he said. "Think about it. We'll make a list tomorrow."

Erik was there with his wife, and Tomi Taimi and Kari from BBB came, both with their families.

"We had to see what you've done with the place," said Tomi.

"It's such a shame it has to be torn down," Kari said.

"Such a shame," Tomi added.

Sara showed up with a teenage girl, both of them wearing denim overalls like they were members of Dexys Midnight Runners.

"Good to see you," I told Sara. "It wouldn't be the same without you."

"Thanks. This is my niece, Eva."

"Hi, Eva," I said, and turned to Sara. "I didn't know you had siblings."

"There's a lot you don't know about me," she said, and winked.

I chatted with everybody, but my conversations got shorter and shorter in direct proportion to the line outside getting longer and longer.

The *Sun*'s editors came to cover the event. They interviewed Dad, who stayed in character the whole time, and Tim, who grabbed the photographer in a headlock and started knuckling his skull.

My heart skipped a beat. Dad had always called Tim a "gentle man," but somewhere behind that gentle exterior lurked a wild man who also brought out the crazy in Dad. I was just about to put a stop to the nonsense when I felt somebody grab my arm.

It was Mom.

"Let them have some fun! It's harmless," she said.

"I hope so."

"Look at Dad's face! I haven't seen him this happy in years. And it's not just the makeup; he looks younger, don't you think?"

I smiled in agreement.

"Thank you," she said, and kissed my cheek.

"Doc" was gesturing wildly with his arms while speaking to some of the guests. I think I heard him say something about a "flux capacitor."

"Well, I think it's best that I get back," Mom said, and rushed away to the other side of the lobby where Tina and Sofie were standing behind the counter, selling soda and candy.

I looked over and saw Rexi, dressed as Strickland, standing in the corner of the crowded lobby, a look of thunder on his face. My heart jumping, I darted over to see what was wrong.

"Everything okay?"

He shook his head slowly.

"Slackers," he said. "Every one of 'em."

I gave a sigh of relief, cursing him.

He grinned. "Get back to your people. Just tell me when you want me to press Play."

I turned back to the line to shake hands with the next person. I extended my hand, and a large bald man grabbed it, shook it, but wouldn't let go. He just squeezed my hand a little bit too hard, stared me right in the eye, and smiled.

"Welcome, I hope you enjoy the movie. Thanks for coming," I said, and tried to get out of his grip. Instead, he squeezed a little harder.

"Thank you for personally inviting me," he said, stressing "personally."

As far as I could remember, the only people I had personally invited were Sara, Jennifer, Kim, and the guy who ran La Favorita. There was something familiar in the man's face, but I couldn't quite place it.

"I'm sorry, I'm terrible with faces—and names," I said. "Do I know you?"

"Come on, Pinhead, look closer," he said.

"Pinhead?"

"Aren't you Pinhead? From the BBS?"

I gasped. "Twisted Sister?"

"Well, yes and no. Haven't quite got the hair these days."

"Wow! Sorry! I thought you were a girl. Also, how do you speak Finnish?"

"Because I am Finnish. From Finland. Little town called Kumpunotko. You may even have heard of me, Peter Eksell, given that we went to the same high—"

But he didn't get the chance to finish his sentence because I'd flung my arms around him in the biggest hug of the day so far.

"Mikke!"

"Peter!"

We jumped around in a big bear hug for what seemed like ages.

And then he let go of me and, aware that the whole room was watching, we both stepped apart awkwardly and said, "Yes, well, great to see you . . ."

"This is awesome," he said eventually, making wild arm gestures. "Absolutely brilliant. I can't believe you now own the Atlas! It's the dream, man!"

"Oh, please, other people want to get in too," somebody said in a loud voice.

"Shut up," Mikke yelled back. "Some of us flew seven thousand kilometres to be here, okay? Sorry," he added, pressed his palms together and bowed his head a little bit.

"Let's talk later," I said, "I need to hurry up here."

"I'm back!" Mikke yelled, and walked in with his arms raised.

The line crawled inside, one handshake at a time. I began to speed up the process, and when there were only about a dozen people left, I stepped outside.

"Get in, everybody, just get in," I yelled. "You're all super-welcome! Some of you might have to stand—just don't tell the fire inspector."

And there she was at the back of the line, radiant and elegant, beautiful and smart.

I grabbed her by the hand and started to run.

I needed a moment with Jennifer all by myself, and I knew just the place.

Thankfully, it was next door.

CHAPTER 42

I THINK WE'RE ALONE NOW

H EY!" was the only thing she got out of her mouth when I took her by the hand and started to run. But when she realized we were only running about twenty metres, she started to laugh.

I opened the door and showed her in, then followed her to the counter.

"Two hot chocolates, please," I said.

"Make mine a skinny one," Jennifer added, which struck me as odd. She used to order extra whipped cream.

"Well, here you are," I said.

She was smiling, looking bemused.

"Here *we* are."

We climbed the stairs to the fancier part of the shop. I waited for Jennifer to sit down first. Our table was by the window, and outside, I could see snow coming slowly down. The first of the year.

"So . . . ," I said.

"So . . . ," she said.

"Here we are."

"We're here."

"You haven't changed a bit, you know."

"Oh, please. See these," she said, and pointed to the crow's feet around her eyes. "They're not just from laughing. But look at you! You haven't changed at all. Not at all. That's almost scary." She glanced at my hair.

"Oh, this?" I said, and flicked my mullet.

"I think it looks good on you."

"So . . . you're back in Kumpunotko?"

"I moved back a few years ago when my parents fell ill. And it felt right. I'd been out there for a long time," she said.

The waitress arrived with our drinks.

"Out there?"

She sighed.

"Well, remember how I left for that French art school?"

"Do I remember?" Now it was my turn to sigh, but I wanted to keep things light. "Yes, I remember. I always expected to read about you in the paper. Big-time Finnish artist in Paris."

"Well, it wasn't exactly Paris. It was Granville, and despite the name, that's not a big city; it's more like a French Kumpunotko."

"But better coffee shops, I imagine."

She smiled. "True."

"Anyway, to make a long story short, let's just say it's not easy making a living as an artist. Looking back, I suppose I'm glad I went. But at the time it was kind of tough, and scary. I was broke, in a foreign city." She chuckled. "Hey, I was young!"

"But at least you followed your dream. Nothing wrong with that."

"Yes, but one day you have to wake up. Dreams change, Peter, especially when you learn how tough it is to make a living as an artist. I moved back to Helsinki, packed up my brushes, and went back to school."

"A doctor . . . ?"

"No! I can't stand the sight of blood, you know that. I'm a speech-language therapist."

"You're . . . you're a wh–what?"

"I help people with speech impediments, such as a stutter," she said, and winked. "What have you been up to?"

"Well, I left Kumpunotko right after high school too. Went to the University of Helsinki, got a job in web design, and blah blah blah, and now I'm back here running a movie theatre."

"I suspect the blah blah blah may be the most interesting part of the story." She lifted her hot chocolate to her lips, but didn't take a sip.

"It was mostly just blah blah blah, actually."

Jennifer looked around the coffee shop and sighed.

My heart was racing so hard I was sure Jennifer would be able to see it thumping against my chest from the inside.

"It's really good to see you, Peter. I spent so long thinking you must have hated me."

That came out of the blue. "What?" I squeaked. "Why would I hate you?"

"The way I just left like that, like our friendship meant nothing. Didn't even say goodbye. I thought I'd wait until I got settled and then write and explain, but by then I thought it was too late. I'd burned that bridge. I don't think you know quite how important you were to me in high school. I had a lot going on at home I couldn't really talk about, but having you there—at school, in the library, sitting at the edge of my front lawn. You really meant so much to me."

I cleared my throat.

I wasn't going to let the moment pass again.

"And you don't know how long I've—"

Right then, the waitress came up the stairs, carrying a tray. "Just so you know, we'll be closing in five minutes," she said. She started to pick up glasses and coffee cups from the tables.

"What time is it?" I asked.

"Five to nine," she said.

I knew I had to leave immediately if I wanted to make it back to the Atlas in time, but I didn't want my moment with Jennifer to end.

Here we were, drinking hot chocolate, catching up, talking about our high-school days—it was everything I'd wanted. She was opening up to me. I'd been important to her. She hadn't contacted me because *she'd* felt bad, not because of something I'd done—or not done.

In my mind, I was back outside her house, sitting on the rear rack of my Crescent, listening to her talk about movies, or art. And once again, I was overwhelmed by that familiar warm feeling inside me.

"Should we be going back?" she said, and I snapped out of my dream.

"Yeah, one more minute. I haven't finished my drink. Hey, Jennifer. Have you ever thought what might have been if you hadn't left Kumpunotko? Or had sold a painting in Paris, or, I don't know, had a different dance partner at the school dance?"

"Sometimes," she said. "I thought of it a few weeks ago. I got this funny letter from our old English teacher, Hanna. She sent me a letter I'd written to my future self."

"Inspiring, right?"

"Mostly hilariously stupid, actually. I don't even remember most of it. We were supposed to write about current affairs or something, but I just went on about the beauty and importance of Wham!'s lyrics. I feel bad because I don't remember Hanna that well, and she wrote that she had *such* high hopes for me."

We both threw back our heads and laughed.

"Too funny. But . . . " She tapped her watch.

"You're right. We're late for the show," I said, and got up in a hurry.

We ran down the stairs. When we got outside, the snow had thickened, and I was glad it wasn't a long run back to the Atlas.

When we got back, I saw Dad standing on the steps, yelling to a group of people still outside, waiting to get in. "Sorry, there's no more space left, but come back tomorrow and you'll get in for free!"

I took Jennifer by the hand again and walked her through the lobby. I gave Rexi a nod and mouthed "two minutes." He nodded back and headed upstairs.

I walked with Jennifer directly to the two seats I'd reserved for her—reserved for us—the only reserved seats that night. The ones by the pillar, the best in the house.

To my shock, I saw a man sitting in one of them. I walked briskly toward him, ready to give him an earful. Who did he think he was, sitting on reserved seats? Jennifer was still a few steps behind me, and I heard her say, out of breath, "Peter, you madman."

"Listen," I said to the man, "I don't think—"

When he got up and turned to me, I saw who it was. That moustache. Sami. The jerk from school who'd always belittled everyone. The guy who'd shouted at me in the street the other day, accusing me of denying young people the right to decent housing.

"Peter," said Jennifer, behind me. "You remember my husband, Sami, from school?"

My jaw dropped.

Impossible.

"Hey," he said, holding out his hand. "Love what you've done with the place. Why don't you sell beer?"

My lips moved but no words came out.

"If you needed a licence, you should've just asked me; I'm on the council." He laughed loudly.

I shook my head in disbelief.

"I'm needed in the projection room," I mumbled. "Excuse me."

At the auditorium's door Tina stopped me.

"I think you should just take this in for a moment." She gestured toward the full auditorium. A loud chatter filled the theatre, and I saw people shake hands with each other and then sit down, hanging their winter coats on the seat-back hooks we'd added.

"Look at this! People are loving it," she said. "And, Peter, you did this. You should be proud."

I turned around and walked out the door.

CHAPTER 43

EVERY TIME YOU GO AWAY

M Y mind was as dark as the Atlas when the house lights went down. I walked around the block with my hands in my pockets, going over the events of the last ten minutes—from the heaven of sitting at a coffee shop with Jennifer, just her and me, to the hell of meeting her husband.

And not just any husband.

It had to be Sami, of all people.

Big-mouthed, obnoxious Sami, with his belittling nicknames and stupid moustache.

In school he'd been the self-appointed class leader, and now he was walking around Kumpunotko in a pinstriped suit like he owned the place. He was a big fish in a small pond. He wasn't worthy of Jennifer. She *got* the feminist message in *Supergirl*. She could read the message hidden between the lines of Wham!'s "Freedom."

Imagine how George McFly felt when he opened the car door and saw Biff pawing all over Lorraine.

Worse: this was like in *Back to the Future II*, where Marty discovers that in the parallel timeline, his mother has married Biff.

And it's all his fault.

I had half a mind to go back inside and knock Sami's block off, but I knew that wasn't going to help.

This wasn't *Back to the Future*. This wasn't Hill Valley. This was my life. And everything in it had just fallen apart.

In my head, Jennifer had always been *my* Jennifer, but I'd forgotten that she had also been other people's Jennifer. And now she was officially someone else's.

I knew that her life hadn't stopped unfolding just because I wasn't there, but it was a fact I had chosen to overlook. Deliberately. Stupidly.

Destiny? Oh, please.

But *Sami*?

That moustache?

I turned another corner and found myself back in front of the Atlas's main doors. I crossed the street and headed toward the market square, throwing my four-point plan into a trash can as I went. Yeah, I'd completed it. And what had it gotten me? Broke and broken.

I stopped at Kim's place and looked at myself in the reflection of the store window. It reminded me of *Back to the Future*. Depending on where I focused my eyes, I either saw Marty or saw through him, saw the crates of records inside. I could see through me. I was fading.

But I didn't want to fade away.

Fuelled by anger and disappointment, I sprinted full speed to the first intersection, and then jogged alongside the market square that was empty and dark, just like the Two Pines Mall parking lot had been in the movie. A car full of guys was driving slowly along Main Street—probably some high-school kids hanging out.

It had stopped snowing, and I could run a little faster without having to worry about falling down. I glanced at the big clock on top of the bank building across the square. The screen was now showing the temperature: zero degrees. Not too cold, but cold enough for my breath to show in the air. I kept on running.

I made a sharp right turn, ran for a block, and then slowed down. On Maple Street, I jogged past Mikke's old house, where we used to hang out after school, and suddenly realized where my feet had been taking me.

I was going back to square one, to the scene of crime, to the place where the wheels had been set in motion. I hadn't planned it this way, but it made perfect sense: it was meant to be.

I was going to our old high school, where Jennifer and I had met and become friends, and where she'd once given me a kiss. Perhaps if I waited there she would come and find me?

When I turned the last corner I saw that the building was completely dark, not a light in any of the windows. There was certainly no dance tonight. The massive stone structure still commanded my respect, and without even thinking about it, I stopped to admire it from afar.

Across the street from the school, I could see the swings and the playground where Mikke and I had met Jennifer that time, before the false-alarm air raid.

I walked slowly to the schoolyard. I let my gaze wander from window to window, and at each one, I muttered the name of the subject and teacher I'd had there.

"English: Hanna," I said. "Art: Siri. Science: Seppo."

I looked at the physics classroom window and thought instead about chemistry—about a particular chemistry that I'd tricked myself into believing existed, even when there was no evidence to support it.

On the other side of the schoolyard was the entrance to the bomb shelter Jennifer and I had run to that day so long ago. I pulled the handle but the door was locked.

I walked to the main entrance and tried to get a peek through the glass doors, but all I could see were lockers, some pieces of paper on the floor, and a couple of jackets and lonely shoes lying around, like in a house whose owners had left it in a hurry.

I spotted my old locker among the many. Four doors to the right was Jennifer's.

Everywhere I looked, I could see signs of Jennifer.

Except right in front of me, the only place that mattered.

I wondered if I was being missed, back at the Atlas.

I wondered if anyone might come looking for me.

I wondered if Jennifer might wander around the corner.

Yes. That would be the perfect final scene. I'd be standing in the middle of the schoolyard, in the pouring rain. Jennifer would see me, and—

No.

It was never going to happen.

I wondered when I was going to stop being so stupid.

I sat down on a bike rack, not knowing what to do next. What I *really* wanted to do was cry. So I did. And when the tears came, they came in a flood.

I sat outside the school crying for thirty minutes, but it felt like thirty years. Crying didn't change anything—the tears didn't magically rewind time and stop me from making so many stupid mistakes—but God it felt good.

When my teeth began to chatter in the cold, I got up and started to walk—very slowly—back to the Atlas.

"Goodnight, school," I said, and gave it a salute.

When I got to Mikke's old house, I saw that the lights were on in the kitchen, and I could already smell his mother's freshly baked apple pie—but the scent disappeared as quickly as it had come when I saw a young couple I didn't know cooking dinner together through the window.

I kept walking. I noticed that the shoe store where I'd gotten a pair of cowboy boots (that I'd only worn once because they gave me blisters) was no longer there. In its place was a mobile phone and game store. The grocery store where the school kids had gotten their candy was also gone; the low building now housed a computer repair shop. The real estate agent was a sushi bar. The fabric store was a coffee shop franchise. The bank had been turned into a health food and supplement store. When I looked at the buildings more carefully, I noticed two new apartment buildings in downtown, and that at least two of the old commercial buildings had been knocked down and replaced with shiny new offices. The old car dealership was now a children's activity centre, with trampolines. Even Video 2000—my home away from home, my film school, my first office—had been turned into its exact opposite: a twenty-four-hour-access gym.

Kumpunotko had changed. The skeleton was the same, the main grid was the same, but the town was a living organism that grew and changed, aged and regenerated itself.

Like a faraway star that has already imploded by the time its light reaches the Earth, Kumpunotko had been radiating ancient light to me, and while I'd been receiving the old signal, it had already become something else.

At the market square I looked at the clock again. At least that was still the same. The digital numbers glowed in the dark to show the time. It was 00:00, which I thought was fitting.

The countdown had stopped. I had reached the end.

Game over.

I looked at the four big zeroes watching over me and felt like just another big fat zero myself.

I wanted to hit my head against a wall. Any wall. The harder the better. I wanted to feel physical pain because at least I knew that would pass. This was not the way things were supposed to go. This was *not* in the screenplay. The hero was supposed to get the girl.

She wasn't supposed to be married to Sami.

He wasn't the hero; I was.

"Look at you all handsome in a tuxedo and everything. I was almost jealous of Sara, snapping you up like that."

That phrase.

For thirty years I'd been haunted by it, had wondered why I hadn't acted. Why I hadn't tipped my head in for a kiss at the bus stop half a second earlier.

But then again, for thirty years I'd been haunted by the *jealous*, choosing not to notice the word that came before it.

For thirty years, my loneliness had twisted a simple friendship into something it had never been.

It was all in my head.

A peck on the cheek. A handful of confidence-boosting compliments.

She's been a friend, nothing more.

But—just as importantly—she'd been a damn good friend.

I shook my head.

Reset my brain.

Thanked God that waitress had come along before I'd had the chance to spill my guts in the coffee shop.

That could have been embarrassing.

So what was I to do now?

There was no reason, logically, that I couldn't just erase all the nonsense from my head and go back to how it had been.

Friends.

I had her details now. I could drop her a line. Go for coffee.

Pick up where we'd *actually* left off. In real life.

WHEN I got back to the Atlas, the red neon sign was still glowing, but the torches were extinguished and the doors were closed. I opened the door and walked in.

Dad, Tim, and a group of Dad's friends were standing in the lobby, holding white plastic cups in their hands. Their faces looked very red and jolly. Both Dad and Tim were still in their *Back to the Future* outfits, and when Tim saw me, he grabbed me by my neck.

"Where have you been, punk?" I squirmed in his grip. "You didn't even see the standing ovation!"

"Just took a walk."

"Got a little nervous there? Too scared to see how it went? What are ya? Chicken?"

I burst out laughing and kept laughing, almost hysterically.

"No," I gasped when I could get some air, "just took a walk."

"Want some of your father's magic potion?" somebody asked me. It was Erik. He pushed his white cup in front of my nose. His breath had a strong stench of alcohol. I looked up and saw Dad raise his cup in a toast.

"Needed to grease the wheels, you know," he said with a big grin. "Hey, I think some people are waiting for you in there," he added, gesturing toward the auditorium.

Jennifer and Sami were still there, talking with Sara and Mikke. I observed them for a while, uncertain of what to do or say, but when Jennifer saw me, her face lit up. "There he is," she said, and then left the group and walked to meet me. "Congratulations!" She pulled me into a hug. "That was such a success. I've always said there's nothing you can't do. Well done, friend."

Then she kissed me on the cheek.

CHAPTER 44

I WANT TO KNOW WHAT LOVE IS

JENNIFER, Sami, and I chatted for a few minutes. Sami showered me with compliments on my work with the movie theatre, and then went on about how important it was for the town to have a community hub like this rather than just more boring apartments.

"You should come for dinner soon," he said. "For old time's sake."

I looked at Jennifer. She was smiling, but she didn't say anything.

"I think I'd like that," I said, and excused myself. The uproarious laughter of Dad's friends pulled me to the lobby where they were telling stories, slapping each other on the back, and spilling Dad's special moonshine on the floor.

Kari gestured for me to come closer.

"Listen, Peter, my hat's off to you, really. You have done such a fantastic job with this. With everything," he said, his cheeks red and a twinkle in his eye.

"Thanks, but it's over now. I mean, the bulldozers will be here next week, right?"

Kari sighed.

"I don't know. To be honest, Tomi and I were talking tonight. You know that old meat-packing factory on the outskirts of town? Well, it's going for a song, and we think we could probably get a couple of apartment buildings on that land. Certainly more than here. I don't know. It would mean scrapping the plans for this place, but plans have to adapt, right? And it would be such a shame to tear this down."

"Damn right," growled Rexi, suddenly at my shoulder.

"So, if you think you might be interested in taking it off our hands . . ."

I was flabbergasted. I was interested, yes—my dream, becoming a reality—but I couldn't see how it would work.

"There's no way," I said with a small sigh. "I can't afford six hundred thousand euro. I've barely got six hundred."

"Well, we'll have a think about it tomorrow. Perhaps in the afternoon, when we've gotten over our hangovers, we can talk about a trial period, see if you can make it profitable. Then you can talk to the bank, maybe. Who knows?"

He winked and raised his plastic cup.

"*Kippis!*"

I clinked my plastic cup against his.

"*Kippis!*"

He knocked back the vodka, and if it made his eyes water I couldn't tell; I was too busy coughing and gasping and clutching my own throat.

I was feeling strange inside—very strange—and it wasn't just my father's home brew. I kept thinking about those four big fat zeroes, and wondering if perhaps they weren't an end after all, but a beginning. Reset and start again. I stood at the front door and looked out. I saw the reflection of the red Atlas sign in the windows across the street. All the praise had lifted my spirits, and I could feel my self-confidence returning. I'd done good! I'd set out to do something and had actually achieved it.

"In a town that had lost all hope, only one man could—" I narrated, but was interrupted when somebody tugged at my shirt.

"So," said Tina. "When do I get to meet your mystery pizza girl?"

"You already know her. From school." I nodded toward the other side of the lobby where Sara was talking to Mom. Her niece was in the auditorium, chatting furtively with Sofie.

"She's cute. Are you guys a couple or . . . ?"

"She is cute. And smart. But tough too. She's a cop, you know."

"You didn't answer my question."

"No, we're not a couple. She thinks I'm a lunatic."

"You *are* a lunatic. Go talk to her, dummy," Tina said, and nudged me forward.

"Stop it."

"You stop it," Tina said. She pushed me so hard that I practically flew across the lobby.

"What *is* your favourite food?" I heard Mom ask Sara just as I landed on the floor between them.

"I'd like to know that too," I said.

"Pizza," Sara said, with a big smile on her face. She helped me up. I looked toward Mom, but she had mysteriously vanished.

"Can we go somewhere to talk?" she whispered to me. "In private?"

I showed her the way to the projection booth. Rexi was still there, sitting on the only stool, running his hand absently over the side of the projector. When he saw us walk in, he excused himself.

"Good show, kid. Same time tomorrow?"

"Sure, Rexi. Thank you so much."

Rexi turned toward the door. "No," he said, a misty look in his eyes, "thank *you*."

Of all the hugs I got that evening, his was certainly the most intense.

I offered the stool to Sara, but she said she wanted to stand, so we both stood.

"Did you like the movie?" I asked, to break the silence.

"Yeah," she said, "but I'd seen it before."

Another pause.

"I like watching the classics," she added. "But you never beat the feeling of seeing it the first time. It's just not as good when you know how it's going to end."

I didn't know what to say. She was totally wrong, of course, but on one level I could see that she might be right.

I'd had enough of awkward pauses for one day. I opened my mouth to say something, but Sara beat me to it.

"I saw Jennifer," she said.

Another pause. Again, I opened my mouth, but again Sara got there first.

"I knew she was married to Sami," she said.

"Why didn't you tell me?"

"I wasn't sure it was important. If you cared, even. I didn't know what you had in mind, really, but mostly I didn't want to scare you away. I've loved having you in town, and, you know, our little chats about everything."

She was smiling, but the smile didn't quite reach her eyes, and for a moment I thought she was holding back tears.

"It's very romantic, you know, to go back in time for a girl. It's crazy, and impossible, but it's very romantic. Even if it was the wrong girl."

I fiddled with the projector.

"You know, I always wanted to go to the dance with you. Back then. That's why I was so excited when we got assigned to each other. That was my dream come true. You were pretty handsome. Back then," Sara said.

I laughed a little. "Thanks, I guess."

"And that's why I was so upset after the dance when you just wanted to hang around with—"

"*That's* why you disappeared?"

"I didn't see the point in hanging around."

"She was my friend," I insisted, stepping closer to her. "Look, I realize now—finally—that that's all it ever was. And you know what? I'm fine with that. And you know what else? For what it's worth, you did look amazing that night. With your fingerless gloves."

Now Sara laughed.

"Yeah, right. New Wave!" she shouted, and raised her fist.

"And that was the first time I ever saw a high-five."

"Get out of town! You're such a lame-o."

We heard loud laughter from downstairs.

"What are you going to do now?" she asked. "I guess you'll go back to Helsinki?"

"Well, I didn't have a plan beyond this moment, but now it looks as if maybe I won't be going anywhere. For one thing, I think I have a movie theatre to run," I said, and made a grand gesture around the small room. "And I'm much happier than I was when I first got here, even if I did lose the plot a bit tonight. I've gotten a lot of wires crossed in my head, lately, but I think . . . I think they're straightened out a bit now."

"You know," she said softly, "I think you got it a bit wrong back there. I think you missed the point of the film."

"How so?"

"Wasn't the whole film about getting Marty back to where he belongs? The future? That is, now, today, 2016?"

I chuckled. She was right.

"So here I am. It took a lot of planning and crazy ideas, but I've ended up back in 2016. And my life *is* a little better than when I left it. Hey, I wonder if my parents play tennis now?"

She laughed, and then said softly, "You know, you're not the only one who's been making crazy and elaborate plans. Do you think it's been easy, serendipitously bumping into you all the time, even in a small town like this?"

I didn't know what to say.

"But I guess I'll just cut to the chase now. Would you like to go on a date with me, Peter Eksell? Maybe go dancing? I know you can dance."

"Don't get your hopes up; it's been a while."

"Oh, but I've always had high hopes for you," she said. "Hey, that reminds me, did you get a letter from Hanna a couple of months back . . . ?"

There was a loud noise at the door. Tina came running up the stairs.

"Dad wants to go to Burgerland!" she shouted. "IT. IS. ON!" She ran back downstairs.

Sara and I looked at each other.

"Won't Burgerland be closed?" she asked.

"I think the guy who runs it is downstairs with Dad . . ."

I turned off the lights in the auditorium and the projection booth, and we walked toward the door.

"I think I'll pass on the burgers," she said. "Maybe next time."

At the top of the stairs there was one of those pauses. She looked a little uncertain. Then she stepped forward and put her arms around me and we hugged—not too tight—and as we let go I think I surprised myself even more than I surprised her when I leaned forward and kissed her on the cheek. Her eyes popped open.

"Cool," I said, with a grin. "I'll text you tomorrow."

As we walked down the stairs, I saw her absently reach up and touch the spot I'd kissed.

I left the neon sign on.

NO MORE LONELY NIGHTS

I got to the Atlas around noon and parked my bike against the wall in the back. The mail was waiting for me in the mailbox. I grabbed it and walked in through the side door and straight to my office.

I turned on Total 80s FM on the lobby's integrated sound system and picked up the most interesting piece of mail amongst a few bills and fliers. It was a large, orange envelope addressed to *Peter Eksell, The Atlas Movie House*, with "DO NOT FOLD" stamped on the front in English. It was postmarked Santa Monica, California.

Curiously, carefully, I tore along the edge and reached into the envelope. Inside was a glossy eight-by-ten black-and-white photo of Christopher Lloyd, signed by the actor. There was no cover note.

Better eighteen months late than never.

I put it down and put my coat back on. I walked out the door, and quickly rode my bike to the bookstore to get a frame. It was perfect. Today was Thursday, which meant that it was Throwback

Thursday Movie Night—an idea Tim and Dad had cooked up. It usually ended up being our busiest night of the week.

Not that Tim was able to make it every Thursday—it was a long drive, after all—but whenever he could come he really threw himself into the theme. Indiana Jones, Louis Winthorpe III, Ferris Bueller: on each occasion his costume was better than the last. I was beginning to suspect that Tina was helping him out.

I had a date at the coffee shop at 1 p.m., and as the clock on the bank building told me, I had fifteen minutes to buy the frame and get there.

Jennifer and I arrived at the coffee shop at the same time: 12:54. I guess she hated being late as much as I did.

"Hello, friend," she said.

We got our hot chocolates and took a table by the window. I told her about the Christopher Lloyd photo, and she laughed.

"You should post that on Facebook," she said. "And Instagram. It's perfect."

"You know I don't do that stuff."

"I know, and by 'you' I obviously meant 'Sara.' You guys. Anyway, the Atlas Instagram account is very funny; she's very funny. It's not surprising the place is so popular."

"Oh yes, she is. Keep it to yourself, though; I'm not sure her boss knows that she's posting on police time."

Jennifer smiled. "Outrageous—especially when there's so much crime around here she should be solving."

We both took sips of our hot chocolate at the same time.

"She was telling me she's thinking of leaving the force," said Jennifer. "Coming to work with you full-time."

"Mmm. We've talked about that. I'm not so sure. Living together *and* working together?"

She shrugged. "I'm not sure how much say you'll have in the matter, to be honest."

I changed the subject. "How are the kids?"

"They're good. It's a busy week with Peter's thirteenth birthday party and everything. It's very kind of you to let us have a private screening. He's been telling all his friends that he knows you. Are you sure we don't need to bring anything?"

"I'm sure. Mom's been baking for a week. There'll be so much to eat, the kids will explode. Dad's going to dress up too."

"He's going to be a Ghostbuster?"

I nodded. "He was just sad we couldn't find him a Stay Puft Marshmallow Man costume."

Jennifer burst out laughing, spitting hot chocolate on me.

"I'm so sorry," she said, and wiped the chocolate off my face with a napkin.

"It's okay. He's really into it, watched all the movies too. How's Sami?"

"He's fine. Excited because we're getting the paperwork for the new apartment this week. We'll be renting it out. It's a great investment opportunity, he says. I'm actually going to meet him at the gym straight from here. Want to walk with me?"

"Of course."

I walked my bike, with Jennifer walking next to me, and when we got to the gym we stood outside for ten minutes, Jennifer telling me all about their new apartment in the old meat-packing building, and me leaning on my bike.

I saw Sami wave from inside the gym. He was running on a treadmill, facing the street. I waved back. He wasn't such a jerk, once you got used to him.

"I should go," Jennifer said. "We'll talk." She waved to me, wiggling her fingers.

I got on my bike and rode through Kumpunotko. It was a nice spring day but still quite cold, so I kept my hands in my jacket pockets, listening to music on my iPod.

Sara was at the Atlas when I got there. She must have seen me through the main doors because when I opened the side door, she came running to meet me. The door was barely open when she grabbed me by the arm and pulled me in—and into a warm embrace that made me forget time and space. I buried my head in her neck.

"You smell good," I said, and I gave her a kiss.

Dad may have been right about the importance of a firm handshake, but this—this was better. Even better than a high-five.

We walked hand in hand through the theatre and into the main lobby, where Sara helped me find the perfect spot for Christopher Lloyd's photo, between two posters of forthcoming events: *Gremlins* and the *Beverly Hills Cop* double bill. (Yes, I know there's a third film in the series, but we do have standards to maintain).

"By the way, the *Ghostbusters* reels just came," Sara said. "I think we need to call Rexi."

To Be Continued . . .

ACKNOWLEDGEMENTS

I'M one of those people who always stay in the stands to see championship teams celebrate their victory, and I weep when I watch Hockey Hall of Fame induction speeches, wishing that I could somehow stand there and thank all the people who have helped me. Well, I think this is my chance. Great Scott!

I'll begin with you right there on the other side of the page. Thank you for reading this.

I owe a great debt of gratitude to many eighties pop culture icons, among them Bryan Adams, Jim Vallance, Jim Peterik, Sting, Andy Summers, Stewart Copeland, Billy Ocean, the Pointer Sisters, Joe Elliott, Joe Lynn Turner, Stock Aitken Waterman, Bruce Springsteen, Prince, Chevy Chase, David Bowie, Phil Collins, Lionel Richie, Corey Hart, Belinda Carlisle, John Lennon, Huey Lewis, Bill Murray, Harold Ramis, Eddie Murphy, Dan Aykroyd, Mike Myers, Tero Vaara, Cyndi Lauper, David Lee Roth, Freddie Mercury, Martti Syrjä, Paul McCartney, Juice Leskinen, John Mellencamp, David Foster, Steve Martin, Brian May, George

Michael, Andrew Rigleley, and Madonna, for inspiration and words of wisdom.

Thank you Michael J. Fox, Christopher Lloyd, Lea Thompson, Crispin Glover, and Thomas F. Wilson, as well as Robert Zemeckis, for giving me Hill Valley.

Maurice Griffith and Mike Messam helped with details regarding VW Beetles and the perils of cinema projection (respectively), and I spent many a wonderful evening listening to Sollentuna Bio's projectionist Kaj Olsson talk about the art of running a movie theatre. Thank you! (Any mistakes and errors in the story are naturally all mine).

This book would never have seen the light of day without the hard work, patience, vision, and guidance of Philippa Donovan, Jamie Groves, Cathryn Summerhayes, the very impressive HarperCollins Canada team, and especially Iris Tupholme, and Kate Cassaday, my insightful editor.

There also wouldn't have been a book if not for Linda Lewis and Val Mindel, who—once upon a time—opened a door that led me onto a new path.

My hat is off to Andrew Applebaum, Mikko Armila, Lucas Aykroyd, Jarmo Betcke, Roberto De Vido, Annacarin Ericsson, Alder Francescut, Kari Halme, Rob Hincks, Mika Kempas, Petri Kortelainen, Timo Kortelainen, Ari Lepistö, Pauli Leppänen, Bryant McBride, Tina McBride, Bert Menninga, Shawn Roarke, Janne Turpeinen, Devin Wilson, Ken Yaffe, and Terry Zulynik, who have, without even knowing it, been my pop culture gurus and mental coaches.

(If I was on the stage at the Hockey Hall of Fame, this is where I'd start to weep.)

Thank you to the Arhammar family—Anders, Yvonne, Jenny, Joakim, and Julia—for making Sweden a true home for me.

Mom, Dad—Asta and Eino—thank you for always believing in me. And for making sure I became a reader.

And finally, Hannes and Hilda, and Jessica, my wife, my best friend, my rock. Thank you for everything. Someday, Jessica, is today.

That's the power of love.